T0304806

The Golden Hour

Also by Jacquie Bloese

The French House

The Golden Hour

Jacquie Bloese

HODDER &
STOUGHTON

First published in Great Britain in 2024 by Hodder & Stoughton
An Hachette UK company

2

A CIP catalogue record for this title is available from the British Library

Hardback ISBN 978 1 529 37736 1
Trade Paperback ISBN 978 1 529 37738 5
ebook ISBN 978 1 529 37737 8

Typeset in Plantin Light by Hewer Text UK Ltd, Edinburgh
Printed and bound in Great Britain by Clays Ltd, Elcograf S.p.A.

Hodder & Stoughton policy is to use papers that are natural, renewable
and recyclable products and made from wood grown in sustainable
forests. The logging and manufacturing processes are expected to
conform to the environmental regulations of the country of origin.

Hodder & Stoughton Ltd
Carmelite House
50 Victoria Embankment
London EC4Y 0DZ

www.hodder.co.uk

'I do not claim to have perfected an art, but to have commenced one, the limits of which it is not possible at present exactly to ascertain.'

William Henry Fox Talbot,
British inventor of photography, 1839

For my friends

PROLOGUE

Brighton, 1896

The body comes up with the spring tide, not far from where the gulls smash clams and winkles under the rusting girders of the pier. It lies blunted and bruised on the glistening pebbles as the sea retreats, and in those few moon-lit hours before it rises again there is a peace of sorts: crabs scuttle from their whelk shells to feast and fight, a thorn ray lays a pouch of eggs in the green shallow waters, a kittiwake swoops silver across the shingle and calls out a blessing.

A fisherman down on the beach at the first shimmer of dawn with his young son sees it first, and he turns his boy's head away and tells him to go to school today instead. He is superstitious, he won't go out on the boat this morning, and then, just as he is deciding what to do, he sees the fellow who's made a mint from selling ice cream, out for his early morning stroll. They confer in hushed tones as the tide creeps in and more boatmen come, and someone covers the body with a blanket, and a boy is given a penny to fetch a policeman, but he spends it on a bun from Medfords and forgets; and by the time word is received at the station and the constable on duty has reached the seafront, the sun is up and so too is most of Brighton, and a small crowd has gath-ered, as crowds tend to do in this shoeless, well-heeled town.

Constable Fisher waits a moment before approaching. He's been in this job for long enough to know when there's been foul play – it's there if you look in the set of a person's shoulders, the shifting dart of an eye. It's in the air too, you can smell wrongdoing, just as you can goodness: he's a religious man and he believes in spirits. Heads turn as he walks down the slipway; but he can't yet see the body. It's a woman, he expects. It's almost always a woman.

Chapter One

One year earlier

The band is mid-way through 'The Sailor's Hornpipe' when Ellen Harper first sees the girl. She is sitting alone on a bench, under the shelters, a half-eaten penny ice in one hand, the other pressed to her forehead, in the manner of an old maid who cannot bear the Sunday afternoon rumpus on the pier and is somewhat regretting the tuppence she paid. But the girl is no old maid. Ellen sees this and so does a young man, clean-shaven in a Homburg hat, who stops uninvited, casting her in shadow and saying something that causes the girl to redden. She looks about her, skittish as a new foal; he lays a hand on her arm and she shrinks back – and this last gesture, the audacity of it, is all it takes. Ellen Harper's feet are ahead of her mind, her boots click-clacking across the wooden boards, the surge of the sea beneath her, and applause for the hornpipe in her wake.

The man eyes her warily. Not brazen enough to brazen it out; a coward in his scuffed boots and cheap waistcoat with its gilt watch chain. He must sense the anger in her, for he mumbles good afternoon and slopes off into the crowd.

'I hope I wasn't interrupting.'

The girl looks up. A face like a heart and clear grey eyes that seem to incline more towards melancholy than merriment. Young – seventeen at a guess – with an older person's weariness about her. A straw hat, bent a little out of shape as if some younger sibling has jumped upon it, a stain or two on her gloves, a pale blue skirt with the colour leached from the hem through laundering. Although clean, her attire borders on shabby; too shabby to be in service in one of the squares, she is perhaps – and now Ellen is hopeful for her – in apprentice as a seamstress, somewhere that over time will pay enough for a hat with trimmings, and lace gloves in the summer.

'No, miss. I didn't know him – nor wanted to neither,' she adds, as much to herself as to Ellen, and she takes a spoonful of the melted chocolate ice, and stares towards the silver horizon, just as the Newhaven steamer passes, with its muffled moan.

'I'd like to go where that one's going.' The girl speaks softly, with the air of someone unused to attention.

'France, you mean?'

She looks at Ellen with interest. 'Is that where it's off to?'

'It's the three o'clock from Newhaven, I expect.' Ellen finds herself sitting then, a handspan away from the girl. 'It'll be in Dieppe by teatime.'

'Dieppe,' her companion repeats tentatively, as if she has just been served up snails on a plate. And then for Ellen, the smallest of smiles. 'Have you been there, miss?'

'In passing. Only at night though.' Ellen laughs for no obvious reason, and tells herself she really *must* go now, that this is time wasted, and that the young ladies from the theatre – if one can call them such – will be squawking and twittering on their favourite table in the west-facing window of the Refreshments Room, and she has arrangements to make with them for tomorrow. But still, she lingers.

'Expect it's the same as here in the dark, is it?' And the girl laughs back, and glancing at her, Ellen fears mockery, but there is nothing except shyness temporarily overcome in her pale eyes.

'I'm Lily,' the young woman goes on, and a gloved hand is being held out for Ellen to take. 'Lily March.'

'Miss Harper.' For a moment, Lily's hand sits snug inside Ellen's own, as if it was fashioned to be there. A baby cries. The band starts up. Ellen's fingers slip free.

Ellen waits until the band has played three more songs, before she asks. By then she knows Lily works with her mother and sister in a laundry, that she lives in the tenements in Albion Hill, that she has never left Brighton in all her seventeen years, nor taken a dip in the sea. And that her pa – and here Lily's face flares a sudden angry red – her pa is in lock-up for a year for doing something he shouldn't, and her Uncle Jack is down from Manchester to keep the house in order. He ain't much of an uncle, she says, her voice turned flat, no matter what her ma likes to think, and truth is, Lily can't bear him, and so she has decided.

'Decided?' Ellen asks gently.

'To leave,' Lily says, with a sniff. For Worthing ... or Margate, or – brightening a little – up north to Blackpool, for she's heard of the pleasure pier, all lit up electric, and she's sure the northerners' clothes must get just as filthy as theirs down here. She'll find a job in a laundry like the one she has now, except without her ma taking every last penny she earns.

'But first ...'

'You need money.'

A nod. A look of both wariness and hope. With a small thrill, Ellen realises she is the first person Lily has spoken to of this; she is a confidante.

'For my train fare and . . .'

'Your first week of lodgings and . . .'

'A case for my things . . .'

'And a little extra for incidentals.'

'*Incidentals.*' Lily tries out the word and smiles. 'Yes.'

How delicious, the ripple of this exchange, Ellen thinks, this sharing of thoughts. And how fortunate that she is in a position to help someone who truly needs it.

'Miss March.' Ellen lowers her voice and leans in towards her. 'How would you like to have your photograph taken?'

'If she's not here soon, the best of the light will be gone.' Reynold Harper emerges from underneath the camera and claps his hands at the tabby cat, flexing its claws with enthusiasm on the worn velvet nap of the chaise longue. 'Stop that, Floss, you little pest.' Scooping the purring cat into his arms, he joins his sister at the window. 'Remind me where you found this one again?'

'The pier.' Ellen tries to keep her voice level, as she scours the terraced street for signs of Lily March. At this hour, soft syrupy sunlight turns the crooked houses of Booth Lane the colour of melted butterscotch, and one might almost turn a blind eye to the peeling paint and rusting windows, the gutters choked with filth. She turns and removes a coil of dark-brown hair from the chaise, and then another, fairer and straight: they'd had the tableaux girls from the Empire in earlier and they were worse than Floss for moulting.

The faintest of taps at the front door draws her back to the window, and yes, there is Lily, in her straw hat with the dent in it, looking anxiously up and down the street, pulling her coat to her as if the day is a cold one – and the burst of

6

happiness Ellen feels startles her and she has to turn away from her brother so he cannot see it in her eyes.

'She's jumpy as a box of frogs,' Reynold grumbles. 'You did tell her she'll have to show her face?'

Of course, Ellen calls out, halfway down the narrow staircase to the front door now, smoothing down her hair as she draws back the bolt.

'Miss March. A pleasure to see you again.'

Ellen believes herself to be smiling, so why is Lily looking back at her as if she is about to have a tooth pulled? She ushers her inside and they stand in the cramped space at the foot of the stairs, Lily's hands twisting inside her stained blue gloves.

'How about a drop of something warming, before we start?' Ellen tries to be brisk as she leads Lily upstairs to the dressing room, feeling somewhat in need of a tot of something herself, as if she too is about to be exposed. She pours a measure of rum, then takes the chipped walnut music box from the sideboard, counting out a handful of coins to a few wheezing bars of 'Greensleeves'.

'Three shillings, as agreed.'

She and Reynold are usually strict on this point: no payment until the work is done, but there is nothing like the weight of a few coins in a purse to lift a young lady's spirits, and sure enough, Lily's colour seems to return as she takes the money, and screwing up her face, she gamely drinks down the rum.

'No one will ever know about this, will they?' she says, taking off her hat and gloves with caution. 'Not those ladies with the boards?'

'The vigilants? The prudes on the prowl?!'

But Lily doesn't smile.

'Of course not.' Ellen passes her the scarlet robe from the back of the door. 'You haven't told anyone, have you, about today?'

'No.'

'Then there's no need at all to worry. And the photographs themselves will be sent far away to the continent.'

'To France?'

'Yes.'

'So I suppose I will go there after all,' Lily murmurs, chewing at a ravaged fingernail, and Ellen says that's one way of thinking about it, and then Lily looks at her and for a brief moment they are back on the pier, under the shelters with the chocolate ice melting and the sun in their eyes. Lily offers up a smile.

'It's a strange enough world, ain't it, Miss Harper?' She takes the robe and disappears behind the Chinese screen in the corner, a forced bravado in her tone. 'Everything off, like I was taking a bath?'

'That's right.'

And Ellen waits as hooks are unfastened, and buttons fumbled over, until the entire mille-feuille of petticoats and stockings and stays are unpeeled, and Lily re-appears in the robe, which trails on the floor behind her as Ellen asks her to sit at the mirror. Such an elegant neck she has, Ellen thinks, as milky and pale as the poor girl's hands are rough and red, hands which are trembling slightly in the dip of her lap.

'Remember,' Ellen says, teasing strands of hair from the pins, 'once you're in front of the camera, you become someone else entirely.'

Lily stares at her. 'Who?'

'Whoever you please! Lily March from the laundry stays

8

here – with your skirts and petticoats.' Ellen waves towards Lily's pile of clothes, that lie neatly folded on a packing crate. 'Ready?'

And together, they go into the studio next door.

As Reynold greets her, Lily keeps her eyes planted to the floor, and he looks askance at Ellen, and she knows what he's thinking – what a waste of plates, and developing fluid, and time spent over the press – the girl's as wooden as Punch! But then Flossy jumps from the windowsill, wrapping herself around Lily's legs, as if summoned to do so, and Lily bends to pet her.

'She's a sweet little thing.'

'And she'll ruin the exposure, given half a chance. Out you go, Floss.' Reynold shoos the cat from the room. 'On the chaise, if you will, Miss March. On your side. Turned towards the camera.'

Her brother is too brusque, too businesslike, that is the problem, Ellen thinks, as Lily perches on the chaise and fumbles with the knotted sash of her robe. This is not one of the tableaux girls who stand on a plinth in nothing but a body stocking, night after night, or an artist's model, so accustomed to shrugging her clothes off that she doesn't bother with stays.

'Let me help you.' Ellen crouches next to Lily, and deftly works the knot loose. 'Let's keep the robe on to begin with. Turn on your side and stretch out, that's right. Lean your head on your hand – and bend your knees a touch.'

Lily relaxes a little and Ellen slips the robe from her shoulders. She smells of lye soap and milk; her breasts are fuller, altogether larger, than Ellen had imagined. And with this observation runs a current of shame, and she wishes then

9

that the girls from the theatre were back, joking and fidgeting and asking for more drink.

A plum-coloured bruise at the top of Lily's left thigh provides an unwelcome distraction, bringing with it unvoiced questions of who and how often; Ellen frowns and reaches for the powder pot.

'That looks sore.'

Lily flushes the colour of a sunset. 'I tripped, carrying the coal upstairs.'

'Won't be too long before you're married and in your own home, I expect,' Ellen says, torturing herself. 'Somewhere the stairs aren't so slippery.'

'Ma says no one will have me,' the girl says with a humourless laugh.

'I'm sure she's wrong about that. May I?' Ellen reaches for the robe, which is now more off than on, but Lily stiffens; and Ellen hesitates. Ignoring her brother's laboured sigh, she goes next door to fetch a drape: Reynold will gripe about the photographs fetching less, but it's that or lose Lily altogether.

'We'll use this,' she tells her, and trying to treat her nakedness with the same dispassionate regard with which she might appraise a statue in the gallery of a fine museum, Ellen arranges the drape so that it falls from the hips, covering Lily's most intimate parts. 'Now it won't feel so strange.' She scoops up the robe. 'And when you're dressed again, we'll take another photograph just for you, if you like – with Floss.'

'Thank you, Miss Harper.' Lily looks down at herself, letting out a sigh which speaks of inevitability, and Reynold instructs her rather tersely to hold still and look at the camera, and to think of her sweetheart if she has one, or a lad she's soft on if not.

As the first plate is exposed, Ellen returns to the window. In the distance, the sea winks at her, a quivering mass of starlings flitting in and out of view to the beat of her brother's instructions.

'Stand up for me, would you? . . . Drop the drape, there's a dear . . .' She won't, Ellen thinks, but oh, she must have, for now he is telling Lily to turn to the side, to clasp her hands behind her back. 'Just so. All right, lower your head, if you must. And hold for three.'

The plateholder slides from the camera; the cat scratches on the studio door, and bidding Lily a cool good day, Reynold disappears upstairs to the attic.

Lily looks after him with a thoughtful expression as she wraps the drape about her. 'What happens now?'

'You get dressed and I'll set up the camera.' Ellen opens the door and lets in Flossy. 'By the window will be best.'

Lily returns, neat in her cotton skirt and shirtwaist. She stares at the array of photographs tiling the wall above the fireplace as if noticing them for the first time, then lets out a little squeal.

'That's Harry Smart! Ain't it?'

'That's right.' If Ellen had her way, there would be no picture of the Empire's most talked-about performer, twirling her cane in her pinstripe trousers and tailcoat – she doesn't care for the woman, who, in her opinion, gets quite enough attention already. Reynold, however, insists it's good for business.

'Is she a friend of yours, Miss Harper?' Lily sits in the easy chair by the window, and coaxes Floss onto her lap.

'An acquaintance, certainly.'

As Ellen stoops under the camera and looks at Lily, now without so much as the nub of a wrist on display, she tries to forget the nakedness that lies underneath. But the dips and curves and puckerings all conspire against her, hammering the image further into her consciousness – the diamond-shaped mole just below Lily's right nipple; even that awful bruise.

She stifles a sigh and re-emerges. Lily's face is washed clean with a smile, and even if this must in part be attributed to Harriet Smart, Ellen is glad of it and hopes that the awkwardness from earlier is behind them.

'I'm sure Miss Smart would sign a photograph for you, if I asked,' she says, taking the cloth from the lens and Lily beams and the tableau is perfect: a ray of sun splintering the clump of cloud through the window, the dozing cat, the young woman whose beauty is a secret which the world has kept from her. As Ellen removes the plate, it strikes her that she has a better eye than her brother gives her credit for.

'I'll develop the photograph this evening.' Ellen glances at Lily and works very hard to sound casual. 'Perhaps I could bring it to the pier on Sunday? With the picture of Miss Smart. We could take tea at the Refreshments Room?'

She has gone too far. Lily looks anywhere but at Ellen, scrabbling to put on her coat and gloves, as if she were suddenly in the most tearing hurry.

'Yes, all right,' she says, and Ellen tells herself it's just shyness and tries not to mind.

Once Lily has gone, Ellen returns to the studio. She kneels and buries her face in the musty velvet of the chaise longue, breathing in what Lily has left behind, as, up and down the terraced street, wheeling seagulls caw and mock her.

Later, Ellen goes upstairs to the attic, which serves as both a darkroom and a place to sleep, a thin green curtain separating one function from the other. She expects to find Reynold preparing the solutions, but the basins are empty, the bottles of developer untouched. The curtain parts and she catches the smell of hair oil as her brother appears in the navy coat and mustard necktie he wears for outings. He smiles, and holds out her jacket.

'I have a surprise for you, Ellie.'

'Don't you want to get the developing done?' She glances at the plate holders. 'They can dry overnight.'

'The photographs can wait. While I, dear sister –' Reynold links his arm through hers – 'cannot.'

'We can't afford surprises,' Ellen sighs. She may only be five minutes the older of the two, yet at times her twin has the knack of making her feel like a punitive parent.

'I beg to differ.'

And Reynold looks at her with such hope in his green-gold eyes, identical to her own, that Ellen swallows her reservations. It is their birthday next week, it is improbable but not impossible that he has money saved; he may have been listening when she spoke of how much she would like to take to the streets on a Ladies' Rambler.

She pats his smooth cheek. 'Then I will fetch my hat.'

Chapter Two

B rother and sister walk along the promenade, past the
attendant line of carriages that run all the way from the
pier. The street lamps are just lit and the tide froths across
the shingle, slowly clearing the beach of the oyster sellers
and the ice-cream carts, the pierrots who juggle and tumble
and perform dumb show, and Dr Esposito who will run his
hands across your scalp for sixpence and tell you what the
future holds. The smell of fried potatoes and onions rises
from the braziers, and the wild-haired Scot who plays the
tin whistle on the slipway counts out the pennies from his
upturned cap and nods to the pair as they pass. The Harpers
are known, by sight at least, by most who ply their trade on
this long, crowded stretch of pebbled beach, but as to who
they are exactly and where they come from, no one can truly
say. They are photographers from Paris, some will tell you,
yet they sound as English as the next person, and the sister
is still unmarried, which is curious for she is handsome
enough, if a little severe, and they can't be living in luxury in
those poky rooms in Booth Lane, with not even a char-
woman to do for them.

They cross the road to the Metropole Hotel, dodging the
hansoms, and walk a little further. Ellen glances at her
brother. He is humming to himself, but whether through
nervousness or good humour, she cannot be sure, and her

feeling of unease returns. A short distance ahead, she sees two men standing outside a shop front – the stouter of the pair raises a hand.

Ellen frowns. 'Is that Wally Clarke?'

'Indeed!' Reynold waves back with enthusiasm, as they approach. 'Well met, Mr Clarke!'

'Mr Harper.' Wally shakes Reynold's hand, then turns to Ellen, his strawberry-ice complexion reddening. 'Miss Harper. Always a pleasure.'

She has nothing against the man, in principle, Ellen supposes, returning his greeting; indeed, it would be hard to find a more affable individual than Wally Clarke, 'Ice King' – so named for his small empire of ice-cream kiosks and parlours – he'd been one of the first to come for a portrait when they'd set up in business at Booth Lane. Yet there is something expectant in the way he looks at her, the hopeful incline of an eyebrow, that makes Ellen want to run.

His companion, introduced as Mr Black, is unlocking the door of what Ellen now realises to be a photographic studio, but one that is as far removed from Booth Lane as a symphony is distant from an organ grinder's tune. She finds herself ushered into a spacious reception room, with the lingering scent of attar of roses, unfurnished save for a large kidney-shaped couch.

'Electric light, naturally.'

Mr Black flicks a copper switch, and a dim light seeps from the tulip-shaped bulbs of the chandelier. Ellen sighs as Mr Black proceeds to outline the merits of this receiving room for the 'clientele', before taking them upstairs – with more flicking of switches and lights to marvel over – while Wally Clarke murmurs that call him old-fashioned, but he prefers gas.

'And so to the beating heart of the operation,' Mr Black intones and they are led into a substantial drawing room, furnished sparsely but with taste, with a carved wooden settee and leather armchair, and a small piano flanking the marble fireplace. Three windows, as imposing as a trio of lady dowagers, rise from floor to ceiling, overlooking the sea.

'The southerly aspect renders the perfect conditions for the photographer's art,' Mr Black goes on. 'A westerly light on one side – and on the other, a studio for the morning.'

'Isn't it wonderful?' Reynold bounds to the middle window. 'Enough light to brighten the shabbiest of days.'

Ellen ignores him, her irritation growing. 'And if this is the beating heart of the establishment, Mr Black, are we to see the other organs which it services?'

'This way, Miss Harper.'

Wally chuckles, as they follow the property agent down a corridor to the darkroom, fitted with multiple basins and rows of shelves, adjoined by a separate annex for printing.

'No more moving like chess pieces in that tiny attic.' Reynold squeezes her hand. 'What do you say, Ellie?'

'I say I have the most foolish brother in the world,' she hisses. She turns to the agent. 'I do apologise for having squandered your time, Mr Black. But this studio, charming as it is, is completely beyond our means.'

The agent glances nervously at Reynold. 'The deposit has already been paid, Miss Harper,' he says.

'Paid! By whom?' But really she means how and with what.

'By your brother, miss.'

'It was a surprise, Ellen. I told you.' Reynold looks at her pleadingly and gestures towards Wally. 'And Mr Clarke is most interested in photography, isn't that right, Walter, and may perhaps see a way to collaborate in the future?'

'It's certainly possible, young man,' Wally says, with a benevolent nod, but it is Ellen whose attention he is seeking and there goes the eyebrow again. The reason Walter Clarke, ice-cream magnate and widower, is here is her, Ellen realises sickly, it has nothing to do with her deluded brother. And in vindication of her point, Wally draws out his watch. 'Isn't it about time for that supper we spoke of, Mr Harper? Your poor sister looks in need of a glass of port.'

Ellen glares at her twin. So, she has been ambushed – she is to sit between them at The Ship like the catch of the day, and be glad about it. She turns to Wally with an apologetic smile.

'My brother forgets that I have work to do this evening, Mr Clarke. I *am* sorry.'

Reynold is about to protest when a crackling sound comes from the ceiling rose. The lights flicker and then go out with a quiet pop. As Mr Black commences a litany of excuses on behalf of the electric lighting, Ellen slips downstairs and out into the busy street.

'Evening, Miss Harper.'

There is an hour to go before curtain-up at the Empire, and the Jolly Players is stuffed to the gills. Ellen asks the landlord for a measure of brandy – damn the expense: she will treat it as supper. The Harpers are going up in the world after all, she thinks bitterly, her head throbbing as she thinks of the money that Reynold must have paid for a deposit on that ostentatious studio – and to what purpose? They'll not afford to heat and light it, much less anything else, and what kind of business will they do in such a place, far too grand for families in search of donkey rides and ices, and not exclusive enough for the 'clientele' who stay at the Metropole and the like. And what of the models? One couldn't find premises more public than the King's Road; they'd have the police on the doorstep before their first week was through.

'Well, if it isn't the Governess.'

There is only one person who greets her with this unauthorised *nom de la rue* and sure enough, there she is, Miss Harriet Smart, short hair oiled back, dressed for her stage turn in top hat and frock coat, and calling to Mr Hobbs to bring a quart of beer for her girls.

'Do-gooders have put the wind up 'em,' Miss Smart tells Ellen, nodding towards a corner table where the tableaux girls – Jemima, Sal and Corazón – better known to audiences as the living statues, and to Ellen as three of Booth Lane's more impudent models, are settling themselves. Corazón spots Ellen and murmurs something to her companions, and the trio convulse with giggles.

'Comes to something when you can't even go to work in peace.' Miss Smart looks with exasperation towards the windows, where a forest of placards bobs up and down above the frosted glass. She starts to sing, her eyes glinting with mischief.

'*We're the prudes on the prowl, and we wear a scowl. Heigh ho, the lifelong day!*'

She winks and cups Ellen's elbow. 'I see you are without your sweetheart this evening, so come and take a drink with us.'

She means Reynold. The joke – if one might call it such – is long established – and honestly, Ellen thinks, she has never met an actress who believes herself to be so very amusing. But as she coolly declines the offer, she remembers Lily.

'I have a friend,' Ellen says, 'who would very much appreciate a signed photograph.' She pauses, made awkward by the sly look in her companion's eye. 'But if it's too much trouble . . .'

'A friend, eh!' Miss Smart's fingers perform a drum roll on the counter. 'No need to look so bashful, Miss Harper. I'll drop one around tomorrow. Booth Lane, isn't it?'

She will have to pretend to be out and ask Reynold to answer the door. Ellen thanks her and makes her excuses, elbowing her way outside with some relief. It suddenly occurs to her that Harriet Smart may have thought she wanted the photograph for herself; the thought makes her want to bury herself deep in her bedclothes.

Ellen lingers for a moment, on the busy street, watching the small but determined group of women attached to the placards.

STOP THE INDECENCY IN OUR THEATRES!
TABLEAUX OUTRAGE – OFF OUR STAGE!

An unwelcome memory arises of her grandmother, her deceptively soft face, fuzzy with down. Had her life extended into this most irreverent of decades, she might well have found a natural home among this bunch of po-faced Mrs Grundys. Faces like shovels, some of them, Ellen thinks uncharitably, an opinion which appears to be shared by a couple of rough types, outside the theatre door, who heckle and jeer. Then, her eyes are drawn to a younger woman, a little apart from the others, bearing a board that exhorts all who lay eyes upon it to 'END THIS PLAGUE OF FILTH!' but whose features bear no resemblance to a gardening implement of any kind. She has high cheekbones and wide blue eyes set in a face that has the luminous quality of a flower in bloom, and Ellen imagines that if the woman were to smile, the effect would equal that of sunlight dappled on water. But she isn't smiling, she is – as if attesting to Harriet Smart's impromptu ditty – scowling somewhat, as she dumps the placard on the ground and says something to a younger girl, next to her. The girl shakes her head and turns her back, and Ellen guesses that for such familiarity to be tolerated, they must be related, sisters perhaps, although they look nothing alike.

The woman frowns, adjusts the angle of her rather fine hat and makes to leave. But as she does so, a missile – soft and red – flies through the crowd, splattering its innards across her companion's placard, swiftly followed by another and then another which hits the woman's right cheek.

'We'll set the police on you for insolence!' one of the vigilants cries out, and in the ensuing commotion Ellen loses sight of the lady. But somehow her path through the surging crowd is such that, a moment later, the two of them are face to face, pressed together like books on a shelf, and close up Ellen sees that her eyes are the delicate blue of Delft china and that her hair bears the reddish-gold tones of autumn and has a kink to it. She smells of scent, richly spiced.

'Do let me pass, would you?' the woman says, wearily but without malice, bringing a gloved hand to her cheek. Her accent is unfamiliar, American perhaps. 'Do I still have that muck on my face?'

'A little.' Ellen delves into her bag and wordlessly offers up her handkerchief.

The woman hesitates, then takes it with a smile. 'Thank you.' She dabs at her cheek. 'The lengths one goes to, to provoke one's husband!' And the intimacy of her tone, the confessional nature of it, sucks any response from Ellen into thin air and all she can do is stare, as the vigilant, her face open and full of trust, tries to hand back the handkerchief. Does she believe them to be equals, does she take Ellen herself for a lady?

'Please – keep it,' Ellen says, and the woman smiles again, revealing a row of small white teeth, perfect save for a gap in their centre.

'You're very kind.'

And then she is gone, just two green feathers in a grey hat, heading with intent towards North Street.

Behind Ellen, someone laughs low and familiar in her ear. 'You'll be handing out the smelling salts next, Miss Harper.'

Harriet Smart again. She tips her hat to Ellen, all twinkle, as she strides to the stage door with the tableaux girls in her wake, their shoulders heaving as if they too are in on the joke.

Damned woman has to poke her nose in everywhere! Ellen is surprised at how close to tears she finds herself – it must be the brandy and then the business with Reynold. And don't forget Lily, a nasty niggling voice murmurs inside her head; she bolted from you like a rabbit out of a trap.

As the theatre bell rings and the street begins to clear, Ellen is hit by a wave of loneliness. All people can do is make fun of her; she knows what they say. She is 'the Governess', buttoned up from her boots to her collar, but who still shares a bedroom with her brother: they are 'the sweethearts', and she is supposed to laugh along and find it jolly when really she wants to seize Harriet Smart by those ridiculous lapels and ask if she has an inkling of what it's like to be tethered to a person you long to be freed from, yet cannot imagine being without.

The theatre doors are closed now, the crowd dispersed. She has no one to see, nowhere to go but back. Picking her way through the tomato pulp, Ellen heads towards Booth Lane, and home.

Chapter Three

Clementine Williams née Brouwer lies underneath her husband of six months' standing, eyes half closed, waiting for the moment when his panting will be replaced by the high-pitched wheeze which indicates that very soon Herbert will grunt like a farmyard animal and empty himself inside her. This morning it's a rather half-hearted grunt, and she guesses with no little satisfaction that her husband is still sore about that business outside the Empire on Friday evening. Herbert rolls off her, and squeezes her hand.

'Which train are you taking?' Clem wriggles free and goes behind the screen to wash, wetting a cloth and dipping it inside her, just as Minnie, her maid in New York, had advised. It was the only way to have any chance of avoiding a child, Minnie had said, if a man didn't pull out before he'd spent himself – that and staying upright for at least an hour afterwards.

Herbert yawns and mumbles something about the 12.10 and lunch with his money man at the club. He reaches for his long johns.

'Now, Clemmy,' he says, and Clem winces – there is nothing worse than a pet name when the pet barely tolerates its owner. 'No more breast beating while I'm away. It sets a bad example to Ottilie. And do try and keep out of the path of flying vegetables!'

Clem lathers the soap and repeats the process with the cloth one more time. 'As I recall, Herbert, not three weeks ago, you explicitly said I should stop moping around the house and wishing myself back in America, and occupy myself with some charity work instead.' She smiles to herself. 'Take a leaf out of your sister's book, you said.'

'I meant go to a few committee meetings, not take to the streets, with my niece in tow, and holler outside the theatre like a couple of cockle sellers!'

Pulling down her nightdress, Clem comes out from behind the screen. 'It was a silent protest, Herbert,' she says. 'And committee meetings don't always yield results.'

'Is that so?' He lolls back on the bed and regards her with deep scepticism.

'Yes.' Clem puts on her dressing gown. 'And as for Ottilie, I suppose you'd rather she was inside the theatre, would you, witnessing that –' she tries to remember the words her sister-in-law, Caroline, had used at the last meeting – 'that "grotesque display of naked bodies, masquerading as art"?'

'Now you're being ridiculous.'

Herbert throws himself into the easy chair, his florid features, weathered by wind and wine, preoccupied. 'We'll have to get her shipshape for Switzerland, or she'll be a laughing stock. Her French isn't up to much, and she needs to stop drooping and lift her head up.'

'She's ashamed of her skin,' Clem says quietly.

'Then lend her some of your potions.' He nods towards the small citadel of pots and bottles on Clem's dressing table. 'Get an advertisement out to *The Lady* today, would you? We could have a tutor in place by the time I'm back from London.'

Clem sits before the mirror and starts to brush out her hair.

She suspects it will take more than a teacher of etiquette to convince Ottilie of the benefits of being sent to be finished in Switzerland, when all the girl really seems to want is to keep house for her uncle, and attend meetings with a group of puritans who appear set on returning the country to the time of Oliver Cromwell.

'I'll see what I can do,' she says.

'Good girl.' Herbert plants a kiss on her cheek, his hand slipping down the front of her nightgown. 'How about another go? One for luck?'

His eyes meet hers, hopeful in the looking glass, but the act has been done once, and now she has the respectable woman's right to refuse. Clem extracts herself from his grip. 'I was about to call for Milly,' she says, reaching for the cold cream. 'You've quite worn me out.'

It is past lunchtime before Herbert eventually leaves. He had been vague as to when he might return, mentioning a possible detour via the estate at Feathers to check on a few things, which Clem had interpreted as passing a few days putting bullets into defenceless birds and feeling clever about it. Upon her arrival in England, she had spent months enduring mud, sub-standard plumbing and afternoon tea with the vicar, before she'd sat Herbert down and insisted on a change. If not for me, for the baby, she said, for she may not have had many cards to play, but his future heir was surely one of them, and her husband's eyes had lit up.

'The baby that will arrive in good time, *if* its mama is contented,' she added, sincerely hoping that this theory would be disproved; and Herbert had hemmed and hawed, and outright refused to consider London, claiming it was too dirty and dangerous and not at all suitable for Ottilie.

And so he had sent instruction for the house in Brighton to be made ready again, and the three of them had arrived here at the tail end of summer, just over a month ago, and taken up residency in a crescent of gleaming white townhouses in the east of the town.

Now, as another long afternoon yawns before her, Clem goes to her husband's study to draft an advertisement for the new tutor. The shelves of dusty books and the papers strewn every which way across the escritoire tell their own story – Herbert is not a man for ledgers and accounts, nor can he spend more than fifteen minutes in the company of a book; his pleasures, he has confessed, come principally on horseback. Yet, there is little to hunt in London, Clem thinks as she fills a pen from the inkwell, and he is there once a week, often for several days.

She taps her fingers on the polished wood, her gaze drawn reluctantly to the wedding photograph on top of the bureau. It had been taken on their honeymoon in a glass-roofed studio in Rome – it had been hot and bright, and there had been much fussing with screens. Herbert stands behind her, like a big hulking bear dressed up in tweeds, pinning her to her seat with his paw. Her dress, a gold silk affair, which he had paid for as he had paid for everything, swarms with pearls. On the eve of their wedding, her mother had called her into the parlour and delivered a pep talk, over a glass of rum punch. *He may be a little older than you, Clementine, but you'll reap the benefits in other ways, you'll see. There really is no point in making a fuss.*

Clem turns the photograph towards the wall. Well, she has done her duty and her family are saved. Her stepfather is back at the shipping offices, giving orders, not sitting desperate in his study with a hand gun in an unlocked drawer; her mother can make calls again on the Upper East Side in her new ermine jacket and ostrich-feathered hat. She has a daughter in England, married to a man worth at least £6,000 a year, with a country estate and a handsome residence by the sea. It is a curious sensation to be sold, Clem muses, making one feel both of value and without worth at the same time.

She reaches for the blotter and puts the advertisement to one side. Idly, she slides the bureau compartments open and shut. Envelopes. Bills. Heavens, but her husband is dull! And then she comes upon an oval tortoiseshell snuffbox. Less dull, perhaps she will try some – she flicks open the catch, before her hand flies to her mouth. On the underside of the lid is a photograph of the type that the vigilants would describe as filth, and that Clem can find no words for, for she has never seen anything of the sort. A woman, slim but shapely, kneeling on a chair, with her back to the camera, in a state of total undress. Her legs are crossed nonchalantly at the ankle, the crease underneath the cheeks of her buttocks seeming to mock Clem in the way the girl's smile would, if she could only see her face. Clem snaps the box shut, hesitates, then opens it again. She wonders how Herbert came by it, she looks at the girl and imagines her husband looking too, and it makes her feel peculiar. And there is no snuff, she notices now, only a tiny key, which lies in the shadow of the model's posterior, like the beginning of a rather unorthodox fairy tale.

Clem tries the locks of every drawer in the bureau. But they are either open and jammed with papers or the key doesn't fit. She studies the mahogany frieze which runs along the centre of the desk. There is a section which is more worn than the rest, and as she slides her fingernail across the seam, the facade comes away to reveal a small compartment with a lock. Her heart thuds. She takes the key and the drawer opens without resistance.

She had expected more photographs, but there are just a bundle of papers and a drawstring pouch. Inside Clem finds a photograph of another woman, but one who is framed in silver and fully attired this time, in a riding dress and hat, her fingers curled around a crop, while a docile spaniel slumps at her feet. There is an imperious tilt to her thickening chin, her eyes are small and her figure imposing. Clem studies the inscription – *'Bibi', Lady Arabella Hawes-Montague.* Bibi, she notes, can be no younger than her own mother. She smells a rat, a whole sewer of rats, and she starts to rifle through the papers.

First a receipt from a London jeweller's for a jet-and-pearl necklace. A calling card from Bibi herself, with a Mayfair address, and several letters, all headed with a school crest, bearing the name of Eton College. The fees for this school could pay the rent on her mother's Manhattan apartment for a year, and her husband has paid them – she flicks through the pages – for the last four years. Then come the school reports – an atrocious Arithmetic result, a lack of application to the study of Classics. Barnaby Hawes-Montague is of a 'boisterous temperament', one master observes, 'which has nonetheless found some application on the rugby field'.

At the back of the drawer, Clem discovers another picture – of the reprobate himself, trussed up in his Eton tails and hat, sturdy and broad, leaning forward as if he might at any moment launch himself into a scrum. It is the same way Herbert sits, Clem realises, Barnaby's hair thick and fair, just as her husband's would have been in his youth.

Clem takes out the freshly laundered handkerchief that the tall stern woman outside the Empire theatre had given her, before realising she has no inclination to cry. She looks at Bibi's photograph with distaste. So, she, Clementine, is to be the dupe, is she, the American whose stepfather lost his fortune in the Panic two years ago, her main duty to lift up her nightgown until her belly starts to swell with legitimacy, while her husband does whatever he pleases?

'I don't think so, Mr Williams,' she says. She puts everything back in the drawer, and returns the key to the snuffbox, wondering if the item was a gift from his mistress and, if that were the case, where one would even come by such a thing? She knows little more of the world than Ottilie, she realises, a state of shadowed innocence in which her husband undoubtedly intends her to remain. Deep in thought, Clem draws back her chair and pulls the bell rope for tea.

Chapter Four

Ellen unpegs the last of the prints which hang across the attic like bunting and arranges them in orderly piles alongside a stack of stamps, envelopes and white tissue paper. Church bells releasing the faithful from their pews sound out across the rooftops, a wasp dips and hovers by the open window. Ellen begins to work, swiftly and methodically, packaging up the prints in white tissue, five apiece, addressing envelopes, ticking names off a list.

They had started the mail order business just before last Christmas, motivated in part by her ambivalence towards their weaselly middleman Mr Meed, who went to London once a month with a battered attaché case, returning with protracted tales of exhaustive haggling in the back rooms of bookshops. Ellen has long suspected that Mr Meed couldn't negotiate his way out of a paper bag, besides which how does one take seriously a man with scuffed boots, whose trouser hems run loose? They were putting all their eggs in one basket, she'd told Reynold, they needed to add more threads to the loom. And so they had set up a postal box address and put out an advertisement, and business since has been brisk, accruing a number of loyal customers, including schoolboys from some of England's most illustrious institutions.

Ellen picks up a print of the tableaux girls. Bent over the

chaise in black stockings, petticoats flung over their heads like parasols blown inside out, the effect is as dramatic as she'd hoped. How they had giggled and snorted in the execution, such a contrast to Lily's quiet composure, her picture all shadows, as she stands with her head dropped modestly, the curves of her body caught in silhouette. Glancing at the order forms, Ellen isn't at all sure that she wants the likes of Mr R. Pritchard Esq. of Wolverhampton putting his greasy fingers all over it, and she slips Lily's print to the bottom of the set, hoping that the tableaux girls might prove distraction enough.

She glances at the clock, wondering where Reynold has got to and when he will be back; they haven't spoken since the ambush at the studio, but she refuses to let this spoil her Sunday. In no less than four hours, she will be sitting in the Refreshments Room, on the sunny corner table behind the potted palm, treating Lily to an ice, a proper one this time, in a glass that is clean. She will arrive early to stake her claim on the table, she will set down Harriet Smart's photograph (slipped through the letter box yesterday evening), ready for Lily's arrival, along with the other of her and Floss. Ellen frowns. Is it perhaps wiser to wait until Lily has come and tea is served, before presenting the gift? A distressing scenario presents itself in which Lily arrives, snatches up the photographs, and in a flurry of excuses leaves immediately.

The front door slams, and Reynold's voice carries up the stairs. A tap on the door jamb – he is waving a white hand-kerchief and wearing a sheepish smile.

'Truce! Please, Ellie!' he says, as she turns back to her work. 'Curse and damn me for being the most feckless of brothers – but enough of the silence, I beg you. It's upsetting the cat.'

And Floss, darting out from underneath the table to greet him, purrs in agreement as he pets her.

'You should have consulted me.' Ellen gives Reynold a sharp look as she seals another envelope. 'And getting the Ice King involved in your idiocy. Luring him there. Poor man's a widower, it's not fair.'

'He enjoys your company! What's so wrong with that?'

She closes her eyes. 'Marry him yourself, if you want his money so badly.'

Yesterday's silence fills the room, and when Reynold next speaks, his voice has a crack in it. 'I want so much more for us than just this.'

Ellen looks up. 'We get by.'

'I want to do more than get by! I'm tired of hiding away in this miserable street, scratching around for business. If it weren't for the girls, we'd be destitute by now.' Frowning, Reynold picks up one of Lily's prints. 'But I hardly think a portfolio of living statues and laundry girls is going to gain me admission to the Society.'

'Oh, Reynold.' Ellen shakes her head. 'The Photographic Society isn't for people like us.'

'It could be!' He starts to pace the attic. 'That's what I'm trying to explain. But not if our customers begin and end with families from Bermondsey, down for a bracer on the prom.' He pauses. 'We could advertise as Paris-trained, you know.'

Ellen's snort of laughter sends Floss scampering behind the curtain. 'Just as long as no one asks for the specifics.'

Her brother ignores her. 'The Season's just beginning, it's the perfect time. The studio could be up and running within a fortnight.'

She stares at him. He is serious. 'How much is the rent on that place?'

Reynold tells her a figure which makes her eyes smart. 'I want to do this properly,' he goes on. 'Wally's even recommended an accountant he uses.'

'And what of the girls, Reynold?' Ellen says, gesturing towards the pile of stuffed envelopes. 'I'd like to see what Wally's man makes of those accounts!'

'We'll keep that side of the business separate. Discreet, here at Booth Lane.' Reynold puts an arm around her. 'Come downstairs a moment. I have something for you.'

With some reluctance, Ellen follows him down to the studio. But there propped against the chaise longue is a bicycle, with a glossy brown saddle, golden spokes gleaming in the light.

'It's the one you wanted,' Reynold says with pride. 'The Ladies' Rambler.'

'I won't be bought off, Reynold.' Yet Ellen can't resist running her hand across the curve of the handlebars, which are painted the deep lustrous black of park railings. She imagines herself weaving through the hordes on Marine Drive, on a sunny Sunday, before disappearing into the hills. A blanket, a picnic, the shadow of a companion eclipsing the sun on her face. She turns to him. 'If this means more debt, you can return it right away.'

He assures her that it is paid for, that he has been saving for it ever since they started doing the mail order, and that he isn't such a cloth-eared fool of a brother as not to know what will make her happy.

'I'm sorry about Wally,' Reynold says soberly. 'You're right – it was madness. How could I ever let anyone take you from me!'

And as he smiles, Ellen sees their reflection captured in the windowpane, and even though the quarrel is over, her heart sinks just a little.

'Mr Clarke has proved himself to be most generous, regardless.' Reynold brightens. 'I have a signwriter booked for Wednesday, and the cards are at the printers – we could be in business by Monday fortnight.'

'*We?*'

'Of course, we.' He takes her hand. 'I don't want to do this without you.'

Ellen looks at her brother. Her heart hurts at his capacity for hope. It doesn't matter how many baronets might patronise their establishment or Photographic Societies Reynold aspires to join, no parent will ever congratulate him, no doting father will ever look at their family name above the door and tell Reynold he's made him proud.

'Take the bicycle back from wherever you got it.' She shakes herself free of his grasp. 'I'm going out.'

'Out? Let me come with you.'

'I'd prefer to be alone.' Ignoring the injured look on her twin's face, Ellen marches up to the attic to fetch her things, trying her best to calm herself. Why – today of all days – must Reynold be so intent on ruining things, on making her cross, when all she wants is to arrive at the tearooms serene as a lily pad on a motionless pond, stirred only by the gaze of the girl in the dented straw hat.

Lily had waited until everyone was safely out of the house to take her Sunday bath and now as she crouches, naked in the enamel tub in the half-light of the kitchen, it crosses her mind that she should perhaps have bathed in her drawers and bodice just in case. She has bolted the door to the street and pushed a chair against the other, in case anyone should come in the back way – her uncle has a habit of creeping up on her when she least expects it, even at times like this afternoon when he's usually settling into the pub down the road with her mother. The first Sunday after he arrived, she had looked up from her bath to see his stupid, grinning, yellow-toothed face peering through the sagging veil of net curtain at the half-open kitchen window. She'd rushed to cover herself, but standing up had just made it worse and he hadn't moved on, like any decent person would, but stayed there, studying her as if she were a picture in a book.

'You're riper than I thought, lass,' he'd said, with a smile, before eventually carrying on down the street, and that had been the start of it, his hand on her arm, then her waist, then her thigh, his breath in her ear, pressing her against the wall, the stove, the table, whenever her mother had her back turned. And how Lily wished at those moments that she was plain like her sister Susan, with a chest as flat as a ten-year-old's and a body like a trunk, for all her looks had brought her was pestering from horrible men. She wasn't so green she didn't know what would happen if her uncle was set upon it, and there was no one who would take her side, least of all her ma.

Lily takes a small towel and steps from the bath. She has a feeling that she is horribly late, which perhaps doesn't matter, for when that strange woman Miss Harper had started talking about Refreshment Rooms and Sunday tea, all Lily could think of was grand ladies in fussy lace blouses and teetering feathered hats. She didn't know why Miss Harper couldn't just meet her at the tollbooth with the photograph of Harry Smart and be done with it, for then she might save herself the cost of the entrance. Still, it wouldn't hurt her to keep on Miss Harper's good side – she'll need to do what she did for that camera again and again if she wants to save enough to leave.

She takes her clothes, freshly laundered and smelling of soap, and starts to dress, thinking about the three shillings she earned, now stashed behind a loose brick in the filthiest corner of the coal cellar. At first she had thought she would die of shame, lying like a doxy on that musty couch, but Mr Harper had behaved as if she'd been as fully clothed as he was. Drop the drape, he'd told her, and Lily had noticed Miss Harper's shoulders twitch, but she hadn't looked round from the window, and thinking she may as well be hung for a sheep as a lamb, Lily had done as he asked. It was over quickly but that wasn't to say she liked it, and the secret she carries around with her now feels a dirty one.

She is just tucking in her shirt, when she hears her mother's voice, slack with drink, outside the window, followed by a pounding on the door.

'Open up! What's she up to in there?'

'I'll set a bob on her talking sweet nothings with some lad,' her uncle responds with a chuckle.

'I'll leather her to next Friday. Lily!'

Lily opens the door. There stands – or rather leans – her mother, propped up against Uncle Jack, whose arm seems to have slipped around her waist. They smell strongly of the pub. Her brothers Christopher and Sammy dodge past them, tossing an India rubber ball across the room with a whoop.

'The Croc's coming, Lil.' Sammy tugs at her skirt, his blue eyes large as saucers. 'He's coming to eat us up.'

Her uncle's work, no doubt, scaring the children witless after a pint or two.

'Uncle Jack's been telling you fibs,' she says, ruffling her brother's matted hair. 'Mr Crocker's not coming here.'

'Says she!' Her mother gives her a look of extreme exasperation as she reaches for the tea caddy on top of the cupboard. 'Cough up, Lil – I need your extras.'

Lily hesitates. It is their agreement that she and her sister are allowed to keep a shilling back from their wages at the laundry each week, although experience has taught her that if she doesn't spend it quickly, it will be called upon for an emergency, such as the one that appears to have seized her mother now.

'I was about to go to the pier.'

'And now you ain't.'

Better not to argue. She takes the last sixpence from her pocket and hands it to her mother, before Uncle Jack, rolling tobacco at the window, lets out a low whistle.

'Wouldn't want to be in his shoes, no, sir.'

Lily follows her mother and uncle out onto the street. It is the boy, Billy, from three houses up, her age or thereabouts, tall and freckled and pale as milk, who goes about as if he has jack-in-the-box springs in his boots. But not now. A man under each armpit, coarse-looking, unsmiling, dragging him up the hill; his red hair is wet, and water leaks from his boots which are unlaced and keep drawing on the cobbles. He coughs feebly, then retches a string of watery bile from his blue lips.

'He's taken a drowning,' Uncle Jack murmurs, and it seems to Lily that the inhabitants of Albion Hill, pressed into their front doorways, are never as loud as when they are silent, for she knows what they're all thinking as well as if they were hollering all hell – it's the Croc's work. And if there should remain any doubt, here he comes, a little distance behind, in a smart grey coat and bowler, flanked by two men burly as farmhands. His is the face that used to haunt Lily's most vivid nightmares as a child; she remembers him standing in their kitchen, cold pale eyes watching her mother as she scrabbled about for the overdue money they owed, his pockmarked skin as rough and pitted as scales. Afterwards Ma would take to bed and cry and Lily and her sister would fall asleep with empty stomachs, to the sound of their parents squabbling.

Now, she hears Ma's sharp intake of breath as the Croc and his men reach their house. Lily thinks of the money in the coal cellar and how she won't give it up for anything. But they walk on, not stopping until they reach Billy's place, where they dump him on the doorstep, and there is a low rumble of voices before the Croc's men step inside, and Mr Crocker carries on up the road, for everyone knows he leaves the roughing-up for others to do.

As their neighbours begin to drift back indoors, Lily looks down the hill, at the sliver of distant sparkling sea. Better to earn money than to borrow it, no matter how. She thinks of Miss Harper, waiting for her in the Refreshments Room. She'll give the photograph of Harry Smart to another girl now, more than likely, someone 'more reliable than yourself, Miss March'.

She sniffs, and her ma scowls. 'Stop your sulking, will you? Me and your uncle are going for a little walk.' Her mother gives Uncle Jack a look that Lily has come to recognise, as if she has swallowed a passing fly and found it surprisingly pleasant. 'You mind the boys for me, till your sister gets back.'

'There's a good lass.' Uncle Jack winks and takes her mother's arm. Christopher hits Sammy and Sammy starts to wail. And Lily closes her eyes and, losing the will to be proper, wonders what's the bleeding point in having a bath if she's to spend the whole of Sunday dragging her skirts through the muck of Albion Hill.

Chapter Five

'Reynold!' Ellen glares at the freshly painted sign above the gleaming bay windows of the King's Road studio, and calls out again to her brother. There it is in bold white lettering, as blatant, as hurtful, as a slap to both cheeks. *Mr R. Harper, Photographer.* She turns on him angrily as he comes outside.

'*Harpers' Photography*, we said. On account of the fact that there are *two* of us.'

She spits out the words and marches back inside, the bell above the door jangling. Reynold follows her, his face pale. 'Ellie, listen . . .'

'I expect these are the same, aren't they?' Ellen breaks the seal on the box of business cards, delivered that morning, and looks inside. *Mr R. Harper, French-trained. Instantaneous method. Highest degree of perfection.* The same insult, repeated a hundred times over and bordered with gilt. 'How could you?'

'I thought it had more authority that way.' Reynold clears his throat. 'That it might be better for business.'

'You won't be needing me in that case, will you?'

Ellen takes her cloak and hat, and pushes past him, collects the Ladies' Rambler from the hall and leaves through the back, wheeling it along the side road at first, before taking courage and joining the flow of carriages and carts on

Western Road. She has been practising every morning at sunrise, up and down the side streets, and the falls and the bruises and the occasional jeers of 'Mornin', mister!' from the hot-potato sellers have only strengthened her resolve. When she'd returned from that wild goose chase on the pier – a scenario in which she casts herself as much the goose as the absent Miss March – the bicycle was still there in the studio, and she had felt so low and dispirited that she had let Reynold persuade her to keep it. The memory of that afternoon still smarts – the table set for two, the pot of cooling tea, the tidal creep of disappointment as it became clear that Lily wasn't coming. Before she left, Ellen had tossed Harriet Smart's photograph into the sea, and as she watched it disappear under the waves, she couldn't rid herself of the thought that she had used it as bait.

Ellen picks up speed. The other day she'd read an article opining that if ladies insisted on taking to the roads, then they should cycle no faster than a ten-year-old child chasing a hoop. The absurdity of it compels her to pedal faster still and the driver of a brougham, idling at the corner, gives her an odd look as she passes. She supposes to others she must seem free to do as she likes, with no maiden aunt to chaperone her, no fretful mother determined to find her a husband. She could leave Brighton this minute, cycling as far and as long as she is able, living frugally in seaside boarding houses, with no one to miss her but Reynold. She could find work of some kind, but what? There is no occupation she is equipped to do, apart from photography, and even her own brother won't extend the courtesy of employing her as anything more than an assistant. She speaks like a lady, but it is clear from the plainness of her clothes that she is not; she could sweat in a factory, or pour quarts of beer in a tavern but no landlord would employ her – she fits nowhere, she and Reynold never have.

She finds herself on the King's Road again, drawn back towards the studio. She cannot leave, she has nowhere to go. Besides – and her heart splits open – she loves her brother, he is all she has, and the worst of it is, he is likely right – since when has a man's name above the door been an impediment to business? In all probability, it was Wally Clarke's suggestion, and at least she has avoided the fate of becoming Mrs Ice King, for it appears Reynold has wheedled the money from him regardless.

As she approaches the studio, the door opens and a middle-aged man appears, accompanied by two young women, whom Ellen assumes to be his daughters. It is clear just by the ladies' millinery alone that they are definitely 'clientele', not customers, and a smart carriage with two glossy black horses awaits them outside. But Ellen is not the only one who has smelt the money, for just as she is applying the brakes of the bicycle, a small boy, intent on opening the carriage door, darts from nowhere and into her path – she swerves and falls.

First, pain – in her shin and the wrist of her right hand; second, concern that the Rambler has been damaged. But looking up, Ellen sees that the gentleman has retrieved it, setting it against the wall, while his companions loom over her with anxious expressions, the younger of the two red-haired and a little spotty; the other a veritable advertisement for Pears soap, and who seems familiar somehow.

'This exactly proves my point about bicycles, my dears,' the man informs the women with a note of triumph. He regards Ellen coolly, as she scrambles to her feet. 'Do you find yourself injured, miss? In need of medical assistance?'

'No. Thank you.' But as she touches her forehead, blood smears her glove.

'You're hurt. Here . . .'

One of the women passes her a handkerchief. Upon it are the same initials as Ellen's own, stitched with such neatness and precision that it was as if this lady had spent hours at the hoop, as Ellen had, overseen by a grandmother who had no qualms about pulling out every last stitch if the end result was anything less than perfect. Ellen looks at her again and then she remembers. The woman is one of the vigilants from that evening outside the Empire, the American, with the face like a flower and the violet-blue eyes, to whom she had lent this same handkerchief. And it seems that the woman recalls her now too, for she is saying that she is glad the item has found its way back to its rightful owner, and at that same moment, Reynold bursts from the studio and runs to Ellen's side.

'Ellie, dearest, are you quite all right?' He examines the wound on her brow, then scowls at the street boy. 'Heavens, you can't move for children getting under your feet in this town.'

'The same might be said for lady cyclists.' The gentleman takes the American woman's arm. 'We look forward to receiving the photographs at your earliest convenience, Mr Harper.'

'I do hope your wife recovers from her ordeal swiftly,' the American lady says, smiling at Reynold and then Ellen, before she follows her companions into the carriage, and Ellen frowns and wishes she could call out after her to rectify the misunderstanding.

'A cabinet photo and a set of cartes-de-visite. Paid up front.' Reynold takes Ellen's bicycle and helps her inside. 'This is a good omen, mark my words.'

Wincing, Ellen sits on the couch and flexes her wrist. 'Who are they?'

'A Mr and Mrs Herbert Williams.' Reynold glances at the invoice. 'Live on the Crescent.'

She looks up in surprise. 'I assumed both ladies were his daughters. They're certainly young enough.'

'Dear Ellie,' Reynold laughs. 'You can be such an innocent at times. Now –' he claps his hands together and beams – 'I have plates to develop! Do you find yourself well enough to hold the fort?'

'Every last ticket sold!' Mr Harty, founding member of the Brighton Vigilance Association, and committee chair, shakes his head in disgust as he helps himself to more caraway cake.

'And is it any surprise? The girls are as good as naked.' Caroline Yorke-Duffy sets down her teacup with force. 'That theatre has been heading towards the sewer for years. And what decent person wants to see a woman dressed as a man, making unseemly jokes!'

'Incidentally, our agent, Mr Jackson, is keeping an eye on Miss Smart's residence,' Mr Harty says. 'Lots of comings and goings at the most irregular hours, by all accounts.'

'Has anyone here seen these living statues?' Clem looks around the table. 'On stage at the Empire, I mean?'

Mrs Yorke-Duffy's poodle, Winnie, looks up at Clem with its tiny currant eyes and growls softly, as all heads turn to its owner who, having introduced her brother's new wife to the group, has been unofficially allocated the task of setting her right on certain matters.

'It's hardly necessary, dear,' Mrs Yorke-Duffy says. 'The reviews speak for themselves.'

'Quite,' Mr Harty agrees. 'Besides, it's no place for a lady.'

Clem sighs. If earnestness has a smell, it is this mélange of lavender, dusty hymn books and damp dog which invades her drawing room every Wednesday. As an animated discussion ensues regarding the unsavoury element who frequent the performances, she slips from her place unnoticed and goes to the window. Fall has arrived and its colours are beautiful, russet and yellow and the icy blue of the sea. She experiences a pang of homesickness as acute as toothache. She has no one to go to the theatre with anyway, even if the committee were to sanction the idea, she thinks sadly. A night in the box with her husband and sister-in-law is hardly what she had in mind.

Her attention is caught by a woman on a bicycle turning onto the Crescent. 'Lady cyclists' are another bugbear of Herbert's – he will bore for hours on the subject. Clem watches as the woman alights directly outside their house, then her spirits lift a little. It is the photographer's wife – Mrs Harper – from the studio on King's Road, a leather satchel looped across her chest. Here is diversion at least, a brief reprieve from this never-ending afternoon.

Turning to the table, Clem asks the committee members to forgive her, but she has an engagement which had quite slipped her mind, and wishing them a good afternoon she makes her escape.

There is a striking resemblance between wife and husband, Clem notes, as she watches Mrs Harper unwrap the photographs. Both tall, and rather handsome, with the same colour eyes that a lazy observer might remark upon as hazel, but which are actually more a shade of honeyed amber, and seem to darken and lighten as the mood does in a room.

A love marriage, no doubt – Clem recalls the look of concern on Mr Harper's face as he'd taken his injured wife in his arms – the rawness of his affection had both touched and saddened her, for she is quite sure that she shall never feel moved to look at Herbert that way. Seeing Mrs Harper now, here in the parlour, so neat in her tweed jacket and shirt, with her hair scooped back from her face in a fetching, if slightly outmoded, style, it is hard to believe that she first saw her loitering unaccompanied among rather a rough crowd outside a public house.

Wordlessly, Mrs Harper passes her the cabinet print. There they all are – Herbert, Ottilie and herself – encased in a thin silver frame and destined for decades on top of the piano. She had not wanted it taken, and neither had Ottilie, but Herbert had insisted. We are like goddesses of Resignation and Frustration, Clem thinks, with Oblivion towering over us.

'It doesn't please you?' Mrs Harper asks, after a moment.

'The composition is flawless.' Clem puts down the photograph. 'But my husband's ward isn't fond of the camera. And I was feeling a little under the weather that day.'

'You are not long married, Mrs Williams?'

'Since the spring.' Clem braces herself for the inevitable gush of congratulation, yet none comes, and she feels rather comforted, as if this tall strange woman has understood something. She gives her a small smile. 'And yourself, Mrs Harper? Are you a newly-wed?'

But Mrs Harper reddens. 'Mr Harper is my brother, Mrs Williams,' she says. 'My twin, in fact.'

Clem's hand goes to her mouth. 'Forgive me.'

'Not at all. You are not the first—'

'To make such a blunder?' Clem says and, gratifyingly,

Mrs – *Miss* – Harper stops looking quite so severe. 'I have no siblings myself,' Clem goes on, 'and nor does Ottilie – Miss Williams. I sometimes think it might be easier for her if she did – she was very young when her parents died.'

'Is Miss Williams out in society yet?'

'Heavens, no! Unless one can class dodging rotten vegetables outside a music hall as being out,' Clem says, and a flicker of amusement crosses her visitor's face.

Indeed, it is unlikely, Miss Harper bats back, that one might find that particular pursuit indexed in an etiquette guide, and she trusts that Mrs Williams has suffered no lasting effects from the incident with the tomato?

'Aside from loss of dignity! Thank heavens you were on hand with your handkerchief.'

'Which became *your* handkerchief—'

'Subsequently returned to its rightful owner—'

'Found sprawled like a drunkard on the King's Road!'

And they laugh then, both of them, and Miss Harper appears as surprised and glad of it as Clem herself is, and oh, it is such a strange sensation to be merry again: she has been so very lonely here in England, Clem realises, and it is horrid. As she looks at her visitor, an idea comes to her.

'Your brother mentioned that he'd worked for some time in Paris. Do you speak French yourself, Miss Harper?' Clem pauses. 'Ottilie requires a tutor – I wondered if you might know of anyone suitable . . . or –' she lets out a little laugh – 'indeed whether the post might be of interest to you?' Her words, born from a sudden longing, come out in a rush. 'As it happens, I am looking to engage a companion for myself – I am new to Brighton, as you know.'

Miss Harper stares at her and Clem feels ashamed. The woman works in a photographic studio and rides a bicycle;

she has an air of answering to no one. Why would she give that up to work in a no-man's-land where she is neither servant nor mistress?

'Forgive me,' Clem says. 'It's a ridiculous notion.'

But Miss Harper's expression has become thoughtful. 'Might I ask,' she says, 'if I would have my own room?'

Chapter Six

E llen does up the top button of her nightgown, takes the mildewed Bible from the window ledge and climbs into bed. The whip of the wind and tremoring candlelight, the vinegar smell of the darkroom and the sound of Reynold stacking plates – these are ingredients that usually combine to soothe her, but not tonight. She selects a passage and starts to read.

> *I will punish you, according to the results of your deeds. And I will kindle a fire in its forest, That it may devour all its environs.*

The print blurs, the words roar loud in her ear. She doesn't read the Bible so much as absorb it into her blood. The salt water of memory stings and stings again.

'Put it away.' Reynold glances at her as he comes in, pulling the curtain taut across the rail. 'Better still, shred it to pieces and feed it to the gulls.'

He undresses with his back to her, shivering in the chill of the attic. As he pulls on his nightshirt, Ellen catches a glimpse of his nakedness, the knobbled ridge of his spine, and wonders if any woman will ever lie watching him from a matrimonial bed. She can no more conceive of it than she can her own marriage. It would make what she has to say so much easier, if there was another who bore responsibility for him; and perhaps she should have done more to encourage some of the models who came to the studio. But they all gave up on Reynold eventually, for where's the fun in pulling a bell that never rings? Not that her brother is entirely innocent – he signs his own confession whenever he returns from occasional trips to the capital, his furtiveness revealing the true nature of his visits so clearly that Ellen feels as if she has accompanied him to the small cold room, where a faceless woman, as worn and used as the bedsheets she lies upon, waits for him to come and be gone again.

Reynold gets into the bed next to her own, without saying goodnight. She is being punished for earlier, for missing the golden hour, for causing Dora, who had a four o'clock appointment at Booth Lane, to seek her out at the King's Road studio, as flashy as a peacock with her cheap paste jewellery and rouge. Reynold, who had been showing a gentleman and his sister a selection of finishes, had been furious.

'So I assume,' he says now, his back still turned, 'that we'll be getting some more business from the American wife? Seeing as you spent the whole afternoon chattering like magpies.'

Her brother is only this sour when he's afraid. Ellen puts the Bible aside, then snuffs out the candle, lies in the blackness with the surge of her thoughts. Two pounds a month, Mrs Williams had said, rising to three after Christmas, if both parties were satisfied, all her meals and a comfortable room on the third floor, with a partial view of the sea. She would teach French to Ottilie for two hours every morning, and keep Mrs Williams company in the afternoons. Ellen realises she isn't quite sure what this entails. Shopping at Hannington's or the Palmeira Stores, she supposes, pretending to care about the sleeves on a dress, walking along the promenade, taking rides, perhaps, on the electric train. Embroidery, flower arranging, the crocheting of doilies for the church bazaar. And there will be visits of course, to this square and that crescent, and all manner of inconsequential nonsense talked over tea and cake, while she sits silent in the least comfortable chair, fodder for the ladies to chew upon once she has left. There will be no trawling the pier or the public houses for models, no chivvying, or scolding, or flattering, no hours spent in the darkroom, gloved hands dipping and drying with the smell of chemicals all around, no aching neck from bending over the press, no addressing of envelopes, no haggling over commission with Meed every time he goes to London, no golden hour, no girls.

She has lost her mind. She cannot do it.

But a voice inside her is telling her that she can, she must. That she cannot live her life hinged to her twin, his decisions made hers – she thinks again of the sign above the studio door. She will have her own room, a thought so novel, so peculiar, that she fears it as much as she longs for it. The thought of crisp clean sheets that it is somebody else's responsibility to launder, the hypnotic lullaby of French verbs, declined in a schoolroom, no one to worry at her for not being married, for she will be assumed a spinster from the minute she is introduced as Mrs Williams' companion. And now she comes to think of it, she has been feeling rather overwrought of late. Ever since Lily, in fact; Ellen stops herself, she must not dwell on the matter further. The girl has no time for her – that much was clear – besides which there was something about the whole episode that had left

Ellen uneasy, and she wishes that Reynold had not been so insistent on Lily dropping the drape.

Ellen sighs, her thoughts returning to Mrs Williams. The woman was a vigilant, committed enough to wave a placard before a jeering crowd, yet she had been quick to laugh about her predicament – and then there was the husband whom she claimed to want to provoke: a strange admission for a new wife. As they'd sat among the sedate ferns in that most genteel of parlours, Mrs Williams had seemed so very dissatisfied, so very alone. Then we shall have one thing in common at least, Ellen thinks, and she closes her eyes and then her ears to the sound of her brother's restlessness, for he calls out several times during the night, as if already sensing what is to come.

'A lady's companion!' Reynold's indignation is matched only by that of the cat, who sits on the windowsill, glowering at Ellen. 'What are you planning to do all day – wind wool!'

'Teach French, actually.' Ellen lays her suitcase on the bed and starts to pack. They will expect her to arrive with a trunk; she will have to lie and say her things are being sent on.

'You're a photographer, not a governess.'

'I'm a photographer's *assistant*, Reynold.' She glares at him. 'And a rather lowly one at that.'

Turning away, she takes Grandmère's Bible, reassuring herself that the photograph is still there, where she concealed it, in the heart of the New Testament. Lily, with Flossy on her lap, her face open and innocent, smiling at the camera – and, Ellen likes to fancy, at her beside it. It is a memento, she tells herself, nothing more – it will remind her of what she is capable.

'Is this about that stupid sign?' Reynold marches towards the bed. 'I'll have it repainted this very afternoon if it matters that much. Ellie, please.' He takes her hand. 'I know you're still angry about the studio, but I'm doing it for us.'

'You're doing it for you.'

She wrestles her hand from his grip, crying at him to stop, as he tips her belongings from the case, and when he finds the Bible, he hurls it at the wall, and Lily's photograph falls from its innards. Reynold frowns as he retrieves it.

'The girl who made a fuss,' he murmurs.

'Reynold—'

'You haven't been the same since.' He nods several times. 'You went soft on her – I've told you before, it doesn't do to let these creatures get under your skin.'

'How would you know?' she snaps. 'She may as well have been a lump of clay, as far as you were concerned.'

'What did you want me to do, Ellie – make eyes at her?' He hands her back the print, and slumps on the bed, defeated. 'You didn't make her do it, you know.'

'That was you, as I recall.'

'And we paid her for the privilege!'

Ellen allows herself anger – and plenty of it – for otherwise she will not find it in herself to put one foot in front of the other and leave the other half of her behind. She jabs her brother's bony chest. 'This isn't about a model who didn't want her photograph taken. It's about you making decisions on my behalf, over and over again. First in Paris and now here. Anyway –' she softens a touch – 'it's time, can't you see? Don't you know what people say about us? That we're . . . unnatural, that we're sweethearts!'

'Since when did you care what people think?' He looks at her wild-eyed, and scoops up Flossy, burying his head in her fur.

57

'I care, Reynold. I just do my best to pretend not to.'

When he looks up, his eyes are red. If he starts to cry, she will falter. As she throws her clothes back into the case, Ellen wonders if this is how their mother felt when she left them, as if her heart was being squeezed very hard and very tight until even the act of breathing would never feel quite the same again.

Elle va revenir. She'll come back. The Harper twins used to whisper this to each other at night, from their separate beds, lying on their sides, fingers interlocking, alert for the sound of Grandmère's footsteps outside their room. They had just celebrated their ninth birthday, the first one away from Papa and London and the nursery with the one-eyed rocking horse and the bookcase of picture books. Maman had taken them to the zoo in Paris for the day – she had begged Grandmère to release them from their lessons. It was cold for September and Reynold had grazed his knee jumping from the parapet outside the monkey house, and Ellen's memory is of the three of them, their mother dressed up for once and pretty like she used to be, while she and Reynold clutched a hand each like miniature jailers, never letting her out of their sight.

Maman took them to a pâtisserie for tea and watched as attentively as she had the feeding of fish to the seals, as they gorged on towering mille-feuilles sandwiched with thick yellow custard, while she sipped steadily on a tumbler of cognac. Reynold's mouth was covered with icing sugar and Ellen had swiped at it frantically with her napkin; Maman had smiled and called her Little Mother, and Ellen had been unable to voice her biggest fear, which was that Grandmère might appear and punish them all.

On the train home to the suburbs, their noses pressed to the window playing I Spy, Ellen remembers turning to see their mother watching them, her face streaming with tears. Ellen had snuggled into her and Reynold had done the same the other side, and the game had ended, and when they alighted at the station, Mama's tears were replaced with a glassy distant expression as if she could see things that they couldn't.

There were no lessons on the morning after she left. Instead, Reynold and Ellen were summoned to the school-room and interrogated by Grandmère. What happened in Paris? Who did they speak to? Where did they go? Did their mother disappear at all, did she talk to any men? Lying was a sin, she didn't need to tell them that, and it wouldn't help bring back their mama. It was only when Reynold started to cry and wouldn't stop that Grandmère let them go.

The twins used to overhear the maid Mélisse and the cook talking about them in the kitchen. 'What kind of mother leaves her own children?' one or the other would say, but it seemed to be one of those questions which adults liked to ask but that had no answer, as neither of the servants ever replied. Their mother had taken Grandmère's money, they discovered, her jewellery too, everything apart from *les pauvres petits*. Reynold started having terrible nightmares, an affliction that only seemed to cease when he crept into bed with Ellen, until one night Grandmère discovered them and threatened to cane them both if they did it again.

Their mother had left nothing behind, forgotten nothing – apart from them. And eventually the twins both reached the realisation that if Maman were unlikely to return, then they would need to look for her. When lessons were over, they would run errands for the cook, buying baguettes and fresh tomatoes and cheap cuts from the butcher at the end of the day. Then they would sit on the steps of the *mairie*, overlooking the town square, and watch the carriages come and go, and the ladies who stepped out of them. They called it I Spy Maman. They scoured the heads of the crowd for blue toques with cream feathers like the one she'd had – or green ones – for she liked green too – before moving through the flow of people like minnows, scrutinising any lady of their mother's height, age and vivacity.

Unbeknown to Reynold, Ellen looked for their mama elsewhere too. She took detours home via the train station, past the women who sat outside begging, who always looked old, even when their faces had no lines. She looked among the women who made their homes under the bridge in the summer, the women with swollen red noses, pinpricked with tiny holes. The women who smelt, the women who drank, the women who wept and grabbed at them as they passed – it seemed to Ellen that her mother was as likely to be found squatting in her own filth as she might be gliding, perfumed and smiling, through the doors of the local theatre.

A whole year later, when the twins turned ten, the cook made them a *tarte au sucre*, and Mélisse took them to the park to play hoop. A little distance away from where they were playing, a carriage drew up and a young woman stepped out. Her hair was the same obsidian black as their mother's, and she moved with the grace that Maman had, the smile when she thanked the driver lifting her face into the heart shape that made it impossible not to smile back. Reynold stopped running, Ellen too. The hoop continued without them, oblivious to the rushing sound in their ears. For a moment, Ellen thought she might be sick; when she looked, Reynold had a hand over his stomach in the exact same spot that she did.

Two children tumbled from the same carriage, accompanied by a nurse with a picnic basket; the woman adjusted the collar of the youngest child's sailor suit, then kissed him on the nose. It wasn't Maman, the twins realised; it wasn't even close.

Ellen retrieved the hoop. When she turned back, Reynold was still watching the woman, who was setting out crockery and glasses, cake and lemonade under a willow tree.

'Grandmère says it's rude to stare,' Ellen said.

Reynold shrugged. Then he took the muddied hoop, and launched it at the woman and her perfect picnic. The woman looked up, puzzled; one of the children shrieked in delight. The hoop came to a standstill on the fringes of the blanket.

'Bitch,' Reynold muttered. Ellen looked at him in shock. It was their word for Grandmère, whispered in bed at night or mouthed behind her back as she wrote sums on the blackboard, not to be released into this warm September afternoon to the pleasant-looking lady in the straw hat, who was now instructing her older son to return the hoop to the 'wicked boy' over there.

Neither Ellen nor Reynold ever talked again about what happened on that day. And although they occasionally still sat outside the *mairie*, watching the comings and goings in the square, they stopped playing I Spy Maman. As Ellen told Reynold, they were both too old now for games.

Chapter Seven

'Is the beef not to your liking, Miss Harper?' Herbert Williams sets down his cutlery and frowns at Ellen's plate, which is almost as full as his is now clean. 'Perhaps you are accustomed to different cuts?'

The fillet is excellent, Ellen assures him, she is simply not in the habit of eating a full luncheon, and he looks pointedly towards his wife, who with a sweet, savage smile tells him that a lady's appetite is not comparable to that of a gentleman's – 'and particularly not yours, Herbert'.

'A *lady's* appetite, certainly,' he says. 'All I know is my old governess used to eat us out of house and home –' a remark which prompts Ottilie to lift her head and tell her uncle crossly that Miss Harper is *not* her governess, and that she has said many times over that she has no interest in either improving her French or going to school in Switzerland.

Her uncle draws back his chair and pats her shoulder as he passes, saying she'll thank him for it later, and looking very much as if she might cry, as Ottilie returns to staring at her plate. Mrs Williams lets out a heavy sigh which encapsulates all of Ellen's weariness too, for this is only her second day here, and she feels as out of place as her scuffed suitcase had looked, set down against the elegant legs of the console table in the hallway, when she arrived. During this morning's lesson, Ottilie had outright refused to say a single word in French and her first afternoon with Mrs Williams had not fared much better, their conversation over cribbage so stilted that Ellen had wondered if she'd completely imagined the hilarity over the handkerchief, the easy sallies back and forth when she'd come to deliver the photographs. Her room itself was airy and pleasant, the mattress almost twice the thickness of her own in Booth Lane, yet Ellen had not slept well, waking every hour to the sound of the grandfather clock in the hallway below. Each time she was momentarily confused as to why there was no other person snoring gently in the bed next to hers, and then she would miss Reynold with such intensity that she had to bite very hard on the pouch of skin beneath her thumb so that one pain might temporarily distract from the other.

Now Mr Williams is saying his goodbyes to his wife and niece – he must hurry to catch the two o'clock train to London and should not be expected back until Friday earliest – and there is one shadow less at least, Ellen thinks, returning his curt nod of farewell, for it has not taken her long to reach the conclusion that she cannot bear the man, a feeling which appears to be fully reciprocated.

As the door closes behind him, the atmosphere in the dining room lightens a touch. Ottilie asks to be excused – she is going with Aunt Caroline to the library this afternoon to ascertain whether *The Adventures of Rodney* has been removed from the shelves as the vigilants have requested. Permission is granted, and then it is just her and Mrs Williams on either side of the large rosewood table, with their half-eaten food before them, and the sombre ticking clock moving inexorably towards the hour. Mrs Williams sighs again and returns her plate to the sideboard. Perhaps, Ellen thinks, in the interest of breaking the silence, she should compliment her employer on her outfit – it has the most extraordinary sleeves, shaped like tennis bats – and she is just about to speak when Mrs Williams jumps in first.

'And how might we occupy ourselves this afternoon, Miss Harper?'

She is the worst companion in the world – she can think of nothing. With desperation, Ellen looks towards the window, and suggests that Mrs Williams would perhaps enjoy a ride on the electric train?

Her employer looks surprised. 'The electric train?'

'It is probably rather chill to be outdoors,' Ellen goes on hurriedly. 'Then – some needlepoint work?'

'Do you enjoy embroidery, Miss Harper?'

'I . . .'

'I thought not.' Mrs Williams takes an apple from the fruit bowl and begins to peel it. 'Forgive me, but I have little inclination either to sit like a lemon on Volk's railway, or to inflict my cross-stitch on a pincushion. What I have in mind is something more diverting by far.'

And when Ellen replies that there is no fault to be found with diversion, a new brightness comes to Mrs Williams, as she sits down beside her. 'I rather thought, Miss Harper,' she says, her eyes shining, 'that you might teach me to ride your bicycle.'

They go to the hills nearby, leaving the house in opposite directions, for the servants, Mrs Williams confides, are terrible gossips and under no account must her husband hear of this. They meet again where the cliffs sheer stark and white into the sea, and walk up to a quiet lane. Ellen shows her employer how to adjust her skirts and sit on the saddle, where to position her feet on the pedals, then with a supporting arm about her waist she guides her along the stony path. Jackdaws cackle in the overhang of a beech tree, as Mrs Williams loses balance over and again.

'It looks so easy for others,' she says, with some despair, 'so why is it impossible for me?' and Ellen reassures her that there are many afternoons ahead in which Mrs Williams may practise and in time her body will remember what to do, without her needing to think.

They stay long past teatime, until the sun has begun its descent into the ocean and the pale sky is streaked with orange.

'The golden hour,' Ellen murmurs, the words out before she can retract them, a wistfulness in her tone that causes Mrs Williams to look at her with some sympathy – and Ellen fears that she might have in some way revealed herself. But Mrs Williams merely touches her arm and says that Miss Harper must miss her brother very much and that she is grateful indeed to have stolen her away, to which Ellen replies, with some truthfulness, that she is the one grateful to be here. They leave then, talking of their plans to return the next day, and the cab they must now find for Mrs Williams so as to keep their secret intact.

When she was a little girl, the highlight of Lily's week was helping her mother with deliveries from the laundry. Every time the cart stopped outside one of the grand white houses that rolled in a horseshoe shape around gardens bursting with more trees than Lily had ever seen in her life, Ma would pass her a small basket of flannels and tell her not to drop them or she'd be for it later. In the sunshine the houses were so bright and sparkling Lily was sure that if she licked one of the stately columns that flanked the entrances, she would come away with a mouth full of sugar. She thought them to be palaces and the people who lived there kings and queens; it was like stepping into a fairy tale, and she thinks of this now with scorn for her younger self as she stands outside the tradesman's entrance at Number Ten, and is scolded for something that hasn't happened yet by Mrs Matthews the housekeeper.

'Mind it's all back by Friday morning,' Mrs Matthews says, as she exchanges the parcel of neatly pressed sheets and towels for soiled ones. 'Not whenever the fancy takes you.'

'Yes, ma'am.'

Lily hovers in the lee of the housekeeper's steely gaze in the hope that experience will prove her wrong and a gratuity might be forthcoming, but Mrs Matthews disappears into the kitchen, closing the back door firmly behind her. Tight as a nun's snatch, as her mother would say, and on this Lily wholeheartedly agrees. She picks up the heavy basket and manoeuvres it up the steep stone steps to the road.

Perkins the driver has disappeared from the cart and she assumes him to be relieving himself somewhere for he says he likes to give the fine folk's flowers a watering when he's down this end of town. Lily sets down the basket and waits. Above her gulls drift like white handkerchiefs against the darkening sky. A smell of woodsmoke in the air and the salty freshness of the sea. Lights come on, one after the other, in different houses across the Crescent, and glow warm and yellow. It *is* like fairyland here, Lily thinks glumly, as a carriage pulls up outside Number Ten and a young lady steps out, her blonde hair coiled, and as she glides up the steps to the front door, it opens magically, without the lady needing to knock, and a smiling maid appears in a black dress with white apron and cap. Lily stares at the servant. What is it like to be her, she wonders, with nothing to do all day but open and close the front door and walk around all neat and proper in a uniform that she hasn't even had to wash herself?

She walks a few paces up the Crescent, then back again. Perkins can take his time, as far as she's concerned he can piss out a river; it's their last delivery and after that there will be nowhere to go but home – and Uncle Jack will be there, making eyes at her whenever her mother's back is turned. Yesterday morning, as she was coming back from the privy, he'd pushed her against the wall in the narrow passageway and tried to kiss her. Lily had shoved her knee into the soft sack between his legs and he'd yelped and let her go, and she'd run to tell her mother exactly what had happened. Is that right, missy, Ma had said, and I suppose you had nothing to do with it at all! But she'd turned frosty on Uncle Jack, ignoring him as he left for work, and when he'd come home again they'd had an almighty row on the street outside, and Lily had sat joyfully with her sister and brothers, crossing the fingers on both hands in the hope that he'd be sent packing at last. But whatever Uncle Jack told their mother in his soft sickening lisp must have worked, because they'd spent the rest of the evening in the pub, and when Lily had woken up this morning, he was still there and her mother had scolded her, saying that telling fibs about her uncle wouldn't bring her good-for-nothing father home any sooner.

'The lass misses her da, that's all,' Uncle Jack had said. 'No hard feelings, eh, Lil?' And the wink he gave her had turned her stomach like soured milk.

A sudden screech of brakes startles her; more startling still is the sight of a woman alighting from a bicycle, and as she turns her face Lily sees that it is Miss Harper. She is so surprised that she forgets what Miss Harper told her that time on the pier and greets her by name.

Miss Harper flinches, as if Lily were a dog that had just shown its teeth, and Lily thinks she will walk straight past her, just as the lady of the house had done five minutes ago. But Miss Harper hesitates.

'Miss March.'

Miss Harper is not altogether displeased to see her. Lily senses this somehow, for there is room enough for Miss Harper to wheel her bicycle past and yet she does not move. And she has no idea what Miss Harper's business might be at the Crescent, but what a piece of luck this is, Lily thinks, for there has been no accumulation in the stash of coins behind the brick in the coal cellar since they last met, and she has even paid admission to the pier a couple of times since to see if she might happen upon Miss Harper there.

She lowers her voice. 'Is there any more of that work, Miss Harper? That we did before.'

Miss Harper frowns and Lily bolts on. 'I'm sorry – about that Sunday on the pier. I wanted to come, really I did. But the littlest was sick, whooping with cough, and—'

'It's of no consequence,' Miss Harper says, so quickly that Lily can't help thinking that the opposite is true. 'Think no more of it. On the other matter –' she pauses – 'I'm afraid I'm no longer occupied in that particular line of business.'

'Oh!' Lily's face falls.

'I'd like to help, but . . .' Miss Harper glances nervously towards the large white house, several of the windows already cheery with lamplight. 'My circumstances have changed somewhat.'

So, you're a lady now, is it? Lily thinks with some bitterness.

She stares at the basket of dirty sheets. 'Doesn't matter,' she says.

A high-pitched whistle carries across the Crescent. 'You going to stand there jawing all day, Lil?'

As Perkins shambles over to help with the basket, Lily follows him to the cart, but how she hopes – right up until the moment when he's geeing up the donkey – that Miss Harper will call her back. But as they set off from the Crescent, Miss Harper and her bicycle have disappeared, and all Lily can see is a figure standing in the shadows by the windows on the first floor of Number Ten, watching them go.

Chapter Eight

In a gentlemen's club, south of Piccadilly, four men gather in a small smoking room, where the leather walls are stained and roughened and the waiters know not to interrupt once the cognac and cigars have been served. The men are known to each other as the 'Thursday Club'; they have in common an enthusiasm for pleasure, married with a respect for the past. They derive much merriment from the cartoons in *Punch*, depicting broad-jawed New Women straddling bicycles in plaid knickerbockers, although they all agree that the construct itself has been exaggerated and that the ladies they know would rather miss three seasons in a row than relinquish their self-respect in such a way. Tonight they are in accord that after the mess the Liberals got themselves into, it is good to have Salisbury back at the helm; and that no gentleman with any dignity would choose to be cremated.

There is a lull in conversation and the man they call Magpie, owing to his extensive collection of back parlour curios and gewgaws, proposes that now might be time to welcome some more guests to the stage, at which he brings his magic lantern from its box and starts to lower the lamps.

'What do you have for us this week, Magpie?' Herbert Williams, commonly known as 'The Squire', on account of his country residence, and penchant for shooting anything that might not look too outlandish stuffed on a lady's hat, takes a swig of cognac.

'Tonight, my friends,' Magpie says, positioning the lantern opposite the wall, 'we are going to France.'

The Thursday Club settle back into their chairs as Magpie inserts the first slide. Through the fug of smoke, two kitchen maids appear on the wall, pummelling dough at a trestle table under the stern supervision of a matronly cook.

The Squire yawns. 'Are you to conduct a lecture on how to make bread, Magpie?'

'*French* bread, Squire!' Mr Groot snorts.

Magpie smiles, enjoying the ripple across the room that accompanies the next slide. The cook has disappeared, and the maids are having a flour fight. Pinafores are discarded, and bodices hang loose, exposing breasts of such pertness that Mr Shaw remarks he'll take up residence in France tomorrow if all the maids are that pretty; and Mr Groot tells Magpie he wants his money back if the next picture shows the cook's bare dugs.

More slides follow and the maids' misdemeanours continue. They are without their bodices once again, this time in a barn, where they play a game of catch with windfall apples, while a swarthy farmhand smirks at the doorway. They peg up laundry, dressed in drawers and little else, while playing a ridiculous, but – the Thursday Club members agree – rather delightful game of hide-and-seek in between the rows of sheets. The finale is met with much ribald cheering from the men, as the cook delivers six of the best to her subordinates over the kitchen table, a punish-ment which she administers bare-breasted in a petticoat, brandishing her birch broom.

'You don't mind 'em on the older side, Squire,' Magpie

says slyly, and Herbert Williams wants to cuff him for insolence, because he won't have his Bibi compared to those
strumpets in the photograph, and certainly not by some
jumped-up stockbroker who spends his spare time grub-
bing around used bookshops, and who, if Herbert had had
his way, would never have been permitted to inveigle his
way into the Thursday Club.

'Good show, Magpie,' he says, swallowing his irritation as
he turns up the lights. 'Where'd you find them?'

'An establishment in Holywell Street – owner imports
from France.' Magpie taps his nose. 'Backroom business,
clearly. I'd be glad to effect an introduction if you're
interested . . .'

Herbert tells him with some condescension that he is not,
and after a circuit of hand-shaking and shoulder-slapping,
he takes his leave and hails a cab.

As he travels through Mayfair, Herbert toys with the idea
of paying a visit to Bibi, but he can't remember if it is today
that Mr Hawes-Montague returns from Dundee. Besides,
Bibi is going through one of her anxious phases regarding
young Barnaby, and Herbert isn't sure if he has quite the
reserves of attention necessary to listen to the most recent
inventory of misconduct. He closes his eyes. He is drunk,
but not drunk enough: images from the magic lantern
are pasted to his eyelids, the sequence replaying over and
over – goosepimpled breasts spilling over the washing line,
the maids with their lowered drawers across the table. That
dirty hound, Magpie, insinuating that he might want an
introduction to some backstreet bookshop owner from the
likes of him! Magpie is just the kind of snivelling chap who
was always running to Matron because his bed was filled
with wet leaves, the sort they used to dangle over the fire at

Eton, making him sing *Hey dilly dilly* from start to finish. An unwelcome image comes to Herbert of Magpie sitting at his walnut desk with a pile of photographs, spectacles fogged as he tugs frantically at his pale member.

He stares gloomily out of the carriage window. He must return to Brighton on Monday latest – he has already been away a week. Hindsight, they say, is a valuable tool, and he is beginning to wonder if he has made a mistake, marrying a foreigner, even one as young and beautiful as Clementine. *Why, at her age she'll be with child in the shake of a lamb's tail,* Bibi had said, when he'd first broken the news of his engagement; *you'll have more heirs than you'll know what to do with,* adding somewhat acidly that she hoped Herbert's generosity would still extend to her Barnaby, once he was a respectable married man. Yet despite regular shaking of the tail, nothing had happened, and sometimes he felt that his wife wasn't even trying. God knows he was bending over backwards to give her what she wanted, even moving the entire household to Brighton, when he would much prefer to live at Feathers on the estate. Ottilie still hadn't forgiven him for getting married in the first place, and as for that peculiar Harper woman, Clem had taken on as Ottilie's tutor and as some sort of companion for herself . . . well, there was something off about her.

The cab pulls up outside his rooms and Herbert tips the driver and goes inside. He settles himself before the fire in the drawing room, wherein a brief internal tussle takes place: he rises, sits down, then with a muffled growl of defeat, gets up again and goes straight to the writing desk, from which he takes a Chinese cigar case from the bottom drawer.

The case contains three photographs, procured at the same time as a snuffbox, from a dealer in the smarter end of

Covent Garden, who had slipped them in as 'a little extra'. Herbert selects his favourite – a dark-haired beauty with a pensive expression and enormous pendulous breasts. He knows he shouldn't for this will be the third time this week, and he will weaken himself, and he cannot dispel the niggling feeling that this propensity to self-abuse is one of the reasons why he has not yet succeeded in producing a legitimate heir. He will strive to do better, he will be generous in his contribution to the collection plate on Sunday, but for now he is like a hound with the scent of the chase. Propping the photograph against a cushion on his lap, Herbert unbuttons his trousers and begins.

Chapter Nine

Miss Harper is an enigma, Clem thinks, sitting astride the Ladies' Rambler and propelling herself towards her companion, who stands, bundled up in a cloak and scarf, at the end of the lane. An enigma wrapped in a convincing disguise of no-nonsense, for although most days it is cold enough up here to turn bone marrow to ice, Miss Harper has never once shown impatience, nor uttered a word of complaint.

'Head up!' Miss Harper calls out, and how different she is now to the person who first arrived, so sombre and silent that Herbert had remarked that he'd had livelier conversations with his sister's poodle. But in the three weeks since they've been coming up here to the hills, Miss Harper has once again become the woman who first drew Clem's attention, the woman who sailed around Brighton on her bicycle and with whom Clem had felt able to talk so freely. Yet while they might now chatter for hours about bicycling or the curious people of the town – the albino pierrot by the Chain Pier who salutes them when they pass, the snaggle-toothed chiropodist on the slipway, who Miss Harper says is no more a foot doctor than she is Queen of England – when it comes to subjects more personal, her companion is a closed book. Miss Harper's drawbridge comes straight down whenever Clem asks too many questions about her brother, or the photography business, or whether Miss Harper herself can operate a camera. Mr Harper's letters arrive with the frequency of a love-struck suitor, yet Miss Harper never visits him, and if they have quarrelled, as Clem suspects, the disagreement must have been a fierce one, for there are certainly no visible signs of rapprochement.

Miss Harper starts to applaud as Clem approaches. I am a lady cyclist, Clem thinks with a swell of satisfaction, and if my mother could see me now, she would choke on her gin daisy. Three, two, one. Gentle pressure on the brakes and she slows to a standstill.

'I did it!' Clem alights from the bicycle, dipping a curtsy.

'And no bones broken.' Miss Harper rummages in her bag and brings out a hip flask and two small glasses. 'A drop of rum to celebrate?'

'Why, Miss Harper,' Clem says, 'I've found you out!' and the light disappears from her companion's face, and anxious that she may have offended her somehow, Clem rushes to explain herself. 'You've been rewarding Ottilie with tots of rum, haven't you,' she goes on, 'every time she correctly uses the subjunctive? Little wonder she's come around!'

And thankfully Miss Harper laughs and the next five minutes are passed most companionably, sipping the rum on an upturned log and discussing how they might best obtain another bicycle for future excursions together without arousing suspicion. Then as the sky darkens and they begin to wheel the bicycle in the direction of town, Clem remembers the piece of news she had meant to tell Miss Harper to begin with, and enquires as to her availability Friday evening next.

'I have secured us a box at the Empire,' she says. 'Do say you'll come!'

'The Empire? Are you sure?' Miss Harper's brow furrows. 'But what about your sister-in-law? And the other committee members? If they were to hear of it, then—'

'It is their idea – or at least I have made it so. I am to report back on the extent of the depravity. It's all agreed.' Clem smiles at her. 'Please come. Or Caroline will insist on accompanying me and the evening will be ruined. Don't you want to see Harry Smart? Milly was beside herself when she saw the tickets on my dressing table.'

But Miss Harper does not seem to share the maid's enthusiasm, and as they reach the road, Clem's gaze is drawn to the worn cuffs of Miss Harper's gloves, the cloak that, although respectable enough, has surely seen out several winters, and she chides herself. How thoughtless she has been not to realise – and crowing about the box can't have helped; one can hardly fade into the background when seated in full view of the stage.

'I have a velvet gown that would suit you very well,' Clem says, and she pictures them then, side by side in the carriage, Miss Harper in the red velvet and herself in her low-necked green satin with the embroidered shoulder straps, the air scented with the ambergris perfume she bought on her honeymoon in Paris. The thought makes her inexplicably happy.

'I'm sure my day dress is good enough for the Empire,' Miss Harper replies, and with this Clem has to be satisfied, and as they reach the fork in the road which indicates that the time has come for their paths to diverge, Miss Harper reclaims her bicycle and disappears into the dusk.

A sulphurous moon glows like a challenge above the black of the sea as Ellen stands in her nightdress at the window, her brother's latest letter in her hand. Reynold has stopped saying he misses her and now is all bluster: the studio is dizzy with new customers, he tells her; he barely has time to eat, to sleep! Wally Clarke may well rub his hands in glee, he writes, but – and Ellen lets out a sigh – the new enterprise has not come without cost to his own health; his cough is back, and the other day Harry Smart said he was like a grasshopper who'd lost its spring, and sent a maid around with an onion poultice and a bottle of Vin Mariani. He lives in hope, Reynold goes on, that his beloved sister will tire soon of servitude and return to where she belongs. Perhaps she might deign to visit soon?

Ellen tosses her brother's note aside. The throb in her right temple – originating from the exact moment when Mrs Williams had announced their excursion to the Empire – intensifies. Whoever heard of prescribing coca wine for a lung condition? All the Vin Mariani will do is agitate Reynold further, but Harriet Smart doesn't have the sense she was born with – what can one expect? The thought of Miss Smart makes her head ache worse than ever. Ellen imagines herself sitting stiffly in the box at the theatre, next to Mrs Williams, with Harriet's mocking gaze upon them – how she wishes she could duck out of it somehow. But Mrs Williams had looked so pleased with herself, and then so disappointed at her lack of enthusiasm, that Ellen hadn't had the heart to refuse.

Before retiring to bed, Ellen takes her grandmother's Bible from the shelf and slips the photograph of Lily from the inner pages. Lily beams up at her, her skin luminous in the afternoon light, Floss's eyes narrowed to such slits of pleasure that Ellen can almost hear her purr. But now as she looks at it, she feels uneasy, remembering the dark shadows under Lily's eyes when she'd approached her outside the house a fortnight ago, the girl's tone almost pleading as she asked if there was any more of 'that work'. Ellen hasn't seen her since – a different girl had brought the laundry last week – and it troubles her to think of Lily at home with the uncle she hates, and the spiteful, negligent mother. Perhaps she should have done more to help her . . . She shakes the thought loose from her head. There will be no more photographs – on that she is decided – and Lily will thank her in the long run.

Ellen holds Lily's picture briefly to her lips. But it does little to soothe her, and as she blows out the candle and climbs into bed, she sleeps fitfully, disturbed by dreams of her old life that will not let her alone.

Chapter Ten

Ellen hasn't been to the theatre since *Dick Whittington* at the Gaiety last Christmas, when she and Reynold had perched like gulls in the eyrie of the gallery, barely able to distinguish the cat from the rats. This evening with Mrs Williams at the Empire is her first time in a box, and her discomfort is such that she may as well be sitting half dressed on a doorstep in Booth Lane with all eyes upon her, and in particular those of Harriet Smart, who is putting on a good show of both pretending Ellen is not there and knowing that she is. They are close enough for Ellen to see the sheen of perspiration on Miss Smart's face, the white line of her scalp when she lifts her hat to take a bow, and Ellen can only feel relief that she refused Clem's offer of the red velvet gown, for it seems to her that Harriet Smart notices everything: the cream shirt with the lace cuffs that so clearly is not Ellen's own, the tortoiseshell combs in her hair – also borrowed – that Clem coaxed her into wearing, the hard glitter of diamonds at her employer's neck.

'Dressed up to the nines, the pair of 'em,' Ellen imagines Harriet telling Reynold, and she groans inwardly as the piano strikes up another tune and Harriet emerges from the wings in a grizzled grey wig, peering through a pince-nez at a dog-eared Bible.

'This one's for the ladies who prowl,' she announces.

'Wheresoever they may be hiding!' and she blows an extravagant kiss towards their box, before starting to sing.

> *'We're the . . . prudes on the prowl and we wear a scowl,*
> *Heigh ho the lifelong day!*
> *We're vigilant and diligent, we leave nothing to luck,*
> *We go to church three times on Sunday and we never*
> *say f— fuh, fuh, fee, fi, fo . . .'*

'She's making fun of me!' Mrs Williams says, looking a little hurt, and Ellen wants to say she may as well scold a cat for mousing; not that there was much that said vigilant about her employer's silk dress – she'd seen more modest necklines in the saloon bar of the Jolly. Instead Ellen gently suggests that they leave, but Mrs Williams shakes her head.

As an explosion of applause marks the end of Harriet's turn, she makes a low, stately bow in their direction, and Ellen is just thinking that she could happily wring Harriet Smart's cravated neck for teasing Clem so, when a waiter appears at the door, bearing two coupes of champagne.

'Compliments of Mr Harry Smart,' he says, setting down the tray, upon which there is a card, scrawled in a spidery hand. Ellen reaches for it but Clem is quicker.

'*To Miss Harper and her companion – for being good sports.*' Clem frowns and looks at Ellen. 'Do you know Miss Smart?'

'No.' A barefaced lie that she regrets as soon as she's said it and one Clem shows no sign of swallowing. 'That is . . .' Ellen takes a sip of champagne, 'she may have come to the studio for her photograph at one time. I don't entirely recall.'

She is about to ask Mrs Williams if she's certain she wants to stay, when she notices a man staring at her from the box next to theirs. He has puffy, deep-set eyes that make her think of marbles set in dough, the right side of his face pitted with craters that not even the kindest lamplight could soften. There is something coarse about him, and not at all respectable, and no more are his two companions, despite the relative smartness of their attire. The man smiles at her, as if it is his right, his gaze drifting like smoke from her to Mrs Williams as he raises his glass in a voiceless toast.

Clem watches Miss Harper watching the man. It is on the tip of her tongue to ask her companion if the gentleman had patronised her brother's studio also, for he certainly behaves as if they are acquainted! As the lights are put out, she frowns – Miss Harper has been in a strange humour all evening – and who would forget the likes of Harry Smart coming to the studio for a photograph; it hardly seems possible.

For a few seconds the theatre is black as pitch. Then a pool of light pours onto the naked hindquarters of a woman lying on a large alabaster dog. 'Ariadne and the Panther,' intones a voice from the wings, and Clem stares, momentarily shocked. So, it's true, the women really are naked, but as she looks more closely, she realises her mistake. The woman's skin is oddly wrinkled in places and the colour of grubby net curtains: she is wearing one of those body stockings which have been the subject of much heated discussion during committee meetings.

'Crenaia!' The disembodied voice comes again. 'The Nymph of the Dargle.'

The light falls on another model, who stands, draped in a thin white sheet. It falls across the right side of her body, in a disingenuous display of modesty – for one has only to look at her naked left side to imagine how the right might mirror it, and this time there is definitely no stocking. Just limbs the milky colour of the foaming sea, a breast plump and pert, supported in the fold of an elbow, and a topknot of straw-berry-blonde curls, not dissimilar, Clem muses, to her own.

She looks across the dark undergrowth of the theatre. What must it be like to wield such power, to hold the atten-tion of hundreds of people, so that all they can think about is you? The drape flutters, and as the plinth rotates, the model shrugs her shoulder and the sheet begins to slowly unfurl. Whistles and cat calls come from the gallery, but the girl does not look up, even when the sheet is at her feet, and for a brief moment she is naked, before the light goes out.

Clem feels her heart beating faster. She is aware of Miss Harper's breathing, her braided scent of hair oil and soap. Two more statues, Venus and Ariadne, strewn with ivy and little else, come to life beneath them on the stage and engage in a game of pat-a-cake. And Miss Harper is gesturing towards the door now, and Clem thinks with some amuse-ment that if Harry Smart wants to brand anyone a prude tonight, it should be Miss Harper, not herself.

'Let's stay a while longer.' She smiles at her companion and settles back in her chair. 'I think the committee will expect a full report, don't you?'

I am very wicked, Clem thinks as she watches the women; there can be no other explanation for it. For what respect-able woman would feel as she does now, this lick of warmth in the core of her, too shameful to admit to anyone.

'Didn't you say you were meeting your brother for supper?' Clem takes Ellen's arm as they walk through the jostling crowd outside the theatre towards the queue of carriages. 'Give Dixon the address and we'll take you there.' She stops. 'Look, it's that ill-mannered man from the box.'

They are like a formation of geese, Ellen thinks, briefly amused, as the man – short, stocky and unsmiling – passes by, shadowed by his two companions, his sense of his own importance sufficient for the crowd to part like the Red Sea. She watches as a driver jumps down from a hansom and opens the carriage door. Mr Crocker, sir, she hears him say, and the name swirls in the rumour mill and Ellen recalls a girl who used to come to the studio, each time sporting a new hat or dress or pair of gloves. He's my crock of gold, my Mr Crocker, she would say, but when the dresses were off, there were bruises, bad enough for Ellen to ask questions – and the girl had stopped coming.

Ellen turns to Clem. 'I've arranged to meet my brother at a chophouse around the corner,' she says. 'There's no need for the carriage.'

'If you're sure?' Clem's disappointment is clear – and for a moment Ellen is tempted to return to the Crescent with her to sip port and chatter in front of the drawing-room fire, not visit her aggrieved brother in Booth Lane, as she'd planned. There is to be no civilised supper at a chophouse, but the lie, she assures herself as she bids Clem goodnight, is unavoidable; she could hardly direct Dixon to 30 Booth Lane.

Habit has Ellen taking the back way home, although the darkness unsettles her: six weeks at the Crescent has made her soft, she thinks, recoiling at the rats whose shadows puddle the narrow alleyways, the drunks who lie in doorways mumbling a rosary of vulgarities, *cunting-fucking-bastard*, over and again. As she approaches the Tom Thumb pub, a bow-fronted top-heavy building, which like its more enthusiastic patrons always seems to be struggling to stay upright, the door flings open and a couple stumble onto the street.

Ellen watches them. The man – thin and stunted with a bushy, unkempt beard – grasps the hand of a young woman in a grey cloak and hood; and this in itself is curious because the Tom Thumb is frequented only by a certain type of woman, and this girl, even with her back turned, does not appear as such, and even if she were, it would likely be her leading the customer. But the man is digging in his pockets for change and handing the coins to the girl, who hesitates, before taking them.

'I've paid you, ain't I, and now it's your turn.' The man grabs the girl's arm, and as he pulls her into the twitten opposite, her hood falls and Ellen sees the pale pretty face that so often visits her at night – but this is no figment of her imagination: this is Lily.

Ellen hurries to the alleyway and peers into the blackness. She hears a scuffling, a squeal like an animal's, and then a glimpse of white flesh as the man hoicks up Lily's skirts.

'Stop making such a fuss, girl. Ain't I paid yer?' and Ellen can bear it no longer.

'Stop! Stop it this instant, or I'll set the police on you.'

She marches towards them as best she can, wincing at the sour smells as she gropes her way along the damp walls. The man, who is fumbling with his trousers, turns and bares his teeth.

'It'll be your turn next, if you don't hop it. I don't care how holy you are.'

'There's nothing holy about me, I assure you.' Ellen gropes in her bag for matches, and with the first flame comes relief: the man is a feeble-seeming specimen and looks more in need of a square meal than Lily. 'How much did you pay, Miss March, Mr . . .?'

The man falters, looks away. 'One and six, or thereabouts.'

'Far below the going rate.' Ellen takes a coin from her purse and thrusts it at him. 'Your money returned, sir, minus sixpence for the nuisance caused. Now apologise to Miss March for the misunderstanding and be off with you.'

The man mutters to himself as he lurches past them, disappearing into the night.

'He won't trouble you again.' Lightly Ellen touches Lily's shoulder, and realises the girl is shaking, crying now too – deep, throaty sobs that resound along the alley until they are all Ellen can hear. She contemplates holding her, then thinks better of it.

'Come along,' she says briskly, guiding Lily along the passageway and back onto the street. 'There's no harm done.'

'I'll pay you back, Miss Harper.' Lily wipes her eyes and then her nose with the back of her grubby glove. 'Soon as I can.'

'There's no need.' They stand there outside the Tom Thumb, the soft drizzle made golden in the light from the pub. Ellen looks at her. 'Have you had supper?'

Lily shakes her head and sniffs.

'Then let's set that right.'

She takes Lily to a tavern off Ship Street and orders them hot mutton and a glass of beer. My brother will be joining us, she tells the waiter, set the table for three, explaining to Lily, sotto voce, that she's sure she's had enough of being pestered for one night and that the third place setting is just for show. Lily drinks the beer straight down, belches delicately and looks Ellen in the eye for the first time.

'I'm so ashamed,' she says. 'And it's all for nothing. I had to drink two gins to get my courage up, and even then I thought I'd die when he asked me how much.'

'He is to blame, not you,' Ellen says. 'You must look at it that way.'

'But I wanted him to ask me.' Another tear slides down her cheek and she looks at Ellen angrily for a moment, as if they are back on the Crescent with the basket of dirty laundry between them.

A sudden gust of wind hurls rain at the bevelled window. Beyond the blurred lights of the esplanade, the sea writhes and froths. Ellen thinks of Lily's photograph hidden in the Bible, and how it draws her most evenings, like the tug of the tide, no matter how hard she resists.

'I'll help you.' She sets down her fork. 'With the work you wanted.'

'You will?' Lily stops chewing mid-mouthful and stares.

'Can you come to Booth Lane next Saturday? At half past three?'

Lily nods and Ellen takes two shillings from her purse. 'An advance on your payment. We'll do a series of photographs – with a Christmas theme.'

She thinks back to the final tableau at the Empire, of Corazón and Jemima and the trailing ivy – yes ivy, and perhaps some rosehip berries – she will see what she can find in the Crescent gardens. Ellen smiles at Lily, and Lily – pocketing the money – smiles back. How much more warming to the soul is a person than a photograph, Ellen thinks, and how strange life is, for who would have thought that this evening would end with her and Lily on opposite sides of a table, enjoying a mutton chop! She is not one to believe in fate, she abhors fortune tellers, would never have her tarot read, yet whatever drew her to Lily that day on the pier has in turn drawn the girl back towards her, not once, but twice . . .

'I want you to put the other thing out of your mind, Lily,' Ellen says. 'There's no need for you to do it. You deserve better, much better.'

'I do?' Lily looks startled.

'Most certainly,' Ellen says, and later, calling for the bill, she leaves a generous tip, barely caring when she discovers that the evening's unexpected turn of events has left her without her cab fare home.

Chapter Eleven

'I will not tolerate deceit, Clementine!'

The thickness of the walls at Number Ten are no match for Mr Williams in a temper, and in the schoolroom above the study Miss Harper and her student set down their copy of the *Petit Larousse* and of one accord creep to the top of the staircase, where they eavesdrop shamelessly.

'It's just a bicycle. You're fussing over nothing,' comes Mrs Williams' response, and Ottilie looks towards Miss Harper with both disapproval and admiration combined, for it would seem that her French teacher and her aunt have been sneaking off in all weathers to ride 'that damned bicycle'. Neither she nor Miss Harper speak as once again her uncle bellows that he will not have his wife making a public exhibition of herself.

'You'll be insisting on crinolines and mob-caps next,' Mrs Williams cries out in exasperation, and at this Miss Harper turns to Ottilie and says it is best they finish their lesson early today. She hurries downstairs and knocks firmly on the study door, entering before she can be told otherwise.

The scene that greets her is predictable enough – Mr Williams, an unbecoming shade of scarlet, in full flow, and Mrs Williams standing before him, her hands bunched into helpless fists. He is trying to pretend he has won, Ellen thinks, when really he is furious because he has lost; and she wishes she could impart this to Mrs Williams directly – but she does what she came for and steps in to help her.

'Forgive me, Mr Williams, but I couldn't help overhearing—'

'Return to your duties, Miss Harper.' Mr Williams glances at her dismissively, as if she were no more than a troublesome maid. 'You're not needed here.'

'I must bear some of the blame,' Ellen goes on, and Mrs Williams looks fearful and gives her an infinitesimal shake of the head. 'My clear enthusiasm for the sport – and the health benefits implicit therein – likely acted as a form of encouragement to your wife.' She pauses. 'We should not have deceived you: I'm sorry.'

The grandfather clock in the hallway is halfway towards chiming noon before Mr Williams speaks.

'When I want an apology from you, Miss Harper, I shall ask for it.' He regards her coldly. 'You are skating on extremely thin ice. Do you understand?'

Clem looks from her husband to her companion and back again. 'I think what Miss Harper meant was—'

'What Miss Harper meant was to be impertinent!' he thunders, and the women flinch as Ellen realises that she has made everything worse not better.

'Occupy yourself for the rest of the day, Miss Harper.' Mr Williams throws open the door and gestures roughly towards it. 'I'm sick of you hanging about my wife like a damned shadow.'

The encounter with Mr Williams leaves Ellen in low spirits, and to cheer herself she takes to the seafront on the Ladies' Rambler, making a silent promise to Mrs Williams that her husband shall not have the last word on this matter, for although she has limited experience of husbands herself, she is no stranger to the workings of the male mind. And speaking of which, she supposes now is as good a time as any to pay Reynold a visit – she needs to tell him of her plan to photograph Lily – and so she continues along the King's Road to the studio. The windows are salt-stained and in need of a clean; the door opening without its customary tinkle, for the bell no longer appears to be attached. Ellen calls out but no one answers.

She glances at the desk, covered with papers, the appointments book submerged under a landslide of back issues of *The Photographic News*. Going to the hallway, she hears a murmur of voices coming from the studio, but there is something hushed and secretive in their tone that tells her Reynold is not with a client.

Ellen goes upstairs. The studio door is half open, and Reynold is standing by the console table, hunched and silent. As she says his name, he looks up in surprise, taking a jerky step towards her as if to stop her coming any further. But it is too late, she is in the studio, and there leaning against the window, hands splayed on the sill, is the man from the theatre, the king goose himself, in the same heavy dark coat and fine leather gloves. Once again he fixes his dull bloodshot gaze upon her, with a smile that has more in common with the cracking of knuckles than a greeting.

'Miss Harper,' he says.

Reynold twitches. His necktie is twisted, as if someone has seized him by the throat. 'I didn't realise you and my sister were acquainted, Mr Crocker.'

'The family resemblance is striking.' Mr Crocker's eyes are cold as he tips his hat. 'Good day to you, Mr Harper. I'll see myself out.'

95

Ellen doesn't speak until the door rattles shut downstairs and Mr Crocker has gone. 'What was he doing here?'

A bout of coughing masks any answer her brother might have given, and she reaches for him, suddenly concerned. 'Are you unwell?'

'What do you care?' Reynold shakes her off, wrinkling his nose suspiciously. 'You smell different.'

'Different? How?'

'Pampered.' He paces to the window. 'What brings you here anyway? Had enough of sipping tea and sewing samplers with Milady of Manhattan?'

Ellen tuts. 'What did Mr Crocker want?'

'A photograph, what else! He's a swimmer – won the race around the pier a few weeks back. Wants a memento.' Reynold flings himself onto the wing-backed chair and lights his pipe, appraising her with narrowed eyes as the room fills with the woody scent of tobacco. 'One letter in six weeks. How lucky am I to have such a devoted sister!'

He coughs again into his crumpled handkerchief, and Ellen goes to him, sinking her hand into his hair, rubbing her fingers across his scalp in the way that has always calmed him. Reynold sighs and leans against her.

'I've missed you, that's all,' he says. 'There were times I thought I'd never see you again.'

'I'm sorry.' And she is. He is her twin, his blood is hers; she loves him. Ellen kisses the crown of his head, then gets up and goes to the camera, running a hand across its smooth polished surface. 'You still have the old one, don't you?'

He looks up with interest. 'It's at Booth Lane. Why?'

'I've found a model,' she says. 'For next Saturday. I thought something seasonal might appeal. Nymphs of the forest.

Mistletoe, berries. Send them out to Eton, Harrow, the usual.'

'This is good news indeed!' Reynold lopes across the room and clasps her hands. 'I knew you'd come back. I knew it.'

'I'm to take the photographs myself, Reynold – you're not to interfere.' She slips away from him. 'And it's only for a few weeks. I can't risk any more. Mrs Williams' sister-in-law is a most committed member of the vigilants – we have to be careful.'

'That's just perfect.' Reynold shakes his head in exasperation. 'Who's the girl?'

Her tongue betrays her and Ellen trips over the name. 'Miss M-March.'

'The laundry girl.' Her brother frowns. 'Why her?'

'Why not her?' And Ellen chooses that moment to enquire as to the merits of the portrait lens on his new Dallmeyer and whether it provides as crisp an effect as the advertising promised, a conversational tangent which has the desired effect of distracting both her twin and herself from the subject of Lily March.

It's easier the second time, Lily thinks, as she undresses behind the Chinese screen in Booth Lane, unlacing and unbuttoning until she stands in just her drawers, shivering as she slips into the robe that smells of other people. The studio door is open and she can hear the spit of a fire just lit and fragments of a song that Miss Harper is humming, but in a way that's too wobbly and uncertain to be cheery, as if Miss Harper is trying to build up courage herself. This, Lily knows, unpinning her hair, is a nonsensical notion, for Miss Harper doesn't seem to be scared of much – hadn't she made that horrible man from the Tom Thumb scarper, and if Lily hadn't been so scared of what was about to happen, she might have almost found it funny, seeing him peg off like that, his trousers still halfway down his legs.

She knocks tentatively on the door frame and goes into the studio. If you didn't know what went on here, she thinks, you might almost think it a respectable place, with framed photographs of nicely dressed families on the wall and dear Flossy asleep on the rug in front of the fire.

'Should I lie down?' Lily looks at the chaise longue with caution.

'We're going to try something different this time. A sequence.' Miss Harper emerges from under the camera, and from the side table takes a wreath, fashioned from ivy and hawthorn berries, which she places carefully on Lily's head. The twigs scratch Lily's scalp; she thinks squeamishly of woodlice burrowing into her hair. It's a crown, Miss Harper explains; Lily is to pretend that she lives in the woods, that she can speak the language of fauns and foxes and understand the call of the birds.

A bubble of laughter forms in the back of Lily's throat, but Miss Harper, she sees, is in earnest.

'You bathe every day in a pond and lie on a rock afterwards to dry yourself in the sun,' Miss Harper continues. 'But this particular afternoon, you notice someone watching you, a mortal—'

'A man?'

'Yes, a man, and you take fright and leave.' Miss Harper places a cushion on the floor and covers it with a drape. 'Now, slip off the robe and sit with your legs tucked under you.'

It is like plunging into freezing cold water; the longer you wait, the worse the anticipation becomes. Flossy blinks at her in the dying sunlight as Lily steps out of the robe and positions herself on the cushion. Her heart hammers. But the world goes on as it had when she was dressed, the sun continues to set, the cat to purr, the children in the street below to shriek and quarrel. Miss Harper produces more ivy, which she drapes around her neck, the tendrils tickling her breasts. Lily feels rather silly. Is this really what the gentlemen in France like to look at to get them going?

'That's right. A small smile. You're caught up in your own imaginings and he hasn't seen you yet.' Miss Harper stands by the camera and instructs her to hold still. 'Perfect! Now I want you to stretch out, with your head on the cushion – yes, like that – lock your hands behind your head.'

A mechanical click comes, after each exposure – Miss Harper tells her it's the sound of the plates moving in the camera. She talks to her as they work, telling a story. Imagine you have never encountered a man before, she says. When you see him you are curious, but your instinct is telling you to run. Lily is standing now, looking over her shoulder at the lenses, staring at her like two pairs of eyes, remembering the shock of Uncle Jack peering at her when she was taking her bath. A little less angry, Miss Harper says, and Lily tries to look less angry and more curious and she must have succeeded for Miss Harper praises her, again and again. It has been a long time since anyone has told her she is good at anything – she is used to complaints, not compliments – and when the last picture is done, and she puts the robe back on, Lily feels a morsel of regret, for now she is in the water, she wants to stay in a little longer.

She asks Miss Harper what happens next, how the piece of glass in the camera becomes a picture like the ones on the wall.

Miss Harper hesitates. She looks towards the door as if afraid someone might come. Then, lowering her voice, she tells Lily to come upstairs to the attic when she's dressed, and she'll show her.

The attic smells of science. Rows of bottles on rickety shelves, three basins and a strange contraption that Miss Harper tells her is a press to make prints. Next to it lies a stack of envelopes, stamped and ready for posting. Lily stares. Behind a fraying half-drawn curtain she sees an unmade bed with a man's nightshirt crumpled upon it. She wonders where Miss Harper slept when she lived here, and whether that was part of the reason for her leaving, for there is no mistaking that the living quarters are modest. Miss Harper puts on gloves and an apron, then takes the bottles and starts pouring and mixing in the basins. They're chemicals, she tells Lily, solutions that will bring her to life, but they need the darkness to do it, and together they draw the curtains against what remains of the light.

Strange to be there in the dark with Miss Harper. The racket of the streets, the call of the barrow man, the sparring gulls all shrink like the pinprick of light underneath the door. Miss Harper, a tall grey shadow, takes the first plate from its box and lowers it into the basin.

'There you are,' she murmurs. 'Look ...' and Lily sees a ghost-like figure emerge on the glass, four times over, but it is all muddled and not as she expected: her hair is white and her skin as dark as the minstrels you see playing the banjo for the crowds on the beach. But those are her arms, made ugly with muscle, and the bosom that she wishes was smaller – or not there at all – for maybe then her uncle would stop his gawping.

'It's a negative,' Miss Harper explains, saying it's just the first stage and the next she will do in the daylight tomorrow, once the plates have dried; with great care she submerges the plate into the second basin and then the third and says that her brother used to make her practise blindfold, with books instead of plates. And she does the same thing again, over and over, five more times, until the plates are dripping in the rack and it is safe, Miss Harper says, taking matches and a taper, to light candles.

Lily scrutinises the pictures. It is her but it is not. The negatives show a girl without shame, courting the camera. Why had she asked to see them, why had she not just left well alone? Water slides from the plates, thrumming steadily on the wooden counter. She looks away, then just as quickly is drawn back. The tufts of hair between her legs are obscene, shocking.

She gives Miss Harper a small smile. 'If the French gentlemen could only see me sweating in the laundry.'

'You're just as good as them, Lily. Better, in fact.' Miss Harper takes a metal box from one of the cupboards, and Lily's heart races in time with the dripping negatives as she takes possession of a shiny silver crown.

'Keep it somewhere safe.' In the candlelight, Miss Harper's eyes are drops of gold. 'Same time next week?'

Underneath Miss Harper's oddness, her stiffness, there is something soft. Lily thinks of the way she handled the plates, the care she took with them, the kernel of pleasure Lily had felt as she watched her work: no one had ever paid her such intimate attention before. She has a desire, unexpected and faintly shameful, to be held by Miss Harper, to rest her head on the swell of her breast. But it is as if the fog of her thoughts has been dipped in the chemicals along with the plates, making what was private public, because Miss Harper turns to the door.

'Yes,' Lily says, 'see you next week,' and Miss Harper shows her out, making remarks about the weather, as if Lily has done nothing more out of the ordinary than deliver a parcel of freshly laundered sheets.

Chapter Twelve

Clem looks out from the rain-lashed window of her bedchamber with a sigh heavy enough to draw the attention of her companion, who sits by the fire, absorbed in a particularly bloodthirsty instalment of the latest Sherlock Holmes.

'December's no month for cycling.' Ellen gives her employer a sympathetic smile. 'Might Mr Williams have changed his opinion, come the spring?'

'He becomes more obstinate with time, not less.' Clem sighs again, then, rallying a little, gestures towards the dressing table. 'Let me do your hair – please, Miss Harper,' she goes on as Ellen hesitates. 'Nothing too fussy, I promise. What about a soft wave at the brow? Something a little less severe?'

'Severe?' Ellen frowns. She has never thought of her hairstyle as severe. A drop of vanity draws her with some reluctance to the mirror. Tomorrow is Saturday and she will be with Lily again at Booth Lane. Last week, there had been a moment up in the attic, as they stood in the half-darkness with the drip-drip-drip of the plates, when Lily had looked at her in a certain way, as if . . . she might be a little fond of her. It had so disconcerted her that she'd started prattling about the weather and shown Lily out immediately, but she hasn't stop thinking about it since.

'Perhaps you're right,' she says as Clem unpins the tight coil of her bun, feeling strangely exposed as she sits before her with her hair loose around her shoulders. A peculiar shuffling of their roles, as if they have been tossed like dice in a shaker, and she has come out the mistress and Mrs Williams her maid. She studies her in the mirror. Since the quarrel over the bicycle with her husband, Mrs Williams has lost some of her usual brightness; she is paler than normal, with dark shadows under her eyes.

Ellen enquires as to her health and Mrs Williams, brushing out Ellen's hair in swift, practised strokes, is silent for a moment.

'There is no cure for a husband such as mine.' She reaches for the hairpins. 'He is so suspicious of late too – it is most tiresome.'

'Suspicious?'

Mrs Williams hesitates. 'He seems to think you gave a false address. On your letter of application.'

Ellen tries to steady her voice, but her heart is pounding. 'But why would I do such a thing?'

'That's what I said.' Clem slides in another pin. 'But he tells me that 42 Keevil Street doesn't exist.' She smiles quickly at Ellen. 'The numbering stops at 40, apparently.'

'That's what I meant.' Ellen lets out a little laugh. 'Number Forty. A slip of the pen.'

'I told him there'd be a simple explanation,' Clem says pleasantly and Ellen breathes again. 'Which is more than can be said for this . . .' and now she is rummaging through the bottom drawer of the dressing table and pulling out a photograph in a silver frame. She hands it to Ellen.

'You've heard my husband has a mistress, I suppose?' she says, with an attempt at nonchalance. 'Not to mention a bastard son.'

No, Ellen says soberly, as she studies the picture, she wasn't aware. There stands before her an older woman, rich, clearly, but big-boned and plain, with doughy skin and small dark eyes. She is dressed in a riding habit, a King Charles spaniel submissive at her feet.

'Why, it's Lady Bracknell –' her eyes meet Clem's in the mirror – 'with a riding crop.'

The corners of Clem's mouth twitch. 'And a stuffed dog, poor thing.'

When they have stopped laughing, Clem picks up the comb with renewed vigour. 'How is it fair,' she says, 'that he does exactly as he pleases, while I cannot?'

'Perhaps it is time,' Ellen says, 'to negotiate.'

'A quid pro quo.' Deep in thought, Clem sweeps up the hair at Ellen's brow, then turns to her, her eyes bright with the excitement of an idea newly born. 'What plans do we have for tomorrow afternoon, Miss Harper?'

Ellen pauses. 'I'm assisting my brother at the studio.'

'Again?' Clem looks at her curiously.

'He finds himself busy in the approach to Christmas. And the assistant Dobson – as I think I explained – fractured his ankle stepping from—'

'An omnibus, yes.' Clem frowns.

Ellen avoids Clem's gaze as she takes in her reflection. The waves, the uplift, do suit her better, although five minutes on her bicycle and she'll be more wreck of the Hesperus than fashion plate.

'I hardly know myself, Mrs Williams. Thank you.'

Clem smiles back, but there is a coolness about her as she

returns the photograph to the drawer. 'Let's call Ottilie, shall we, and play a game of hearts before tea?'

Ellen is in agreement. And as she follows Clem into the hallway she asks further as to Mrs Williams' plans for tomorrow and whether they might work as well on Monday, but her employer will not be drawn further, claiming that it no longer matters.

Clem stands alone in the dressing room of the Palmeira Stores in a dark tweed riding dress, leather gloves and an ugly three-cornered hat, cross-checking each detail of her attire with that of the redoubtable Lady Arabella in the photograph. A more than satisfactory match, even down to the riding crop with the fox's head – little matter that it is silver plate, for the camera will not discern the difference. She must use what limited resources she has, Clem thinks; her husband has underestimated her and it is time that he – and those around him – are made to know it.

As she calls for the assistant, her thoughts return to her absent companion. It pains her more than she can say that Miss Harper should choose to keep secrets from her. On the surface of it, there is nothing untoward about Miss Harper assisting her brother at the studio on a Saturday afternoon, yet the story about the assistant and the omnibus and the sprained ankle is almost too well conceived to convince. She recalls that stocky bull of a man in the box next to theirs at the Empire, well dressed but clearly low-bred; he had raised his glass to Miss Harper as if he knew her. Could she be meeting him, or some other man? Miss Harper had once said rather stiffly that she had no interest in marriage, but is it really so hard to picture her, chestnut hair swept back and scented with lemon oil, wrapped in an embrace?

Frowning, Clem goes to the counter and pays for her purchases. Ever since Miss Harper burst into Herbert's study in support of her – an act of solidarity which had left Clem deeply touched – Herbert has been on the warpath, muttering that he doesn't trust the woman as far as he can throw her. And while Clem does her utmost to defend her companion, is it really feasible that someone as precise as Miss Harper would be so absent-minded as to write down the wrong house number in her address? Yet Miss Harper had looked her in the eye, and told her that that was exactly what had happened.

Once outside, Clem summons a cab. 'Harper's Photographic Studios,' she calls up to the driver as she settles into her seat. 'The King's Road.'

As the hansom sets off, she looks once again at the photograph of Herbert's mistress. It is time, she thinks, staring out at the to and fro of the crowd from the grubby window, to set the cat among the pigeons.

'Mrs Williams.' Mr Harper glances at the appointments book, as he extends a slim hand. 'What an unexpected pleasure. But I was expecting . . . a Miss Brouwer.'

'My maiden name,' Clem says, looking about her. The place is as quiet and subdued as a library. 'I would like my picture to be taken in the style of this lady,' she goes on, taking Lady Arabella's picture from her bag, and gesturing to the pile of boxes by her side. 'My costume is prepared.'

'Without the spaniel, I assume.' Mr Harper gives her a small smile, as he studies the photograph. 'Follow me, Miss Brouwer, and you shall effect your transformation.' He hesitates. 'I assume a maid is coming to assist you?'

'My maid has influenza,' Clem says as they walk upstairs.

She tries to sound airy as she takes off her hat. 'I rather thought your sister might help me dress. She's working with you this afternoon, I understand?'

The briefest of pauses.

'That's right,' Mr Harper says and Clem's heart lifts. She is a foolish and mistrustful person; Miss Harper will appear directly.

'But I'm afraid Ellen is out at the framer's at present.' He holds open the studio door, guileless. 'Should I send for a girl instead?'

That won't be necessary, Clem tells him, she will manage, and her thoughts, as she follows Mr Harper into the studio, are not charitable. He is lying, she is sure of it, and something tells her that wherever it is that Miss Harper may be at this moment – and it is almost certainly not the framer's – she is there with her brother's blessing.

Ellen presses the scalloping tool into the border of the print. Laid out on the table are forty-eight Lilys – crouched, reclined, in flight. Their appeal – she decides – lies in what makes Lily Lily: her gentle, open nature and her sweetness, with not a trace of the impertinence so often evident in the other models. Reynold would have been horrified if he'd known she'd allowed Lily into the darkroom, but Ellen couldn't see the harm; why, she and Lily might almost be friends. When Lily had arrived this afternoon, she'd noticed her new hairstyle straight away, remarking that it looked 'very pretty'. It had made the trouble of styling it this morning worthwhile, and Mrs Williams had been kind enough to lend her tortoiseshell hair combs again, leaving Ellen to wonder if she had imagined yesterday's froideur.

As the church clock strikes six, she hears the front door

open, then Reynold's loping footsteps on the stairs as he bounds up to the attic. He kisses her cheek in greeting, as he glances at the prints.

'She's come along, hasn't she, the little laundress?'

'Don't mock her.'

'No need to be touchy. Now –' he perches on the table edge – 'don't be cross but the Three Graces heard we were back in business. They want to come next Saturday.'

The tableaux girls. Ellen closes her eyes. 'Reynold, no. I told you it was just Lily.'

'Come on, Ellie, it's Christmas. Or it will be, soon as blinking. Which reminds me, Harry Smart's having a knees-up on Christmas Eve. She was most insistent that you should come, told me not to let you wriggle out of it.'

'Charming,' Ellen says drily, reaching for an envelope. 'But I'll be expected for dinner at the Crescent.'

'Oh, fa-di-lah!' Reynold makes a face and mutters that it's a funny kind of person who prefers to spend Christmas Eve away from the company of her family and friends, even if Mrs Williams is rather more of a lark than he first thought.

Ellen looks up. 'What do you mean?'

'She came to the studio this afternoon. Wanted a photograph in some kind of disguise. All very curious. Don't look so worried – I told her you were at the framer's.'

'And she believed you?' Ellen frowns. 'She's watching me. We need to be careful.'

They wouldn't need to be so careful, her brother reminds her, if Ellen hadn't decided to up-end their lives by going to live with a signed-up member of the Vigilance Association, and what now should he tell Harry Smart when he next sees her – he folds his arms peevishly – for she is certain to ask about the party?

'Send my apologies.' Ellen puts on her cloak and bids him a curt good evening. As she steps outside onto Booth Lane, she reflects that she'd rather endure dinner à deux with Herbert Williams himself than be part of Harriet Smart's entourage of smirking acolytes. At least with the former she knows where she stands: he tolerates her for his wife's sake, just as she does him.

'I was sorry to miss you at the studio this afternoon.' Ellen lays down a jack of spades. The candles on the Christmas tree flicker and sway, paying court to the gold dots on Mrs Williams' dress, the coppery tones in her hair.

'Unfortunate timing,' Clem says. Her eyes make contact with Ellen's above the fan of cards.

'I was collecting prints from the framer's,' Ellen goes on. 'It was quieter today than we expected.'

'Why did you go to Mr Harper's studio, Aunt Clem?' Ottilie throws down an ace and declares herself out.

'A surprise for your uncle.' Clem gives her a quick smile. 'You know how to keep a secret, Ottilie, I'm sure.'

The words land on Ellen as surely as if Clem had lobbed a ball across a net for her to catch. She proposes a quick round of hearts, but Clem suggests that she and Ottilie should continue without her: she is not in the right humour, she tells them, to play any more games.

Chapter Thirteen

Clem watches and she waits. Two Saturdays pass in which Miss Harper leaves for the afternoon with her hair coiffed, eschewing the Ladies' Rambler and walking to the King's Road studio instead. She has had enough of arriving all wind-blown and ruddy-faced, she tells Clem, her brother says it's enough to frighten off the customers. She returns with stories – of the baronet whose lurcher relieved itself on the carpet, the dowager who upon receipt of her photograph demanded a refund, finding it in no way a good likeness. It is as if Miss Harper concocts something amusing each week to tell her, Clem thinks, more certain than ever that she is being deceived. And so when Christmas Eve comes, drizzly and half-lit, she decides to follow her.

Dressed in her plainest cloak, with the hood pulled low, Clem watches from the drawing-room window as Miss Harper sets off along the Crescent. Then she hurries downstairs, slips outside and follows her companion onto Marine Parade, thankful that Miss Harper is a good half-head taller than most around her.

They weave in and out of the chestnut sellers lining the route to the Chain Pier, dodge the shoeshine boys and the carol singers, and the Romany women selling mistletoe. A small boy tugs at Clem's skirts and begs for a penny, and when she gives him a shilling, multiple siblings cluster about her and she has to shoo them away with her umbrella. She fears she has lost sight of Miss Harper altogether, until she spots her a little distance ahead, crossing the King's Road, just past the Metropole Hotel.

Angling her umbrella to conceal her face, Clem trails her companion through one side street, and then another, before they reach a hilly terrace of ramshackle houses. Miss Harper strides to the top of the road and stops outside a shabby front door. Clem hangs back in a doorway as three young women, dressed in all the colours of a sweet shop window, approach from the opposite direction, and in a blur of hats and feathers disappear with Miss Harper inside the house. So Herbert had been right: she had lied about living on Keevil Street.

Clem shivers. Dirty rainwater drips from the window ledge above her. *Might I suggest, Clementine, that if you spent a little more time tending to the needs of your husband and substantially less indulging your fertile imagination, you might be rather more satisfied in your marriage.* Her mother's presence is always at its most forceful in the wake of recent correspondence and she had received a letter just yesterday, along with a Christmas parcel. She can only imagine what her mother would say if she saw her now, lurking on a filthy doorstep, shadowing one of the staff. A woman carrying a squawking infant, with two children trailing at her heels, looks at Clem with hostility as she passes. Clem is stern with herself – she must leave: Miss Harper has no sweetheart, she is passing the afternoon with friends, ladies who are clearly not as respectable as they might be, and she is embarrassed to mention it: that is all. Yet there had been no warm exchange of greeting when the women arrived – it hadn't seemed like a social call.

The Golden Hour

Slowly Clem walks to the top of the street and back again, rain driving against her face as she thinks once more of her mother's letter.

You tell me that your husband is often absent, <u>but</u> it is <u>your</u> responsibility, Clementine, to ensure that Herbert does not stay away for longer than is necessary in the city . . . .You must be loving, affectionate, attentive etc. My dear daughter, you have many charms, <u>but</u> allow me to be frank: children cannot be made when husband and wife are apart! I cannot emphasise enough the importance of your duty in this regard.

A responsibility she never asked for, a duty she has no interest in carrying out, not with a man who was chosen for her. If only she could exchange places with Miss Harper, Clem thinks, and then she might do as she pleased, even if it meant living in a drab little street like this one – for she assumes that these are the lodgings where Miss Harper used to live with her brother.

She is on the verge of returning home when she notices another woman waiting outside Miss Harper's house. Clem strains to see her face, but the hood of the girl's thin cloak shields her. She is small, soberly dressed, unassuming – as different from the sweet-shop women as a pigeon from a parrot, and, curiosity freshly piqued, Clem draws back into a needle-thin alleyway and watches. The door opens, the women from earlier tumble out in a giggling gust, and the girl steps inside.

An icy wind blows down the sour-smelling alley, rubbish skitters at her feet. I know very little of the world, Clem thinks, and if I go home now, I will know even less. And whatever is going on behind that scruffy front door amounts to more than tea and chitchat. Besides – self-righteousness rallies her – Miss Harper is in her employ, doesn't she have a right to know? She waits a few minutes, then emerges from the alley. She looks up and down the empty street, but no one tries to stop her, no manifestation of her conscience pulls up a window and tells her to mind her own bleeding business. Clem stands outside Number Thirty, as others have before her, and turns the door handle in her gloved hand. It opens without resistance.

Clem steps into a narrow hallway, where a grey-veined carpet, worn to its threads, marks a path upstairs. Above her she hears the low murmur of voices, and as she creeps up towards the landing she sees a door left half open, and the conversation becomes more distinct.

'Are you warm enough?' Miss Harper's voice. 'A little powder here, I think.'

Holding herself still, Clem peers through the gap in the door, but the room is empty save for a tortoiseshell cat dozing on a pile of clothes on a packing box. A pair of muddied boots lie abandoned on the hearth and a corset, the laces gaping, dangles from the top of a Chinese screen.

Go now, Clem tells herself, you don't belong here. Her mouth is dry and she feels peculiar. But she cannot go back, she has come too far. She walks into what seems to be a dressing room with an adjoining door. Next to the screen is a dressing table, where two empty tumblers coated in a sticky dark residue share company with a hairbrush and comb, and multiple hairpins. Clem sniffs one of the glasses. Rum.

Behind the door, someone laughs. 'Silly theatre girls,' says Miss Harper. 'Stiff as a board, one of them!'

Clem crouches down and looks through the keyhole. She sees a parlour, the stumpy legs of a green velvet couch. The blur of Miss Harper's skirts, and then the shiny nub of a bare ankle, passing so quickly that Clem wonders if she has imagined it, before the ankle and the foot to which it is attached settle on the floor, and then are gone again.

'Let me take the drape,' Miss Harper says.

A white sheet falls to the rug and is retrieved. A hush descends, interspersed only with the creak of a floorboard, the crackle of the fire. Hold still, Miss Harper says, and for a second Clem imagines the removal of an eyelash or a splinter, until the phrase echoes back to Mr Harper three weeks earlier, standing by the camera in his draughty studio, preparing to expose the plate. The cat stirs and flexes its claws on a petticoat hem, as if sensing her unease, and it is at that precise moment, for it must be said that the house is not the cleanest of places, Clem's nose begins to itch uncontrollably, and before she has time to reach for her handkerchief, she sneezes.

The door flings open and there stands Miss Harper, and behind her, crouched on a chaise longue, her head burrowed in her hands, is the girl with the fine ankles, with, as Clem's own Manhattan mama might have put it, nothing between her and her virtue. Clem scrambles to her feet, the words she searches for not yet born, and it doesn't matter that Miss Harper is closing the door on the scene and asking her to calm herself, for these women – the photograph on Herbert's snuffbox; the living statues glazed with light at the Empire; and now this girl, anonymous, naked – these images once seen are impossible to forget.

'Let me explain.'

Miss Harper grasps her arm, but Clem shakes her off.

How dare you, she hears herself saying in a voice that no longer resembles her own. She is shaking with an emotion that she cannot name, something more delicate, more easily bruised, than anger. She has taken this woman, not just into her home, but into her confidence: she has told her things about her marriage, about Herbert, that she had admitted to no one, they have spent hours wheeling that damned bicycle she will likely never be at liberty to ride again up and down the dirt track in the hills, talking and joking, sitting on a tree trunk like tramps and drinking rum, when all along Miss Harper – and her brother too – must have been laughing at her.

'I am your mistress!' Clem's words come out in a sob. 'And you are . . .'

She cannot finish. Her gaze lands on the tortoiseshell combs in Miss Harper's hair that had given her such pleasure in the lending, and she can bear it no longer: she runs down the rickety stairs and out onto the desolate street. The feeling of seasickness that she has been trying so hard to ignore over recent days overwhelms her as she reaches the bustle of the King's Road, and she cannot help herself – she retches into the gutter, her humiliation complete, as a well-dressed woman walks by, shielding her children's faces from the spectacle and telling them not to stare.

It is the hardest thing in the world to calm a distressed person when every unwelcome thought she chooses to express stokes the anxiety in one's own mind. Lily's voice, as she dresses behind the screen, is fretful.

'But who was it?'

'I told you,' Ellen says. 'Just a nosy parker from opposite. I should have bolted the front door – I'm sorry.'

'What if she goes to the police?' Lily emerges, her hair half up, half down as she fumbles with her hairpins.

'*She* go to the police?' Ellen forces out a laugh. 'Why – I've a mind to report her for trespassing! Here, let me help you.' She sits Lily down in front of the mirror. 'French bun?'

Lily nods. Ellen takes a few drops of oil and smooths out Lily's hair, the motion soothing her a little, as she works out what to do. She must hide the plates, and the prints too, take them to Mr Meed's, although he'll charge them through the nose for it. Lily is right, the shock may send Mrs Williams to the police station, or at the very least to her husband. And if Mrs Yorke-Duffy and the committee get wind of it, everything is over. The thought of having to pack up and leave crushes her. The two of them again, her and Reynold, back where they started, cheek by jowl in some Parisian garret. And then there was Mrs Williams herself. That look on her face as she fled from the room. I thought you were my friend, her eyes seemed to say, but I don't know you at all.

Lily pats the topknot, which sits in a neat twist on the crown of her head. A strand of hair falls, brushing the nape of her neck, and as Lily reaches for it, so too does Ellen, their fingers briefly touching.

'Let me,' Ellen says, and she feels Lily's soft gaze reflected upon her, and she thinks of her as she was five minutes earlier, lying on the couch. There in the studio, she'd imagined another world where she might lie beside her, daring to touch the curves of her body, pressing her mouth to the delicate arch of her back. It had felt so real as to be almost possible. Now Lily – dear Lily – is asking her something. Are you feeling unwell, Miss Harper?, and yes, she is far from well, she is found out, her feelings as raw and tender as if she had plucked out her own heart for the gulls to scavenge upon.

It seems to Ellen that Lily reaches for her. And she will go over and over this moment in the days and weeks to come, but it happens without warning – Lily turning from the mirror to face her, her hand feather light on Ellen's own, the pulsing warmth of it; and Ellen's body reading this as a sign, as sure as the arrangement of tea leaves in a cup. And so Ellen kisses her. And Lily – Lily doesn't pull away – at least, not immediately. Better if she had for then it would have spared Ellen later agonies, when after a few dizzying seconds, Lily's chair had scraped across the floor and Ellen read in her eyes that she had endured rather than desired the embrace, and worse still, pitied her.

Ellen turns away. 'I think you should leave.'

'Miss Harper, I . . .'

'Miss March. Don't trouble yourself. Please – go.'

And Lily does as she is told, not even stopping to button up her coat or pull on her gloves, calling out a forlorn Merry Christmas that hangs like wilting mistletoe in the darkening rooms.

Chapter Fourteen

'And how might the festivities differ across the Atlantic, Mrs Williams?' Herbert's closest friend, Thomas Shaw, smiles at Clem in a fashion that could pass as charming, had his gaze not darted to her bosom directly afterwards, as if it were her breasts who might speak up in unison and give him details of turkey and carols and pumpkin pie.

Clem gestures to the butler – hired for the evening – for more wine, earning herself a look of disapproval from Ottilie. Well, perhaps she is drinking more than usual – little matter that it is making her feel more nauseous than ever – and if Ottilie knew what she does about her French tutor, then the girl might be reaching for something stronger than fruit cup too. And the more she drinks, the more questions Clem has, for she is not naive enough to believe that the model she came upon was the only one, nor the first, and what do Miss Harper – and her brother – do with the photographs afterwards?

She glances at Miss Harper's empty chair. Blaming her absence on illness, Clem had afflicted Mr Harper with a bad case of pneumonia and put his sister in the role of nurse: she has told Ottilie that she can't be certain when Miss Harper will return, news that filled Herbert with much festive bonhomie.

'Mr Shaw was asking about your Christmas traditions, Clementine.' Her husband clears his throat.

'I'm sure you Americans have a merry time of it – hush, now, Winifred!' Mrs Yorke-Duffy slips a scrap of beef to her whimpering dog.

We do, Clem says, drawing back her chair. And might she suggest that they take advantage of this lull between courses to each exchange a small gift, just as her German ancestors used to do on Christmas Eve. She retrieves a package, gaily tied with red ribbon, from under the Christmas tree and walks to Herbert's place at the head of the table.

'In honour of an absent friend,' she says. 'Happy Christmas.'

'*Danke schön, mein Schatz!*' Herbert squeezes her hand, then fumbling with the ribbon, unwraps the parcel, drawing out the photograph from the folds of tissue paper. His colour heightens as he studies it, the cheap gilt frame winking dully in the candlelight, and the look he gives her – fierce with humiliation – is brand-new: she is no longer his Clemmy, his '*Schatz*'. Then he laughs and, swallowing a mouthful of wine, holds up the picture to the assembled guests.

'It seems that my wife will be accompanying us to Feathers for the Boxing Day hunt after all!'

No one responds. They know already, Clem realises, as she looks around the table; the silence says it all. Mrs Yorke-Duffy is petting the poodle. Mr Shaw, his eyes alive with mischief, is pinching his lips together; his wife stares at the tablecloth. It is only Ottilie who looks puzzled.

'But you loathe hunting, Aunt Clem.' She frowns. 'Why are you dressed like that?'

'Ask your uncle.' Clem reaches for her wine glass, her eyes drawn to the space where Miss Harper should be. It has taken all the pleasure from the performance for there will be no reliving it with port and crackers later, when everyone has gone to bed: she is more alone than when she first arrived, for now her memory has seized Miss Harper in its jaws and will not let her free.

'Your aunt's having a little joke, Ottilie.' Herbert's chuckle has more in common with a growl and Winnie starts to bark. 'You can join us for the hunt, Clementine, and I'll hold you to it too!'

And then the butler is instructed to bring up cigars and brandy forthwith, as the ladies, Herbert says with some firmness of tone, will be retiring to the drawing room without delay.

It is a little after midnight when Herbert comes to Clem's room. He enters without knocking, and Clem's heart quickens as she lays down her hairbrush and turns from the mirror. He has with him the photograph, which he tosses on the bed.

'I suppose I should be flattered.' He lets out a dry laugh. 'You went to no inconsiderable trouble to humiliate me, Clementine.'

'Flattery was not my intention.'

'And what was your intention exactly?'

'Stop playing me for a fool, Herb.' She gets up from the dressing table. 'I know about your mistress and I know about your son. And do forgive me if I expect a little more from my life than to just sit here, waiting to give you an heir.'

'*Expect!*' And then Clem sees that she has misjudged the situation: her husband is furious. For a moment he looks as if he is about to hurl the photograph straight at her. 'You and your mother and that useless excuse for a man she married would be on the street, if it wasn't for me.' He paces towards her. 'Your mother begged me to take you off her hands.

Begged! Do you understand? And all you can do in return is insult me.'

'You'll wake Ottilie,' Clem says, but he becomes louder still.

'You know I could cut your mother off without a penny, don't you? Who do you think's paying for that Upper East Side apartment she's so fond of? And the goose she'll be tucking into tomorrow lunchtime? And the brand-new four-poster that she and your stepfather will be fucking on afterwards?'

'How dare you!'

'Take off your nightdress.' His breathing is ragged and erratic, like a horse about to tantrum. 'That's an order.'

'An order!' He sounds so ridiculous she wants to laugh, but the look on his face scares her. 'For heaven's sake, calm yourself.'

'You want to play games, Clemmy, here's one for you.' He seizes her and flings her onto the bed, holding her down as he fumbles with the buttons of his trousers.

'Herbert, stop!' The impulse to prevent what is about to happen overwhelms Clem. 'I'm sorry.' She stares at the needlepoint swallows on the embroidered bedspread, a wedding present from her mother that she has always hated. An apology is just words, she tells herself. 'I'm sorry for embarrassing you.'

He stops. His penis droops. The wildness in his eyes disappears; he wipes his forehead and looks about the room as if he has no idea of how he came to be there. He turns away and rearranges his clothes, and when he looks back the temper has drained from him, and he is the husband Clem knows again: selfish but uncomplicated, unreasonable but not wilfully unkind.

'Please return the photograph of Lady Arabella to where you found it,' he says quietly as he goes to the door. 'It was wrong of you to go through my things.'

Standing in the corner of Harriet Smart's expansive parlour, feigning interest in the mosaic of photographs on the wall and trying to ignore the whoops and shrieks from the crowd gathered around the piano, Ellen realises it was a mistake to have come. Reynold – still furious with her for letting her guard slip – had insisted, saying that if their rooms got searched, far better to be out than in. Not that there was anything left to find – every plate, every print had gone to Mr Meed for safekeeping, who had not only charged them handsomely for it but invited himself to the party. Harry won't mind, he'd said, she'll barely notice, but Harriet Smart had answered the door to them herself, and had both noticed and seemed to mind.

'Your Mrs Williams was much prettier, dressed for the theatre, Miss Harper,' she'd said with a wry smile, warning Meed not to go worrying at her girls for she wouldn't stand for it.

Ellen takes another sip of punch and looks about her. Although it is commonly known that Miss Smart has done well for herself, Ellen is still somewhat surprised by the smart cream-and-yellow villa, with its dainty iron balconies and view onto the sea. It is undeniably genteel, which is more than can be said for the present company. The tableaux girls had descended upon Reynold the minute they arrived, and Corazón hasn't left him alone since, sitting on the arm of his chair and playing with his hair, twisting each strand into springing curls. He is drunk or he wouldn't tolerate that kind of fussing, and Ellen wishes that she could find similar oblivion at the bottom of her glass. The events of the afternoon are branded upon her, and every time her mind is left to wander, it takes her either to Lily by way of Clem or Clem by way of Lily, and with each revisiting her memory adds cruel detail: the way Lily had wiped her mouth with the back of her hand as she moved away from her; the force with which Clem had snatched her sleeve free from her grasp, as if Ellen were some clawing animal.

The piano stops, and a maid starts to lower the lamps. An older woman in a shapeless orange dress, hair loose around her shoulders, instructs the men to push the furniture back for there is dancing to be done. That decides it. Reynold may do as he likes, Ellen thinks, but she is leaving, and she makes a path towards the door.

'Stay for the dancing at least.' A firm hand on her shoulder, masculine smells of cigarette smoke and cologne – Harriet Smart's dark eyes glitter. 'Let's find you a seat.'

And ignoring her protests, Harriet escorts her to a couch, telling those upon it to 'budge up', and Ellen finds herself squeezed between Mr Meed, who shows every sign of staying put until the party's dying breath, and one of Harriet's maids.

'Ladies and gents!' Harriet climbs onto a dais in the corner of the room, where the woman in orange lies smoking on a chaise longue. 'Show your appreciation for Les Filles d'Artifice!'

The woman smiles lazily at Harriet as she makes room for her to sit. Ellen stares. There is something intimate in the way they inhabit the small space, but as the piano starts up, Harriet catches her watching them and she looks quickly away.

Seven girls dressed in red petticoats, yellow bodices and

wide hats exploding with exotic plumage high-kick into the parlour to much cheering and applause. As they dance, inching their skirts higher and higher, the floorboards creak and strain, photographs tremble on their fittings, the very walls seeming to shake. Ellen's head throbs. She smells lavender water and sweat, and the ripe odour of alcohol. Mr Meed has gone quiet, his eyes glazed, and Ellen sees what he sees, which is black stockings and white dimpled flesh, feels his terrible longing for the skirts to go higher and higher still. She sits with her hands folded in her lap, because she does not know what else to do with them; she wants to leave but she cannot move; she drains her glass of punch.

'Terribly energetic, aren't they?' she says to the maid, whose mouth twitches in the same way as the models' when they think she's not looking.

'Yes, miss.' She turns her back.

Oh, why did she come? Ellen scours the room for Reynold but sees no sign; Harriet and her friend have vanished from their spot on the dais too. All the better – she will be able to slip away now unnoticed. Ellen pushes her way through the crowd to the quiet of the hall, where she comes upon another maid, dressed in a butler's jacket and trousers, whom she asks to fetch her cloak.

'Tessie's coats and carriages, not me,' the girl says cheerily. She nods towards the staircase. 'It might be quicker if you get it yourself, miss. Up top in Miss Smart's study.'

Miss Smart's study indeed! More likely an excuse to display more photographs of herself. Wondering how and why Harriet puts up with such slapdash behaviour from her servants, Ellen goes up the next flight of stairs, finding herself in a dimly lit hallway from where an open door leads to a small study. A white cat yawns lazily amidst a nest of cloaks and scarves, and after locating her own, Ellen looks about her, mildly curious. In the centre of the mantelpiece stands a framed print of a much younger Harriet, in top hat and tails, in front of a music-hall billboard, flanked by two beaming individuals who look fit to burst their buttons with pride. Ellen reads the inscription – *The Smart Family, 1885*. How different might her own life be now, she thinks, if she and Reynold had had even one parent who cherished them in that way – little wonder Harriet Smart walks through the world with such swagger.

She moves on to the bookshelves, piled high with papers, on which are scribbled half-written songs and fragments of sketches, alongside a scrapbook of newspaper cuttings and reviews. There are just two books: a collection of plays by Oscar Wilde and a tatty Bible in a cheap cloth binding. It is a prop, Ellen supposes, for one of Harriet's turns at the Empire – she can't imagine the woman anywhere near a church otherwise, or any congregation who'd welcome her for that matter. On the inside cover she sees a faded dedication to a Teresa Middleton of St Mark's Orphanage, Bermondsey, and she wonders fleetingly who she is, and what, if anything, she means to Harriet Smart.

Ellen is about to leave when a sudden cry, high-pitched and keening, carries down the hall. Silence follows, yet if she listens hard it is not silent, for she can hear gasps and the heaviness of breathing, and yet another cry, too short-lived for pain, too scented with pleasure for sorrow. Ellen pauses. She has drunk too much, she should leave directly, but the call of the unknown is more powerful than her logic and so she inches, step by guilty step, in the direction of the sounds, towards a room at the end of the hall.

The door is ajar, candles are lit. She sees two long pale legs parted on a bed and Harriet Smart's dark cropped head bobbing between them. The cries intensify and tug at somewhere deep and private inside her. She hadn't even known that what she was witnessing was possible, that one woman might do this to another. Then the legs spasm and shake, and a raspy groan is released from their owner, followed by a murmur from Harriet Smart, who sits up, wiping her mouth. The woman in the orange dress – for of course, it is her – leans forward, mussed-up hair tumbling down her back, and the two of them embrace. As Ellen turns to go, a floorboard creaks, betraying her, and the woman looks over Harriet's shoulder, suddenly alert.

'Why, Harry!' She stares straight at Ellen. 'We have company.'

Ellen runs. The riot of the party is spilling now from the parlour and she pushes her way through the throng, a song of Harriet's repeating over and over in her head. *I'm a ladies' man, I am, I am, I'm a ladies' man, for certain!* She has always known deep down what Harriet is, as surely as she knows that salt stings, but why, why did they have to leave the bedroom door open – it felt like a trap that she had been lured into. Glancing upstairs, Ellen sees Harriet leaning over the banisters, shirtsleeves rolled and puffing thoughtfully on a cigarette, as she looks down at her. Ellen's cheeks scorch red. How Harriet and her friend would split their sides laughing if they knew what had happened with Lily earlier. *We should have given her a seat and charged her a shilling, Harry,* she imagines her friend saying in her drawling way. *The poor thing can't so much as steal a kiss!*

'Your brother's gone.' Corazón appears from nowhere, flushed and loosened with punch. 'Went home to find you.'

'Warming up the bed, Miss Harper,' Sal pipes up behind her, and the girls erupt with laughter.

Ellen's skin prickles, her neck chafes against her starched collar. Then, through the din of the party comes a hammering at the front door and the sound of raised voices.

'It's the peelers!' someone shouts, and there is a change in the current, as dozens of guests burst from the parlour and try to force their way out. Ellen catches a glimpse of Harriet in the mêlée, before a policeman and then another and another advance up the stairs to the first floor, their stern expressions a poor disguise for the enjoyment they are clearly taking from all the flesh and feathers. The Filles d'Artifice shriek and struggle as their wrists are forced into metal cuffs, Corazón and Sal and Jemima enduring a similar fate, but no one pays attention to Ellen, and she hurries downstairs.

'This is a respectable neighbourhood, Miss Smart.' In the dark recess of the hallway, a man with a stringy moustache and the self-righteousness of a newly ordained curate is lecturing Harriet. 'No one is above the law, little matter what day of the year it is.'

The man is familiar. Ellen recognises his voice and then she remembers. He comes occasionally to the Crescent for committee meetings – she has passed him on her way in and out of the house. He is an agent, she realises, paid by the vigilants to snoop and inform. Putting up the hood of her cloak, she heads for the open door, but just as she is about to leave, a policeman with an unpleasant smirking countenance blocks her way.

'Work here do you, miss?' he says, taking in her sober attire.

She is about to say she'd rather sweep streets for a living, when it strikes her it is far better to collude in this assumption than have the police asking questions about her at the Williams' household. Nervously she eyes the police cart across the road, the horses made skittish by the cries of the women inside.

'Miss Harper, housekeeper,' she says. 'And I shall be handing in my notice directly.'

'Will you now?' His smirk deepens. 'And I don't suppose you knew anything about tonight's activities either, did you, Miss Harper?' He calls over to the cart. 'Another one for the cage, Bob.'

And Ellen struggles and cries out and the policeman who is securing the cuffs laughs and calls her a wildcat, worse than the trollops in the cage, his hands lingering on her, before Ellen finds herself shoved into the back of the cart with the girls.

Chapter Fifteen

The women are kept in the cell until the slop bucket is full and Christmas Day is over. As the first slivers of daylight move across the floor, they are given a piece of bread and a pail of icy water to wash in, and by this time even the tableaux girls are tight-lipped and miserable, huddling together on the bench for warmth. Ellen sits alone, hunched against the wall, the thought of where she should have spent Christmas, and where she now finds herself, flattening her. She thinks of Clem, sipping claret over lunch, cheeks pinkening in the warmth of the dining room. All it will have taken is a few glasses for her to have told her husband that he was right, that Miss Harper was not as suitable a companion as she had hoped, and he would ask what had changed her mind, and then she might have told him. And Mr Williams would confide in turn to his sister, and Caroline Yorke-Duffy would seize upon this news like a seal leaping for fish. Ellen closes her eyes. She will be an item on the next committee-meeting agenda, before she can blink. And the worst of it is, she is the agent of her own downfall, for if she hadn't been at Booth Lane with Lily, none of this would have happened: she would have spent Christmas Eve at the Crescent with Clem, where she wanted to be, not at Harriet Smart's party, which had only served to remind her of how alone she used to feel. The golden hour must end – she thinks again of Lily pulling free from her – all it has brought her is humiliation and now disgrace.

'You.' A warder approaches, pointing at her through the bars. 'Do you want to get out or not?'

Ellen is lightheaded with relief. Reynold has come for her after all. When she had not returned home, he would, of course, have gone to Harriet Smart's directly – in all likelihood he was at the police station the whole of yesterday, awaiting her release. She runs a hand through her hair. The filth of the prison clings to her, her shirt cuffs are grey, the hem of her skirt wrinkled and sodden. She needs hot water and plenty of it, she will scrub herself raw, then they will sit down to the Yorkshire ham she ordered from the grocer.

But in the waiting room there is no sign of Reynold. A woman, in a coat too elegant for the surroundings, hands encased in a fur muff, stands with her back to her, staring out of the window. On hearing footsteps the woman turns; Ellen's heart leaps – it is Clem. But Clem looks her up and down coldly, as if running an inventory and finding it lacking, and only then does it occur to Ellen how much, up until now, Clem has always strived to please her, as if Clem herself were the companion whose livelihood depended on her mistress's good will.

'The carriage is waiting,' Clem says, unsmiling, and silently Ellen follows her outside.

'I've seen photographs like the ones you take.'

Clem and Ellen sit in the empty drawing room, a low fire crackling in the grate. Number Ten has a melancholy feel, as if the festive season were an unwelcome guest, deserted by its hosts. Mr Williams and Ottilie have gone to Feathers for the Boxing Day meet; it was fortunate, Clem had informed

Ellen icily, that when the message arrived that morning from Agent Jackson, it had fallen into her hands, and not her husband's.

'There's a picture in Mr Williams' snuffbox.' Clem goes to the window and looks out at the silver sea. 'No doubt I'd find more if I troubled myself to look.' As she returns to the fire, her tone is harsh. 'I want to know everything, Miss Harper. Don't insult me by lying, not about your acquaintance with Miss Smart, or anyone else for that matter.' She looks at her sharply. 'If I'd a mind to, I could send for the police.'

'I know.' Ellen looks at her companion, tense and pale and seemingly furious, and she understands the anger for what it is – pain that she herself has caused. And the root of this pain lies not in the act of deception itself – she is no disgraced housemaid called to account for stealing – but rather because Clem has come to care for her: they are more than just companions, they are friends. And this realisation fills Ellen with a feeling of such warmth, such gladness, that all she wants is to set things right. If she cannot be completely truthful, she tells herself, then at the very least, she will not lie.

It started, she tells Clem, when she and Reynold first arrived in Brighton from France. Neither of them held much fondness for their mother's country, and although it was wicked to say it, their grandmother's death had been more blessing than curse. Reynold had been apprenticed to a photographer in Paris for a short time and they'd set a little money by for their passage to England, but once they arrived Reynold had contracted pneumonia – and they'd found themselves short of money to pay doctor's fees, and then the rent. And so the golden hour had begun. The models were actresses mostly – living statues, or dancers. But there were others too, factory workers with more mouths to feed than money; seamstresses half blind from toiling fourteen hours a day and not yet twenty years old.

'Is that who she was?' Clem asks. 'The girl you were with? A seamstress?'

She isn't at liberty to say, Ellen tells her; the sensitive nature of the work means she must protect each model's identity. Mrs Williams will doubtless understand why the young lady took such pains to hide her face, when she discovered them in the studio.

'We pay the women fairly,' she goes on, 'and they come of their own free will.' She pauses. 'If they weren't doing this, they'd be forced to do much worse, some of them – you'll know that from your committee meetings.'

'The world is an imperfect place.' Clem paces again to the window. And when she next turns, her face is wet with tears, so that Ellen finds herself offering her employer her own handkerchief, just as she'd done three months ago outside the Empire, but this time she lays a hand on her arm.

'What has happened?' she asks.

Clem sniffs angrily. 'I am very much afraid that my body has betrayed my will and that my husband has got what he brought me here for.'

'You're . . .'

'Yes.'

The look in Clem's eyes troubles Ellen: it reminds her of girls who have come to the studio in the same condition, fierce but desperate.

Clem grips Ellen's hands tightly; her fingers are cold. 'I need your help, Miss Harper,' she says.

Chapter Sixteen

The New Year comes. Flurries of snow apply a confectioner's hand to the curlicued railings along the promenade and to the domes and minarets of the Brighton Pavilion. The rooster atop the weather vane at the end of the pier acquires an icy elegance as it stares eastwards across the oily dark of the sea. Pebble-eyed snowmen pop up on the beach, and families travel to London for skating parties on the Thames, for roasted chestnuts and ginger wine. The snow melts, freezes, melts and freezes again. The world turns from white to grey and clouds slump heavy across the town. A woman and her newborn are found dead in a ditch, their lips frozen to identical shades of lilac. In the slums north of the centre, the street sellers huddle around braziers, scraps of bandage wrapped around red swollen fingers. The queue for the workhouse has never been longer, the dread and misery among the unfortunates who shuffle towards it in the sleet never more acute.

The Empire theatre has gone dark, and will stay that way, Mr Juniper the manager says, until the first of February at least. Time for the dust to settle, for the vigilants to calm themselves and find something better to do. It hasn't been shut down though, that's just idle gossip, and all that talk about disorderly behaviour at Harriet Smart's house on Christmas Eve is rumour, nothing more, although it is said that half the performers on Mr Juniper's pay roll woke up to Christmas morning in a police cell, and Miss Smart went to war with the police over it – but now she's vanished, reported to be holidaying in the south of France with a friend. They are dull without their Harry, complain the girls they call the living statues – Jemima, Corazón and Sally – who prance around the pier like restless ponies, before scrabbling loose change together for a cup of cocoa in the empty Refreshments Room.

Anyone seen Miss Harper? one will ask the others, but Miss Harper and her brother haven't been seen since Christmas, and Sal says it's because Corry tried to steal Miss Harper's sweetheart at Harry's party, and now the Governess has got her brother under lock and key, and the women splutter into their teacups.

They don't notice the small pretty girl in a thin coat, speaking to Mrs Larr at the counter: the girl is looking for Miss Harper too, and she is holding an envelope with her name on it. Tall, neat-looking, I know who you mean, Mrs Larr says, submerged in a cloud of steam from the tea urn, but this is a refreshments room, not a postal service, and would Miss like to buy anything or will that be all?

And Lily goes outside, screwing her face up against the wind and the spray from the sea, and wonders, for the hundredth time since Christmas, if it would have been better for her in the long run if she'd kissed Miss Harper back, because now she feels as if she is worth nothing again, and if she is honest, she misses the way Miss Harper used to look at her, almost as much as the money she earned. And so, the next time she is put on deliveries at the Crescent, she flits up the front steps of Number Ten, while the driver is taking a leak, and slips the envelope addressed to Miss Harper through the brass letterbox. It can surely only make things better, Lily thinks, as they drive away in the cart, for it is hard to imagine how they might be worse.

The hot iron sizzles as Lily presses the first in a pile of white lawn napkins. This afternoon Mrs Hadley has moved her from mangling to ironing for it needs to be done quickly but well, and returned to Brunswick Square by five, or the customer has threatened to take their business elsewhere. Lily doesn't mind the ironing room, which is warm at least, and she has been spared sheets, unlike her mother, who is sweating at the press opposite, her face wan and exhausted as she pulls down the metal bar. But then her mother stops, quite suddenly, and rushes from the room, her hand clasped to her mouth, and Mrs Hadley looks up from the counter, where she is checking the packages for delivery, and frowns, before quietly beckoning to Lily to come to her office.

Mrs Hadley sits under the embroidered sample that had taught Lily to read the words 'cleanliness' and 'godliness', when she was just eight years old, and comes straight to the point.

'What's wrong with your ma, Lily?'

'She's got the sickness,' Lily mumbles. Faces peer through the box window in the door as they pass, murmuring that goody-two-shoes Lily March is in for it; but the look on Mrs Hadley's face is kind.

'Your uncle still at home with you all, is he?'

'Mostly.' Uncle Jack's evenings in the pub have been more frequent, since her mother started being sick every morning, absences that would have been a blessing, had drunkenness not made him bolder than ever.

'Is he kind?' Mrs Hadley asks. 'As an uncle should be?'

When Lily doesn't reply, Mrs Hadley sighs and shakes her head. 'I thought not. You're a good girl, Lily.' She looks at her severely. 'It's easy to get sick like your ma is now, you know that, don't you?'

Lily nods and Mrs Hadley sighs again. 'All right. Back to work.'

When she comes out of Mrs Hadley's office, her mother is back at the press. She scowls at Lily – and Lily wants to say that she hasn't been telling tales – Mrs Hadley is just sharper than most – and soon the whole laundry will know she's in the family way with Uncle Jack's bastard child. Later at home, Lily does express these sentiments and her mother hurls a plate at her. When Lily arrives at the laundry the next day with a split lip, Mrs Hadley goes straight to her office and composes a letter to an acquaintance of hers from the church, a Miss Hinchlin who is on the board of the Brighton Vigilance Association, asking for her help with a decent young woman whose moral and physical wellbeing is giving pressing cause for concern.

On top of a hill, with the countryside rolling bleak around them, Miss Harper and Mrs Williams, eyes and noses streaming like those of labourers in the field, contemplate the rough stony path that cleaves the valley beneath. It is hardly the weather for cycling, but Mrs Williams sits upon the Ladies' Rambler, her face rigid with intent.

'Gentle on the brakes,' her companion reminds her. 'You don't want broken bones on top of everything else.'

And Mrs Williams sets off, unsteady on the uneven

ground, brambles tearing at her skirts, an arc of mud flying in her wake. She passes the rotting carcass of a dead rabbit, writhing with maggots, and her insides heave; she reaches the bottom of the hill and pushes the bicycle back up to the top. Go again, Miss Harper tells her, and this is not exactly what Clem had in mind when she asked her companion to help her, but Miss Harper had assured her it was a safer way than any other, and the pills Clem had bought by mail order had done nothing but upset her stomach.

She keeps going up and down the valley until her legs are blancmange, and she is retching up the remains of her lunch in a ditch.

'Just once more,' Miss Harper says, patting her back, 'and then we'll go back to Feathers,' and Clem wipes her mouth and wordlessly climbs back onto the bicycle.

The scalding bath and half bottle of gin had the advantage of sending Clem into a deep sleep at least, Ellen thinks, as she sits by her bedside in the flickering candlelight. The servants have been given the evening off and the house is strangely quiet – even the wind has dropped, as if it too is holding its breath in anticipation of what comes next. Ellen has never thought of herself as one for the countryside, but this week of hibernation at Feathers, while Mr Williams is visiting finishing schools with Ottilie in Switzerland, has not been entirely unpleasant even given their present circumstances.

Gently, Ellen touches Clem's arm. Reassured that she is fully asleep, Ellen takes Lily's note from her pocket and reads it again.

Dear Miss Harper,
I am sorry that I made you angry.
Sinseerly,
Miss Lilian March

It is so neatly, so carefully, transcribed, that it pains Ellen to
see it, the handful of words transporting her back to that
moment in the dressing room, when, foolish woman that she
is, she had confused Lily's sweet nature for something else
entirely. But for Lily to march up to the front door of
Number Ten with a letter for her that anyone could have
opened and read, well, that was reckless, and couldn't be
allowed to happen. Better for both of them if they never set
eyes on each other again – Reynold was right: she had let
herself go soft. Besides, there is no more work, the sun has
set on the golden hour; she has told Clem as much, and
upon their return to Brighton, she will tell Reynold too.

Ellen looks at Clem, her tangled hair, the frown lines on
her brow that tell of the ache in her head to come. She has
been as honest with her as she can, but there are some things
she could never share. For if Clem ever came to learn of
who and what she desires, of where she comes from and
who she really is, there is no doubt she would despise her.

They had woken one morning, she and Reynold, a few
weeks after their eighteenth birthday, to find Grandmère
dead in her bed, her face slack down one side as if it had
melted during the night. Sudden as a curse or an answer
to a prayer or both. Mélisse, the maid, urged '*les pauvres*' to
pray, and on her knees by her grandmother's bedside Ellen
had thanked God, over and over again, and she guessed
Reynold felt the same, for when she looked at him, his eyes

were shining. With Maman gone, they were Grandmère's only living relatives, and the house, although in need of repair, had to be worth something. But their grandmother's final punishment was a vicious one that caused even Monsieur Lafalle from Léopolde & Fils to frown as he read out the will: Madame Georgette Abadie had left the house and everything in it to the church.

The curé took pity on them, this pair of gangly adult orphans, with their English accents, who spoke so properly, but whose clothes were old-fashioned and worn. He let them select two pieces of hefty mahogany furniture each, along with the pearl choker that Ellen had tried on once, without Grandmère's permission, and received a beating for. Neither of them had ever had their own money before and the sum the dealer, Monsieur Cloutier, gave them for the items seemed huge.

'Enough to buy a camera,' Reynold had said, at which Monsieur Cloutier produced a card with an address of a photographer in Paris. Tell him Cloutier sent you, he said as he slipped away from the house, and when he thought he was out of sight, a smile spread like oil across the sharp edges of his face.

They left for Paris and found lodgings in the 18th arrondissement on the second floor of a house which was as riotous as Grandmère's residence had been silent. The inhabitants squabbled, wept, shouted and drank, seemingly without end, and as the little money they had began to run out, Ellen realised that Cloutier had swindled them. There was no money for a camera, there was no money for anything but survival. She couldn't bear to spend her days in the lodgings, and so she roamed the city, the phantom of her grandmother marching ahead of her, casting judgement at every turn. Obscene. Disgusting. Sinful. Girls as young as thirteen standing in their shifts in doorways, calling out to passing men. Desire and its consequences everywhere she looked, the pant and grunt of it from open windows, the wailing babies, the loitering men who stared at her, no matter how high her collars or long her skirts. Ellen would return home every evening and boil water to wash in, scrubbing herself clean of the city until all she could smell was Pears soap, her one luxury.

One morning, Reynold took out Cloutier's card and went to visit the photographer on the Rue Marcadoux. He returned with a job as an apprentice and snapped at Ellen when she asked whether this Monsieur Fourbier was respectable. Ellen found out for herself soon enough, when she saw the trickle of young women who passed through the doors of the dingy studio that bore a few dusty family portraits in the window, an alibi so unconvincing that she almost wanted to laugh. Almost. Fourbier had spotted her and come outside.

'You'll keep the police at bay, dressed like that, mademoiselle,' he said. He was a short, squat, greying man, his moustache stained with tobacco, a hardness to his small eyes. Ellen couldn't bear the thought of Reynold getting in out of his depth, and so she found herself asking Fourbier if he needed any help – with accounts or paperwork – and he laughed and said he'd pay her a few sous to clean the studio after a photograph '*en groupe*' and pour drinks beforehand for the *artistes*. Ellen had agreed.

She never witnessed what went on in the grubby studio every Friday afternoon, but there was no mistaking what it was. The smell afterwards, the creamy stains on the tatty upholstery, the way the women would hurry out with their heads down. But the men, Ellen noticed, swaggered. The photographs were developed and printed in a room above the shop that was always kept locked. And then there were the girls, the ones Fourbier called his *poules*, his *puces* – they posed alone or in pairs sometimes – and compared to what happened on a Friday, these pictures seemed almost innocent. Reynold took his first photograph of a model called Pierrette – short and tubby with meaty calves, who sucked on pear drops throughout and flirted with Reynold relentlessly. He was so proud of the result that he put her print on the bookshelf, next to Grandmère's Bible, where Pierrette's insolent gaze followed Ellen around the room. Before long, it was the Englishman Monsieur Harper, not Fourbier, whom the girls wanted behind the camera – Reynold combined good looks with an innocence that made him easy to tease; and he never took liberties like Old Man Fourbier, whose hands always seemed to stray into places they shouldn't.

Months passed. Spring rolled into summer and then autumn. Now they lived on their earnings, and after a while Ellen found there was a little spare every week to put by. The details of what she was saving for were vague but her aim was precise – to leave Fourbier and find her and Reynold a more respectable position. But then one day Pierrette didn't come for her appointment, and everything changed.

Fourbier slid Ellen two silver coins across the counter. 'We have a model,' he said, 'standing right here. Isn't it about time you showed us who you are, mademoiselle? If you want your brother to keep his job, that is.'

Ellen had thrust the money back, her face hot. 'I'll find you a girl,' she said, and then she'd walked through the back-streets until she saw a young woman sitting on a doorstep in her nightdress, yawning like a cat in the afternoon sun. Unbrushed hair, her breath sour with last night's wine, but her eyes were clear and bright and hopeful, and she was still young and pretty enough to wear her profession lightly.

At first, the girl – whose name was Margie – refused. But Ellen told her that if she came with her now and did as she said, she wouldn't need to do the other work later this evening, or at least not as much of it – and wasn't there always a customer who she wanted to say no to, but couldn't? Yes, said Margie, her face darkening, and then she'd put her cloak on over her shift, and had gone with Ellen to the studio. The relief Ellen had felt was overwhelming. Reynold took the photos, Margie was paid; she left, smiling.

Fourbier had turned to Ellen with a gleam in his eyes. 'Good work, mademoiselle,' he said, and that was the start of it. He doubled Ellen's wages and employed a cleaner. *La flâneuse des filles*, he called her, a rather grandiose title, Ellen thought, as she trawled the dogleg alleyways and gloomy courtyards for new girls. But they were grateful mostly, and if it wasn't them, it might be her, and although Grandmère's voice bled into her, calling her all manner of names, Ellen didn't – in fact couldn't – stop.

Chapter Seventeen

The women travel back to Brighton three days later, a journey made lengthier by the frequency with which they call up to Dixon to stop so that they can take some fresh air. The sound of Clem vomiting in the copse stirs the wood pigeons from the branches and causes Dixon, waiting on the platform of the carriage, to grin, and Ellen fears that if it carries on, there won't be a person below stairs that doesn't know that Mrs Williams can't keep anything down, and before long Mr Williams will learn of it too.

'It hasn't worked, has it?' Clem says flatly, as they pull into the Crescent, and although Miss Harper tells her that it's too early to be thinking that way, Clem can't deny what she feels, which is sick as a dog, and unmistakably pregnant. Her heart sinks when Milly tells her that Mr Williams is back from Switzerland already, sinks further upon the news that Mrs Yorke-Duffy has come to call, and that both would like to see her, at her earliest convenience, in the study.

The trip to Switzerland has done nothing for her husband's good humour. No, it was not a success, he informs her, greeting her with a brusque kiss; Ottilie remains as obstinate as ever, and her French – and here he and his sister exchange weighted looks – is appalling. He passes Clem a letter from his desk.

'All it requires is your signature,' he says. 'Miss Harper was your appointment, after all.'

'Not that this is a criticism of your judgement, Clementine,' Mrs Yorke-Duffy pipes up. 'You're still so young. Why, the staff I've had to dismiss over the years – I've had half the cooks in Brighton come through my kitchen!'

'Dismiss?' As she scans the letter, Clem feels sicker than ever. Certain behaviour had come to light which made Miss Harper's position untenable etcetera; she is to leave the household immediately.

Her sister-in-law draws herself up. 'There is a residence in Hove, belonging to a Miss Smart, which has been under surveillance by our agent, Mr Jackson, for some time. Miss Harper was a guest at a party there on Christmas Eve. It was most disorderly, so much so that the police were called.'

'It's no crime to make merry at Christmas, is it?' Clem tosses the letter aside.

'Miss Harper spent the night in a cell,' Herbert says with disdain. 'I don't suppose she told you that while the two of you were toasting your feet by the fireside at Feathers!'

Clem is about to reply, when the roll of nausea returns. Clapping her hand to her mouth, she rushes upstairs to the water closet, tugging hard on the chain to drown the sound of her retching.

When she returns to the study, Mrs Yorke-Duffy has disappeared.

'My dear. Is everything quite all right? Caroline has sent for ginger tea.' Herbert springs to his feet and eases her into a chair, hopeful as a child on their birthday. 'Is there something you wanted to tell me?'

'Miss Harper will remain as my companion. I'll hear no more about it.' Clem scrunches the letter into a ball and throws it in the wastepaper basket. 'I'll be more in need of her than ever –' she is done for, she realises, the rest of her life stops here, for saying the words makes the thing deadeningly alive – 'when the baby comes.'

'Clemmy!' Herbert has her in his arms, the pet who has pleased him, clumsy kisses crowning her head. 'Precious girl.' He stands back, his eyes bright. 'I knew you'd do it in the end.'

Ellen sits in the Refreshments Room on the pier, sipping tea that she doesn't want. She should have gone directly to the King's Road studio to break the news to Reynold about the golden hour, but she is delaying the task: it will cause a row, and part of her still remains angry with her brother about Christmas, for not being brave enough to at least try to secure her release from prison.

'Miss Harper!'

Ellen looks up to see the Ice King hovering awkwardly by her table, his face full of the pleasure of seeing her.

'Mr Clarke.'

'And a happy new year to you!'

Wally is to her as she is to Lily, Ellen realises; she pities him for looking at her this way, for daring to hope. Her impulse, just like Lily's, is to be kind, as one would to a docile animal in need of petting, and she enquires as to his health, his business, his enjoyment of the festive season.

'And how is Harpers' Photography?' he asks. 'I noticed the studio's been closed since Christmas.'

She tells him he must surely know more of that than her, and he smiles and asks why so.

'Why, as my brother's investor, Mr Clarke.'

Wally wets his lips and frowns. 'I'm sorry if you've had

cause to think otherwise, but I have no involvement with your brother's business.'

'I must have misunderstood.' Ellen stares at him, then recovers herself. 'I leave the business affairs to Reynold these days.'

'And yet, you're the one with the head for it.' His gaze is shrewd, and as he tips his hat in farewell, Ellen is left feeling that it is she who is the fool.

She pays the bill and hurries outside. Reynold must be ill; he has always been susceptible to colds, and it is winter, after all. She remembers him as a child in France, not long after their mother left, white as the sheet he lay shivering under, blue lips calling for Maman. A doctor came with a Gladstone bag and a grave expression, matched only by the severity on Grandmère's face when the time came to unlock the safe and pay him with two gold coins.

When she arrives at Booth Lane, Ellen notices a pair of gulls on the doorstep of Number Thirty, and her first thought is how curious this is, for gulls conduct their business on chimney stacks and rooftops. But as she gets closer, she sees that they are pecking at something with great appetite – a dead mouse, or rat, perhaps, although Flossy is no mouser. As she tries to shoo them away, a smell assaults her, rotting, sulphurous, and then the birds take flight and Ellen wishes they hadn't, for what she sees makes her cry out in horror. It is Flossy, her tortoiseshell fur matted with blood, a wound at her neck beaded with black flies that hum with industry.

Her bicycle falls to the ground, the wheels spinning. A face appears at the window opposite as Ellen fumbles for her keys, fear consuming her. She would give all she had now to find Reynold sick in bed with a head cold, or even a mild case of pneumonia; once inside, she takes the stairs two at a time, calling his name. She thinks of the models who dislike her, the contretemps she'd had before Christmas with Jemima whom she'd accused of stealing a feather boa from the box. Yet all the girls love Flossy; there's not one of them would do such a thing.

The house is as cold as a crypt. Ellen goes up to the attic, and flings back the curtain. Reynold lies in bed, curled up in a tight ball, his face swollen with tears.

'Reynold!' She kneels down next to him. 'Are you hurt?'

He stares blankly at the soot-stained walls. 'They made me watch.'

'Who?'

He doesn't respond. 'Rather they'd taken the cheese wire to my own throat.' He clamps his hands to his ears. 'She screamed, Ellie, she actually screamed.'

Ellen pats his wrist and looks around the room. The chamberpot is unemptied, the air fetid and stale. 'How long have you been up here?'

'I don't know.' He begins to cry again. 'Since it happened.'

'Have you told the police?'

'Don't be ridiculous.' He will not meet her eye.

Ellen gets up. She stands on a chair and forces open the skylight. Then, she empties and cleans the chamberpot, and pays the passing rag-and-bone man half a crown to dispose of the cat. She lights a fire, makes toast from stale bread, and when the desire to shake her brother until his bones rattle has subsided, she returns to the attic with tea on a tray.

'How much do you owe? I assume this is to do with money.'

Reynold sniffs, swallows, then implores her not to be angry. He is two months behind on the rent for the studio, and there are other debts still unpaid, the new Dallmeyer, furnishings for the studio – regrettably, he says, his investor has not turned out to be a patient man.

'Investor!' she snaps. 'I just spoke to Wally – you don't have an investor! Who is it, Reynold? I can't help you if I don't know.'

And he shifts uncomfortably under the covers and the fear in his eyes reminds her of the time she'd surprised him in the King's Road studio, with his necktie all twisted and that man, Mr Crocker, with a smile that would freeze a Turkish bath. Those pale puffy eyes studying her over the rim of a champagne glass in the box at the Empire.

'It's not . . .' Ellen pauses, hoping that she has this wrong, that her intuition is flawed, but as she says Mr Crocker's name, Reynold flinches and then she knows. Ellen closes her eyes. 'And where might Mr Crocker be found?'

'You mustn't go to him, Ellen.' Reynold sits up in alarm. 'It's not safe.'

'It's safer for me than it is for you,' she says. 'And I can't see we have much choice.'

Her brother hesitates. Then he puts down his teacup and tells her what he knows.

It takes Ellen some time to pinpoint the exact whereabouts of Mr Crocker. Her boots become sticky with sawdust, for the public houses in this area are not the most salubrious, nor their patrons the most helpful, and she is met with grunts or silence. But eventually she finds a man who tells her there's not many who'd choose to go knocking on the Croc's door, but last he heard he was up the road at Number Eleven.

A stench rises from the gutters as Ellen walks up the terraced street. Filthy curtains sag at darkened windows; a front door hangs from its hinges, the splintered panel bearing the recent imprint of a boot. Hardly surroundings to match Mr Crocker's tailored suits, she thinks, or a seat in the best box at the Empire, but this is clearly a neighbourhood whose residents don't ask too many questions. She is about to cross the road when a woman in a plain navy cloak comes out of a pink bow-fronted house a little way ahead. She is inconspicuous in almost every way but one: her dark shockingly short hair revealed by the jaunty angle of a library-green hat. Ellen stares, as Harriet Smart – for she is certain it is her – disappears around the corner.

How strange. And stranger still, when, upon reaching Number Eleven, Ellen sees that it is the same rose-coloured house from which Miss Smart has just emerged. But perhaps there is nothing odd about Harriet Smart visiting a moneylender – that villa in Hove can't come cheap, with every room ablaze with light and all those maids running to and fro. It occurs to Ellen that it may even have been Harriet who put Reynold in the way of Mr Crocker: the thought enrages her, giving her courage as she knocks on the door. After a while, it opens a fraction and a hulk of a man appears, with a bushy old-fashioned beard.

'I need to see Mr Crocker most urgently,' she says, giving him her name, and he chuckles and says that's as may be, then slams the door in her face, whistling as he walks away. Ellen hammers on the door again, and a few minutes later the whistling returns and the door opens wider this time.

'He's in his office,' the man says, and leads her down the hallway to a shabby flight of basement stairs. He stands, watching her, as she descends in the semi-darkness, the only light coming from a half-open door at the bottom. There is the crackling sound of a fire, and as Ellen gets closer, she hears a yawn and the rustle of a newspaper, sees bare hairy ankles protruding from Moroccan slippers on the arm of a settee.

'Is that you, Miss Harper?' His voice as soft as treacle. Ellen remembers how she'd had to strain to hear him in the studio, how it rendered him more powerful in a peculiar way. Swallowing hard, she reminds herself of Flossy on the doorstep, of Reynold huddled in bed.

'Mr Crocker.'

As she walks into the room, Ellen averts her eyes for the man is in a state of undress, lounging in a paisley robe, a rolled-up cigarette smouldering in a saucer at his side. It is uncomfortably hot and dimly lit, the curtains drawn against the January afternoon, an unpleasant smell of paraffin from the lamp which hangs from the low ceiling. In the corner of the room is a cloudy fish tank, home to a tangle of brackish weeds and a solitary goldfish which swims desolate among them. Pinned to the wall above the fireplace, presiding over an assortment of photographs, and a grimacing pewter crocodile, with an inkwell in its back, is a yellowing newspaper article with the headline: LOCAL SWIMMER, 30, WINS RACE AROUND THE PIER.

'Close the door, dear. I can't stand a draught.' Mr Crocker turns the page of his newspaper. 'Is this a social call?'

'I'm sure you know why I'm here, Mr Crocker.'

There is nowhere to sit, nor does he invite her to do so. Ellen takes an envelope containing her wages for the month from her bag and lays it on the table. 'That's the first payment of six.' She passes him a grid of figures, outlining her calculations. 'I've drawn up a plan. We'll pay the next at the end of February, the third end of March and so on, until June, by which time my brother will have given notice on his premises and will no longer need your assistance.'

'Did you fight his battles in the school yard too, Miss Harper? No wonder the man's such a milksop.' Crocker glances at the ledger. 'This doesn't take into account the interest he owes. Twenty per cent.'

'You garrotted his cat! He hasn't been back to work since.'

'Poor puss.' He smiles. 'I must have a word with my men. But it could have been so much worse, Miss Harper, wouldn't you say? Come, don't look so sour.' He pats the settee. 'Sit down a moment.'

She cannot leave without the assurance that he won't hurt Reynold. Reluctantly, Ellen does as he asks, and Mr Crocker leans back, enjoying her discomfort. Turning away, she stares at the mantelpiece, where among the photographs she sees Harriet Smart, in costume with her arms outstretched, a white carnation in her buttonhole, a kiss curl on her forehead. What had she been doing here in this dismal room? Had she sat where Ellen is now, hands clammy inside her gloves, trying to keep the fear from her voice? Or was she on altogether friendlier terms with Mr Crocker?

'Is it true?' Mr Crocker's eyes narrow as he exhales a plume of smoke. 'What they say about you and your brother?'

Ellen gives him a terse smile. 'I don't trouble myself with gossip, Mr Crocker.'

'A woman after my own heart.'

The smell of him becomes stronger and he is suddenly close to her, too close, although she hadn't seen him move.

'You're too good for him, you know.' His eyes slide the length of her. 'You're a handsome woman, when you lose the scowl.'

He is sitting forward now, his knee almost touching hers. His robe gapes open. The thick muscle of his calves, carpeted with whorls of dark wiry hair, renders her almost physically ill.

Her eyes dart to the fireplace – a poker, long and sharp, lies across the grate.

'I want you and your men to stay away from my brother,' she says firmly. 'Any financial matters can be dealt with by me in future.'

'Can they now!' Mr Crocker laughs, then slides one hand across her thigh, the other around her waist. 'I can think of other ways you can pay off your brother's debt, Miss Harper.'

'Get your hands off me!' Ellen has never been this close to a man who wasn't Reynold in her life. He repulses her, his scarred, damaged skin, the dull flare of his eyes, the strong trunk of his body that presses against her as she struggles. He chuckles as if they are engaged in some kind of parlour game, pinning her arm behind her back before suddenly letting her go.

Ellen stumbles to her feet. 'You'll get your money.' She can still feel him upon her; her hands shake and she cannot still them. 'Just leave us alone.'

'I'll see you next month, Miss Harper,' he says, and Ellen tries not to run, not to show she is afraid, but to what purpose? The man has made terror his trade: he can smell fear at fifty paces.

As she reaches the top of the stairs, the bearded man steps from the shadows with an animal's stealth and silently shows her out.

Chapter Eighteen

'I'd like to introduce our new member.' Clem smiles at the committee members assembled around the table. 'Miss Harper will be familiar to most of you as my companion – and Ottilie's French tutor.'

'Nominated by whom?' Mr Harty's voice is icy, and Ellen wishes she could tell him that her desire to leave is as strong as his to be rid of her. It had been Clem's idea – you are my companion, she had said, and the sooner everyone, particularly my sister-in-law, accepts it, the better.

'By myself,' Clem says firmly. 'Miss Harper has an excellent knowledge of the town and its people from her work at her brother's photography studio – a very fine establishment on the King's Road.'

'Along with Miss Harper's superior knowledge of a prison cell, I suppose!' Mrs Yorke-Duffy says. 'I apologise for being blunt, but the facts remain.'

'The facts –' and now it is Clem's turn to bristle – 'are that Miss Harper was brutally treated by the police, incarcerated on Christmas Day – and subsequently released without charge.'

And her colour heightens, and there is much rustling of paper, for everyone knows a lady who's expecting should not be upset.

'No need to distress yourself, Clementine. You've made

your point most clearly. Welcome, Miss Harper.' Mrs Yorke-Duffy's lips tighten as she checks the agenda. 'The first item is yours, Mr Harty.'

'A familiar case of moral lassitude in the home.' Mr Harty checks his notes. 'Man of the house in prison, his wife now pregnant by her brother-in-law, who is resident with the family and a very dissolute individual by all accounts. Fears for the safety of the eldest daughter, whose current employer, a Mrs Hadley of the Mayo Road Laundry, has concerns for her wellbeing and notified the association. Background notwithstanding, the girl is of good character and a hard worker. We're seeking a place for her in service, as a laundry maid or housemaid. I suggest we put an advertisement in the—'

'But does the girl want to be helped?' Mrs Yorke-Duffy interrupts. 'You know what happened to the last one we placed. Her own room, three square meals a day, and she still ran off – with a set of napkin rings no less.'

'This girl from the laundry can hardly be held responsible for that,' Clem says.

'All I'm saying, dear, is that some of these young women can be difficult to set on the right path.'

'She can come and work here,' Clem says crisply. 'No need for an advertisement. I'll interview her myself.'

'Are you quite sure?' Mrs Yorke-Duffy lets out a small laugh, as she looks around her. 'You have so many beautiful things here. Temptation at every turn.'

'Let's assume, Caroline, that the girl is not a thief.' Clem glares at her sister-in-law.

'All the same, Mrs Williams . . .' Mr Harty frowns.

'I'm decided, Mr Harty.' Clem smiles sweetly. 'Let the girl know I'll see her as soon as she's able. Heavens, in a house this size, we'll find something for her to do. What did you say her name was?'

Mr Harty glances at his file. 'Miss Lilian March,' he says and Ellen feels as if she is in the gallery at the theatre, looking down at the drop. She tries to collect herself, but her companions are not called the vigilants without reason, and looking up, she sees she is the object of Mrs Yorke-Duffy's scrutiny.

'Are you quite all right, Miss Harper?' the woman asks. 'You look as if you've seen a ghost.'

Ellen replies that she is perfectly well, and Clem says that's the matter settled then, and Mrs Yorke-Duffy marks a neat tick on the agenda next to the laundry girl's name.

'We send our laundry out, Mrs Matthews, always have.' The cook hurls the dough onto the table and begins to pound it with her ample fists. 'Besides, we've nowhere to dry anything here, you'll be asking to hang the linen in my pantry next.'

The cook throws a sceptical look at Lily, who stands helpless by the housekeeper's side. She has barely been here five minutes, yet already she seems to have made everyone cross. A kitchen maid, stirring a pot on the range, looks at her slyly.

'Where do you live, missy?' the cook enquires.

Lily tells her, feeling more like a walking apology than ever as the cook makes a face and says she hopes she hasn't done anything she shouldn't: this is a respectable house.

'And I'll see it remains that way. Thank you, Cook.' Mrs Matthews turns to Lily, glancing with disapproval at her muddy boots. 'Mrs Williams would like to see you. Take those filthy boots off and don't speak unless you're spoken to – understand?'

As the entire kitchen watches her fumble with her laces, Lily wishes for a moment that she hadn't come. Her mother had been right. They'll look down on you, she had told her, they'll treat you like something they've stepped in and expect you to be grateful for it. Lily had sat there, her eyes lowered, clutching the cream envelope addressed to her in handwriting so elegant that even Uncle Jack had delayed his visit to the pub until it was opened. Lily had had to read it twice over, to make sense of it.

If convenient, the short note said, Miss March was requested to present herself at Number 10, The Crescent the following afternoon for an appointment with Mrs Matthews, the housekeeper, to assess her suitability for the live-in position of housemaid with a monthly wage of a pound.

Her mother had declared her a wicked ungrateful thing for wanting to leave her family, and said if she found out she'd been going around selling sob stories to the fancy folk in those grand houses, she'd belt her from here to Eastbourne. They needed her pay from the laundry, she said, and she was needed at home too, especially now, and Uncle Jack had agreed and told her to listen to her mother. Lily had snatched the letter from his grubby hands and asked him why he didn't mind his own business for once. And in the row that ensued, something curious happened. She heard Miss Harper's voice crisp in her ear, as clearly as if she were standing behind her in the cramped kitchen. *You deserve better.* And she had looked again at the address and recalled the monogrammed sheets she ironed every week, the two giant icing-sugar pillars by the front door: 10, The Crescent was where Miss Harper lived now. And then Lily had smiled to herself. Miss Harper wasn't angry with her any more, in fact quite the opposite: she had received her note and made arrangements to help her.

Now, in her stockinged feet, Lily walks in the wake of Mrs Matthews' bustle up two flights of stairs, emerging in a hallway so spacious that it seems impossible that its only function is as a thoroughfare from one room to another. As the housekeeper knocks on a door, she reminds her on no account to touch anything, before Lily follows her into a room so bright and flooded with sunlight that it could be mistaken for heaven itself. And there reclining on a green couch, not dissimilar in style to the one she herself has lain upon at Miss Harper's, is Mrs Williams, in a white blouse and a skirt the colour of lavender, with tiny jewelled earrings which wink and flash in the light. Movement at the windows calls Lily's attention and she sees Miss Harper, standing by the curtains.

Lily drops her gaze to the floor. If she looks at Miss Harper and Miss Harper looks back at her, and Mrs Williams should catch them doing so, she will betray herself. Miss Harper is more accustomed to seeing her naked than dressed; how is she able to look upon her as if their acquaintance is a respectable one? But Miss Harper, Lily reassures herself, is clever, she will know what to do, and sure enough, Miss Harper settles herself in front of a curious-seeming contraption with two lenses like spectacles, paying no more attention to Lily than she does the potted plants.

'Miss March –' Mrs Williams smiles and sets down her magazine – 'I believe you work at a laundry, is that right? And you're seeking an alternative position in service?'

'Yes, madam.'

'You are able to read and write too, I understand?'

'Yes, madam, passably well.'

'Very good.' Mrs Williams nods at the housekeeper. 'See that Miss March has tea and a bun before she leaves, please, Mrs Matthews. And ask Milly to make ready the box room, so that Miss March can join us as soon as possible.'

Mrs Matthews falters. 'The box room, madam? Next to Miss Harper's room?'

'Indeed.'

'I thought Miss March might sleep in the scullery – so she can get the fires lit in the morning,' the housekeeper adds, but Mrs Williams shakes her head.

Miss Harper looks up. 'Could Miss March not share with one of the other maids in the attic?'

How cold her voice is when she is with her lady friend, Lily thinks, as if she is practising at being one herself.

'All the beds in the attic rooms are occupied, Miss Harper,' Mrs Matthews says curtly, and Lily sees Miss Harper and Mrs Williams exchange glances, and understands that they like to make fun of Mrs Matthews when she isn't there.

'Then that's decided,' Mrs Williams says. 'There'll be no more talk of sleeping in the scullery, Mrs Matthews – we're not living in the Dark Ages.' She laughs, although she sounds angry.

'Very good, madam,' Mrs Matthews says. 'Come along, Miss March.'

The housekeeper doesn't speak to her again until they are halfway down the stairs. Then she turns to Lily with a cold expression. 'It'll be the worse for you now that Mrs Williams has made a pet of you – you'll see. The other girls won't like it.' She tuts to herself. '"Make ready the box room" indeed!'

And she continues to grumble as they descend to the kitchen, where Lily finds herself summarily dismissed with a sharp reminder to report for duty in a week's time, and no more mention of tea and a bun.

'Have you ever noticed how Mrs Matthews' neck becomes redder and redder, the crosser she gets?'

Idly Clem runs a finger across the piano keys, as Ellen inserts another card in the stereoscope and peers through the viewer.

'And the puffs of green smoke that come from her nostrils?' Ellen smiles and consults the index paper. 'Lake Lucerne,' she says. 'Rather similar to . . . Launensee. Which in turn is almost identical to Arnisee.'

'Could Ottilie have found a more dreary gift!' Clem says and they both laugh. The stereocard set featuring the 'Lakes and Mountains of Switzerland' had come in a velvet pouch, which had borne false promise: Clem had been hopeful for jewellery. She glances at Ellen. 'You don't mind the girl – March – being next door to you, do you? There's just nowhere else suitable to put her.'

Ellen stares at the jutting peak of the Matterhorn, the symmetry of its reflection in the glacial waters beneath, and wonders what the photographer intended her to feel. Awe? The desire to explore and frustration that she cannot? Lily in the box room? A terrible idea and she wishes she could say so. But oh, the poor girl in her stockinged feet, blushing so hard that Ellen's own discomfort had lessened and she had managed to retain a semblance of calm.

'Miss Harper?'

Ellen looks up from the viewer. 'I'll barely hear a peep from her, I'm sure,' she says. From the hallway comes the sound of the baby grandfather striking three, sonorous, as the afternoon sun dazzles a reminder. She cannot put it off any longer: she must tell Clem what she has agreed now with Reynold, that the golden hour will continue until the debts are paid.

'Mrs Williams, there's been a development.' Ellen lowers her voice. 'Not one I would have wished for at all, but unavoidable under the circumstances.'

Clem frowns. 'You're talking in riddles, Miss Harper.'

'My brother – he – he's in need of money. His new premises haven't come without cost. And with the season not underway until September, and so much competition when the good weather starts, he finds himself in a predicament.'

'Indeed?' Clem looks at her thoughtfully, then goes to the bureau. 'How much of a predicament? One pound. Two?' She pauses. 'Three? Come, Miss Harper, no need to be coy. We're friends, aren't we?'

'The amount is substantial, I'm afraid.' Ellen hesitates. 'Reynold and I have discussed it at length and we will need to resume that part of our business that I told you was done with.'

'The golden hour,' Clem says quietly, and as she walks to the windows it is as if those three words have sucked all the stale air from the room, replacing it with vapours that are altogether more potent. She turns to Ellen. 'Is it lucrative?'

'There is consistent demand.' Ellen gets up and in silence they look out onto the grey-green stretch of winter sea, the mesmeric roll of the waves.

'And your customers are whom? Gentlemen with money to spend?'

'Largely, yes.'

'What do you charge per photograph?'

When Ellen tells her, Clem raises an eyebrow. 'Herbert's cigars cost less.'

'They are just photographs, Mrs Williams.' Ellen thinks of Paris, of the goings-on in Monsieur Fourbier's back room on Friday afternoons when Reynold had always refused to work. 'And they're not as bold as some that are available.'

Clem returns to the fireside, and picks up the box of Swiss stereocards. 'These are "just" photographs, and how much do you think Ottilie paid for them? No less than a pound for the set, I'm sure.' She turns the box over in her hands, with a mischievous glint in her eye. '*The Golden Hour portfolio*,' she intones. 'Exclusive collectable photography for the discerning gentleman. And in issue one, we bring you . . . housekeepers!' She laughs. 'Can you imagine Mrs Matthews as nature intended?'

'It's hard to imagine Mrs Matthews without her key set, much less anything else!' Ellen smiles and sits down beside Clem, suddenly thoughtful. 'But there may be something in it. A portfolio, with our customers' favourite models.'

'And a little joke at your customers' expense.'

'Meaning?'

'Each set of prints includes a woman from a respectable profession. A housekeeper to an aristocratic family in St John's Wood.' Flushed with enthusiasm, Clem gestures towards the piano. 'A music teacher at an exclusive girls' school. A governess to three young ladies on a Brighton square. Don't you see – the men will have fun guessing!'

Ellen stares at her. Is this one of the risks of the first trimester of pregnancy – that the expectant mother might completely lose her mind? 'But, Mrs Williams, I could never propose such a thing to a music teacher. Or a housekeeper. Or . . .'

Clem laughs again. 'Dear Miss Harper, of course not. The piano teacher is –' she waves her hand vaguely – 'the living statue from the theatre, the housekeeper – the seamstress who comes to earn a little extra. It's all nonsense naturally, but who will ever know! What fun we'll have!'

'We?'

'Miss Harper, I have nothing to do for the next six months, other than split the seams of every garment I possess, and knit booties. Let me help you and your brother.' Clem takes a sheet of paper from the bureau and gestures to the empty chair next to her. 'Shall we start with the figures?'

When she was at school, Lily read a story about a poor beggar man, old and sick and crooked, who was out collecting kindling for firewood, and such was his misery and distress that he had called upon death to release him from his worldly troubles. But Death had appeared – skeletal and terrifying, with a scythe that was ready to be used – and the beggar man had changed his mind about his desires and hurried on his way. Lily thinks of this now as she looks up from the bed she is making in Miss Harper's room and catches sight of herself in the wardrobe mirror, barely recognisable in her navy twill dress and white apron, her hair tucked under a crocheted cap. What had the moral of the story been – something about being mindful of what you wished for – and although she is warm, well fed and better dressed than she has ever been, at times she finds herself longing for the noise and squalor of Albion Hill. It had been home, at least, and she belonged there, whereas from the moment she arrived at the Crescent a fortnight ago, she has been made to feel as if she doesn't fit.

'No trunk, I see,' Mrs Matthews had remarked, casting a scornful look at the hessian laundry bag in which Lily carried her belongings. 'You'll be needing a uniform too – we can't have you walking about the place dressed like that.'

Lou, the other housemaid, had sniggered and all hopes of future friendship disappeared as she took her to the box room next to Miss Harper's room, which was both airless and dirty, a spiteful gleam in Lou's eye as she told Lily it would need a good going-over. It had fallen to Lou to teach her how things were done, and every time Lily made a mistake, such as using a duster, rather than a silk handkerchief, to clean the piano keys, or washing the skirting boards with the same water she'd used to wipe down the mantelpiece, Lou would exclaim that anyone would think Lily had never cleaned anything in her life.

As for Miss Harper, it seemed as if she was positively avoiding her. Whenever Lily saw her in the house, she was either in the company of Miss Ottilie or Mrs Williams, and Miss Harper's gaze would slip and slide anywhere but upon Lily. For the first few nights, once her duties were over, Lily had sat in her room, expectantly waiting for Miss Harper's tap at her door, but she had not come on the first night, nor the one after that, and now she wonders if she ever will.

Lily looks about the sparse bedroom. Miss Harper doesn't have a trunk either, just a suitcase under the bed; in fact she doesn't have much of anything. No books or photographs, just a Bible. Lily takes it from the shelf, and fans out the gilt-edged pages, wondering how many years it would take to read it all, when something slips from inside. It is a photograph – and as she picks it up, she sees her own self smiling back, with the cat Flossy on her lap. Her hand goes to her mouth. How strange to see herself pressed inside the middle of a book like a dead flower; quickly she returns the Bible to its place. So Miss Harper does still have a soft spot for her, and likely she doesn't mean to be as cold as she behaves; what they know of each other must be kept secret from the mistress, that's all, for how might it look if Miss Harper were seen jibber-jabbering with the new maid the very minute she arrived?

Heartened by this development, Lily decides to linger a few minutes more – the grandfather clock is just striking midday, and any moment now Miss Harper will be back from Miss Ottilie's French lessons to tidy herself before lunch. And so Lily sets to work giving the grate a polish and it is there that Miss Harper finds her five minutes later, on her hands and knees on the hearth.

'Miss March!'

'Miss Harper.' Lily jumps up and tries to smile but it is hard to play catch with only one person, and Miss Harper does not smile back. 'I wanted to thank you,' Lily goes on.

'There's no need.' Hovering by the open door, Miss Harper hesitates, then steps inside. 'I've been meaning to . . . to ask how you were settling in.' Her face reddens and it is as if they are back in Booth Lane again after the kiss at Christmas, Lily thinks miserably, when all Miss Harper wanted was to be rid of her.

'I'm glad you're safe,' Miss Harper says, softening a little, and Lily is reminded of that first time in the studio, as she lay trembling on the couch, with the sun setting and Mr Harper losing patience. 'But please understand – no one must know of our former acquaintance, not Milly or Lou or any of the other servants.'

'They don't talk to me anyway,' Lily says, and Miss Harper seems pleased about this, and nods, satisfied.

'Silly creatures – you don't need them.'

They stare at each other, the first shafts of afternoon

sunlight sloping across the gleaming floorboards, before Miss Harper looks away.

'I have a few things to do before lunch.'

Yes, Lily says. She picks up her mop and bucket and is about to leave, but she feels so hollow and disappointed that she can't stop herself from asking the question that has kept her awake, night after night. 'Aren't you glad, Miss Harper, that I'm here?'

A long, terrible pause.

'Of course,' Miss Harper says, a look in her eyes that speaks more of pain than pleasure; so that it is almost impossible to believe, Lily reflects later, that Miss Harper is the same woman who swooped upon her with such longing in Booth Lane.

Chapter Nineteen

The hoardings are down at the Empire, the spring programme has rolled from the press, and love them or loathe them, the living statues about whom there was all that fuss now have a permanent slot. 'And there ain't nothing the prudes can do about it,' says Sal as she walks along the seafront, arm in arm with Corazón and Jemima, smiling at a man in overalls who is pasting an advertisement with their names upon it to a board by the slipway. Yes, winter is over, and the girls have daffodils bobbing in their hats, picked from the flower beds outside the town hall when no one was looking. Corazón had wanted to keep a couple for Reynold Harper, but the others said it was he who should be giving her flowers, and in any event the Governess had said nothing about her brother being at the studio, when she'd approached them on the pier.

'I'm almost looking forward to seeing the Governess again,' Sal muses, popping a sherbet lemon in her mouth.

'Looking forward to the money more like,' Jemima says, and the others agree, and they pass a pleasant five minutes, deliberating over how they shall spend it – dancing slippers for Corazón, violet scent for Sal, while Jemima will buy a penny ice and put the rest in the tea caddy under her bed.

Soft, orange sunlight with a hint of warmth bathes the girls as they flit across the road, and then a hansom stops, and their very own Harriet Smart steps out, carrying a wicker basket with a lid. She is dressed in what she calls her 'civvies' – a skirt and riding jacket, and simple green hat with a feather, and as she pays the driver from her purse, not her pocket, she appears almost ordinary.

'My ladies!' Harriet says, tipping her hat as she catches sight of them. 'What mischief might you three be up to?'

'Tea,' they chorus, for Miss Harper had reminded them most sternly when they'd met last week that if anyone asked, no matter who, they should say they are coming for afternoon tea, and if they ever said otherwise, it would be the worse for everyone.

'I happen to be visiting Booth Lane myself,' Harriet Smart says, and just as the girls are wondering how she knew and what Miss Harper will say, a plaintive wail comes from inside the basket.

Yes, Miss Smart confirms, as the girls crowd around her, it's a kitten, just a few weeks old, and en route to its new owners, and they walk together to the Harpers' lodgings, Jemima muttering to Sal that Harry better not stay jawing all afternoon or the light'll go and then it'll be goodbye three bob.

Harriet Smart raps on the door of Number Thirty. She tucks a stray hair behind her ear and rolls back her shoulders, just as she does in the wings while awaiting her performance. Miss Harper appears, and the tableaux girls hang back uncomfortably, for it looks as if they have invited Harry along with them, and the Governess is frowning so hard that if the wind changed direction, she'd turn fifty in a second.

'Miss Smart,' she says. 'I wasn't expecting you.'

'Four for tea is much the same as three, isn't it? Well, four, and this pretty miss.' Harriet shows her the basket. 'My cat's just had a litter and a little birdy told me you might be in need of a replacement.'

Miss Harper eyes the basket warily, then stands back from the door. 'You'd better come in.'

'Don't worry, Miss Harper,' Harriet murmurs, as the girls troop up the stairs. 'Mum's the word. You're no more tea and chatter than I'm evening gowns and ribbons.'

And she taps her nose and follows the models.

Ellen bolts the front door, feeling rather scrambled. Had Mr Crocker told Harriet Smart what his men had done to Flossy? Is she feeling guilty for recommending the Croc to Reynold in the first place, as Ellen strongly suspects she had, no matter her brother's half-baked story of first meeting the man in a tavern on West Street. She should have sent her away, told her they had no need of another cat and certainly not a kitten. But before she is halfway up the stairs, she can hear Reynold exclaiming with delight, and by the time she has joined them in the studio, he is cradling the kitten like an infant and mulling over suitable names.

'I christen you Blanche Neige!' He holds up the mewling cat. 'Snow White.'

And the girls cheer, and from the arm of the chaise Harriet Smart applauds, and says Blanche's own mother couldn't have named her better, and Reynold shakes her warmly by the hand.

'It's the least I could do, after that song and dance at Christmas.' Harriet turns to Ellen, and for a moment all Ellen can see is her head, as slick and dark as a seal, between her companion's trembling legs, and she finds herself almost breathless with fear that Harriet is about to tell everyone that she caught her snooping.

'I hope you didn't suffer any ill effects from your night in the cells, Miss Harper?' Harriet goes on, in a tone more vexed than sly. 'I've lodged a complaint with the station.'

'I was lucky Mrs Williams came to my assistance so promptly,' Ellen says stiffly.

'Fortunate indeed to have such a lady on your side. And a vigilant, no less – little wonder the peelers rolled out the red carpet.' There is a glimmer of curiosity in Miss Smart's gaze, before she gets up and nods towards the camera. 'It must be nearly teatime, ladies. I'll see myself out.'

As Harriet leaves, Ellen checks herself. She remembers the white Persian cat dozing on the coats in the study: the woman is fond of Reynold – it is possible she is just being kind.

'Miss Smart.' She hurries down the stairs after her. 'Thank you. Reynold was most attached to Flossy.'

Harriet looks up, with a brief smile. 'Let's hope Blanche Neige doesn't suffer a similar fate. Her mama would never forgive me.'

'There's no question of anything like that happening again,' Ellen says quickly. 'I've seen to it.'

'Have you?' Miss Smart gives her a searching look. 'I'm glad. Be careful who you and your brother play with, Miss Harper.'

Is she in debt too? It is on the tip of Ellen's tongue to ask, but as they reach the bottom of the stairs, Harriet draws a little closer.

'I don't suppose there's any demand for a slightly more mature woman in your line of work?' She gestures up to the studio. 'I've been told I have a most pleasing silhouette for my age. And unspoilt by childbirth to boot.'

Ellen pauses, her mouth suddenly dry. 'There are . . .' She

swallows and starts again. 'As it happens, I am looking for new models.'

And then, too late, she realises her mistake. She has let her guard down and here is the punishment, the mockery she had so feared just minutes earlier – Harriet Smart throws back her head and roars with laughter, and nothing Ellen can draw upon will stop the colour flooding her cheeks.

'I was teasing you, Miss Harper. I don't sell myself to anyone.' She leans forward and dares to chuck Ellen under the chin, smiling as Ellen shrinks back. 'Not even you, ducky.'

And bidding her a good afternoon, Harriet Smart walks away without a second glance.

It takes Ellen several moments to compose herself. When she returns upstairs, the girls are lolling around in the dressing room, teasing the cat with a feather boa. She tells them that they aren't paid three shillings apiece to play with kittens, and banishing Blanche Neige to the landing, she orders the girls to take everything off except shoes and stockings and to be quick about it.

Ellen removes the last prints from the basin and pegs them to one of the strings which criss-cross the attic, the bromides fluttering in the breeze from the open window. Six girls, their image repeated over and again, until she feels she is more familiar with their bodies than they are themselves: the roll of flesh around Corazón's belly, the delicate sprinkling of freckles across Jemima's breasts. Nakedness notwithstanding, Jemima has more airs and graces than a debutante at her first ball, with a natural haughtiness not dissimilar to Mrs Matthews herself, attributes which made her a rather convincing housekeeper, Ellen thinks, particularly with the addition of the chatelaine around her waist. Jemima had complained bitterly, saying it felt peculiar and she'd rather have nothing on at all.

The front door slams and Ellen hears voices: it is Reynold with Mr Meed, come to collect the first consignment. The attic door opens and Mr Meed steps inside without being invited, peering at the photographs as he walks the length of the room.

'My, my.' He turns to Reynold. 'Is this the new crop?'

'It's the first edition of the Golden Hour portfolio, yes,' Ellen interrupts. 'We have several boxes ready for you to take to London, Mr Meed. Shall we discuss downstairs?'

Meed winks at her brother. 'It's a tight-run ship you've got here, Mr Harper, and no mistake.'

Not tightly run enough, if they are still paying commission to wastrels like Meed, Ellen thinks, as she follows them down to the studio. She wants to ask when he last visited a barber or laundered his clothes; there is a distinctly mossy smell about the man.

Reynold unlocks the chest where they keep the boxed-up prints. 'Each set of photographs has a theme,' he explains to Meed, passing him a box. 'Something a little playful. A guessing game of sorts.'

Her brother had been dismissive of Clem's idea at first, an opinion Ellen suspected had more to do with his aversion to her employer's involvement, for he seems proud enough of the photographs now.

'We want a little more from your distributors than usual,' he goes on, as Meed removes the prints from the drawstring pouch. 'To account for the superior nature of the product.'

'We want double,' Ellen cuts in.

'Dawson drives a hard bargain.' Meed studies a

photograph of Corazón with such intensity that it is all Ellen can do not to snatch it from him. 'You're not the only ones in this game, let me tell you.'

'May I?' Ellen takes the pictures and returns them to the pouch. 'When were you planning to go to London, Mr Meed?'

He leans back on the chaise and yawns. 'Friday suits me best.'

'As it does me,' Ellen says. The men gawp at her.

'Ellen . . .' Reynold begins with caution, 'if you feel Mr Meed needs a companion, it might be better if I accompany him myself?'

Mr Meed nods vigorously. 'Holywell Street is no place for a lady, Miss Harper.'

'My brother has a business to run,' Ellen says, 'and as for Holywell Street, allow me to be the judge of that. Does the half past nine train suit?'

'I suppose . . .'

'Very well. You'll take responsibility for bringing the prints, of course, but I think it best if we travel separately, under the circumstances.' She gives him a brief smile. 'My brother will see you out.'

Once Meed has gone, Reynold turns on her. 'For heaven's sake, Ellie, what were you thinking?'

'I don't trust him to get the price we want.' She snaps shut the lid of the chest.

'And you will, I suppose?' Reynold collapses gloomily onto the chaise. 'No matter that you'll get us arrested if you're found out.'

'No one's getting arrested, Reynold.'

'How can you be so sure?' He ducks his head under the couch and calls out to the kitten.

Like all the best ideas, the plan comes to Ellen in an instant. 'Because I will be accompanied by a woman whose respectability is beyond question,' she says. 'I shall ask Mrs Williams to come with me.'

Chapter Twenty

The nine-thirty train shrieks into Victoria Station, and two ladies emerge from a first-class compartment, inconspicuous enough save for the black lace veil that shrouds the features of the more smartly dressed of the two. Passers-by might reflect, as the ticket inspector had done earlier, that it is a great shame to be widowed so young, yet the woman's cloak is navy, not black, so perhaps she is not widowed but scarred, which is an even greater misfortune. The women pass into the arrivals hall, where they are met by a short, scraggy man, with sagging trousers, who with an unseemly eagerness asks for an introduction to Miss Harper's companion.

'That won't be necessary, Mr Meed,' Miss Harper says, and behind the veil her friend smiles. 'Shall we go?'

And the trio take a four-wheeler to the cocked dog's leg of Holywell Street, accessible from the Strand by way of a foul-smelling alleyway in which bodily fluids are expelled and exchanged on a nightly basis. Long trestle tables, covered in books, run the length of the road, and as the two women follow their guide, the lady in the veil nudges the other.

'Look!' she says. '*The Adventures of Rodney*. Shall we take a copy back for Caroline?'

And the women smile.

They accompany Mr Meed to a smoke-blackened building

halfway down the street. Two gentlemen are perusing the wares in the shop window with such concentration that they barely hear the veiled lady exclaim as she catches sight of a book which makes Rodney's amorous adventures appear mild in comparison. Her companion draws her to one side.

'Are you certain about this, Mrs Williams? We could arrange to meet later at the Strand Hotel instead?'

'Don't spoil my fun, Miss Harper,' the lady murmurs, adjusting her veil, and, taking her companion's arm, they follow Mr Meed into the musty interior of Dawson's New and Used Bookshop.

Mr Dawson, unpacking a box of romance novels at the counter, looks up and stifles a groan. It's that tedious fellow from Brighton who always outstays his welcome and whose name he can never remember – Merryweather? Meadows? He shouldn't complain for it's bread-and-butter stuff he brings with him, titillation for schoolboys or for those gents who like to dip their toe in from time to time. But he looks again and sees that the man has two ladies with him – one in a peculiar veil; the other, respectable enough but with a brusqueness about her that lacks gentility.

'Mr Merryweather.' Surreptitiously, Dawson scours the counter for any remaining evidence of a recent delivery of postcards from Paris – he doesn't like the way the brusque woman is looking at him. A sudden terrible thought occurs. The women are vigilants, and Merryweather himself an agent. A gang of policemen are primed and waiting in Half Moon Alley. A raid, three months in prison, the wrath of his wife.

'Mr . . .'

'Meed,' the man from Brighton says, with grudging good humour. 'I have a new consignment for you, Mr Dawson.'

'A superior offering,' the brusque woman adds, unsmiling.

Dawson stares at her. 'I don't believe we're acquainted, Miss . . .?'

'I – we –' the woman nods towards her veiled friend – 'are interested parties in this business. Might we adjourn somewhere more private?'

If Meed is gulling him, he'll chop off his shrivelled testicles with a meat cleaver and feed them to the pigeons. But Meed blinks, hopeless, as if to say, what can I do, they insisted on coming. They're New Women or similar, Dawson supposes, as he calls a boy to mind the counter, and leading his visitors upstairs, he wishes they'd stayed on their bicycles and out of his shop. But now they are here they can lie in the bed they've made for themselves, and he enjoys the flicker of revulsion that crosses the brusque woman's face at the sight of 'Matchgirl atop a bedpost', a photograph he keeps propped against the inkwell on his desk – and a source of much comfort, after a long day in the shop.

He draws out a couple of rickety chairs for the ladies and asks Meed to show him what he's got.

A slim black box, with *The "Golden Hour" portfolio* inscribed in gilt copperplate, is placed on the table.

Dear Sirs,
We trust you will enjoy our assortment of artistic photo-
graphs, taken at the 'golden hour', as the sun begins its
journey to the exotic hinterlands of our great British Empire.
As exquisite a moment as the subjects of the photographs
themselves – models of the highest calibre with the utmost
languour and grace. But in their midst, an imposter, dear

reader, a housekeeper to the aristocracy, overseer of a large country establishment in Sussex, who keeps her secrets as close to her bosom as her chatelaine. Which is she, gentlemen? The ladies eagerly await your inspection …

'Housekeeper?' Dawson takes the photographs from a fuss of tissue and ribbon and spreads them across his desk, studying them in the rays of half-washed light that force their way through the filthy window. One woman dangles a set of keys from her little finger, her smile too impudent to be anything other than the seaside doxy she undoubtedly is; another with an alluringly ripe physique lies with her head dipped, an old-fashioned chatelaine around her waist, a series of chains and keys falling towards her shadowy mound of Venus. It's likely nonsense and yet …

He sets the box aside with a shrug. 'Eight shillings a box,' he tells Meed. 'I'll take fifteen – see how they sell.'

Meed opens his mouth to speak, but the brusque woman jumps in. 'A pound apiece,' she says. 'For ten boxes. As we explained, Mr Dawson, these are an exclusive product, a limited edition. And you are not the only proprietor we shall be visiting today.'

Dawson is tempted to show the woman the door, before a merry-go-round of potential customers passes before him. The gentlemen who pop in for something extra after luncheon at their clubs, who like things all the better if the price tag is high. The men who like to collect, the men who keep company too refined to purchase the likes of the matchgirl on the bedpost, hypocrites all of them, but what does he care?

He addresses the woman directly. 'Ten shillings – for twelve,' he says. 'And a bob on top if this one –' he jerks his head towards the woman in the veil – 'shows us her face.'

'You are impertinent, sir! Mr Meed, we shall leave.' She nods towards Meed and the veiled woman rises, and Dawson catches a glimpse of white teeth behind the quivering black lace. The bitches are laughing at him! But as the Golden Hour portfolio disappears into the agent's bag, Dawson reminds himself that business is business, and he doesn't want to hear that Mr Stokes, from a few doors down, has beaten him to it when they convene for a drink at the Rose and Crown later.

'Twelve shillings,' he says.

'Fifteen,' the veiled woman says sweetly. 'And a deposit for the next consignment – to compensate for the offence caused.'

A genteel voice, refined, she is a lady, no doubt of it, and a long way from home, too. Who *are* these women? Dawson stares, then defeated goes next door to his safe and takes out the money. He returns and counts it out to Meed.

'Pleasure doing business, Mr Dawson,' the darker-haired woman says, pointedly averting her gaze from the assortment of photographs on his desk, before she and her companion head back down to the shop.

Dawson draws Meed to one side. 'Who are they?'

But the agent's commission must be higher than Dawson had anticipated, for he just shakes his head and tells the proprietor that it's more than his life's worth to say.

Ellen brushes out her hair, tutting at the specks of soot that fall on her nightdress. London was a filthy place, and she has no desire to rush back, although she can't deny that the trip was a success, with all boxes sold, not to mention some advance orders for the portfolio's next edition. But the men though – all of them making her skin crawl in different ways; the owner of the curiosity shop in Covent Garden with his greasy eyepiece and soft stutter, and as for Mr Dawson, he is best described as a rat in a hole. Those appalling photographs in full view on his desk, and one in particular that still haunts her, of an older woman with a sag of a belly and silvery stretchmarks rising like seaweed from the thatch of hair between her legs. She wore black stockings and nothing else, legs parted wide, as she prised herself open; her eyes, as she stared into the camera, were dead.

Ellen reaches for the pot of cold cream. 'You're too old for I Spy Maman,' Reynold had snapped when she told him of it on her return, and as he disappeared into the darkroom, she had resisted the urge to cry out that he was too old for fairy stories. When they were children, he had found comfort in concocting elaborate fantasies explaining their mother's whereabouts – she had run off with the elderly Belgian gentleman who used to sip hot chocolate in the park pavilion and they were living in his mansion in Bruges; or she had taken the train south to the heel of Italy and was in a cat-filled apartment in Naples, waiting for Grandmère to die so she could return and fetch them. Ellen, on the other hand, had always feared the worst – picturing her poor and bruised with festering sores and ragged clothes – knowing somehow that the wildness in their mother's eyes made her weak not strong. It was Mama's weakness after all that had had the three of them banished at their father's behest to Grandmère's in France; her weakness for men other than Papa that had killed him, or so Grandmère liked to surmise, for he'd gasped his last breath on a pavement in Pimlico only a month after they'd left.

She stares at her reflection. One of her earliest memories

is of her and Reynold, sitting at opposite ends of a dusty hallway, rolling marbles back and forth while they waited for Maman to finish whatever it was she did every Thursday with the man with curly ginger hair who gave them Turkish jellies, and put his finger to his lips, before he took their mother into his bedroom. There were other men too, bearded and bald, dark and fair, and when she and Reynold tired of marbles, they used to dare each other to look through the keyhole while the other counted to ten. If Ellen closes her eyes, she can still see the images: their mother bouncing naked on a bearded man's lap; or a big white hulk of a man crouched over her, the thing between his legs as purple and swollen as a sausage. She and her brother had been in agreement – that they would never take their clothes off and do that disgusting thing that Maman and the men do with anyone – not ever. This, Ellen knows, is why Reynold has made his nest behind the camera where he is safe, rebuffing the advances of Corazón and her ilk; the reason also for the shame they both feel whenever he returns from his trips to London.

Ellen sighs. The establishments in Holywell Street should not surprise her, no more the likes of Dawson, but still the experience had proved unsettling, more than she cares to admit. She thinks of Reynold, burrowed in his darkroom, developing prints of women for whom he feigns no desire; she thinks of herself, similarly content to hide under the camera or in the attic, operating the press, ignoring the truth of where the photographs travel. She can't accompany Meed to the capital again: she will tell Clem tomorrow.

She is about to climb into bed when there comes a succession of light taps at the door, tentative yet insistent. As Ellen opens it, she sees Lily, barefoot in a thin cotton nightdress so carefully pressed that the lines from the iron are still visible. Her hair is tied back in a neat braid, the watery grey of her eyes rippling with such unhappiness that Ellen wants nothing more than to take her in her arms, senses too that Lily might let her.

'Lily.' Ellen's voice is cautious. 'Is everything all right?'

Lily doesn't reply. Her candle gutters in the draught, there is a scorch mark on the delicate nub of her wrist.

Ellen glances down the hallway. 'Come in a minute. Would you like a glass of water?'

Lily nods and follows her inside, watching as Ellen pours water from the jug on the washstand.

'Now, what's the matter? Are you not happy here?'

Miserably, Lily shakes her head. 'I'm grateful, Miss Harper, really I am. But . . .' Her words tumble out. 'Lou and Milly hate me because Mrs Williams gave me the best room, and my supper's always cold, because Cook's taken against me, and yesterday I overheard Mrs Matthews say that charity began at the workhouse and that that's where I should be.'

'What an unpleasant woman she is,' Ellen says, and Lily offers up a small complicit smile.

'Yes.' She takes a sip of water and, emboldened, carries on. 'And you, Miss Harper, you don't like me any more!'

Ellen looks at Lily. The shape of her body is clear through her nightdress; Ellen turns away. 'What nonsense – I'm busy, that's all. Mrs Williams is to have a baby and needs my attention, you know that. And I have Miss Ottilie's lessons and—'

'What about the photographs?' There is a note of defiance in Lily's voice. 'I'll come to the studio again, Miss Harper. I want to.'

Ellen thinks of Dawson and his grubby hands on Lily's picture, of men like Meed, in dank bedrooms, and Herbert Williams, in gentlemen's clubs.

'No,' she says sharply.

Lily stares at her. 'You said I was good. You said the gentlemen liked me.'

'And so they did.' Ellen tries to smile. 'But when you first came to me, you needed money, didn't you, to leave your situation, and that's no longer the case.'

'*You* came to me, Miss Harper.' Angrily Lily wipes away a tear, setting the glass on the washstand with force. 'You –' her face twists as if she has sucked on something sour – 'you kissed me!'

'Hush!' Her tone is made harsh with humiliation. Ellen's skin prickles with shame as Lily backs away, just as she had on Christmas Eve, but this time the look on her face is knowing, almost cruel.

'Lily – Lily!'

They both freeze as Lily's name bounces down the hallway, accompanied by frantic footsteps and a pounding on the door of her empty room. 'Wake up, girl!'

At first, neither of them moves. Then Ellen opens the door a crack and there is Mrs Matthews, red-necked and flustered, in her dressing gown.

'What on earth's the matter?' Ellen says.

'It's Mrs Williams.' The housekeeper lowers her voice. 'There's bleeding.'

Ellen senses movement behind her, and as Lily steps into view, Mrs Matthews' mouth opens and shuts again like a goldfish. 'Clean sheets and hot water,' she says, collecting herself. 'Quick as you can.'

As Lily runs down the hall, Ellen forages for an excuse.

'Poor girl had cramps,' she says. 'She was calling out in her sleep so I gave her a dose of Lydia Pinkham's.'

A hostile silence follows, but it is the housekeeper who is first to look away.

'Mrs Williams is asking for you,' she says curtly, and disappears downstairs.

The room smells of blood and relief. There is a large inky stain on the rug by the side of the bed where Clem lies, pale as the pillows around her. But the light in her eyes reassures Ellen, and as she sits down Clem gives her a small triumphant smile that goes unnoticed by the doctor, scrubbing his hands in a bowl of hot water.

'You'll find the discomfort will lessen over the next few days, Mrs Williams.' The doctor looks up, as he dries his hand on a towel. 'You are young and in excellent health. As I said to your husband, there is no reason to suppose that you shouldn't go on to have armfuls of children.'

'How heartening, Doctor.' Clem's lips twitch. 'Please tell Mr Williams he can retire for the evening as you leave – I need to rest.'

'Of course.' The doctor wishes her goodnight, closing the door behind him with a discreet click.

'Mother Nature decided to be kind, Miss Harper,' Clem murmurs. 'No need for the bicycle after all,' and Ellen takes her employer's warm slim hand and holds it in her own, and when she draws back to remove it, Clem does not let go. They sit that way for a long time, listening to the distant moan of the sea, until the lamps have burnt down to the wick, and the rest of the household are fast asleep again, oblivious to the cries of the new housemaid on the floor above, troubled by dreams of half-dead babies washed up in a tide of blood.

A few days later, while they are out walking, Clem gives Ellen a gift. They stop under the shelters on Madeira Drive and Clem watches, bright with excitement, as Ellen opens the smart black box from a jeweller's on St James's Street to find a gold wristwatch, lying on a bed of creamy satin.

'It's Russian gold. Do you like it?'

Ellen holds the watch up to the light. Each delicate link of the bracelet holds the burnished hues of a sunset, the numerals on the watch face plain and unfussy, and inexplicably pleasing to the eye.

She turns to Clem. 'I can't possibly accept this.'

'You must. I'll be terribly offended otherwise.' Clem smiles. 'Besides, it can't be returned – it's engraved.'

Ellen looks at the back of the watch, where *The Golden Hour* is inscribed in extravagant flourishes and twists. She smiles back in spite of herself, slips it onto her wrist.

'Most discreet.'

'Naturally,' Clem replies. 'Shall we go to the pier?' She loops her arm through Ellen's, and the women walk in the direction of the sinking sun.

Chapter Twenty-One

$\mathbf{I}$t is Palm Sunday and St Mary's church is full. Little Frankie Humphreys, scion of the Humphreys of Sussex Square is to be baptised this morning, and the infant cries inconsolable in his nurse's arms as the vicar wades through a lengthy sermon on the importance of hope. Pinioned between her husband and Ottilie, Clem reflects that the man may be long-winded but she agrees with the sentiment: to live without hope is to cease to live. And – she eyes the squalling bundle across the church – now that her prayers have been answered and the baby has gone from her, she has never felt more vividly alive.

She looks along the pew to where Miss Harper sits, hands clasped in her lap, face upturned towards the altar. It gives Clem a hum of pleasure to think of her putting on the Golden Hour watch each morning, concealing it under the cuff of her blouse. Miss Harper had seemed most touched by the gift, as Clem had hoped she might, for she felt she owed her companion a good deal.

'You've brought me back,' she told her one evening, mawkish after too much wine at dinner. 'Who I used to be, I mean. Before all of this.'

She meant the person she was before she married, Clementine Brouwer from New York City, brimming with half-formed dreams and desires that she had naively believed to be her own to forge. She would choose who she married, and it would be someone amusing and easily amused – and he would see beyond the beauty that was both a gift and a noose about her neck to who she really was inside. There would be plays performed at dusk in a garden pavilion – *A Midsummer Night's Dream* – and herself as Titania, lying in a hammock in white gossamer with her ankles showing, spellbound. An audience in lawn chairs with her amusing, amused husband among them, and her companion, the English lady in the front row, calling out 'Brava, brava!' when she takes her bow.

'Let us pray.'

The congregation stirs, and she gets to her feet. *Lead us not into temptation.* Well, she can't deny she wasn't shocked by what Miss Harper was doing in her parlour in Booth Lane, but in many ways the golden hour has been the best thing that could possibly have happened. She waits for God to smite her dead; he does not – she continues to pray. It has shown her something of the world that the vigilants could never understand, for as Miss Harper explained it is just men paying, as well they should, to look at something which brings pleasure, like admission to a gallery or museum; and no one is touched or harmed, and the girls are saved from doing other, terrible things.

Amen. The Humphreys are called to the font and the grizzling baby passed to Mrs Humphreys – next to her Herbert squeezes Clem's hand. He means to be kind, but he may as well squeeze her heart in his fist until it stops pumping, for she knows she can only keep him from her bed for so long with complaints of cramps or fatigue. Only last night he had come to her, saying he'd spoken to Dr Phillips and it was perfectly safe for relations to be resumed: she had resisted and he had gone, leaving her free to do what she has grown accustomed to doing every night: setting loose her imagination, and forgetting she is a lady.

She imagines she is one of the girls in the Golden Hour portfolio, whom the men can't touch. She is the woman on Herbert's snuffbox, pressing herself against the velvet nap of the armchair, until she is roused, and then she turns, legs parted, ready for an imaginary tongue or her own real hand or the fine silk tassels on the curtain sash. Her memory calls up a cast of characters – the gondolier in Venice with walnut-brown forearms, his eyes as dark and bitter as olives; the living statue with hair like her own in a translucent peignoir that she lifts slowly from her body. Yesterday, she had tried to coax Mr Harper from the wings, but he would not show himself and her desire had waned. Then something curious had happened. Miss Harper had appeared instead; she had stood severe before her, then unbuttoned her blouse and skirt, unlaced her corset, and stepping from her drawers, she'd lain on her, her body as hot and heavy as a man's. It had felt so real that Clem could barely look Miss Harper in the eye over the breakfast table, in case her companion might somehow intuit her depravity, and she had resolved not to let it happen again.

'I baptise you in the name of the Father, the Son, and the Holy Spirit.'

The infant squirms. Water trickles. Sunshine flares through the stained glass, the red apple, green serpent, Eve dimpled and white and naked. As the vicar invites them once again to pray, Clem stares across the bowed heads of the congregation. There is another edition of the Golden Hour to be done and an idea wraps itself about her and thrums like another pulse.

Clem glances at Ellen, who is fidgeting with the corner of her hymn book. She looks back, as if she has heard Clem's thoughts, and the corners of her wide, sensual lips, that unbeknown to their owner were doing such unspeakable things to Clem only a few hours earlier, lift into a small smile.

'It's out of the question!' Ellen wades deeper into the cold sea and looks towards their dipper, who stands, arms folded, on the steps of the bathing machine some distance away.

Clem swims a few strokes, then lifts her right arm above her head, tilting her jaw in the direction of the sun.

'Crenaia of the English Channel!' she intones. 'Remember the living statues? When I was as wet behind the ears as a newborn!' She drops the pose, and gives Ellen a playful splash. 'I don't understand why you're so upset. My head would be turned or lowered – no one would know it was me.' Holding out her palms towards the shore, she adopts a grandiose tone. '*From the diamond bracelet on her wrist, 'tis clear she is a lady of breeding and wealth. But who is she, gentlemen?* We could ask your man Mr Meed to spread the word with the distributors.'

Ellen shivers. She dislikes bathing, hates undressing in the tiny hut, the dragging, clinging weight of the wet flannel costume. 'Think of your sister-in-law,' she says. 'The vigilants.'

'Should we ask them too?' Clem says roguishly. 'Miss Hinchlin has a playful manner at times, granted, but Caroline may take a little more persuasion.'

Ellen looks away. The end of the month has come and later she must take Mr Crocker his payment. The thought weighs heavy on her, although to her relief she has only seen him once since January, her business usually conducted with his henchman in the hallway.

'The Golden Hour will be drawing to a close soon anyway,' she tells Clem, who starts to swim in sweeping elegant strokes in the direction of the pier, not turning back until the dipper has called out several times. Ellen recalls the determination with which Clem had freewheeled down the valley in the frozen countryside, less afraid of breaking a limb than she was of the baby growing inside her. It is the grit in the oyster which makes the pearl, she thinks, with a surge of fondness, as Clem swims back, seawater beading her eyelashes, strands of wet hair that have come loose from her hat clinging to her bare neck.

'I can't let you do it,' Ellen says gently. 'What if people found out? Your reputation would be . . .'

'In tatters. Yes.' Clem's voice is matter-of-fact. 'Heavens, my husband might even divorce me.'

'Don't say that!' Two women bathing nearby turn and stare, and Ellen lowers her voice. 'He'd leave you with nothing!'

Clem turns and starts to wade towards the machine.

'I already have nothing, Miss Harper,' she says, looking back over her shoulder. 'Can't you see? And I'm afraid that I never will.'

It is just after five when Ellen reaches Mr Crocker's house. The bearded man lets her in as usual, but when she passes him the envelope, he shakes his head and indicates she should go down to the basement instead. Ever since the first meeting, she has taken the precaution of slipping a pair of nail scissors in her pocket before she comes, and she feels for them now, pricking her finger against the sharp steel tip.

This time Mr Crocker is dressed and sitting at a table by the window with a sheaf of papers, the curtains half drawn. A second goldfish has joined the first in the tank and they circle each other listlessly in the murky water. As he looks up to greet her, a shaft of sunlight falls across the toughened scar tissue that spreads like scales along the right side of his jaw.

'Miss Harper.'

From the tarnished frame on the mantelpiece, Harriet Smart, suspended in mid-bow, catches Ellen's eye as she hands the Croc the envelope. He empties the contents onto the table, stacking the coins into a small pile.

He frowns. 'Is that all?'

'It's as we agreed.'

'But that was before.'

'Before?'

'Before I knew about the insurance.' Mr Crocker leans back as if he is basking in warm sunshine. 'I like to know who I'm doing business with, Miss Harper, and it has been brought to my attention that you and your brother haven't been entirely honest with me. Trust is very important in my line of business, you understand.' He waggles his finger at her. 'I can't risk having the constabulary on my trail.'

He unlocks a drawer and takes out a Bible, a different edition to Ellen's own, yet it seems somehow familiar. A number of photographs fall from the pages as he opens it, and she sees the tableaux girls with their petticoats over their heads, Dora on the arm of the couch with Jilly on the other, a plump chorus girl whose name she can't recall in a pair of black stockings, holding an apple in her right hand. They were pictures Reynold had taken when they first arrived in Brighton, fleeing from Paris after Fourbier's arrest. The deposit they'd paid the landlord for the lodgings in Booth Lane had cleaned them out, and they had other expenses too. 'Just until we're on our feet,' Reynold had said, but of course, they had never got on their feet; there had always been this bill or that, a doctor's fee, a new camera to replace the old.

'How much do you get for them?'

Ellen fixes her gaze on the goldfish for she can't bear to look at him. Where had he got them? They didn't pay Meed to go to London for nothing – they never sold on their own doorstep.

'I don't know what you're talking about,' she says.

'I think you do, Miss Harper.' Mr Crocker laughs. 'Don't look so glum. You'll find my rates very reasonable.'

'What do you mean?'

'I'd hate these to fall into the wrong hands,' he says, gathering up the pictures. 'My men can be so careless. Loose with their tongues too.'

'You're threatening me.'

'No.' He smiles, long and yellow. 'I suggest an ongoing arrangement.' He names a figure. 'You keep your business and we can all sleep soundly at night.' He looks at her steadily as he starts counting on his fingers. 'You, me, your brother. Your pupil with the spots. That charming companion of yours.'

Ellen stiffens. 'My employer has nothing to do with this.'

'But she does, Miss Harper, don't you see? Because what Mrs Williams and I have in common is you.' He shakes his head, runs a hand over his ruined skin. 'Such a pretty face she has. I'd hate an accident to befall her.'

'What do you mean?' Ellen has the sensation of being

underwater, the air sucked from her as she is dragged deeper and deeper down.

'No midnight flits, Miss Harper.' Mr Crocker's voice hardens, as he returns the Bible to the drawer. 'Your brother seems the type. Make sure he knows it.'

'You'll get your money.' Is this to be her life now, Ellen thinks with despair, in bondage to this man and his coterie of thugs, paying for Reynold's old errors and new whims, over and over.

'Yes, I will,' he says amiably, as if she is some kind of servant and he the benevolent master, and what can she do but leave, as quickly as she is able, out of the squalid house and into the spring evening with the relief of a creature released from a trap.

Loathsome man. She hurries down the street, back towards the bustle of town. He knew about Ottilie; he knew Clem's name, he had made it his business to know, and in turn someone had made it their business to tell him about the photographs. *It has been brought to my attention . . .* Ellen thinks back to the night at the Empire, sees him again in the front box, applauding as Harriet Smart took her bow. And then something occurs to her. That Harriet Smart is not in debt to Mr Crocker at all; far more likely, in fact, that she is some kind of informant, for wasn't she always poking her nose in, hadn't she turned up uninvited with the tableaux girls with that mewling ball of fur as an alibi, her quick bright eyes all over the studio, with Reynold too gullible to notice.

By the time she reaches the King's Road, Ellen is convinced. It was Harriet Smart who had betrayed them to the Croc – the proof had been staring her in the face from the man's own mantelpiece.

★

'What utter nonsense.' Reynold dips a plate bearing the imprint of four generations of the Humphreys family into the basin, then slots it on the rack. 'Why would Harry want to make trouble? She's our friend – or at least she would be, if you'd let her.' His voice comes irritated from the gloom. 'Then you wouldn't have to go chasing after American socialites for company.'

'Mrs Williams is hardly a socialite. Besides . . .'

'She pays you. She needs you,' he chants in a mincing tone. 'Sing a new song, Ellie, I'm tired of that one.' He submerges another plate. 'You belong here and you know it too. Why else would you keep coming back?'

'To clean up your mistakes!' Her temper rises. 'Nothing has changed, Reynold. Nothing! A King's Road studio that you can't pay for isn't going to turn you into the person you want to be. Don't you understand how much trouble you've got us into?'

'At least we know where we are with the Croc. It wasn't me who led a vigilant to Booth Lane – and then told her everything!'

'I had no choice. Anyway –' Ellen pauses – 'you don't need to worry. We can trust Mrs Williams.'

'And how can you be so sure?' He peels off his gloves, and she follows him back into the studio.

'Because Mrs Williams will be our next model.' Once out, the words take life. They will take the photographs here in the King's Road studio – in fact, *she* will take them.

'Don't be absurd.' Reynold walks to the window and pulls up the sash, glancing at her when she doesn't reply. 'You're serious, aren't you?' He sits on the sill and lights his pipe with a frown.

'It will give the portfolio an edge. It's a good idea.'

'Her idea, I assume?'

'Our idea,' Ellen says, but he ignores her.

'Why doesn't she stick to church bazaars and watercolours, like the rest of them?'

Ellen stares at her brother. He is no better than Herbert Williams, forbidding his wife from riding a bicycle and forcing his niece to go to finishing school. Hadn't Reynold shown that he would have been blissfully content for her to work as his assistant for the rest of their days, her only permissible way out marriage to a man rich and foolish enough to subsidise a business that Reynold would invariably struggle to keep afloat. But as he sits smoking in the recess, Ellen sees he has no notion of any of it; he is as oblivious, in his way, as Mr Williams. Her temper subsides.

'Mrs Williams isn't like the rest of them,' she says quietly, the truth of it bursting like the flare of the sun. As she leaves, she tells her brother he should expect them both here at the studio Saturday next, and she would much appreciate it if he could ensure that the charlady had visited beforehand.

Chapter Twenty-Two

Tea for eight – and a caraway cake – makes for a heavy tea tray. Lily reaches the top of the stairs and sets the tray down upon the trolley with more relief than care, and tea slops onto the white linen cloth. She repositions the cake to cover the stain, but now the cloth is wrinkled, and Lily wishes bad things upon Milly whose job it is to do this, but who has returned to her village to dance around a maypole. Adjusting her cap, she pushes the rattling trolley towards the drawing room, from where she can hear Mrs Williams' soft barley-sugar voice.

'What's your opinion, Miss Harper?' she is asking, and Lily's heart starts to beat faster. Since that terrible night when Mrs Williams lost her baby, word seems to have got around the other servants that Mrs Matthews found her in Miss Harper's room, and she has been teased relentlessly, with even Roderick, the groom, barely old enough to have hairs on his chin, asking with a wink if she'll come and tuck him in at bedtime. As for Miss Harper, Lily curses herself now for ever mentioning the kiss, for now if they ever come upon each other when no one else is about, a thick fog of discomfort descends, through which Miss Harper's curt greeting cuts like a whip.

Lily knocks on the door and enters the drawing room. A group of ladies sits around the table, with a gentleman at the head of it. There is Mrs Williams, with Miss Harper by her side, Mr Williams' sister – and that horrid fluffy dog that goes everywhere with her – Miss Ottilie, and three other ladies, one with a small blue bird pinned to her hat. The dog lets out a low growl as Lily approaches.

'What we need,' Mr Williams' sister is saying, 'is first-hand intervention! We need to go to the public houses, find these girls and nip it in the bud.'

'I would be happy to offer my services in this regard,' says the man at the top of the table, and when Mrs Williams next speaks, she sounds more grit than barley sugar.

'I believe the intervention would be more effective if a woman were to carry it out, Mr Harty,' she says, 'and I would like to recommend Miss Harper.'

The teapot trembles in Lily's hand. Tea slops into the saucer as she sets the first cup on the table, and Mr Williams' sister glowers at her. Everyone else, Lily sees, is looking at Miss Harper.

'Miss Harper has much experience with young women from her time spent as a tutor.' Mrs Williams nods towards Miss Ottilie. 'She understands the workings of their minds.'

Lily's hands are clammy inside her gloves, the cloth with which she grips the teapot seems to have a mind of its own. She glances from Mrs Williams to Miss Harper. They are looking everywhere but at each other, as people with secrets do. Is it possible, Lily wonders, that Mrs Williams know about the photographs? And if this is so, does she then know about her? She looks up to find Miss Ottilie's gaze upon her, as if she is an object of much curiosity, and Lily feels as if her insides were turned out and her wickedness uncovered. Her hand slips, the hot china burns and with a yelp she drops the teapot. It lands on the floor, where it rolls lidless on the Turkish rug, dispensing a moat of brown tea about itself.

'For heaven's sake!' Mr Williams' sister tuts loudly, and everyone turns to look.

'She's new, Caroline. There's no harm done.'

Mrs Williams tells her to fetch hot water and cloths and, mumbling a string of apologies, Lily hurries to the door. Hand on the doorknob, the last thing she sees is Miss Harper, turned to Mrs Williams like a flower towards the sun, with a smile that although small brightens her whole face; and it is like hearing a familiar tune that causes pain for the memories it evokes. It is the way Miss Harper used to smile at her at Booth Lane, when it was just the two of them alone.

The poodle barks, and Lily wonders what would happen if she kicked it. Instant dismissal, she expects, she'd be cast onto the street. Too proud to return home, she would be forced to colour her cheeks and lips, and take men into alleyways, and this time there'd be no one who cared enough to help her. Miss Harper has found a new pet, Lily thinks, dully, as she returns to the kitchen, and she doesn't matter any more.

Recently Clem has found herself somewhat distracted by the strand of hair that always comes loose from Miss Harper's pins, around lunchtime, and curls like a comma about her collar. Miss Harper will re-pin it and later it will come free again, and then it will be tucked behind her right ear, or assertively pinned back, but to no permanent avail. During dreary committee meetings, or games of écarté with Ottilie, Clem likes to imagine playing the maid and removing her companion's hairpins one by one, then brushing out Miss Harper's chestnut hair into a wild, frothy mass.

Miss Harper would be in her nightdress of course, with the top two buttons undone, the hollow of her clavicle steeped in shadow ... How impossible it is, Clem thinks, looking at her companion, fully dressed in the armchair opposite, to forbid oneself from thinking of a thing, for what is prohibited becomes more enticing than ever.

Laid out on the table before them is everything they will need for the Golden Hour tomorrow – the latest issue of *The Sentinel*, left behind by Mrs Yorke-Duffy, a teacup and saucer, an embroidery hoop, with the outline of a bluebell stitched upon it, and a pink parasol. Miss Harper is just suggesting the addition of a pen and inkwell, for doesn't Mrs Williams detest the daily labour of responding to unwanted invitations for tea, or lunch or dinner, when there is a knock on the door and Milly appears with the bottle of champagne that Clem had requested. Milly will later remark to the other servants that the mistress is always happier when Mr Williams is away in London, and that she and that Miss Harper were having a fine time of it, laughing away, in the sitting room adjoining Mrs Williams' bedchamber, which is an odd place to take a drink when the evening is over.

When the servant has gone, the two women raise a toast.

'To the Golden Hour,' Clem says, thinking how apt it is that her companion's eyes take on a gold hue in the lamplight, and how glad she is that Miss Harper reconsidered her proposal.

'The Golden Hour,' Ellen replies. She is filled with nerves – but pleasant ones – like the bubbles racing up the side of the glass, as she questions once again whether she is making an error by allowing Clem to do this, and then looks again at Clem, so animated, so alive, that the question whimpers and dies.

'What are you thinking, Miss Harper?' Clem asks softly.

'How brave you are, Mrs Williams.'

Clem is quiet for a moment. 'My husband came to me last night. I wasn't able to refuse him.' She shakes her head as if clearing her mind of the memory. 'It makes me all the more determined. To do as I please, while I still can. To be utterly wicked.'

She raises an eyebrow towards the items on the table and they both laugh.

Ellen takes another sip of champagne. 'Do you not wish for children at all? Ever?'

'Perhaps.' Clem considers this. 'One day. If it is of my choosing. A bright-eyed terror of a boy, with pockets stuffed with twigs and pebbles, who will jump up and down on the furniture and make apple-pie beds for the nanny!'

Ellen's smile costs her: it is not the answer she realises she desired. She glimpses a future where this evening, this conversation will be remembered by herself alone, because Clem, this friend she has made, will be lost to her. Isn't it only a matter of time, before Clem has affairs as her husband does, with no one batting an eye as long as she remains discreet – and before long the bright-eyed terror will be conceived, and life will have changed.

'And you, Miss Harper?' Clem settles into her chair. 'Can you not see yourself . . .?'

'No,' Ellen says quickly.

'And Mr Harper similarly?'

Ellen pauses. 'My brother appears content enough with his cameras and his cat.'

'And he lives all the better for it, I'm sure.' Clem studies her over the rim of her glass; the bubbles hiss as she smiles. 'Although you, Miss Harper, are far too handsome to be an old maid.'

It is just a compliment, such as ladies give each other, Ellen tells herself, like saying that your hairstyle suits you well, or asking from which milliner you purchased your hat. So why does it feel different, the way Clem is looking at her – and not just now, but over the weeks and months since Christmas? She feels something stirring inside her and tamps it down. Hadn't Lily been lesson enough?

She looks at her watch. 'I should let you get some rest.'

'And I, you.' Clem gets up and accompanies her to the door. 'Until tomorrow, Miss Harper.'

'Until tomorrow.'

Their voices are low, almost whispers. But the hum of the secret they hold is enough to rouse Ottilie, dozing in the bedroom along from her aunt's. She sits up, alert to the prospect of some unexpected danger, but all she can hear is the soft sound of Miss Harper's slippered feet passing through the hallway and upstairs to bed.

Chapter Twenty-Three

'The navy skirt, please, Milly.' Clem smiles briefly at the maid. 'No need to bother with a bustle. Not that one,' she adds, as Milly takes out a shirt with a row of fiddly buttons down the back. 'The white cotton will do.'

The less fuss and fumbling, the fewer the layers to remove later, the better. Yolky sunlight fills the bedroom; in the flower beds outside, delphiniums – pink, lilac and blue – sway in the breeze. The sea is frisky, a glint in its eye at what the day might bring. *No one will see my face.* Clem blushes deeper at the wickedness to come.

A knock at the door – it is Ottilie, run out of hair oil. She settles herself on the window seat and watches idly as Milly puts up her aunt's hair.

'Did you enjoy the time in your village, Milly?' Clem asks. 'I heard you were Queen of the May!'

'Yes, madam, thank you.' Milly chatters on for a while, then glances at Clem rather slyly in the mirror. 'I hope you weren't put to any trouble, madam?'

'Not at all. The other girl – Lily – stepped into the breach.' Clem frowns. 'Why the scowl, Milly? She seems good-natured enough to me.'

'I don't like to tell tales, madam. But . . . she's got ideas above herself, and there's those that let her too.'

'Meaning?'

'She wasn't in her room, madam. The night you took ill.'

'Then where was she?'

'Next door. With Miss Harper.'

A short silence, in which Ottilie loses interest in the view and gives the sudden turn in conversation her full attention.

'Well –' Clem rubs a nub of cocoa butter onto her bottom lip – 'I'm sure there was a good reason.'

'Cramps, Mrs Matthews says. But—'

'Then we should commend Miss Harper for her kindness, wouldn't you say?'

Milly reddens at the reproach, dipping her head as Clem tells her that she will finish her toilette herself. Ottilie watches the maid leave, then gets up from the window seat with a yawn. 'They're friends, you know.'

'Who?' Clem slides a mother-of-pearl comb into her hair, her mind scampering ahead to this afternoon – later she must go to the safe box and take out the diamond bracelet Herbert gave her on their honeymoon.

'Lily and Miss Harper.'

Clem looks up at her. 'Don't be ridiculous.'

'They know each other anyway.' Ottilie speaks with the pride of someone who holds privileged information. 'I saw them talking outside the house before Christmas, when Lily was delivering the laundry.'

Clem pauses. 'Miss Harper's never mentioned any previous acquaintance.'

'No,' Ottilie says airily, 'she denies it. Try asking her.' And telling her aunt she'll be sure to bring back the bandoline as soon as she's finished with it, she returns to her room.

★

'I don't know why she couldn't come to Booth Lane, like all the others,' Reynold grumbles, wiping the camera lens with a cloth.

'It's hardly suitable – surely you can see that.' Ellen looks down from the studio window at the ceaseless flow of activity on the King's Road, the tide of carriages, the bobbing parasols along the promenade. 'Ah, here she is.'

How she tries to keep the tremor from her voice, as she watches Clem alight from a cab, in a duck-egg blue jacket that sets off her complexion. She must just imagine she is a model like any other, Ellen tells herself; there is no need whatsoever for the nerves that prevented her from barely eating lunch.

She turns to her brother. 'Remember, you're not to disturb us.'

'Yes, ma'am.' He delivers a cool salute and trails behind her downstairs to the reception.

'Miss Harper. Mr Harper.' Clem rises from the couch and extends a gloved hand to Reynold. 'A somewhat different proposition to the last time we met.'

'Indeed.' Reynold darts to the door and flips the Open sign to Closed, turns the key in the lock. 'Although this time it will be my sister behind the lens.'

'I'm sure I will be in most capable hands.' And the smile Clem gives Ellen is of reassurance, as if Ellen is the one who will be removing her clothes. 'Shall we?'

Clem moves towards the stairs, and, calling out to Reynold to bring them tea in a quarter hour or so, Ellen follows her.

The room burns with a thick apricot light. Clem disappears behind the screen to undress, politely refusing Ellen's offer of help, as outside the afternoon continues: children shriek, fishing boats bump up onto the shingle with the day's catch, the gulls squabble and squawk. Ellen adjusts the tripod and fiddles with the plate holder, hearing none of it, only a rustle of petticoats, the snapping of laces, the swift threshing of a button hook. A sigh. Is Mrs Williams in need of assistance, she asks again, or perhaps a drop of brandy, but 'I am able to manage' and 'possibly later' come the measured replies. How can Clem be so unflustered, so collected, when Ellen herself feels as if she has been turned upside down and given a good shake. She stares through the viewing screen at the piano, seized with a sudden desire to stay there, under the hood in the dark.

'Miss Harper.'

Ellen emerges. Clem stands by the mantelpiece, wearing a robe Ellen has never seen before, a long sheath of creamy silk through which the sunlight streams, inviting one's gaze like a half-open door. In the light, her hair holds the best of nature's colours – the drop of the sun and the early morning rise of it, her skin the tone of a peach, one day ripe. She wears nothing underneath, Ellen notes, not a stitch, and hadn't they discussed drawers or perhaps she had assumed, in any event, the robe is shrugged to the floor and Mrs Williams positions herself on the piano stool, her shoulders as straight as those of a seminary student who has endured a lifetime of rapped knuckles for slouching.

'Do you have my bracelet in the picture?'

'Yes.' Ellen returns to her refuge and assesses the composition. The smooth curves of Clem's hips call to mind the shape of a violin, the shadowy dimples at the base of her spine perfectly symmetrical, like two thumbprints in clay. Inverted, it has the shape of a heart.

'Turn your head to the window a touch,' she says.

A shadow falls across the plane of her cheekbone, but

Clem's hair is just a little too neat. Ellen is firm with herself. Do as you would with the girls. She goes to Clem and adjusts her hairpins, releasing a wispy curl, and then another. The cuff of her shirt brushes Clem's skin. Naked, her scent is less like a lady's and more like herself, and as Ellen returns to the camera, it is all she can smell.

'Hold still,' she says.

Light floods the lens, drenches the plate. One second, two. Time enough for Ellen to know that what happened with Lily is happening again, and that she is helpless, a moth trapped in amber, for the harder she tries to push the feeling away, the more forcefully it makes itself known.

The women are upstairs for an hour. The hurdy-gurdy of the seaside, the shouting, grunting, cursing mass of it evaporates like mist, and it is just the model and her photographer and the camera's eye. Occasional snatches of laughter cause Reynold Harper to raise his head from the columns of figures in the ledger and frown: he is a spare part in his own studio, damn it, little more than an errand boy, bringing tea on a tray.

'Leave it outside, would you?' his sister calls as he knocks, and what a song-and-dance they are making of a few photographs, and using up valuable studio time too. If Mrs Williams isn't too grand to take her clothes off, then she isn't too grand for Booth Lane, not that present company seems to care too much for what he thinks. And on this point at least, Mr Harper is correct – Mrs Williams and his sister are having far too much fun.

Mrs Williams reclines on the chaise longue, legs bent to preserve a little modesty, her sister-in-law's copy of *The Sentinel* covering her blushes, should she have any, which she doesn't, not any more. She has after all stood in nothing but her shoes and stockings with the pink parasol – new from Hannington's – covering her face, and allowed Miss Harper to apply drops of cold water to the nipple of each breast, and watch them pucker and crimp. She has sat bare-breasted in the leather armchair, with her head bent low, applying cross-stitch to the petal of a bluebell. And she has taken tea, quite naked in the stream of light from the window, the diamond wedding ring on her left hand sparkling like a second sun.

As the sun begins to set, they take one final picture. No embroidery or piano playing or tea drinking but Mrs Williams by the marble mantelpiece, one arm resting lightly upon it, her head lowered in contemplation. She has taken down her hair and it falls across her back and shoulders in restless waves. As Ellen slides the final plate into the camera, she promises herself that she will find a way to keep this one from the jackals in Holywell Street; she will tell Clem it has suffered some misfortune, breakage or overexposure.

While Clem dresses, Ellen restores the studio to its previous state of innocence, taking a clothes brush to the piano stool, lighting a sandalwood pastille in the burner.

'Almost as if it had never happened,' Clem says, looking about her, as she comes out from behind the screen, respectable again, with not a button left undone, nor a hair in a place where it shouldn't be. 'But you hold the evidence, Miss Harper!'

She picks up her carpet bag. And then she moves towards Ellen and kisses her very lightly on the cheek, a gesture so unexpected that Ellen finds herself without the words to reciprocate a farewell of any kind, a discourtesy which does not seem to trouble Mrs Williams, who can be heard humming to herself on the staircase as she leaves.

Chapter Twenty-Four

Lily steps over a steaming pile of horse dung and gives a penny each to the two boys who have been trailing her the length of Albion Hill. Barely more than ten years between them, yet they can sense the money in her purse, like baby wolves smell blood, and she supposes her new boots don't help, although she has made a point of wearing her tatty straw hat – she has not come home to gloat.

She reaches the house and peers through the open window. Her mother dozes, slack-jawed, in her chair by the fireplace, a pile of mending in a basket next to her, her hand resting on the new swell of her belly. In the corner of the room she glimpses the legs of her two youngest siblings jumping on the bed.

'Stop that or I'll belt yer!' Her sister's voice, followed by a scream, a wail, loud tears. Lily hesitates. Is this really what she wants? Her mother wakes and rubs her eyes, then looks straight at her, her face hardening.

This was never going to be easy. Before her mother can tell her to scram, Lily opens the battered front door and walks into the room where she used to live.

'Lee-lee!'

Christopher toddles across the room, encircling her skirts with his tiny arms, and for a moment there is joy, as Lily scoops him up and kisses his grubby cheek.

'Look who it isn't.' Her mother, arms folded, makes no move to greet her, her gaze sweeping over Lily and settling on her basket. 'What you got in there? Susan!' she calls out back. 'It's your sister, all high and mighty, with new boots an' all.'

Susan appears in the doorway in her laundry clothes, the grey skirt and shirt with dark patches under the arms that Lily looks upon with a pang of pity. Her sister has their mother's build and sweats accordingly. Susan seizes the basket and begins to rummage through the contents, tossing the waxed-paper packages onto the table. The children gather round, their eyes wide.

'Bringing us your leftovers? Very nice, I'm sure,' her mother says as they unwrap what Lily went without supper yesterday to bring: a quarter of a chicken pie, two slices of ham, and some stale fruitcake that was about to be thrown out. 'Anything else?'

She gives Lily a pointed look, and dutifully Lily takes out her purse and hands her mother a week's wages. Her mother stares at the coins, her jaw working as she nods to herself.

'Put the kettle on, Susan, will you?' She moves a bundle of clothes from a chair and motions to Lily to sit. 'Expect your sister might like a cup of tea, before she goes.'

It is as close to a truce as she will get. Lily sits down and shares out the fruitcake between Christopher and Sammy, as Susan slams the kettle onto the stove.

'Look at those hands.' Her mother gives a sour laugh as she glances at Lily's palms. 'Managed to wheedle your way out of the washroom?'

'They've put me on maid duties. There's not really anywhere to dry the laundry so . . .'

'You can make the tea then, Lady Muck.' Susan abandons

the stove and sits down next to her mother, who slaps her shoulder merrily, saying that's the way.

Lily gets up and spoons tea leaves into the chipped teapot. 'How's the laundry?' she asks cautiously.

Complaints follow. The other day Mrs Hadley had Susan work two hours past hometime doing deliveries, and she still hasn't been paid extra for it. She's got it in for Susan, and everyone says it, even though Sue does nothing but work her fingers to the bone in the woman's pigging laundry.

Lily makes sympathetic noises. 'I was thinking –' she looks warily at her mother – 'I could come back.'

'Back? What do you mean?' A look passes between her mother and Susan, and Lily's heart sinks. They will make her fight for it, make her bleed.

'Back to the laundry.' Christopher snuggles into her and she strokes his head. 'Back home,' she continues more boldly. 'I'm sure you need the help, Ma.'

'I've needed help since the day you left, you selfish wretch,' her mother says. 'You made your bed, my girl, when you went telling all sorts to Mrs Hadley. She's a do-gooder and you can never trust them.'

'What do you mean?'

Her sister sighs, exasperated. 'She got you out of there, Lil. Wrote to one of her church friends about poor little Miss March, always so quiet and sad-looking.'

'No!' It is suddenly of the utmost importance that they are wrong. Her mother and sister stare at her in surprise. 'It wasn't her.' Lily shakes her head. 'It was someone else.'

'The Queen of Sheba, I suppose.' Ma rolls her eyes. 'It was her, Lil. The woman told me so herself – ah, here comes trouble.' She turns to the open window with a familiar note of affection in her voice that makes Lily wince, for there is her uncle, ash from his pipe dribbling onto the sill as he grins directly at her.

'My, my,' he says. 'If it ain't the prodigal. How is our Lady Lilian?'

'Never mind her.' Her mother frowns. 'Get yourself in here.'

Susan's sigh is audible, as their uncle saunters in, singing.

'*Oh, it's pretty Polly Perkins of Paddington Green. Ain't she got the sweetest . . .*' He smirks at Lily. '*Ain't she got the sweetest . . . smile a man's ever seen.*'

'Uncle Jack.' Lily gives him a terse smile.

'*Uncle Jack,*' he minces, winking at her. 'Butter wouldn't melt, eh, Susie, what do you say?' He chucks her sister under the chin and, flinching, Susan draws back her chair and mutters something about an errand she has to run.

'Lily was just leaving too, weren't you?' Her mother fixes her with a gimlet eye, and Lily understands that in spite of everything, it must still be going on, the five minutes of panting and squealing on the sagging corner bed, while Christopher plays marbles underneath, and, bribed with a ha'penny, Sammy keeps watch at the door.

'You'd best stop bleating and make the most of what you've got, miss,' her mother goes on. 'Besides –' she eyes Uncle Jack with suspicion – 'there's no room back here now you're fully grown.'

'You listen to your mother,' Uncle Jack says, then makes a low bow. 'May I have the honour of escorting you down the hill. There's some rough sorts round these parts.'

'There's no need,' Lily says, a sentiment echoed most vehemently by her mother, but there is nothing for it, she has barely had time to kiss her brothers goodbye before she finds her left arm looped through her uncle's and kept in a firm grip as they step out onto the street.

'You're a rum 'un,' he says, once they've walked a little way down the road. 'Lady Lily.'

She tries to wriggle free. 'Ma's waiting for you, ain't she?' But even this doesn't shame him.

'You should be thanking me, milady. Oh yes.' He nods to himself, and looks at her slyly.

'Thanking you?'

'Got summat to show your ma, ain't I? Thought I'd show my special girl first.'

His arm drops to her waist and Lily finds herself steered into a twitten and pressed up against the filthy wall.

'You touch me and I'll tell Pa everything.' She gives her uncle a shove. 'And when he gets out, he'll throttle you.'

'No, you won't.' He releases her, and delves deep in his trouser pocket. 'You'll never guess what I found,' he says in a sing-song voice, and at first Lily is relieved that he is just toying with her and what she thought might happen won't. But then he holds up a photograph and she has nowhere else to look but at a girl, naked and timid-seeming, with a lopsided crown of ivy in her hair. At first she refuses to recognise herself – she whimpers, tries to look away, but Uncle Jack holds her chin in a vice.

'Someone,' his voice drops to a whisper, 'has been up to all sorts.'

Lily squirms. She looks again and thinks it can't be her, it can't be because hadn't Miss Harper told her that all the photographs were sold to gentlemen in France, and her uncle's never been anywhere close and is anything but. But it is her – her breasts, her buttocks, her lips curved into a shy smile.

'Bought it for a shilling,' her uncle says with triumph. 'And you always so proper! Who'd have thought it?'

'Who sold it to you?' Her lip trembles. 'Someone foreign?'

'Foreign!' He laughs. 'My eye! No girl, I got it from a fellow I know from the George. English as they come.'

'Let me go.' Lily's voice is quiet. 'Or I'll scream blue murder.'

He leans in close. 'I think it's time you started being a bit more grateful, Lil. You know what I mean, don't yer?'

The stale smell of his breath, the yellow stains on his moustache, make her want to vomit. She tries to snatch the photograph from him, but he holds it out of reach.

'Come on.' Uncle Jack glances towards the street, then shoves his hand under her skirts and starts to fumble with the tie of her drawers. 'Be nice – then I won't have to show it to anyone else, will I? And I know some as would like to see it, and no mistake.'

For a moment Lily hesitates, goes slack against him. Then she feels his rough fingers against her bare skin, and she cannot do it, will not do it: she knees him hard between the legs and he cries out in pain and lets her go. She leaves him there, clutching himself, but as she reaches the road he calls after her, and for once he isn't smirking or grinning or leering, and the look on his face makes her afraid.

'There's more where these come from, in't there?' He clutches her picture in his curled fist and shakes it at her. 'Best you think about what I said, girl. Do you understand? Do you?'

Ellen washes the last plate and sets it to dry in the rack. The negatives of Mrs Williams have a ghostly, ethereal quality, as if what has happened might yet be reversed, but she knows already that the final prints have the potential to be very fine indeed, blending long shadows and soft diffusion of light upon skin that looks warm to the touch. A diamond winks in an earlobe, a cheekbone slants, curving towards a secret that cannot be told. The plates drip oblivious, mundane as crockery left to drain. If only one could view a photograph instantly, as soon as one had exposed the plate, Ellen muses, yet perhaps it would detract from the pleasure of anticipation, for there is a kind of magic in it; and she knows she will sleep only fitfully tonight.

A knock on the door and Reynold appears. 'Finished?' He strides to the rack and studies one of the plates. 'She'll tire of you eventually, you know. Her sort always do.'

'And you're familiar, are you? With her sort?' Ellen begins to rinse out the basins.

'I worry for you, that's all.'

He spends too much time alone, Ellen tells herself – it is solitude, not spite, that makes her brother jealous. She must be kind. She turns to him. 'Let's have a quick supper. Go to The Ship for some flounder?'

'I don't think so,' he says, a dull reproach in his eyes. 'Blanche needs company. She's been on her own all day.'

Ellen takes a cloth and wipes the basins. She should offer to go with him to Booth Lane and make supper. They will sit as they used to at the wobbly card table, by the open window, gossiping about the neighbours who pass in the street below. The thought of it sucks the life from her. She does not want an evening alone with Reynold, his need for her eclipsing the light of this most extraordinary of days.

'I'll be back tomorrow afternoon to do the prints,' she tells him, turning away and busying herself with tidying, until the door to the darkroom clicks shut and he has gone.

★

It is past ten when Ellen returns to the Crescent, and the house is so still she can hear the surge of the waves combing the shingle. She goes directly to her room, and as she steps inside, she sees a folded piece of paper, slipped under the door. Smiling, she picks it up. She should have known better when Lou told her everyone had retired for the evening: it will be an invitation from Clem to take a drink in her rooms. But the writing is untutored, written in stubby pencil on wax paper.

Miss Harper. I <u>must</u> speak to you.
LM

Ellen sighs. Does Lily really expect her to weigh in at every harsh word from Mrs Matthews, every imagined slight from the other maids? Can the girl not fight her own battles? She tosses the note aside and gets ready for bed, puts on her nightdress, takes down her hair. If she could only turn back time, she would walk right past the girl on the pier with the heart of a face and the troubled grey eyes, eating a chocolate ice under the shelter.

She is about to get into bed when there is a knock at the door. The girl is impossible, Ellen thinks, she cannot pander to her any more. Uneasily, she recalls their last encounter, the angry look in Lily's eye. *You kissed me, Miss Harper!* A second knock follows and, telling herself she will have to be firm, she goes to the door.

A smell of sandalwood, not the vapours of the kitchen or starch and sweat. A bold eye staring back at her, the iris a dark pool in the candlelight, a blonde coil of hair brushing a cheek.

'Oh,' Ellen hears herself say. And later she will not be able to remember the exact choreography which brings Clem over the threshold and into her room. But somehow the door opens, as if she has been expecting her, and Clem comes inside.

She is in her nightdress. She does not look around her, she does not hesitate: she reaches straight for Ellen's hand and holds it in hers.

'Dear Ellen,' she murmurs, her eyes liquid and glittering. Dipping her head, Clem presses her mouth into the delicate skin of Ellen's wrist, and Ellen sees with terrible clarity the path she should take, one where she draws back and suggests that perhaps Mrs Williams has had too much to drink. But she finds herself unable to move.

Clem comes closer, her breath warm in Ellen's ear. 'You must tell me to go if it displeases you,' she says, running a finger along the curve of her neck, 'but somehow I suspect it will not.'

A sound escapes from Ellen's throat, as if her body knows before she does what is about to happen, and Clem holds her face and kisses her. And at first Ellen hesitates, as if it is some kind of practical joke, for it seems so strange that what she has spent so many years longing for is being given to her without suffering. But it is not a joke, Clem's lips are on hers, her tongue is in her mouth and her body is pressing her now against the wall next to the washstand.

Ellen's breath comes faster. She trembles like a flame, as Clem cups her gently through the thin cotton of her nightdress and moves her palm against her, just as Ellen has done to herself many times before. But this is different. The weight of Clem's body against her, Clem's mouth on her skin, at the base of her throat, fingers fumbling with the buttons of her nightdress, before Ellen feels the teasing, flitting sensation of Clem's tongue on her breasts. She cannot help herself, she moans, and the pressure between her legs becomes more intense. She opens her eyes and sees Clem, pink-cheeked, breathless as she is, and she thinks of her as she first saw her, standing among the vigilants with a placard, she thinks of her naked in the studio, the jutting brown tips of her nipples, and how much she'd wanted to touch her: Ellen thinks of her now. Her crisis comes quickly and Clem swallows her cries with a kiss, pushing her hard against the wall, replacing her hand with the firm cushion of her leg, and with it comes another ripple of pleasure.

Ellen pants. She sobs. She is made dizzy by the extraordinary sensation of Clem's tongue flicking against her own. Her legs are blancmange, and her mind . . . is lost.

Clem strokes her hair, her eyes as luminous as stars. 'Dear Ellen,' she murmurs again, taking her hand and drawing her to the narrow bed. She lies down and lifts up her nightdress.

'Now it's my turn,' she says.

In the room next door, Lily stares into the darkness. She knows what they are, the sounds that have been seeping through the wall for the past half-hour, the stifled moans, the sudden calling out. She has heard them often enough from her mother's bed. But the voices – when they speak, which isn't often – are soft, female: Miss Harper is with another woman, doing with her what she'd wanted to do with Lily. Her cheeks become hot. It is what the men in the kitchen were sniggering about, she realises, when Mrs Matthews found her in Miss Harper's room.

As the clock downstairs begins to strike midnight, Lily hears the creak of a floorboard, then the turn of the door handle. Footsteps – light and stealthy – pass her room. She gets out of bed, and waits a moment before opening the door. A familiar smell scents the narrow hall, woody, expensive, a lady's perfume. Lily creeps towards the staircase, just in time to see a blur of white, a pale hand on a banister, as the mistress, Mrs Williams – for who else could it possibly be – returns to her bedchamber on the floor below.

Chapter Twenty-Five

The household at Number Ten is up unusually early for a Sunday. Mrs Williams is dressed and calling down to the kitchen for eggs for her and Miss Harper before eight, and there is something odd, Milly thinks, about the quiet in the sun-soaked breakfast room, as she brings up the tea. At first she thinks Mrs Williams and her companion have quarrelled, but as she leaves she catches Mrs Williams smiling at Miss Harper, as if she is somehow to be praised for taking the master's place at the table while he is away, and Milly remarks upon it to Cook upon her return to the kitchen.

'That woman's on borrowed time, mark my words,' Cook says, setting two poached eggs on a plate, and Lily comes forward and offers to take them up.

As Lily enters the room, Mrs Williams acknowledges her with a brief smile, but Miss Harper is buried in a newspaper the size of a window and does not look up. A jolt of anger runs through Lily. So she is still to be ignored, is she, no matter that yesterday had been the worst day of her life, and that she barely slept a wink.

'Miss Harper.' Lily hovers by the fluttering edges of *The Sunday Times*. 'May I speak to you after breakfast?' She searches for a reason. 'There are mice on our floor and I need to put down some poison.'

The newspaper lowers. Miss Harper's amber eyes are cool. 'Mice? Really? I hadn't noticed.'

'You can hear them in the wainscot at night.'

'Very well. Show me after breakfast.'

The newspaper comes up again. Lily bobs a curtsy to Mrs Williams, who is now studying her with some interest over her teacup, and returns to the kitchen.

'What exactly is the matter, Lily?' Miss Harper stands in Lily's room, wearing an expression so stern that Lily wonders how she could ever have thought of her as kind. 'I have to tell you I do *not* appreciate—'

'He knows,' Lily blurts out, 'about the photographs.'

Miss Harper's face changes. 'Who? Who knows?'

'My bloody uncle. He bought one from a man in the pub.' The shame of it returns afresh and Lily's bottom lip quivers. 'You told me they were going to France. To *gentlemen* in France.'

But Miss Harper has no answers, only questions. 'Did you tell him about Booth Lane? About Mr Harper's studio?'

Lily shakes her head.

'Good girl.' Miss Harper paces to the window, tapping her finger to her lip. 'You must tell no one else of this, do you hear?'

'Why would I tell anyone? I'm so ashamed.' Lily sits on the bed and starts to weep. 'He had a photo of me, Miss Harper, don't you understand?'

'Lily, listen to me.' Miss Harper hesitates, then sits down next to her and pats her shoulder. 'It's just a photograph.' She grimaces. 'Your uncle will likely have seen much worse, believe me.'

'You lied to me,' Lily says harshly, reaching for her handkerchief, and Miss Harper moves away.

'It's done now – and there's an end to it. The whole thing is best forgotten.' She looks at Lily pointedly. '*I'm* best forgotten.'

'What do you mean?'

'I mean –' Miss Harper's hand is on the doorknob – 'that if you no longer find this position to your liking, you should seek out another. Didn't you once have plans to go to Blackpool?'

'Blackpool!' But that's a two-day journey away, Lily is about to say, before she sees the look in Miss Harper's eye, and realises that the distance from there to here is precisely the point.

'I'm sure Mrs Williams would give you an excellent reference,' Miss Harper goes on, and Lily stares at her then, until a blush stains Miss Harper's cheeks and she looks away.

'I'd better get ready for church,' she says.

'Suppose you'd better.' Lily turns her head towards the window, and keeps it there until Miss Harper has gone.

Clem had never imagined that what happened between her and Ellen would take up so much space. It was as if the pleasure they had received from each other had become a person in its own right, an unwelcome chaperone, accompanying them on their walk to church with Ottilie, there to ensure that they will never do similar again. How quiet Miss Harper had been at breakfast, hiding behind the newspaper just like Herbert, and as for herself, she was suffering the after-effects of last night's champagne and could barely eat a thing. The alcohol had made her bold, and given courage to her convictions, convictions further endorsed by below-stairs gossip – Lily had been found in Miss Harper's room; Ottilie was sure they knew each other. And this – coupled with her own imagination, the boundless possibilities of what could happen – had spurred her on, naked beneath her nightdress, as she crept upstairs to her companion's bedchamber.

Clem glances at Miss Harper. Imagination was one thing, but Miss Harper's muffled cries had been real, as had the smell and the dampness of her when they'd lain on the narrow bed and she had shown Ellen how to touch her. The invisible chaperone taps her shoulder and a terrible thought occurs to Clem. What if Miss Harper had just been obliging – or worse – doing her duty? She must speak, say something, anything, to break the thickening silence.

'I forgot to ask, Miss Harper,' she says, 'did you rectify the mouse problem Lily spoke of?'

'A fuss over nothing,' Ellen says. 'A figment of the girl's imagination, most likely.' They walk on a few more steps, and then she speaks again. 'Although I had a little trouble sleeping myself last night.'

'There is always something to keep one awake.' Clem keeps her eyes fixed on the distant pier. 'Even when one is quite exhausted by the events of the day.'

'Indeed.' And Miss Harper turns and looks at her fully just as she had last night, her eyes bright and alert, despite the dark shadows underneath. 'Pleasurable thoughts can be as much a barrier to sleep as worrying ones.'

'I barely sleep these days either,' Ottilie says in her matter-of-fact way. 'For thinking about how much I don't want to go to school in Switzerland.'

'Then perhaps it should be postponed,' Clem says suddenly. 'What do you say, Miss Harper? How is Ottilie's French progressing?'

'There has been much improvement.' Miss Harper smiles

at her student. 'Which is not to say that there isn't room for more . . .'

'What would you recommend? Another six months of lessons perhaps?' And it is as if Ottilie has vanished and it is just the two of them, and now Clem is almost certain that Miss Harper feels the same powerful desire that she does to find a quiet spot under the arches and kiss until their legs give way underneath them.

'Yes,' her companion replies. 'Six months at the least.'

Ottilie becomes ten again and claps her hands, then looks anxious. 'What about Uncle Herb?'

'Leave your uncle to me,' Clem says, nodding at various acquaintances as they reach the church gates. 'Perhaps we might discuss your contract later, Miss Harper, over tea in my rooms?'

'I'd be delighted, Mrs Williams,' Miss Harper says, without an ounce of duty, and as they walk up the steps to church, Clem reflects that on this morning, in particular, she has much to give thanks for and resolves to leave half a crown extra in the collection plate.

They wait long enough for the tea to cool in the teacups and for Milly to be safely back in the kitchen, before Clem draws the curtains. Then she stands before Ellen and slowly unbuttons her blouse, and then her skirt, removing petti-coats, bodice and corset until she is wearing nothing but her chemise and drawers. As the clock strikes four, Ellen thinks of Reynold waiting for her at the studio to develop the prints, before pushing the thought away. She steps into Clem's arms and they kiss for a long time. When Clem starts to undo the buttons of Ellen's shirt, she stops her, and says they may have locked the door, but what if someone should come: it is wise for one of them at least to be fully dressed.

Wise, Clem says teasingly, why yes, Miss Harper, I suppose you're right, and then she leads her through to her bedroom and climbs onto the wide, plump bed and draws Ellen on top of her.

'I think you make rather a fine husband, Ellen,' she says with a sigh, and this time, in the shadowed afternoon, with the chaffinches singing songs of sin and springtime in the cherry trees, Ellen doesn't need to be shown the way.

Reynold has resolved that if his sister hasn't come by a quarter past, he will do the prints himself. Until then he lounges on the couch in the reception room, with the door locked, and Blanche Neige, whom he brought along as a Sunday treat, dozing on his stomach. Someone taps on the window and he sees Harry Smart, come to invite him for a stroll and an ice, for was there ever a better day for it, she says, and he tells her he must work. She'll keep him company, if he'd like it, she tells him, for if Blanche is anything like her mother, she isn't much of a one for conversation, and Reynold laughs and invites her in. Too bad, he thinks darkly, if Ellen should come after all and find her there, for Harry has been a good friend to him since Ellen left, besides which she's the only woman apart from his sister he feels truly comfortable with: she doesn't flirt, or fuss, or expect anything that he is unable to give.

They go upstairs to the darkroom and Harriet exclaims when she sees the plates from the previous afternoon.

'Oh my!' she says. 'The girls from the Empire have competition!' And she and Reynold sip tea and chatter as he prepares the prints, until each set is washed and dipped and pegged on string to dry.

'Extremely diverting.' Harriet strolls among the photo-graphs, chuckling as she appraises each one. 'Although the humour will doubtless be lost on your customers!' She stops and looks again at a photograph of Clem, naked by the mantelpiece, and turns to Reynold. 'Is that who I think it is?'

He couldn't possibly say, Reynold tells her, and Harriet raises an eyebrow and remarks that it just shows that you shouldn't pay attention to hearsay, for she'd always had the impression American ladies would give Queen Vic a run for her money when it came to prudery.

'She's using my sister as a plaything. A diversion.' Reynold stares out of the window at the scrubby piece of garden below. 'But Ellen can't see it.'

'Perhaps she is equally diverted?' Harriet suggests, but Reynold shakes his head.

'Ellen's suffered more than I realised from being without a mother,' he says thoughtfully. 'I never knew it until recently. She lacks those natural feelings women should have.'

'And what natural feelings might they be, Reynold?' Harriet says archly, brushing the fluff from her trouser leg, and he sees that she is teasing him and smiles.

'You're different, Harry. You're a performer. One of a kind. Unique.' He leans on the counter with his chin in his hands. 'No, I mean marriage and so on.'

'You'd like to see your sister married?' Harriet looks up in some surprise.

'I'd like to see her content,' he says. 'Not to mention provided for. She'll tell you herself I'm hopeless with money.' He walks to and fro, examining the dangling prints. 'I good as found her a husband a few months ago.'

'Really?'

'The Ice King, no less. Pots of money – and it was clear Wally adored her – he'd have let her stay working, if Ellen had wanted it.'

'But she refused him?'

'He never got the opportunity to ask!'

'Ah, well.' Harriet looks at her hands and shrugs. 'It seems as if your sister knows her mind.' She slaps his shoulder in farewell, taking a last look at the photographs as she goes to the door. 'Do congratulate Ellen for me when you next see her. She really does have a good eye.'

If it's not one thing, it's another. Herbert Williams straightens his necktie in the mirror and tries to adopt a paternal countenance. As if managing the household in Brighton wasn't difficulty enough. Finally his wife settles down and does what is expected of her, only to lose the baby mere moments later – a common enough occurrence, according to Dr Phillips, yet rather than getting back in the saddle, as any sensible woman would, Clementine treats him like a leper and he has the devil's job persuading her to let him near her. That blasted Harper woman is still skulking around the place, Ottilie throws regular tantrums about finishing school, and now even his dear Arabella, usually a veritable Doric pillar of self-possession, is showing distinct signs of crumbling. Barnaby has been sent down from Eton and will not be allowed back until he has apologised for his misdemeanours, which he is refusing to do. Nor is it clear exactly what the boy has done, for the headmaster had told Arabella it was a delicate matter, not for female ears, and with Mr Hawes-Montague on the high seas to the Orient, she has begged Herbert to talk to the boy.

An assault on the door and Barnaby bowls in. Such a

shame that the boy was *nullius filius*, for really Herbert finds it hard to conceive of a son of whom he might feel more proud, no matter what the school reports might say.

'Now, young man.' Herbert pours them both a measure of port. 'Why don't you tell me what's been going on? Man to man,' he adds as Barnaby looks warily towards the door. 'Your mother need know nothing of it.' He gives the boy an encouraging smile. He knows what goes on even at the best schools, young men cooped up together; all it took was one rotten apple in the barrel. 'Bit of tomfoolery, was it, with the other chaps?'

'I didn't do anything, Uncle Herb.' A self-righteous flush stains the boy's ruddy cheeks. 'It was Brown. He was the one that bought them. All I did was look.'

'Bought what?'

'The photographs.'

'Ah.'

'He got them sent. To different fellows each time so as not to arouse suspicion. I told him I didn't want any part of it, but he didn't listen – and I got caught.'

'And took the blame. I see.' It is all making sense. Herbert leans back in his chair. 'And am I to assume that the content of these photographs would not be suitable for your mother's eyes?'

Barnaby does battle with a grin and loses. He nods.

'And have you kept any of these pictures? Aside from those that the master confiscated.' When the boy doesn't reply, Herbert raises his voice a notch. 'I can't help you if I don't know what I'm dealing with.'

They lock eyes. Barnaby scratches his jaw, then disappears from the room, returning with a brown envelope, which, with some reluctance, he passes to Herbert. It bears

231

a London postmark and is addressed to a Mr B. Hawes-Montague Esq., with 'Art Supplies' penned in an authoritative hand across the top corner.

So this is what it's like to be a father, Herbert thinks, rather enjoying himself as he removes a bundle of photographs from inside the envelope. He flicks through the pictures. The usual – waifs and strays from the East End reclined on ottomans, sprawled open-legged on armchairs – right up Magpie's street, in fact he wouldn't be surprised if they came from the same supplier. He stops at a picture of a girl perched on the arm of a battered easy chair, stockinged legs outstretched. Large breasts, but a slight, muscular frame – one of the working classes, no doubt of it. Almost something familiar about her. Herbert puts the envelope into the breast pocket of his jacket and pats Barnaby's shoulder.

'All of this will blow over before you know it.' Herbert goes to the writing desk and beckons to his son. 'You are going to take some dictation, young Barnaby. Best handwriting if you please. Remind me of your housemaster's name.'

'Mr Lamb.' Sighing heavily, Barnaby sits down at the desk.

'Dear Mr Lamb . . .' Herbert begins, pacing across the room. 'I would like to offer my most profound and sincere apologies for recent unfortunate events . . .'

Chapter Twenty-Six

Lily is peeling potatoes at the kitchen table when her sister comes. Susan's bulky frame hoves into view as she stomps down the basement steps, and Lily looks up from the pail of potatoes, the sick anxious feeling in her belly worsening as she stifles a childish impulse to crawl under the table and stay there. An accident at the laundry, her mother scalded. Or worse, one of the boys – little Christopher scarlet with fever, gasping for breath.

'Three minutes, and not a second longer. You know the rules.' Cook decapitates a rabbit with a force that makes the table shake, and Lily hurries to the back door.

'Sue.'

'Lil.' Her sister looks at her long and hard. 'You look done in.'

'I ain't been sleeping.' Lily braces herself for an onslaught, for Susan to say she should be so lucky, sleeping in a bed of her own with no brats keeping her awake half the night. But her sister remains strangely quiet. She draws Lily away from the kitchen window and lowers her voice.

'I know what you done.' Susan's heavy brow darkens, before her words come out in a torrent. 'That gibface uncle of ours showed me that . . . that picture, and I won't be the last. He's going to get you in trouble, Lil, now you won't give 'im what he wants – he'll see to it.'

Lily swallows. She turns away and presses her head against the cool whitwashed wall. Over a week has passed since her encounter with Uncle Jack, and every morning she has awoken filled with dread about what the day might bring; now it has come home to roost, as she knew it would. A buzzing starts up in her ears as Susan talks on.

'It's disgusting what you did. Wicked. But I don't care what Ma says, you're still my sister, and it's not your fault he's been sniffing round you like a dog. I know it's why you left and so does Ma, even if she won't admit it, but there's nothing our precious uncle likes more than to stir the pot.'

Lily looks up. 'What do you mean?'

'He's going to send the picture here, Lil. To the house.'

The fear in Susan's eyes reflects Lily's own, and as they stare at each other they are children again, hiding in the coal bunker from Ma and her leather strap.

'You should leave. Tonight.' Susan takes a couple of coins from her pocket and presses them into Lily's hand. 'It ain't much, but it'll get you to Worthing.'

Lily looks at the money. Her sister could give her ten times the amount and it would make no difference. Her photograph – her nakedness – is everywhere. Every man she encounters – the butcher in the market who winked at her this morning as he jointed a chicken, the stable boy with fluff on his chin who comes to the kitchen for meals, the drayman unloading beer barrels at the George – all of them will either have seen the photograph or she'll imagine they have: either way, she'll have no peace, she will never be free. Better she had parted her legs in an alleyway, like so many before her; at least that way it was done and forgotten. She remembers the contraption in the attic that Miss Harper explained was the press they used to make copies of the photographs. But how many had they made? How many pictures of her were there? Twenty? Fifty? More than that? She shudders.

'Lil.' Susan is shaking her shoulder. 'You all right? You're awful pale.'

Voices come from overhead, the sound of footsteps as the front door closes.

'Over the hill to Rottingdean, I think, Miss Harper?' Mrs Williams' voice drips like honey.

'An excellent idea,' comes Miss Harper's response.

I never want to hear that woman again, Lily thinks, not one word that she speaks, not one part of a word.

Susan looks up at the departing women. 'Is that the mistress?'

Lily doesn't reply. She puts her arms around her sister and kisses her downy cheek, not caring when Susan stiffens with surprise.

'I have to go,' Lily says. 'Give the boys a kiss from me.'

As the kitchen door closes, Susan sees the cook through the kitchen window, hands on indignant hips, as her sister, head bowed, slopes back to her bucket of potatoes. Leave her be, you silly bitch, she says to herself, feeling rather grateful suddenly for Mrs Hadley and the laundry. It is only then she notices the money she gave Lily left on the window ledge, and if the cook hadn't looked so fearsome she'd have knocked again to give it to her sister, whose kiss she can still feel on her face, and whom Susan realises she loves more than she'd ever let on.

Lily lies curled up in bed, still in her work clothes, listening to the sound of Miss Harper readying herself for bed in the room next door. The biggest mistake she's made, bigger even than taking her clothes off over and over again like a slut, was believing what Miss Harper told her. That there was no harm in it. That she was just as good as anyone else. That she was special. She thinks of her uncle in his soiled tinker's trousers, his stunted handwriting on a grubby envelope, the envelope delivered to Mr Williams in his study, the frantic ringing of the bell as Mrs Matthews is summoned, the photograph confiscated, the rumour circulating from housekeeper to cook, then from Milly to Lou to Dixon. Perhaps even Mrs Williams will get wind of it, but she will keep Miss Harper's secret before Lily's, that much is certain. She imagines them laughing about it, on one of their walks, or in bed, when they tire of doing things that should only happen between man and wife.

Her thoughts unspool and tangle. Voices come for her in the dark, coarse and knowing. Better for her if she'd been more like Susan and Ma, tougher, harder – instead she has always been too trusting, too eager to please. Downstairs the clock strikes on and on. She has never become accustomed to it, has never slept right through the night, not since she arrived; she has always hated it here. Lily gets up and laces her boots, and goes downstairs to the kitchen. There is something that needs her attention before she leaves.

She takes a pencil and opens the drawer where Cook keeps the receipts for the grocery orders. On the back of the latest order she writes what she has to, doing her best to spell each word correctly. She was always good at school; her teacher used to praise her. Lily tries not to think of Miss Bunting's kind, open face as she folds the paper and goes upstairs, hesitating before sliding it under the door of Mr Williams' study. Her heart quickens. It is no more than they deserve. She fetches her cloak from the basement, unbolts the back door and lets herself out.

Lily walks down the steps to Madeira Drive, gusts of wind ballooning her cloak. A drunk calls out from the recesses of the arches; she looks behind her, but it is too late to protect her honour – Lily hurries on. Ahead the creaking chains of the pier glint in the sullen moonlight. She has heard that it is to be destroyed, that it is weak and rusting and broken. A memory comes from years ago of her and Susan, each buying a shiny painted pebble from one of the kiosks: she had gone to bed with it curled in her tiny hand.

She reaches the old tollbooth where a rotting door swings loose on its hinges. Ignoring the sign that exhorts her to keep out, Lily delivers a well-aimed kick and then another, and as the door comes looser still, she squeezes through the gap.

Her feet beat out a rhythm on the wooden boards. Beneath her the sea churns, salt spray stings her eyes. She walks under one arch and then another. Halfway along, she stops. Her name called, footsteps hurrying after her? Lily squints into the dark. A gull swoops and shrieks – *fool, fool.* There is no one.

As she approaches the end of the pier, she slips on the uneven wood, a sharp splinter searing her palm as she falls. The pain, in a peculiar way, is welcome. Shivering, Lily grips the railings. She has never been more than ankle-deep in the sea, never set foot in a bathing machine. A wave baptises her, and then another. She looks back at the lights of the town, studding the blackness like the faintest of stars, and for one hopeless moment she wishes that this night could last forever, for there is safety of sorts in the cave-like dark. But she is trapped, nonetheless, for whenever she closes her eyes, all she can see is the photographs, and when the daylight comes, so will her uncle's act of revenge and she will be exposed.

Lily hauls herself up onto the top of the railings, swings her legs over so she is directly facing the sea. Her fingers grip the rusty metal, they won't let go, they won't let her do it. She thinks of the note under Mr Williams' study door, she thinks of herself with Miss Harper in the attic, watching her body emerge white and ghostly on the glass. She need not worry about her eternal soul, she thinks, for it has been taken by science and Miss Harper and her brother: she is already in hell.

The waves reach up to take her and Lily lets herself fall.

Chapter Twenty-Seven

How, Ellen thinks, can she be expected to give any subject her full concentration ever again, when Clementine Williams is the distance of an outstretched arm away, idly running a finger back and forth across her bottom lip, with the sole intention – Ellen is certain – of teasing her. Granted the room is warm and Caroline Yorke-Duffy has been droning on about the difficulty of finding a suitable laundry matron for the Penitents' Home at Albion Hill for far longer than is tolerable, but nonetheless. Four whole days since she and Clem have been alone together in the only way that matters, four days since she has tasted her on her fingers. Their eyes meet; and with this a tug like a bell pull. In a few hours Mr Williams will return to London, and they will be rid of him.

A knock comes at the door and Mrs Matthews appears, flushed from her neck to her hairline. The effect is not a pretty one and Clem must have had the same thought, for under the table her foot nudges Ellen's own.

'Might I speak to you, madam?' Mrs Matthews is breathless, as if she has charged full pelt up the stairs.

Clem gets up. And as the housekeeper murmurs in her ear, Clem's face changes, and this, Ellen realises, is no below-stairs crisis, no broken vase or change to the dinner menu. Her heart beats a little faster – and then her name is being called, and excusing herself from the meeting, she follows Clem and Mrs Matthews into the hall.

'Lily March has gone missing,' Clem says, her expression troubled. 'She hasn't been seen since last night.'

'We wondered if you might have seen her at all?' Mrs Matthews looks pointedly at Ellen. 'Seeing as her room's next door to yours.'

So Lily had finally done as she'd suggested, and left. Ellen tries not to let her relief show. 'I can't say I have,' she says. 'I retired early last night and slept like a log.' She pauses. 'Miss March seemed rather unsuited to service. Is it possible she may have just left?'

'Unlikely.' There is a hint of accusation in Mrs Matthews' tone. 'Not without collecting her wages first.'

Clem lowers her voice. 'They've found a body, washed up by the pier.'

'A body?'

'A young woman, fitting Miss March's description,' Mrs Matthews adds.

'But that's impossible.' Ellen's mouth trembles like an old woman's, and now it is she who is breathless. She turns on the housekeeper. 'Isn't it time, Mrs Matthews, that you put a stop to the incessant gossip among your staff? It's far from harmless, and frankly it's . . . cruel!'

'Miss Harper.' Clem lays a restraining hand on Ellen's arm, as Mrs Matthews stares at her unsmiling.

'I only wish it were gossip, Miss Harper,' the housekeeper says. 'But if my word isn't to be trusted, why not go and see for yourself?'

Ellen runs from the house like a madwoman, hatless, glove-less, her hair coming loose as she tears across Marine Parade and down the steps to the seafront. She can think of nothing but Lily. How she'd avoided her, when Lily first arrived at the Crescent, because she couldn't bear to be reminded of what had happened at Christmas in the studio. Mrs Matthews' harshness, the spite of the other maids, the rattling tea trolley with Lily's unhappy face behind it. *You came to me, Miss Harper.* She, Ellen, should have been her ally, but she had done her utmost to bury their association; in her own way, she had been just as cruel as Mrs Matthews. Then the scrawled note under her door and her disappointment that it wasn't from Clem. And that awful last exchange, a fortnight ago, where, struggling to hold back the tears, Lily had told her about her uncle and the photograph, and all Ellen had thought about was her own safety, hers and Reynold's. She had told her to leave, she had been callous and unfeeling, she had told Lily to forget her. And then she had put on her best hat and gloves to rub thighs in a church pew with Clem.

Not far from the Chain Pier, a small hushed crowd has gathered on the shingle. Ellen hesitates as she sees one blue uniform and then another, moving among them, their helmets shining like wet pebbles in the sun. Her pace slows as she walks across the beach. There are the tableaux girls – Sal, Jemima and Corazón – and Harriet Smart behind them, her mouth a thin sombre line. She nods in greeting as Ellen approaches, and Sal nudges Corazón, who whispers something to Jemima, and the girls stare, their gaze as unyielding as marble.

'One of yours, wasn't she?' Harriet's voice is barely audible above the sound of the waves, and Ellen doesn't reply. A short distance away in the shadow of the pier, she sees Mr Crocker standing alone, his hat pulled low.

There is a sudden vicious logic – the photographs he keeps in his Bible; Lily's uncle sliding a grubby coin across the counter in the pub. Could it be that, having acquired the pictures somehow, he is selling them on? She marches towards him.

'Is this your doing? Is it?' Distress makes her shrill – a few bystanders turn and stare. From the corner of her eye, Ellen sees Harriet Smart giving an almost imperceptible shake of her head.

'My doing, Miss Harper?' Mr Crocker looks her up and down with amusement. 'What a peculiar woman you are.'

Ellen flushes as she returns to the crowd, edging closer to where the body lies under a blanket. *Move along now,* the constables are saying, *there's nothing more to see,* and the shingle crunches as the onlookers begin to disperse. A hand on her shoulder tries to restrain her but she has to do it, she must know: Ellen lifts the covering from the woman's head.

Her face – young, unlined – is bloated, grotesque; an engorged tongue lolls obscenely between swollen blue lips. But it is Lily's grey eyes that stare back at her, Lily's dark hair, usually so neat, now knotted into snake-like tendrils, stiff with salt. A strand of knobbly seaweed rests in the dip of her throat. Ellen turns away, her hand to her mouth. She needs her brother – where is he?

'It's a terrible thing.' A policeman with a kind face stoops to adjust the blanket. 'Take a drop of brandy when you get home and try not to dwell on it – that's my advice, miss.' He studies Ellen with grave curiosity as he gets to his feet. 'Not someone you knew, I hope?'

Her scalp prickles in the wind; despite the morning sunshine, she feels desperately cold. She is suddenly aware of how she must look, with her head uncovered, her hands bare. She must pull herself together.

'No, poor soul,' she says. 'It's the shock, that's all. Thank you, Constable.'

She feels his eyes upon her as she walks away. The horror of it stalks her. What good a whole vat of brandy, after what she and Reynold have done? Lily is dead – and it is all her fault.

'So you weren't aware of anything untoward, Mrs Williams? Miss Williams?'

Constable Fisher looks up from his notebook at the two young women sitting on the Chesterfield in the dark study, as Mr Williams thrums his fingers on the desk.

'No, indeed. Ottilie?' Clem turns to her husband's niece, wondering if the horrors of the day will ever cease. The house is in uproar, with everyone from the stable boy to Mrs Matthews being questioned, Herbert has postponed his trip to London and has gone strangely silent, and most worrying of all, she hasn't seen hide nor hair of Ellen since she bolted from the house this morning, an absence which will not be possible to conceal from Constable Fisher for much longer.

'Miss March was unhappy,' Ottilie says, glancing at Clem, who wills her not to say more. Surely she will not be so foolish as to mention Miss Harper's name.

'Her background was rather troubled,' Clem says quickly. 'As I told you, we took on Miss March out of charity, rather than necessity.'

'My wife is devoted to her charity work, aren't you, my sweet?' The look on Herbert's face is far from friendly and Clem frowns.

'Of course, we would like to contribute towards the funeral,' she goes on. 'If you could inform Miss March's family, Constable?'

He will do so, the man assures her, and he is about to take his leave, when Herbert asks if he might see the photograph of the March family again. Clem sighs. What good will it do poring over some mildewed picture, which had just made her feel sad when Constable Fisher first brought it out. Lily and her dumpy sister, with a father who looked fond of the drink, and the mother holding a babe in each arm with no more pride than if they were sacks of freshly dug potatoes.

As he studies the photograph, her husband's expression is thoughtful. Handing it back, he calls for Milly to show the constable out.

Once he has gone, Clem is the first to break the silence. 'Who can say what was going on in the poor girl's head?' She wanders over to the window. Where *is* Ellen? She turns to Herbert. 'Will you still be leaving for the city later? I'll ask Cook to—'

'If I were of a suspicious nature,' Herbert joins her at the window, locking his arm around her waist, 'I'd say you were trying to be rid of me. What do you think, Ottilie?'

Ottilie stares at them and says nothing.

'Cat got your tongue?'

Clem doesn't like his tone. She doesn't like the kiss he gives her either, before he leaves – a slapped wrist of a kiss that leaves her lips smarting as she looks out across the placid treacherous sea, pondering once again what Lily March had really meant to her companion.

The wages of sin is death. The words revolve and tumble with each turn of the wheel as Ellen cycles along the King's

Road, the spirit of Grandmère so strong it is as if she is back in the schoolroom, writing lines at a woodwormed desk, as their grandmother patrolled with the hazelwood switch. Three hundred lines once, when she and Reynold had returned home late from their errands on a hot August afternoon after swimming in the river with some of the neighbourhood children, and the more lines Ellen wrote, the less she had understood what the words even meant.

Damned woman. If only death had silenced her. There are tears in Ellen's eyes as she crosses the road. She and Reynold had spent years hating Grandmère for driving their mother away, yet in the end, hadn't she been proved right? *The wages of sin is death.* I am no better than our mother was, Ellen thinks, I am the same – I have sinned with Clem and now Lily is dead. It is as just a punishment as any meted out by a wrathful god, an exquisite cruelty inherent in its application, for like the worst punishments, her suffering will never end. She would write lines every day for the rest of her life if it would bring Lily back, she would work in a laundry and scrub stained sheets until her spine was crooked and her hands as tender and swollen as ripe fruit.

She reaches Booth Lane and unlocks the door. Upstairs, she hears the murmur of voices. What had she expected? That the golden hour would just disappear, that she would find Reynold in his King's Road studio, with all his debts paid, photographing a lord? She marches up to the dressing room, where traces of cheap scent still linger, and flings open the studio door.

'Oh!' The model sits up in surprise, her hands over her breasts, just as Reynold is exposing the plate.

He looks up and growls with frustration. 'Ellie, for heaven's sake! The picture's ruined now.'

'Get dressed.' Ellen empties the contents of her purse and thrusts the coins at the model, whose name she can't recall. 'Take it and get out.'

The girl gives Reynold a sideways look, but he nods, his fist curled to his mouth. As the door closes behind her, he seizes Ellen's arm.

'Have you completely taken leave of your senses?'

Ellen pushes him away. She goes to the camera and releases the plate holder, hurling it to the floor. 'It's over, Reynold. We have to stop.'

He frowns, then picks up the holder, the broken glass rattling inside it. 'Is this because of Lily March? Your laundry girl?' He looks up. 'I heard about the drowning this morning. It's all over the town.'

She stares at him. She has always made excuses for her brother's coldness, understanding it as the armour they both forged in the years after their mother left them living with Grandmère. But now, as he stands fretting over the broken plate, Ellen feels as Lily must have done when she came to her for help and comfort, for reassurance that she refused to give. She digs her nails deep into her palm.

'I can hardly let some scrap of a girl bring business to a halt.' Reynold shrugs. 'Besides, I can't see what it has to do with us. We haven't used her for months.'

'She was not a scrap!' Tears roll down Ellen's face and she reaches for her handkerchief, trying desperately to compose herself. 'I feel responsible, I suppose.'

'How on earth are you responsible?'

'I should never have brought her here. She was too sensitive for it. Too good.' The tears continue and she sits on the chaise and sobs, and her handkerchief is soaked through before Reynold finally comes to sit beside her.

'I can't go back to the Crescent.' She lets herself lean against him. 'Not yet.'

'Then you should stay here.' There is a hint of triumph in her brother's voice as he draws her closer, the afternoon sunlight sliding with oblivion across the well-trodden floor-boards of the shabby room.

Chapter Twenty-Eight

M r Dawson, crumbs from breakfast still in his moustache, stands at the entrance to his bookshop, beneath a pair of copulating pigeons, and scours Holywell Street for signs of Mr Meed. He'd never thought the day would come when he'd be so anxious to see the man, but he has only one set of the Golden Hour portfolio remaining now, and he could sell it fifty times over if he had the stock. It's enough to make a man choke on his pipe to see a lady of class and distinction showing everything she has or as good as – the piano photograph being his own personal favourite. There is a kind of genius at play, for the photographs of this woman make a man long for more, to do what the pictures would never show. That she would sit astride him as she does the piano stool, his hands on her tail as she . . .

'Mr Dawson – well met!'

He is a dozing dog, woken with a bucket of cold water. Can a man not daydream in peace? But then he looks into the windburnt features of Mr Meed and he greets him warmly, inviting him inside the shop.

The men go upstairs. Dawson endures a minute or two of chitchat about some fantastical-sounding electric railway that is to run on stilts across Brighton seafront, before his attention moves to Meed's scruffy leather bag.

'New edition, eh, Mr Meed? I'll take as many as you have.'

But Meed appears flustered as he opens the bag, drawing out just a selection of prints wrapped in brown paper. Dawson rifles through them – just the usual roll-call of seaside doxies – and one of them cross-eyed to boot.

He tosses the prints aside. 'What about the others? The Golden Hour?'

'The enterprise has ceased trading,' Meed says sombrely.

'Ceased trading! In God's name, what for?' Dawson hesitates. 'It's not trouble with the law, is it?'

'No, nothing of that nature.' Meed leans forward. 'I understand it relates to a domestic matter – a disagreement – yet to be resolved.'

'Then our business here is done.' Briskly Dawson gets to his feet. Always a mistake to involve women in business – they were too capricious, too unpredictable altogether. 'Good day, Mr Meed.'

And he calls to the boy to show Mr Meed out.

The day rolls on. Dawson passes an enjoyable hour, pepping up a dreary selection of romance novels with salacious additions to the front pages, in the hope of shifting them from the shelves. Five of the French postcards that he keeps locked in a safe box sell to a regular who's been coming to the shop for months, yet Dawson's heart still galloped as he took the man's money, but in this business you learnt to be brave, and if he didn't sell them, there's others that would.

And then, just as he is about to close, he sells the last set of Golden Hour editions to a gentleman he hasn't seen in a while, moustachioed and furtive, whom he suspects, in all honesty, would prefer the Parisian collection in the safe box to the women gilded in sunlight. But what's good for a man in the privacy of his own home and what can be shared at the club are two different things, and notwithstanding the money he receives from the sale, Dawson is left with a melancholy feeling. After all it is highly likely, he reflects, drawing down the shutters, that he will never set eyes on the lady from the Golden Hour again.

Herbert Williams inhales a plume of cigar smoke and leans back, eyes half closed against the Cuban fug induced by a pleasant half-hour sampling the latest arrivals from the humidor at the club. God, but it was wonderful to be back in the company of men again! Every single one of his recent problems could be directly attributed to the fairer sex – and his wife in particular, who had proved herself utterly incapable of running a household, even with every resource in the world at her disposal. First, there was that wretched maid, who Herbert of all people knew was no better than she should be – and when Constable Fisher had brought out the family photograph, Herbert could have wrung the girl's neck, if she hadn't already saved him the bother. Later that evening he'd gone to his study and looked again at the photographs that had so offended young Barnaby's masters at Eton – and yes, it was the same girl. Butter wouldn't melt in one – and the kitten with the cream in the other. That was women for you – they couldn't be trusted – and as he was learning to his cost, this weakness of character was not solely confined to the lower orders.

As Herbert drains his glass, he toys with the idea of sharing what has been tormenting him with his friends. Not disclosing the whole of it, naturally – rabid wolves wouldn't drag from him the contents of the quietly venomous note he found slipped under his study door, just before all the upset with the drowning.

Your wife is a haw.

Clearly some below-stairs malice at play, but he is less interested in the provenance of the note than he is in the veracity of its message. He had called up Dixon immediately. Had there been any untoward visitors to the house, while he was in London? Any outings of a suspicious nature that Mrs Williams took in the landau? But the coach driver had little of interest to impart. Mrs Williams rarely called for the carriage, he said, preferring to take walks instead, with her companion, Miss Harper. And at the mention of that woman's name, Herbert's right eyelid had begun to twitch, and he'd resolved there and then to do what he should have done months ago, and dismiss her upon his return from London. He didn't like the way she looked at him, for one thing, it wasn't respectful, and he was damned if he was going to have some jumped-up servant knowing more about his wife's business than he did.

'More brandy, squire?' Mr Shaw refills Herbert's glass, remarking that he hopes there is nothing too weighty troubling his old friend, for he seems elsewhere this evening.

Herbert looks at him. How to tell another man that he can't control his wife, that his marriage is a failure which he spends a little more time each day regretting?

'Three sheets to the wind, my friend,' he says. He seizes on Magpie for distraction, for he isn't so preoccupied that he hasn't noticed that it's that time in the evening, when the waiters know to stay away – although he can't honestly say he's in the mood. 'What's on the menu tonight, Maggers?'

'Something of a rather playful nature.' Magpie clears a space on the card table and brings out six small boxes.

'Causing quite a stir in certain circles,' he goes on. 'One of the models is a member of the aristocracy, by all accounts.'

What poppycock! Herbert returns to his cigar as the other men crowd around the table. What is there to see that hasn't been shown a hundred times over? It was downright depressing the power that a woman's naked body could wield over a man, causing fine young men like Barnaby (back at Eton by the skin of his teeth) to act without caution, putting their very futures in jeopardy. These women who stripped for a coin or two got what was coming to them – they were no innocents. As the guffaws around the table become louder, Herbert's curiosity gets the better of him, and he wanders over and picks up one of the photographs. A parody of an afternoon stroll, in which the model in question wears only shoes and stockings, her open parasol covering her head, but little else.

Herbert pauses. Something about the angle of the cocked leg – and the shapely calves – that is familiar, and now Groot is saying that there's more of her, if he likes it, and passes a picture of the same woman, sitting at a piano. Wisps of hair fall loose over her shoulders and she wears a bracelet, studded with diamonds which catch the light. Fake, without a doubt, Herbert thinks; replicas were easy enough to come by. The woman's left hand is hidden. Her back is straight, the vertebrae an arrow towards her firm buttocks, head tilted slightly to the sunlight, as if someone has just entered the room. He stares. He would pay good money to see that face, that face belonging to the body which in form and posture bears an uncanny resemblance to that of his wife.

Herbert's mouth is suddenly dry. His companions' voices fade, leaving him terrifyingly alone with his thoughts, which are absurd yet persuasive, as the evidence – diamond bracelet, wavy hair, a sprinkling of freckles on the woman's right shoulder – steadily accrues.

'He's struck!' someone says, as another picture comes his way (the sipping of tea by a mantelpiece, a hint of a dimple – he had complimented her on them on their wedding day), and then another, and it is then the seashell is plucked from his ear, and the roar of his thoughts stops. The same woman reading a copy of *The Sentinel*, legs on a sideways slant, the wedding ring on her left hand winking at him as she holds the paper aloft. He can hear her now, laughing at him, and there are others laughing too, as that room, that studio, splits its sides with mockery.

Herbert shoves the picture in his pocket. Magpie opens his mouth to protest, and that is all it takes – Herbert seizes the man by his scrawny neck, upending the card table and its contents, and slams him against the wall. Restraining hands pull him back, Shaw's voice in his ear – 'what in heaven's name's got into you, man!' – while Magpie – better he should be named Maggot – chokes and splutters and squirms, his colourless eyes wide with fear.

It takes two of them to pull him off. A hush falls upon the room. Magpie gathers up the photographs, Groot rearranges the furniture. Neither will look at him. Shaw – his oldest friend, his truest – hands him a drink.

'I don't understand,' Shaw says, his face, usually creased in the anticipation of merriment, now solemn.

'I . . .' Herbert cannot find the words. He closes his eyes and sees his wife and Miss Harper, their heads together, whispering. And then that beanpole brother of hers in his King's Road studio with the marble fireplace and corner piano, and he feels like turning his fists upon himself for being so slow.

Herbert wipes his brow. He will eviscerate them, he will douse them in developing fluid and set them alight, he will show this pair of seaside smudgers what happens when someone inveigles their way into his household and corrupts his wife. But first . . . first, he must deal with Clementine.

He strides across the room towards Magpie, hand outstretched. 'Touch too much of the sauce, old man. No hard feelings, I hope?'

Chapter Twenty-Nine

'Moving to the final item on the agenda . . .' Mr Harty's joyless face slips into profound gravity, a state usually reserved for discussions around opium dens or women who have fallen to particularly low depths. 'Miss Lily March.'

Clem lowers her head. Over the past few days, it has felt as if Miss March is haunting her, exacting some kind of revenge from the grave. Her eyes are sore from lack of sleep, her head aches from fretting about Ellen. There has been no word from her for three days now – and the servants are starting to talk. Yesterday, she'd overheard Mrs Matthews tell Cook that there was no smoke without fire, that was for certain, and that Miss Harper had 'bolted like a horse out the gates'.

'It seems the police are launching an investigation into her death,' Mr Harty goes on.

'What can there possibly be to investigate? Surely they don't suspect foul play?' There is a tightening in Clem's chest as she looks around the table.

'A lewd photograph of Miss March has been handed into the police.' Murmurs of condemnation abound from the committee members as Mr Harty consults his notes. 'Her sister, Miss Susan March, came to the station in some distress, having retrieved said photograph from a family member.'

'Well, really!' Mrs Yorke-Duffy's jowls quiver.

'Indeed,' Mr Harty says. 'And as we know from experience, it is extremely likely that there are more. Detective Horlock has asked that we share any insights with the force. And meanwhile, I suggest that we increase our surveillance on certain photographers in the town.'

Clem swallows, her heart hammering with such force that she is sure the very pigeons, roosting on the chimney stacks, can hear it. So this must be the reason for Ellen's sudden and unexplained absence – Lily had been one of her girls.

She turns to Mr Harty. 'Are you quite sure this is necessary?'

'Necessary, Mrs Williams?' He looks at her oddly. 'I'm not sure I understand.'

'Surely there's been some mistake.' She can feel her face turning pink. 'I always found Miss March to be a polite, decent girl. I really couldn't think of anyone less likely to enter into . . . this vulgar trade.'

Mr Harty shakes his head gravely. 'Which is exactly why we need to hunt down the perpetrators of this crime, Mrs Williams. This young woman – decent, polite – as you note, has nonetheless been persuaded to take off her clothes for money. Miss March was no harlot, touting her wares on Elm Grove. She was a woman of the lower classes striving – but sadly failing – to lead a respectable life.' He brings out a sheet of paper. 'I have drawn up a list of all the studios that we feel it would be prudent to investigate. And Mr Jackson will be keeping a close eye on the beach photographers.'

The table buzzes with a new-found energy as the list is circulated. Clem scans the page, and the name she'd hoped she wouldn't see springs up: Mr R. Harper, Photographic

Studios, King's Road. She wants to protest – *see reason, it's tantamount to harassment, trying to entrap respectable photographers in this manner* – but she feels the scrutiny of Mr Harty upon her, as she might a heavy hand on her shoulder, and she can do no more than nod in agreement.

Once the vigilants have gone, Clem sits at the escritoire and writes a hasty note to Ellen, which she slips into her pocket. She creeps down to the front door like a fugitive, ducking around a corner to avoid Mrs Matthews, for the sight of the lady of the house in her hat and gloves will only bring forth an unwelcome torrent of questions – should Dixon be called with the landau, should Milly hail a cab? But to her relief the house is quiet, and she steps out unnoticed into the soft warm air.

Clem walks to the end of the Crescent and is about to cross the road, when she hears a discreet cough behind her. She turns to see Dixon, bowing his head in greeting.

'I have been asked, Mrs Williams, to escort you back to the house.'

She stares at him, then signals to an approaching hansom to stop – no matter that it is going in the wrong direction: she has an animal's instinct to flee. The cab slows, then drives straight past her, and Clem turns to see Dixon waving the driver on.

'My husband shall hear of this,' she says angrily. 'How dare you.'

But Dixon dares to do this and more, and now he is taking her arm and steering her as if she were a prize cow, back along the Crescent. Clem tries to shake him off, but his grip is audaciously firm, reminding her of her husband, whose orders, she now realises, the coach driver must be following.

'Dixon.' Briefly she stops struggling, the smile she gives him costing her greatly. 'My head aches to high heaven and I need to take some air. Just five minutes along the promenade.'

'I'm so sorry, Mrs Williams.' The grip on her forearm is reprised. 'But I'm under strict instruction. You're to stay at home for your own safety. Your husband was very clear.'

Ellen takes a sip from the cup of steaming black tea that Reynold has just brought her, along with a triangle of toast, and for the first time since her return to Booth Lane, derives a faint sensation of pleasure from its sweetness. A patch of blue sky is framed in the attic window and a starling perches on the ledge, peering at her with a gentle curiosity in its beady eye. Reynold reappears with Blanche in his arms and the bird takes flight, betrayed.

He sits on the edge of the bed and eyes her tangled hair. 'There's hot water left in the tub, if you want to . . .'

'I might, yes.' Ellen looks away. 'In fact, I was planning on returning to the Crescent today.'

'Are you sure?' Reynold's face falls.

'I can't just vanish. Ottilie has lessons. Besides –' the next mouthful of tea tastes less sweet – 'I need to tell Mrs Williams about the new living arrangements.'

'Indeed!' The light returns to her brother's eyes. 'We always knew you'd come back, didn't we, Blanche?'

The cat steps daintily from his lap, flaring her claws through the thin weave of the eiderdown. She fixes Ellen with a blue-eyed glare, as if she can smell her secrets. For a moment, as Ellen looks around the poky attic bedroom with the two narrow beds, and the faint odour of the chamber-pot, she feels close to despair. If only she didn't have to do this, if she could just wash and dress and set her hair, and return to the Crescent, blaming her absence on a sudden fever, a contagion she hadn't wanted to bring to the house. The room that was Lily's would become storage for linen, and she and Clem would continue as they had done before, and while Ottilie is reading *Les Misérables* out loud in the schoolroom, Ellen will daydream about Clem's pink tongue, and the dip of her throat, the sensation of softness made hard.

Reynold paces to the window. 'I've been thinking that it might be time for us to move.'

'Move?'

'Away from here. Back to Paris, perhaps?'

A city to hide in, crowds in which to pass unnoticed. Ellen looks at her brother. He will draw them back into the trade as soon as blinking, she knows it. They will need money urgently for the month's rent, and he will know of some girls who are willing, and 'be reasonable, Ellie,' he will say, 'you cannot mope after a dead girl forever'.

Ellen shoos away the cat. 'And what about Mr Crocker?'

'I doubt he'll go to the trouble of crossing the Channel to recover fifty pounds.'

'He told me he'd hurt her. If we left.'

'Who?'

'Mrs Williams.' She puts down the toast: suddenly she cannot swallow.

'I think a change of surroundings may be worth considering –' Reynold looks at her steadily – 'given the circumstances. Miss March has left something of a stench behind her.' He picks up Blanche and goes to the door. 'I'll be at the studio if you need me.'

Ellen takes another mouthful of toast. The butter is rancid, the bread holds the mossy aftertaste of flowering mould. Impossible to delay what must be done any longer – she puts the plate aside, and gets out of bed.

The sea glints like an executioner's blade. Ellen averts her eyes from the pier with its rusting chains, the frothing, surging waves. Her heart beats faster as she passes the spot where Lily was found, sees two fishermen emptying the morning's catch from a rowing boat. How can life just continue as if nothing has happened, how can the universe remain so undisturbed? And then a familiar voice calls her name, and she pretends she hasn't heard and walks all the faster, but the voice is persistent, footsteps breaking into a run behind her, and she turns to see Harriet Smart, dressed in a plain skirt and plaid jacket, and her green hat, with the feather. Ellen remembers it, the splash of colour on Mr Crocker's doorstep, the sleek darkness of Harriet's hair underneath.

'I'm in rather a hurry.' Ellen ups her pace, but her companion does not take the hint and falls in step with her.

'Is Reynold at the studio?'

Harriet does not sound as she usually does; she is serious, sober. Yes, Ellen tells her, what of it?

'You know Mr Walker, the antiques dealer, shop at the top of the Steine? A chap came in asking questions earlier – same ferret face as the gentleman who so rudely interrupted our festive celebrations.'

'Questions?' Ellen glances at her.

'"Do you happen to stock any 'Gentlemen's Relish', kind sir? We're all men of the world here," and so on.' Miss Smart clasps her arm, forcing her to a standstill. 'You understand me, I hope, Miss Harper?'

How dare she. Manhandling her, knowing far more than she should about their private business, and now causing trouble, when, no matter what Reynold thinks, Ellen still suspects that it was Harriet who let slip the provenance of the photographs to the Croc.

'Oh, I understand you.' Ellen glares at her. 'I understand the company you keep. A certain Mr Crocker, for example.' A flicker of discomfort crosses Harriet Smart's face, and Ellen pushes on. 'You told him about our photographs, didn't you? Our Booth Lane business. That's why you're always hanging around my brother, poking your nose in. How does Mr Crocker pay you, Miss Smart? In cufflinks and cigars?'

Harriet Smart recoils as if she has been spat upon. She turns towards the sea, the set of her shoulders rigid as iron. When she looks back at Ellen, her colour is high.

'I am sorry you believe me capable of such a thing,' she says quietly. 'Clearly, I have misjudged you. Take good care, Miss Harper.'

And she walks back in the direction she came from.

Ellen watches her go, her heart racing. For a brief moment, she feels a pang of guilt: Miss Smart had looked so hurt. Then she reminds herself that the woman is a performer, accomplished at manipulating emotions. As for the news she'd been so keen to impart, Reynold wasn't born yesterday – he can sniff out an agent when he sees one. Still, as she crosses the road to the Crescent, her insides writhe with nerves.

Number Ten is strangely quiet. It is almost mid-morning, but the drawing room shutters are closed, and no sound comes from the basement. Ellen lifts the brass knocker and raps firmly on the door.

It is a few minutes before anyone comes. But when the door finally opens, it is Mrs Matthews who stands there, not Milly, and her face hardens as she takes in Ellen.

'Miss Harper.'

'I have come for Miss Ottilie's lesson – I've been ill,' Ellen adds, for the housekeeper is making no attempt to let her pass.

'Miss Ottilie has gone to the countryside with Mr Williams' sister.'

'I see.' Ellen pauses. 'Well, is Mrs Williams at home?'

A long, inexcusable silence. Then the housekeeper takes a step forward, and Ellen glimpses in her something violent, a need to slap or push or shake.

'You'd best be on your way,' Mrs Matthews says. 'Or he'll do the same to you.'

The door slams with such force that Ellen's face tingles as if Mrs Matthews had done as she desired and struck her. Her breath comes faster, as she retreats down the steps. In desperation she picks up a handful of gravel and hurls it at the window of Clem's room. But the stones scatter and fall, and the heavy drapes remain undisturbed. Reluctantly, Ellen starts to walk away, but on looking back, she notices that the drawing room shutters have opened a crack and that someone is standing there, watching her. It is Ottilie – Ellen raises her hand and waves. She must talk to her and find out what's happened, she must knock again on the door and insist. But her student turns quickly away, as if summoned or scolded, and although Ellen waits several minutes, she does not return.

He'll do the same to you. What had Mrs Matthews meant? There is no doubt the police would have come to the house after Lily's death – had Mr Williams started asking questions? Hurrying along the promenade towards the King's Road, it occurs to Ellen that Mr Williams may have found out about her and Clem. She recalls the distaste in the housekeeper's gaze. If that man has hurt so much as a hair on Clem's head, God help her but she will pay a street urchin a sovereign to slip a knife into the soft pouch of his belly, just see if she won't. Ellen's eyes swim with tears.

As she approaches the studio, she sees there are people gathered outside, and not just people, but policemen in their domed helmets, two of whom are keeping guard outside the door, forbidding entry. Passers-by stare and whisper, and now one of the policemen is telling her that she'll have to get her picture taken somewhere else – the premises are temporarily closed. She doesn't want a photograph, she wants her brother, Ellen hears herself say in a breathy, tearful voice that isn't hers, and the constable's face changes as he asks her who she is.

'Your brother's assisting with our enquiries, Miss Harper,' he says, and if Ellen had been the fainting kind, she would have swayed like a poppy and been glad of the fall. But the world remains vivid with edges that cut – she nods with as much curtness as she can muster, and mindful of being followed, takes the backway home to Booth Lane.

Chapter Thirty

Her room is south-facing and overlooks the bowling green, a not unpleasant aspect, had it not been for the iron bars at the window, which go some way to spoiling the view. Nonetheless, with little else to occupy her, Clem spends long hours observing the shambling inhabitants of Ticehurst House who are deemed harmless enough to be let outside: the middle-aged man, impeccably dressed in waistcoat and jacket, watch chain glinting, as he picks up balls and drops them, over and over; the old woman with the girl she used to be still inside her, long grey hair flying as she twirls and twirls across the manicured grass. Her features are delicate, aristocratic, and Clem thinks of her mother's regard for the English upper classes, and how wonderfully 'civilised' she might think her daughter's new abode in the rolling Sussex countryside, where a room costs as much as a suite at the Metropole. Clem laughs out loud, partly to test her voice, which she hasn't used all day, and partly to unsettle Miss Ford, who is paid to watch her and sits, prim as a nun, on a wooden chair in the corner, like an attendant in a gallery.

'My wife likes company,' Herbert had said to the doctor, when they arrived, the doctor whom Clem is sure he must have bribed to lock her up. 'I wouldn't want her to be lonely.'

His solicitous tone had made her want to spit and growl and struggle, as she had a fortnight ago, when white with fury, Herbert had as good as dragged her into the carriage to bring her here: a chain of betrayal which began with the arrival of Dr Phillips and his gentle questioning about her state of mind, and ended with her things packed in a case, while Herbert's wretched lackey Dixon smirked widely enough to eclipse the sun. And they had ridden at quite a pace into the Downs and beyond, and she had asked again and again where they were going, and Herbert's grip on her wrist hadn't let up until he removed the black Golden Hour box from his inside pocket and held up her photographs, one after the other.

'You're a whore,' he'd said, almost matter-of-fact. 'Either that or mad. And if you insist on behaving as such, Clementine, you shall be protected from yourself.'

Miss Ford comes to the window and unlocks it, opening it a crack. The sound of the outdoors washes the stuffy room. If Clem listens hard, she can hear the desperate tweeting of the songbirds in the aviary next to the pagoda – she imagines hundreds of brightly coloured wings – yellow, emerald, turquoise – batting frantically against the glass.

'Would Mrs Williams like to take a walk in the grounds?'

Is it Clem's imagination or is there a hint of a plea in Miss Ford's question? They have not been outside for days.

'To what purpose?' Clem cocks her head, opens her mouth, widens her eyes. Let's play at being mad, if that's the game. A faint stain tinges Miss Ford's sallow cheeks and turns her almost pretty. Oh, Ellen. Clem closes her eyes and moves from the window, her jeu d'esprit extinguished. There is no game. There is only her and Miss Ford and the ticking clock above the mantelpiece, chiming out breakfast and luncheon, tea and dinner, until night falls and she is finally left alone.

'I need paper,' Clem snaps. 'And a pen.'

'You know that's not permitted.' Miss Ford rises from her chair, her gaze darting to the door. She has called for help before, when Clem hurled the tea tray against the wall, causing a muddy-brown stain to bloom among the sprigs of jasmine on the wallpaper. Four nurses had come running – one for each limb, Clem realised later, and wordlessly they had 'put her to bed', tying her wrists and ankles with sheets to the iron bedstead and leaving her there, until the sun was replaced by a sliver of moon and the room stank of the urine which had gushed from her after she'd called and called and no one came.

It had changed nothing. There was no communication from Herbert, or anyone else; she had sulked and cajoled, pleaded and demanded but the instructions from her husband were clear: she was neither to write nor receive any letters.

A knock comes at the door. Miss Ford takes a key from the ring on her belt and unlocks it. Whispered voices, before the door closes again. She turns to Clem.

'You have a visitor, Mrs Williams.'

For the briefest of moments, her dying heart revives. 'I do?' Ellen, she prays, looking hopefully towards her jailer, let it be Ellen.

'A Mrs Yorke-Duffy,' Miss Ford replies. 'Shall I call for tea?'

Miss Ford and Mrs Yorke-Duffy would likely get on like a house on fire, Clem thinks – she should leave them to set the world to rights over a piece of currant cake and take her insane self for a walk in the gardens. She is about to tell Miss Ford that she has no intention of receiving Mrs Yorke-Duffy for tea or anything else, before the old adage 'Beggars can't be choosers' unfurls like a sampler, and she reconsiders.

'Perhaps I should like some fresh air after all,' she says. 'Ask Mrs Yorke-Duffy to wait downstairs, would you?'

'Oh, Clementine.'

Clem had never thought herself to be anything other than tolerated by her husband's sister, but Caroline Yorke-Duffy embraces her with a teariness that takes Clem by surprise, as they stand outside on the back lawn, the sound of a harpsichord stuttering through an open window.

'What a place!' her sister-in-law goes on, actually wringing her hands, as if she has been transported to Bedlam itself. A high-pitched shriek from the direction of the pagoda startles her and she draws her hand to her chest. 'What on earth was that?'

'One of the birds, I expect,' Clem says, coolly.

'Birds?'

'They keep them to amuse the inmates.'

Mrs Yorke-Duffy winces. 'Patients, dear.'

'And yet I find myself perfectly well,' Clem says. They start to walk along the gravelled pathway. 'It is rather my husband who should be committed for insanity for bringing me here.' She glances at her companion. 'Do you happen to know when I might be permitted to leave?'

Mrs Yorke-Duffy's fleshy features pucker. 'But, Clementine –' she places a hand on her arm – 'you *aren't* well. Your recent actions ... well, they speak for themselves.'

So she knows. Or at least she knows a part of it. Clem opens her mouth to speak, but her sister-in-law talks over her, with a fluency that suggests she has spent some time airing her views on the subject.

'I'm not defending your behaviour, Clementine. Sin is sin.

But as I said to Herbert, you are not the truly guilty party here. You arrived in our country a newly-wed, without friends or family. Herbert has left you more alone than he should and I have told him so.' The woman nods decisively. 'He left the door wide open, and you have been corrupted – there is no other word for it – taken advantage of by that . . . no, I cannot bring myself to even say her name.'

'Miss Harper?' It is the first joy of the day to say Ellen's name, the second to witness Caroline's reaction.

'You must not speak of her,' Mrs Yorke-Duffy says sharply. 'If you are to recover, you must put her from your mind.'

They have reached the aviary. The birds flit from branch to branch of the stunted trees, their cries shrill and anxious. There is a sharp unpleasant smell. Clem's neck prickles. 'Where is Miss Harper?'

Her sister-in-law does not reply. She peers through the glass panes. 'A pheasant,' she murmurs. 'How very peculiar.' She takes Clem's arm. 'Shall we have some tea, before I go?'

'Caroline, please.' How she hates to beg, but what else remains to her – she cannot be left in this place to rot. 'Help me. Take me home with you. Take me back to Herbert and we'll talk sensibly –' her words trip over each other – 'I've shamed him, I know it, and I will gladly release him from our marriage. Why, he could be free by the end of the year, and . . .'

'Release him?' Mrs Yorke-Duffy stares at her.

'Divorce, yes.' The words come out with more force than Clem intends, and her sister-in-law looks at her warily, as if she is a troublesome child whose care has become her responsibility for the afternoon.

'Hush!' she says. 'You don't know what you're saying.'

'But I do! Caroline, I'm perfectly sane.' They stop in the middle of the path and Clem grips her hands. 'I don't want to be married to Herbert, nor he to me. He never did – you know that. Please . . .' To her embarrassment, large messy asylum tears begin to fall. 'Help me. I shouldn't be here.'

'There now.' Mrs Yorke-Duffy hesitates, then passes her a handkerchief. 'That's enough. There'll be no more talk of divorce – it won't help matters. I know Herbert.'

The other morning, Clem had watched a howling man tear across the lawn in his pyjamas and fling himself face down onto the grass, pounding at the ground with his fists. She understands now how he felt.

'I should like to return to my room,' she says. 'I find myself rather fatigued.'

It is the first thing she has said that afternoon that would seem to indicate acceptable levels of rationality, for her sister-in-law nods vigorously, saying of course she must rest, and Clem barely has time to ask when Mrs Yorke-Duffy might return before Miss Ford appears, silent as a ghost, to take her back upstairs.

'We have to leave, Ellen, can't you see?' Reynold scoops up an armful of clothes and throws them in the battered suitcase lying on the bed. 'Back to Paris, and the sooner the better. Harry has said she'll take Blanche.'

Blanche looks up from her inspection of the case's contents with a suspicion that matches Ellen's own.

'You've discussed our plans with Harriet Smart?'

'If it wasn't for her, I'd be in a police cell, awaiting trial.' Blanche mewls and Reynold picks her up, holding her close. When he next speaks, his voice is unsteady. 'We got the prints out in the nick of time, let me tell you. Meed was jimmying up the wall at the back as the peelers were hammering down the door. Six-foot drop and he almost broke a leg, he told me.'

Ellen trails behind her brother as he strides into the dark-room and starts wrapping the bottles of fixer and developer in newspaper. He glances at her. 'Could have done with you there, Ellie; the police may have taken a bit more care with a woman around. But no –' he rips up the *Brighton Gazette* with venom – 'you were off like a bunny in springtime to see Mrs Williams.'

'How was I to know there'd be a raid?' Ellen thinks again of her encounter with Harriet Smart on the seafront. She pauses. 'Doesn't it strike you as odd that Harriet Smart was the first to know of it?'

Reynold scowls at her. 'Don't start that again, or heaven help me, I'll—'

'You'll what?'

'I told you it was a mistake to let a lady pose for those photographs.' He shakes his head. 'I never thought I had a sister who couldn't say no.'

'You're being absurd.' The blood rushes to Ellen's face. 'Anyway, the police don't know anything about the Golden Hour.'

'Yet! This is just the beginning. The vigilants are working with the police – they're trying to build a case around Lily March.'

Ellen stares. 'But there's no evidence. They didn't find anything.'

'They got a photograph of her from somewhere. They were very keen to show me that at the station.' His face twists. 'If it wasn't for that girl, we wouldn't be in this mess.'

Ellen can't speak. Her breath won't come without effort;

it is as if a pair of rough strong hands have seized her about the neck.

'*We're* the reason, Reynold!' She takes him by the shoulders and shakes him. 'It's not Mrs Williams or the vigilants or poor, poor Lily. Can't you see?'

Her brother meets her eye and there is a coldness to it, and an image comes to Ellen of a girl, naked on their couch, wishing she were somewhere else, as the plate slides into the camera.

'Oh, I see, all right, Ellie,' he says, looking at her with the same disdain as Mrs Matthews had earlier. 'I see.'

Chapter Thirty-One

'Insufficient evidence!'

If it were possible to die from sheer indignation alone, then Herbert Williams would surely have passed away on the spot, there in the airy drawing room, with his guests – his sister Caroline, Mr Harty and the vigilants' man of the law, one Cyril Steadman – each wondering how best to pacify their host. It is Mr Steadman who steps in first.

'One must be realistic, Mr Williams,' he says. 'The police found nothing untoward on Mr Harper's premises during their search.'

Herbert harrumphs. 'And what about the unseemly photograph of that wretched March girl? The one the girl's sister brought to the station?'

Soberly, Mr Steadman informs him that there is not a shred of evidence which might connect the indecent photograph of Miss March with Mr Harper's establishment.

'We're still keeping an ear to the ground for witnesses who are willing to testify,' Mr Harty says. 'Although I'm afraid that it is a reflection of the times we live in that the tolerance for this type of photography is higher than we'd like.'

Steadman pauses. 'Are you certain, Mr Williams, that there is nothing you have found or seen – by chance, naturally – that could attest to this man Harper's involvement?'

'Quite certain.' Herbert avoids his sister's eye. 'It's a hunch, that's all. Intuition of the strongest kind.' A scowl, lately as much a part of Herbert as his jacket and deerstalker, settles in deep. 'For mercy's sake, the girl took her own life! How's that for evidence?'

'Miss March's unfortunate demise is certainly of interest,' the lawyer agrees. 'But it is circumstantial.' He pauses, coughs discreetly. 'And from the number – and nature – of the photographs we have since found of the young woman, it appears she was not altogether unwilling.'

'She was corrupted!' barks Herbert. 'And what of Miss Harper? Have the police taken her in yet?'

'Mrs Williams' companion?' Mr Harty frowns. 'Aren't we rather clutching at straws?'

'As an employee in your household for the best part of a year, Mr Williams, the police had no good reason to bring Miss Harper in for questioning,' Mr Steadman says.

Caroline Yorke-Duffy sighs and puts down her teacup. 'Herbert, might I speak to you in private?'

'Well?' Visitors dispatched, Herbert pours himself a whisky and slumps into an armchair. 'I won't have my wife in the witness box, if that's what you're proposing, Caroline. I'd rather shoot us both.'

'Are you not going to enquire as to Clementine's state of mind, when I visited?' his sister asks tartly.

'I told you not to go.'

'I was concerned for her!' Caroline tuts and shakes her head. 'She may have made some grave errors of judgement, but your wife is far from insane. As you well know.'

'I'll teach her not to make me a laughing stock.' Herbert takes a swig of whisky and stares grimly at the glass.

'What woman in their right mind asks their husband for a divorce?'

'She did? When?'

'On the way to Ticehurst, when I showed her those infernal photographs. As cool as you like, as if she were asking for no more than a new gown! Damned Americans – I should never have married her.'

'Remember why you married her, Herbert. It will be somewhat challenging for Clementine to produce an heir from a locked room.' Caroline pauses. 'If you want to see Miss Harper and her brother receive their just deserts, then you will need to give way a little.'

'Give way?'

'Just enough to get what you want. And to do what's best for your wife too.'

'What are you proposing exactly?' Herbert drains his glass and is about to pour another when his sister stops him.

'Put that bottle down and I'll tell you.'

And Mrs Yorke-Duffy proceeds to tell him her plan.

Ellen is cleaning – scrubbing and pummelling and buffing to a sheen. She has applied lumps of wet magnesia to the ancient grease spots on the chaise longue, trying not to think about all the girls who have lain upon it, the layers of skin shed and turned to dust, emerging now like puffs of frozen breath as she beats the velvet with a paddle. She has taken an axe to the Chinese screen in the dressing room and chopped it into pieces for firewood, and the jagged remains lie forlorn in the wicker basket, an air of reproach in the dragon's emerald eye.

It is not enough of course, Ellen thinks, plunging net curtains into soapy water, it will never be enough. The girls

277

are all around her, their whispers sighing down the chimney breast, snatches of stifled laughter, so real at times that they make her stop, imagining someone is there. The everyday haunts her, every object, every piece of furniture a trap. The sea-green cushion where Lily had sat that Christmas, in her crown of ivy, legs tucked under her, as Flossy purred by the fire. The stilted notes of 'Greensleeves' as she'd opened the music box to pay the models, the gilt tray and glass tumblers and the sticky bottle of rum, the dressing-room mirror which had reflected so many faces, had borne witness to Corazón's tussles with her curls, to Jemima's fussing over pimples. How many lips pouted, cheeks powdered, hair pinned and unpinned; at the end of a week she'd sweep up balls of it, fair, dark and russet, the strands twisted together – and the other kind too, coarse and wiry.

Lily had avoided the mirror. Lily had not been like the others. Ellen had known this from the start – it was this difference, this innocence, that had drawn her to Lily that day on the pier. You are no better than a man, she tells herself. She dispenses with the dolly and plunges her hands straight into the near-boiling water, crying out with the pain but keeping them submerged for as long as she can bear. No better than that miscreant uncle of Lily's, driven by what hung between his legs: her impulses are the same, and they have brought her and those who have made her heart beat faster nothing but suffering. She withdraws her swollen hands from the tub.

Ellen goes back to the studio, where Blanche sits on Reynold's packed suitcase. Over the past few days, the cat has been as sullen and sulky as her owner, doing nothing but sleep and mope in silent complaint at the absence of diverting company. The room still holds the echo of her and

Reynold's last – and worst – altercation, just a few hours earlier, when Reynold had demanded that she be packed and ready by the time he came back, before storming out to buy two tickets for the night boat to Dieppe. But how can she leave with no word from Clem? How can she live freely, knowing that Clem might be hurt, or in danger?

A rap comes at the front door. At first Ellen ignores it, but the knocking continues. Blanche Neige yowls. If it is Mr Crocker . . . A deadening sense of inevitability draws Ellen to the window. But on the street below there is just a woman, whose extravagantly trimmed hat and smart attire has already attracted the attention of a gaggle of children, who appear to have followed her up the road. The woman turns and scolds them sharply, and her tone of outrage is horribly familiar, calling to mind the torpor of committee meetings, the clink of teaspoons on china. As she looks up at the window, Ellen flinches and moves out of view: it is Mrs Yorke-Duffy, and it seems the woman has lost her mind, for now she is bellowing like a street seller with the last of the day's catch as she hammers on the door.

'I know you're in there, Miss Harper!'

As unwelcome a visitor as the vigilant might be, she may have news of Clem at least. Ellen wipes her brow with a handkerchief and goes downstairs to open the door.

'Miss Harper.'

Mrs Yorke-Duffy sweeps inside as if the house is her own, reviewing her new surroundings with a grimace.

'I have news which I suspect will be of interest to you, Miss Harper,' she says. 'Perhaps you might show me to your parlour – if indeed such a room is to be found here.'

Ellen forgives her tone, forgives the wretched woman anything – she has seen Clem, she brings communication from her. With some haste, she takes Mrs Yorke-Duffy up to the studio, and the woman installs herself on the chaise longue where so many models have reclined before her – how Clem will laugh, Ellen thinks, taking a chair by the window, if she is ever able to tell her of the scene.

'Is Mrs Williams well? When I went to the Crescent, Mrs Matthews said . . .'

Mrs Yorke-Duffy ignores her, her gaze alighting on the suitcase. 'About to go on a trip, I see. How convenient.' She sniffs. 'As to your question, I am afraid to say that when I last saw Mrs Williams, she was very far from well.'

Ellen's mouth is dry. The Croc has got wind of Reynold leaving; he has carried out his threat. 'I don't understand,' she says. 'Where is she?'

'In a madhouse, dear.' The words fall like a blow to the head. 'A madhouse with feather mattresses and a few screeching parakeets, but let's call a spade a spade, shall we?'

Ellen stares. Her wits have left her, she cannot – will not – understand what this woman is taking such vindictive pleasure in telling her.

'An asylum?'

'Yes, an asylum.' Mrs Yorke-Duffy's anger comes off her in waves. 'Actions have consequences, you see, although not, it seems, for the likes of you.'

'He put her there, didn't he?' Ellen's words come out in a sob. 'Her damned husband.'

'You watch your tongue,' her visitor snaps. 'Mrs Williams had taken to certain behaviour that gave every indication of an unsound mind.' She gives Ellen a long, hard look. 'I think you know what I'm talking about, Miss Harper, don't you?'

Ellen calls the cat to her lap and looks away. How much does she know? 'It's not right,' she says, when she has collected herself. 'How long is he intending to keep her there?'

'That all depends on you.'

'Me?'

Mrs Yorke-Duffy draws an envelope from her bag. 'This contains Mr Williams' authorisation to the doctors at Ticehurst House to release his wife from their care. Read it, see for yourself.' She passes Ellen the letter. 'Mrs Williams' freedom can only be secured under a certain condition,' she goes on, '– that you – and your brother – should present yourself to the police and be tried for your crimes.'

Ellen can't speak. A courtroom. The dock. Eyes upon her, wherever she looks. Better to be pronounced mad; at least that way she would stay hidden.

'You can't fool me, Miss Harper. I believe you preyed upon those girls, decent hardworking girls like Miss March – you lured them here, to this very room in all likelihood.' Mrs Yorke-Duffy looks about her with distaste. 'They trusted you and in return you corrupted them. Nor did you stop at the lower orders, as Mrs Williams knows to her great cost. Although that matter shall never be spoken of, neither in court nor elsewhere, do you understand?'

So Mr Williams had found out about the Golden Hour. The realisation hits Ellen like a punch to the guts. He will never forgive Clem now, he will not rest until both of them are locked up, Clem with the parakeets in the asylum, herself with women run desperate with poverty, who had tricked or thieved or sold themselves.

'How do I know I can trust him?' Ellen returns to the letter, frowning at Mr Williams' scrawled signature.

'Do take that look off your face, Miss Harper. You should be thanking me. Male pride is a formidable opponent, let me tell you. I don't like to see a woman locked away, even if it is for twenty pounds a week. Mrs Williams' place is by her husband's side – he knows it, and now so does she.'

Mrs Yorke-Duffy looks at the suitcase once again. 'I believe the duty sergeant is at the station until seven this evening. In any event, Miss Harper, I wouldn't sleep on it. Mr Williams is not noted for his patience.' She stands up. 'I'll see myself out.'

As she reaches the door, she turns, her nose wrinkling in the manner that Clem used to mimic with such precision. 'That cat's in litter. You should put it out.'

Blanche Neige yawns with admirable nonchalance, as Mrs Yorke-Duffy descends at speed down the creaking stairs, the door slamming with finality behind her.

'You've lost your mind.' Reynold folds up the tripod and puts the camera into the wooden carrying case. Outside, the street is darkening, the candle on the mantelpiece weeping wax onto two boat tickets to France. 'I'm damned if I'm going to offer up my throat to be bled just because the vigilants want a scapegoat. No more will you – I won't allow it.'

Ignoring Ellen, he picks up Blanche, the sprawl of her belly spilling from his arms. 'You're going home to your mama, Blanchey, to have your babies, you naughty, silly puss.'

'He'll keep Clem locked up for the rest of her life,' Ellen says flatly. In the distance, the church clock strikes nine. She has tried hard reason and soft tears, she has coaxed, raged, threatened, but to no avail: her brother will go nowhere near the police. He insists on the artistry behind the photographs, repeating that they are no more obscene than Raphael's paintings of nymphs and goddesses. It is on the tip of her tongue to remind Reynold that he is not an acclaimed Renaissance artist, but it won't help matters and so now, hating herself, she pleads instead.

'It's very likely that the court would show us lenience. You've said yourself that one need only walk into any book-shop in Holywell Street to see much worse.'

'I'm not taking that chance. And to be frank, Ellen, I find it inconceivable that you would even ask it.' Gently he places the cat in the basket she arrived in and secures the buckle, making soothing noises as Blanche starts to wail. He looks up at Ellen, his shadowed face unknowable. 'You're choosing some woman – who you've known for five minutes, who *pays* you to be her friend – over me, your brother.'

'When all of this is over,' she says, her heart as heavy, as unforgiving, as a boulder about to roll, 'I will live with you again. We can go where you want – France, Belgium, Holland, I don't care. If you come with me to the police, if we do this together.' She pauses. 'As we always have.'

Reynold lets out a dry laugh. 'We haven't been together since you left me for the American.' Ellen opens her mouth to protest but he stops her. 'You think I'm some kind of idiot? That afternoon in the studio, the two of you were like animals on heat.' He walks to the mantel and slips a single boat ticket into his pocket. 'You know who you remind me of, Ellen? Our precious mother.'

A truth wrapped in an insult: it whips and stings. Hasn't the same thought occurred to her? Isn't he right?

'Reynold.' She reaches for him, wraps her arms about his chest, but it is like expecting comfort from a marble pillar and he stands stiff and hurt and betrayed in her embrace.

'The last train to Newhaven is at ten,' he says, his eyes red as he pulls away. 'I'll be there, waiting.'

And Ellen feels sorry then because it is one of the worst feelings in the world to be left by a person you love, and no one knows that better than her and her brother; and Reynold must have felt the same as she does now, when she left for the Crescent all those months ago. He picks up his case with the same resolve as she had; he takes Blanche and the camera, and he looks at her just once, wiping his streaming eyes with his curled fist, a mannerism as old as their twenty-two years in the world together.

Ellen follows her twin to the top of the stairs, waits for him to turn back, to relent; he does not. The last thing she hears as the front door shuts behind him is the yowl of Blanche Neige, clawing at the soft insides of her, tattering her heart.

Chapter Thirty-Two

The cell is small, surprisingly clean, and very, very white. There is a wooden bed which Ellen is too tall for, a stool on which to sit when she tires of the bed, and a small hole, crudely carved in the door, just above the grille. It is this feature which disturbs Ellen above all else, even more than the metal bucket in the corner with its odours of the farmyard. Over the long, dreary hours she often fancies she hears whispering and muffled laughter; she calls out, tells them to leave her in peace. The warder is a solid red-faced bull of a woman who looks more like an inmate than some of the inmates themselves, and Ellen suspects her of taking bribes, of showing her off to the other prisoners like some freak at a sideshow.

It would be easy, Ellen reflects, sitting hunched on the bed, to lose your wits here, as the days pass, until you can barely recall who you used to be, and all there is is the person you are now – in the dress in which you left your home, now soiled and wrinkled, the gold watch that was once yours confiscated, along with everything else. Every day she hopes for a message from Mrs Yorke-Duffy, but none comes. She has nightmares – Clem, in the public gallery in the courtroom, wearing her black mantilla veil, lifting it slowly as Ellen is brought up to the dock, revealing scalded, puckered skin. She dreams she is a goldfish trapped in a bowl in Mr Crocker's gloomy basement, watching him smile as he feeds drops of vitriol onto a photograph of Lily that writhes and hisses and smokes. And she awakes with her first thought always of Reynold, damning him for leaving her, but understanding why he did. Not knowing where her twin is, or whether he is safe, is as unmooring as her conflated nightmares.

Footsteps come now in the corridor, stopping outside her cell. The key turns. A thought so strange that she can hardly believe it comes from her own head: her mother is here.

But it is not her mother. It is a man with a large smooth forehead and wispy greying hair; his eyes are calm and thoughtful, as, thanking the warder, he steps into the cell as if it is his own front parlour, and offers Ellen his hand.

'Mr Limbrick,' he says. 'Your lawyer.'

There must be some mistake, Ellen tells him, her voice hoarse with disuse, she has no funds for a lawyer. But the door slams shut and Mr Limbrick draws up the stool and pulls a sheaf of papers from his case.

'No need to concern yourself, Miss Harper. My fees are already paid.'

'By whom?' She stares at him. She thinks first of Reynold, but quickly dismisses the thought – the boat tickets to Dieppe had left him with barely a penny.

'An interested party –' he gives her a brief, professional smile – 'who has asked to remain anonymous.'

'A friend?'

'That would be my interpretation,' Mr Limbrick replies, and for the first time in this miserable fortnight, since she turned herself in at the station, Ellen feels a spark of happiness. Here it is – the message from Clem, whose spirit is unbroken and who has found a way, as of course she would, to help her.

'Now,' he says, 'there are two charges against you.' He starts to read from the indictment. 'Assisting in the production and distribution of an unspecified number of indecent photographic prints. Secondly, procurement of young females with . . .'

'With intent to corrupt.' Ellen struggles to keep her voice steady. 'Yes.'

'Quite. And based on your statement, and the voluntary manner in which it was obtained –' the lawyer looks over the top of his spectacles – 'may I take it that your plea will be a guilty one?'

'Not fully,' she says, and Mr Limbrick frowns. 'I plead guilty to the first charge but not the second.'

'I see. But my understanding is that you were responsible for sourcing the women who posed for the photographs?'

'It was never my intention to corrupt, Mr Limbrick. I saw it as a simple transaction.' Ellen pauses. 'I made every effort to employ only those suited to the nature of the work.' Suddenly there is nowhere more appealing to gaze upon than the floor. 'On one occasion, I may have made – I *did* make an error of judgement, that I now deeply regret.'

'Are you referring to Miss March?'

'Yes.'

'May I suggest, Miss Harper, that you make every effort to dissociate yourself from that young woman's tragic death.' His tone is firm. 'There are any number of reasons that might drive a person to take their own life – a troubled mental state exacerbated by a morally corrupt home life, for one. One must search for root causes, rather than an isolated event, and in this case they were extremely tangled.' Mr Limbrick draws out a paper. 'As this letter from Miss March's former employer to the local branch of the Vigilance

Association might attest. It seems this lady – Mrs Hadley – had "grave concerns" that Miss March would be coerced or forced into an incestuous relationship with her uncle, who had also had relations with his sister-in-law, that resulted in pregnancy.'

'It was my fault.' Ellen looks directly at Mr Limbrick. 'I know it and so does God.'

'But what of your brother – Mr Harper? The King's Road business is in his name, as was the lease on your rooms in Booth Lane. If he could be found and convinced to stand trial, it would be the better for you, Miss Harper, I assure you.' He leans towards her. 'Do you know where he is?'

At first, Ellen doesn't answer. 'You would pit us against each other,' she says.

'I would make a case that you were drawn into these illegal activities through loyalty to your brother, rather than of your own volition. Did you not attempt to leave the photography business behind you, last autumn, for a respectable position as a lady's companion?'

'It's of little consequence now.'

'On the contrary, Miss Harper.' The man regards Ellen solemnly, a skein of pale sunlight from the high window falling across his face. 'Now ... we will need to call upon witnesses to attest to your good character. I . . .'

'There is no one.' Ellen feels sorry for the man as his face falls. 'Mr Limbrick, I appreciate your efforts. But I am here in this cell because, in many respects, I am guilty.' She presses her hand to her chest. 'I *feel* guilty. I don't require your services. I shall speak for myself.'

He shakes his head. 'You are making a grave error, Miss Harper. This case has received much public attention – the Vigilance Association is not to be trifled with. I am very much concerned that they will make an example of you – and that your sex will further complicate matters.'

'Because I am a woman?'

'Precisely.'

Ellen gets up, walks across the cell. Her limbs are stiff and do not move as they used to; her body feels like that of someone much older. 'I don't think there is anything else to say.'

'But . . .'

'Please –' she turns to him – 'please leave.'

Mr Limbrick sighs. A good man – Ellen knows it, she feels it – and this too is a problem. How could he ever understand that she desires the punishment, for it is as close as she will come to atonement, after all the sins she has committed, and those she continues to commit in her head, lying alone at night, blocking out the wails and cries from the other cells, and thinking of Clem.

The lawyer is on his feet now. He shakes her hand again and reminds her that the trial has been set for next Tuesday, and she should send urgent word if she changes her mind. She imagines him returning to his offices and composing a letter to Clem – *I am sorry to say that Miss Harper is most adamant . . .*

'The person who sent you –' Ellen hears the quiver in her voice, and hopes Mr Limbrick cannot see the cracks in her – 'is she well?'

He looks at her gravely. 'I am not at liberty to say.'

The warder comes and, as Mr Limbrick leaves, the cell door seems to slam with particular force, the echo of it hovering in the cell long after he has departed.

In the days that precede the trial, Ellen tries very hard to pray. She does it properly, both knees on the cold stone floor, three times a day, just as she had to when they first arrived at Grandmère's house in France, she on one side of her mother and Reynold the other, as their grandmother stood behind them reading extended passages from the Bible. Each time she and Reynold fidgeted or sighed – or their mother audibly wept – Grandmère would stop her recitation and they would hear the squeak of chalk on the blackboard as she added five minutes to prayer time. Ellen often feared that she would never walk again, for whenever prayers were finished, she found herself unable to move, her lower legs and feet left without sensation as if God had seen fit to remove them, and she was always relieved to feel the fiery darts of pain that brought them back to life.

She does the same now, praying first for Lily, and then working her way through the entire roster of models who came to Booth Lane – Corazón, Jemima, Sally, Jilly – the girl with the squint, the girl who ran off with the rum, the girl who had a birthmark shaped like a heart at the base of her spine. She prays for Reynold and the soul of their mother, and their father, on and on, not stopping until the discomfort in her knees and her spine is significant and she has the feeling of being a child again, with rules to obey and consequences to suffer.

From time to time she is allowed out into a dismal yard to exercise. The warders mock the way she speaks, and an ungodly hatred of one in particular whom Ellen overhears calling her a deviant takes seed. And then on the night before the trial, as she is turning the pages of the Old Testament, straining her eyes in the dim light, something inside her snaps. She hurls the Bible across the cell, and swears loudly. She does not believe in this god, she is not sure she ever has, and if he exists at all, he is heartless and cruel and indifferent to suffering, and she wants no part of it. Ellen bangs on the door and calls for the warder. She must see Mr Limbrick immediately, she shouts, she cannot stay in this hellhole a minute longer. Far down the corridor she thinks she hears laughter, but no one answers, no one comes.

Chapter Thirty-Three

They do not handcuff her at least. It is a hot, humid overcast day that compresses the very human smells of the packed courtroom – market-day sweat and ale breath, lavender water and unwashed hair, Mrs Yorke-Duffy's peppermints that she allows herself the comfort of sucking in testing situations, and the faint but pervasive smell of horse dung smeared across the sole of a tableaux girl's boot. They are all here, Ellen sees, looking up to the gallery, as two policemen deliver her to the dock – the vigilants and the girls from the theatre, the costermonger she used to buy cloths from, her next-door neighbour from Booth Lane, with a lap full of children. Housework will have been abandoned, shops temporarily closed for this; they could have sold tickets for three shillings apiece: she feels suddenly terribly afraid and doesn't know how she will stand without trembling. She scours the gallery for Clem, but sees no sign of her or of Mr Williams.

The jury shuffle in and Ellen examines their faces for hints of compassion, wondering how this can be called justice when they are all men. The judge calls for silence and eyes bear heavy upon her as the charges are read. *Production and distribution of indecent images. The procurement of young females with intent to corrupt.* Gasps come from the gallery, as if they didn't know the show they came for, Ellen thinks with scorn, and this thought takes the weakness from her voice as the judge asks her how she pleads.

'Guilty to the first charge, my lord. Not guilty to the second.'

A stirring across the courtroom like a murmuration; Mrs Yorke-Duffy, front row of the gallery, performs a succession of indignant bird-like nods. Their eyes meet. *What have you and your brother done with her, you sanctimonious old bat?* Ellen's hands grip the wooden bar of the dock, as the prosecutor, a Mr Steadman, who even in a wig bears a whiff of the men who loiter among the bookshelves on Holywell Street, presents the case, before calling an Inspector Barrett to the stand. The inspector explains how on the morning of 28th May, a young woman by the name of Miss Susan March had come to the station in a state of distress and handed in an indecent photograph of her sister that had recently come into her possession.

'Miss March's distress was clearly exacerbated by the fact that her sister, Miss Lily March, had been found drowned only a few days earlier.'

'And what were the causes of her drowning?' Mr Steadman asks.

'Regrettably, there is every indication that Miss March had taken her own life, sir.'

The prosecutor bows his head. 'Please continue, Inspector.'

Using intelligence from a source at the Brighton Vigilance Association, with whom they collaborate on occasion, the inspector says, he ordered his men to search the premises of a photographic studio on the King's Road, belonging to a Mr Harper, with the expectation of finding more photographs of a similar nature.

'And what did you find?'

'The storage room where the photographic plates and prints are kept showed signs of recent upheaval – but nothing of an incriminating nature was uncovered. However, we then began a thorough investigation of all possible points of distribution throughout the town – public houses, itinerant booksellers, curio shops and so on. We found several more photographs of Miss March, along with other women, taken in identical surroundings, a selection of which have been submitted as evidence.'

'Exhibit A.' Mr Steadman nods to the clerk, who passes a folder to the jury foreman, and Ellen watches as prints are passed from one man to the next.

'How would you describe the contents of these images, Inspector?'

The man pauses. 'They'd be best described as . . . titillating, sir.' A faint flush rises from his neck. 'Although I regret to say I've seen much worse.'

'Ain't you the lucky one!' comes a voice from the gallery and laughter follows, causing the judge to call sternly for order.

'Miss Harper –' and now Mr Steadman turns to Ellen, and the clerk is collecting up the photographs and passing the folder to her – 'might you tell us what this folder contains?'

She opens it. There, the first photograph Reynold ever took of Jemima, in the pose of the Greek Slave, with the alabaster replica it was based upon on the mantel behind her. Next, the hindquarters of a girl who is unrecognisable, another with no such coyness – Fanny – lying on her side on the couch, then sitting astride the arm of the easy chair, the image slightly blurred. There are more, different girls in varying degrees of modesty, all photographed in Booth Lane, but none – to Ellen's relief – of Lily.

She looks up at Mr Steadman. 'Portraits of young ladies, sir. Taken in our studio in Booth Lane.'

'Portraits of young ladies,' he repeats. 'A rather misleading précis, wouldn't you say, Miss Harper? Would we see these pictures framed on a wall or atop a piano? I think not.'

'They are of an artistic nature, sir, and as such not to everyone's taste.'

'No respectable person's taste, certainly. Did you take these photographs, Miss Harper?'

'I did not. My brother was the photographer.'

'Yes, your brother, Mr Reynold Harper. A warrant out for his arrest too, I understand. And your role in this enterprise?'

'I assisted him.'

'You found these young women. You gained their trust and enticed them to your home.'

'There was work to be had and the women were glad of it.'

Mr Steadman looks towards the judge. 'Permission to bring Exhibit B, my lord.'

Ellen is presented with an envelope. She draws out several prints, aware of the eyes of the court upon her. There are the photographs of Lily playing the nymph at Christmas time, with her crown of twigs and ivy. Ellen feels faint, insubstantial.

'Would you like to tell the court the name of the young woman who is the unfortunate subject of these photographs, Miss Harper?' Mr Steadman nods to the clerk who takes the pictures and distributes them among the jury, their hands and eyes roaming, as Lily is passed along the row. Better Lily were dead than to see this, Ellen thinks, looking away. Better she were dead herself.

'Miss March,' she says finally. 'Lily March.'

'Yes. Miss Lily March. And how did the two of you become acquainted, Miss Harper?'

'We fell into conversation on the pier. She was receiving unwanted attention from a young man and I intervened.'

'Quite the good Samaritan, aren't you? Go on.'

'Miss March confided that she was very unhappy at home. Her father was in prison and his brother – her uncle – had moved in – the two of them didn't get along. She wanted to save money so that she could leave.'

'And so you took advantage of her vulnerable state?'

'Not at all. I wanted to help her.'

'Help her, Miss Harper! Next you'll be claiming you and your brother were running a charitable organisation!' Steadman puffs up his feathers a little more. 'And so you persuaded Miss March to come to your "studio" as you call it, to be photographed naked by your brother?'

'Yes.'

'And three photographs were taken, which were then distributed in the usual manner –' he reviews her statement – 'via mail order and specialist bookshops, is that correct?'

'Yes.'

A sudden movement from the gallery catches her eye and she sees Mr Williams take a seat next to his sister. He sits back, arms folded, his gaze trained upon her. Ellen wonders if he has found out about Mr Limbrick, if he has kept Clem away from the courtroom as punishment.

'And what was your arrangement with Miss March?'

'There was no arrangement.' She remembers Mr Limbrick's counsel. 'Shortly afterwards, I found a new position as a live-in companion and tutor.'

'Quite a change in circumstance, Miss Harper,' Mr Steadman says drily. 'One might even be forgiven for thinking that you had seen the error of your ways.' He indicates the photographs. 'Yet your association with Miss March was far from over, it seems.'

'She wanted more work,' Ellen says quietly. 'She was desperate.' She pauses. 'She would have sold herself otherwise – indeed, I found her in the very act of doing so.'

'And instead you convinced her to sell herself to you!' He looks at her shrewdly. 'What puzzles me, Miss Harper, is why you would go to such great lengths to help this particular young woman, risking your new position, along with the threat of imprisonment.'

'I . . . felt sorry for her.'

'A selfless act of compassion?' He is goading her now, prodding her like a bear in a pit. 'I put it to you, Miss Harper, that you developed an unnatural obsession with Miss March.'

'What nonsense . . .'

'To the extent that you used your influence to secure her a position as a housemaid at the very household where you yourself were posted, installing her in the room next door to your own, no less!' Mr Steadman's voice fills the court. 'You befriended her – an uneducated working woman with few resources – with the sole aim of corrupting her, not only for financial gain, Miss Harper, but to satisfy your own ungodly desires.'

'No!' Her cry is carnal – and she blushes at the sound, and then again at what he is suggesting, there in front of the whole town. For the first time Ellen notices the court reporter, his scratchy pen running away with him – she will be in the newspapers, she realises, her face in the

Illustrated News for all to look upon. She is foolish to have turned away Mr Limbrick: had he not tried to warn her of this?

'No?' Mr Steadman is nothing but a penny-gaff performer playing to the gallery, but how they enjoy him, Ellen thinks dully, how they hang on for the words to come. 'Then how might you explain the photograph of Miss March that you kept among your personal affairs?' He turns to the judge. 'Permission to call the next witness, my lord.'

Photograph? He is lying – she had kept no photograph. But then she remembers, and it seems that every hat in the gallery tilts forward, every neck cranes as the courtroom door opens and the next witness steps forward. Ellen recoils in surprise. It is Mrs Matthews, the housekeeper.

A girl with a cat on her lap, dressed and respectable, hair neat and swept back from a face that is open and hopeful. Ellen cannot look at the photograph for long. It was found, Mrs Matthews is eager to explain, in Miss Harper's Bible when her room at the Williams' residence was cleared out by the maids. Crimson with her determination to exact justice or revenge or to earn whatever the reward which Mr Williams – glowering from the gallery like some vengeful god – has promised her, Mrs Matthews is now telling the court about the night she found Miss March in her night-gown in Miss Harper's room.

'Miss Harper said that Miss March had cramps, sir, and that she was giving her a dose of Pinkham's herbal compound.'

'And did you believe Miss Harper?'

'No, sir. She had no such medicine in her room – I took it upon myself to check the very next day.'

A month or so later, Mrs Matthews continues, when she was locking up last thing at night, she heard sounds coming from Miss Harper's room.

'What kind of sounds, Mrs Matthews?'

'I can't say exactly, sir. Sudden cries – a calling out.'

Better to have had each item of clothing stripped from her, to stand there before the court shivering in her drawers and chemise, than this. Ellen fixes her eyes on the court-room clock.

'And how would you describe these cries precisely?'

'Sir?'

'Were they cries of pain, for example? Was Miss Harper in distress, perhaps?'

'Oh no, sir.' The woman shakes her head. 'Not like that at all.'

'Forgive me for being indelicate, Mrs Matthews, but is it possible these cries denoted pleasure?'

'They did, sir, yes.'

'And what did you do next?'

'As I passed Miss Harper's room on the way upstairs to my own, I heard whispering between her and another woman, whom I took to be Miss March. I was even more convinced that this was the case when I witnessed Miss Harper's reaction to the news of the drowning, barely a fortnight later.'

'And what was that reaction?' Mr Steadman asks softly.

Mrs Matthews turns and looks directly at Ellen. 'Her attachment to Miss March was plain to see.'

Tears slide down Ellen's face as Mr Steadman's voice distorts and fades. Intent to corrupt? What no one but herself knows is how much she'd resisted. She tries to steady her voice as the judge asks her if she has any questions for Mrs Matthews, anything to say in her defence.

'Miss March was lonely,' Ellen says. 'She had not been made to feel welcome by Mrs Matthews or her staff. She came to me for comfort, as one might a sister or aunt.' She turns her attention to the housekeeper. 'Mrs Matthews is very much mistaken in her assumptions.'

'I know what I heard,' Mrs Matthews says stiffly, 'and what I saw too.'

And there is nothing Ellen can say that will not incriminate herself further, or have the meaning mangled out of shape by Mr Steadman, and so she stays silent. As the court adjourns for lunch, animated chatter comes from the gallery – the vigilants are in fine spirits and she hasn't even been sentenced yet. If only Clem were there the pain would be more bearable, she would feel a little less alone. As two policemen come to escort her back to the cells, Ellen senses someone watching her. She looks up. There, sitting alone in the back row, is Harriet Smart, and her demeanour has nothing in common with those who mill about her; she is neither tutting like the vigilants nor joshing like the girls from the theatre. Rather she looks at Ellen with the most profound sympathy, as if she can see straight and clear into her heart.

'Would you like to share with the court how you came to be acquainted with the accused?'

Ellen had thought he wouldn't dare. Yet there he is, her former employer, bristling in the witness box.

'Miss Harper was my wife's companion, and French tutor to my niece, from September last to May, a position which I very much regret authorising.'

Steadman inclines his head. 'Were you not satisfied with the way Miss Harper carried out her duties?'

'Not at all,' Herbert snaps. 'She was something of a charlatan. My niece made little progress – and as such her admission to finishing school was delayed.'

'And how would you describe Miss Harper's relationship with your wife?'

'She took liberties,' he says shortly. 'Took advantage of my wife's good nature. Put ideas in her head. The woman is not to be trusted, sir. She weaselled her way into my house and exploited my wife's generosity – I've recently discovered that Miss Harper was the recipient of a gold watch, worth a considerable amount.' Mr Williams clears his throat. 'Naturally, I cannot comment on the specific charges put to this person –' He looks at Ellen with revulsion and she feels trapped in his gaze, as if she is a specimen in a bell jar, unnamed, unnatural. 'Suffice to say, I found Miss Harper to be a disruptive, indeed, a corrosive presence in my household.'

How much does he know about her and Clem? Ellen looks from Steadman to the judge, who is asking if there is any testimony from Mrs Williams, or Miss Williams, for that matter.

'Mr Williams did not wish to expose his niece to a case of this nature, my lord,' the lawyer says. 'And Mrs Williams is currently incapacitated.'

The judge frowns. 'I see. And may the court know as to the nature of your wife's incapacitation, Mr Williams?'

'Mrs Williams has an acute nervous condition, my lord, for which she is receiving ongoing treatment.' Herbert looks at Ellen with challenge. 'At Ticehurst House.'

He has betrayed her; how could she have believed otherwise? Ellen looks up to the gallery at Mrs Yorke-Duffy, whose expression is hidden under the broad brim of her hat. She thinks again of Mr Limbrick, her certainty that it was

Clem who had sent him, a trick her mind must have played to save her from despair. The judge is addressing her now, asking if she has any questions for Mr Williams, and no, she replies, she doesn't, although she does have an observation to make.

'Mrs Williams was perfectly well,' she says, 'when I saw her last. The illness lies with those who have wrongly committed her to that place—' And what she says next is lost amidst the outburst from her adversary which causes the judge to insist that Mr Williams compose himself, reminding him that they are in a court of law.

It is over now, Ellen tells herself, and her punishment, her sentence, is worse than anything the judge could mete out: her brother has abandoned her, Clem is locked up; Lily is dead and she is the cause. For the first time in her life, she is utterly alone.

Head bowed, Ellen doesn't notice the note the clerk passes to the judge after Mr Williams has left the box, nor the tilt of the judge's left eyebrow that indicates to those that know him best that Judge Hooper is slightly taken aback.

'Miss Harper,' he says, and here it comes, the sentencing, and everyone's eyes upon her, and perhaps they have decided to dispense with the jury, Ellen thinks, for what purpose can they serve when the whole world believes her guilty. 'A witness in your defence has come forward,' the judge goes on, 'who would like to attest to your good character. A Miss Harriet Smart.'

The gasp that resounds through the court echoes Ellen's own: she is confused; it is a trick. But here is Harriet, in a tweed jacket and a high white mannish collar, stepping into the witness box, and most extraordinary of all, her hair has grown into a lustrous dark coil swept up into her green hat.

As the clerk passes her the Bible, she touches the hairpiece; it must feel strange, Ellen supposes, if one is used to hair that is short and close to the scalp. She pictures Harriet at her dressing table, telling the maid that she must be made to look as respectable as possible and today is not the day for cuflinks or gentlemen's hats. Has she come for Reynold's sake, perhaps, a promise made before he left? And now the judge is asking Miss Smart the nature of her association with the accused, and Mr Steadman is sighing and shuffling papers at his seat.

'We moved in similar circles.' Harriet smiles briefly. 'I won't beat around the bush, my lord. I was fully aware of the nature of the Harper photography business, due to my professional acquaintance with several of the models, on whose behalf I would like now to speak.'

They are not here to waste court time with hearsay, Mr Steadman grumbles, taking to the stand, but the judge orders that Miss Smart should continue.

'I am uncertain, my lord, how much the jury might know of the challenges that a life in the theatre presents, particularly for women.' Harriet's voice projects across the court. 'You must travel wherever the work may be; you must sleep in shabby lodgings that are often unsafe. You are your own protector; you must negotiate with theatre managers who will try and cheat you, you are enslaved both to the fickleness of an audience and the outrage of moral crusaders –' she becomes stern as she looks toward the gallery – 'intent on peddling the myth that to tread the boards is tantamount to prostitution. At times – the bad times – it can seem as if one's very life hangs precarious on a thread. You may be paid in free suppers, or pairs of silk stockings, the Queen's currency, or nothing at all; you may sing and dance until your throat is hoarse and your feet blister, and still earn little more than a hot eel seller on the seafront. Is it any surprise, then, that young ladies might seek to supplement an unpredictable income with one that is infinitely more reliable, and for which I am told there is consistent demand?'

Mr Steadman gets to his feet. 'This is all most illuminating, Miss Smart, but may I remind you that it is Miss Harper who is on trial today – not one of the unfortunate women whose circumstances are exploited by the likes of her and her brother.'

'This is exactly my point, sir.' Harriet turns her attention to the jury. 'Do you know, gentlemen, what the models called Miss Harper, among themselves?'

She has come to laugh at her, Ellen thinks miserably, to punish her for what she'd said the last time they met on Marine Parade.

'"The Governess."' Harriet Smart tosses a wry smile to the gallery. 'Yes, amusing in its way, but it is a compliment of sorts. Miss Harper was always – *is* – fair. Proper in her conduct. The models I know were paid well and treated with respect. To claim that this lady –' and she turns to Ellen for the first time – 'had the primary aim of corrupting the models she sourced is disingenuous at best, coming as it does from an organisation so devoted to winkling out invisible sin.'

'There is nothing invisible about an indecent photograph, Miss Smart,' Mr Steadman retorts.

'Save for the gentlemen who choose to purchase them, sir,' she replies, to more laughter, but Harriet's expression is serious. 'And it is doubtful we will ever see any of them standing where Miss Harper is now. It is not an irrelevance to say that my own home was under surveillance by the very organisation whose efforts helped bring this case to court today. Surveillance that resulted in a raid, I might add, on Christmas Eve of last year, where several of my guests – Miss Harper among them – spent Christmas in the cells. As you may be aware, I have since received an apology from the station.'

Her face hardens before she turns her attention back to the jury.

'It is my belief that Miss Harper is being made an example of, because it suits certain people to do so. I commend this woman, gentlemen –' her voice becomes more strident as murmurs of disapproval ripple across court – 'I commend her bravery for giving herself over to the police, when she might well have fled; for taking responsibility for a crime that is as much the fault of the society we live in as it is Miss Harper's alone to be blamed for.' She pauses. 'I ask you to reflect upon this when passing judgement. Miss Harper –' her dark bright eyes settle on Ellen and it is as if it is just the two of them in the room together, and Ellen grips the bar so tightly the veins in her knuckles protrude like cords – 'your brother should be deeply ashamed to have abandoned you in this way. I am sorry.'

She doesn't wait to be thanked. Harriet nods to the judge and steps down from the stand, is gone from the courtroom before Ellen can corral her thoughts, before she has a chance to stutter out a Morse code of apology that only she and Harriet might understand. Ellen recalls in sharp, cruel detail the look of hurt – of betrayal – on Harriet's face when Ellen had accused her, without a jot of real evidence, of being in league with the Croc: how unjustly she has always treated the woman. Little wonder, Ellen thinks, that she has spent her whole life lonely, for she cannot see true goodness, even when it knocks on her front door and delivers a mewling kitten to replace the one that her brother had so loved.

The jury do not adjourn; they huddle. If Mr Limbrick had been there to offer counsel, he would have seen this as an unfavourable sign indeed, but the hearing has overrun as it is, and people would stay all afternoon if they could, for it's not every day you see Harry Smart in a hairpiece for free, fighting the corner of "the Governess" – and a cold, lonely corner it was too; you almost felt sorry for the woman. Hard to imagine her doing things she shouldn't with that housemaid who drowned, but she had blushed so hard when she was accused of it, it seemed true enough. And there's no one can speak for the dead, though that Mr Steadman had a good go, and he got very fierce at the end, calling Miss Harper a 'predator' and the housemaid a 'wretched creature' whose 'overwhelming feelings of shame had led to her sin further by taking her own life.' And Miss Harper had got out her handkerchief then, and told the judge she would never have intentionally hurt her, nor any of the women who came to her studio for their picture, and then she had looked up to the gallery and said she was sorry if that had been so.

Now the jury stop their murmuring and the foreman rises. He is a young man, clean-shaven; his Adam's apple bobs as he swallows, and what reason has he to be nervous, Ellen thinks, when it is her in the dock?

Guilty, your honour, he says, on both charges, and he doesn't look at Ellen once as he takes his seat.

The judge's countenance is weary. Someone's stomach rumbles loudly as he begins to deliver his sentence. He denounces the trade as repellent, and the part she has played in it extraordinary. He can only assume that she was coerced in her turn by her brother, and as such her sentence will be reduced from three months' hard labour to two; and he hopes – and here his attention turns to Mr Steadman in particular – this will bring an end to the whole sorry matter.

Chapter Thirty-Four

On a hazy September morning, when the birch trees that line the approach to Ticehurst House are shedding their golden leaves like tears, and wasps hover over the windfall apples rotting in the orchard, Mr Williams draws up in his carriage to collect his wife. Clem has been told of his coming and is waiting for him; it has been suggested that she might want to make herself 'look pretty', but her face remains shiny, her hair pulled back into what she privately calls a jailer's bun. She sits in the reception room with the matron, her suitcase at her feet, the cloying scent of lilies wrestling with the strong smell of carbolic soap.

'This must be him,' the matron says upon hearing the horses, and calling for a boy to help with the luggage, she goes to the entrance. Clem tenses as the low murmur of voices in the hallway becomes louder.

'Has she eaten breakfast?' her husband is asking and then he is there in the doorway. 'Clementine.'

He looks a little different, Clem thinks, as he crosses the room to greet her, older, slacker, a weariness etched into new lines around his eyes. He kisses her cheek, and the bristles of his moustache prick and graze, and his eyes linger on the middle of her, although there is nothing yet to see. Neither of us will ever truly know, she thinks, as she is led outside, if he would have released me were it not for the child.

But the joy of being out of Ticehurst House, as the countryside flies past the carriage window, green fields and nonchalant cows and hay stacked into bales. The sky stretching on forever as people – ordinary people who do not scratch or weep or rage – thresh corn and cut hedges and take chickens in cages to market. How she longs to see the sea again, to sit at the drawing-room windows at sunset, to walk the length of the pier with the waves acrobatic beneath her, to lie in her old bed with the curtains drawn and memories of Ellen all around. She will find Ellen, wherever she may be, she will sell her jewellery and bribe whoever she needs to; Clem glances at Herbert. He thinks he has won. Well, let him believe it – he will find out soon enough.

'Is Ottilie well?' she asks, but her husband does not turn from the window. And the pleasure of her first glimpse of the sea from the crest of the Downs is short-lived, when instead of taking the descent, the driver presses on deeper into the hills.

'Where are we going?' Clem shakes Herbert's arm, but he tells her coldly that she should calm herself and they'll be home soon enough. And that word – *home* – tolls relentlessly as the carriage rocks across the stony path that leads to Feathers, where he had brought her when she first arrived in England, with the lumpy beds, and cold heavily draped rooms stuffed with dark furniture, and nothing to look at through the windows but fields and trees. The servants are lined up outside and she doesn't recognise a single one of them, and there is still no sign of Ottilie. Welcome home, madam, they chant one after the other, as she follows Herbert to the door, and he stops before a stout older woman with rosy weathered skin, introducing her as Mrs Gately, her maid – 'five children of your own, isn't that right, Mrs

Gately?' and Mrs Gately beams and says yes, sir, there's not much she doesn't know about what a lady needs when she's expecting.

'Where's Milly?' Clem hisses as they go inside.

'Dismissed.' Herbert hands his coat to the servant. 'I thought a new start was called for.' He turns to face her, a severity to him that she cannot reconcile with the man who likes to drink and hunt and finds it amusing to keep a snuffbox with a photograph of a woman's posterior on the underside of the lid. 'I think it's better for all concerned if we keep what's past behind us, don't you?'

It is not a question that she is expected to answer. And just as he is telling her that Ottilie has begun her first term at the Institut Brelmar in Lausanne, information which makes the hollow feeling inside her hollower still, Clem hears a familiar voice.

'Clementine, dear. I do hope you are fully recovered.'

And Caroline Yorke-Duffy steps from the drawing room and wraps Clem in her lavender-scented embrace, before taking her hands and looking at her searchingly. 'I am delighted to see you again – and in such blooming health, too. Now –' she takes her arm – 'I expect you'll want to rest before lunch. I've asked Cook for poached salmon – a favourite of yours, as I remember.'

'You're very kind.' As they start to walk upstairs, Clem is consumed with unpleasant apprehension, as if she is back again at Ticehurst House. 'But surely you are needed in Brighton, Caroline? I don't need looking after.'

Her sister-in-law chuckles. 'Why, I'll stay for as long as I might be useful, dear,' she says. 'Until the baby's safely delivered, at the very least.' She wags a finger at Herbert who stands at the foot of the stairs watching them. 'I've told my brother he has to see about plumbing for the bedrooms. Anyone would think we're living in the Middle Ages!'

And Clem finds herself steered, like one of the cattle she had gazed so fancifully upon from the carriage window, along the dark hallway to her room.

Every morning at seven, a basket of thick matted rope is delivered to Ellen to unpick, and at first she doesn't mind being on her own. Sometimes when the warder has left, the other prisoners call out to each other, and Ellen has been asked several times who she is and what she's in for, but she stays quiet. By the end of the first day, her fingers are swollen and shooting pain flares along her arm when she picks up a spoon to eat her gruel at supper. Midway through the first week, she catches a cold and gets behind with her work, and the warder tells her that if she doesn't step on it, she'll have to do a week extra of picking, and the thought crushes her. Once a week a smiling postwoman walks along the corridor and the other women twitter like sparrows and the air is thick with 'thank you, mum' and 'bring another soon, mum', but later sounds of weeping seep through the walls, and Ellen feels more alone and wretched than ever, for the postwoman never stops outside her cell; and one evening, lying in the dark, she answers her next-door neighbour's hollered request for information.

'My brother and I took photographs,' she says, and she imagines the whole wing, the whole prison listening, as she forces herself on. 'Of women with their clothes down.'

But her neighbour laughs. 'They'll lock you up for breathing next,' she says, before calling out a cheery goodnight. Her name, Ellen later finds out, is Mary; her crime, stealing from the house where she was a maid of all work.

'It was just a shilling or two here and there,' she tells Ellen, as they turn the handle of the wringer in the laundry, where they are both put to work after the first fortnight. 'The master would leave it lying around, like he wanted me to take it. Took him weeks to even notice.'

She can quite imagine, Ellen says, reaching for another pile of sheets. Although her arms ache and her face streams with sweat, she doesn't mind the relentless carousel of bedding and towels, the stained yellowing drawers and petti-coats – she'll volunteer for the jobs the others hate – the scrubbing and the wringing – and she's so fast and efficient that she's heard the women say they like to be on with Harper for their load gets done all the sooner, and the screws don't keep such a tight eye on them either. She is accustomed now to the damp and the clouds of white steam and the squeak of rubber boots across the floor, and as Mary chatters on, Ellen's mind drifts. Last night, she had dreamt about Reynold; he was standing at an open window with a black-and-white cat in his arms – she could hear it purring, and the rise and fall of it was immensely soothing: he-is-well-he-is-well-he-is-well. She had stood awhile in the street below, but when eventually he looked in her direction, his hand had gone to his mouth in horror and the cat had sprung from his arms.

'Ellie!' he cried out. 'Where are your clothes?'

And she had looked down at herself – and saw that she didn't have a stitch on her, and the street filled with people, staring and pointing. She ran through a door and found herself back in the courtroom, naked in the dock, with Harriet Smart on the witness stand, her hairpiece scrunched up in her fist, declaring that she 'doesn't sell herself for anyone, ducky.'

A shriek, followed by laughter, returns Ellen to the laundry.

'They're at it again.' Mary jerks her head towards the troughs across the room, where two of the women are playing snowballs with a sodden flannel.

'That's enough, Fan, you'll get us into trouble,' one squeals to the other, ducking behind the tub, and her companion bobs down next to her out of view, and there is silence.

Ellen glances towards the door. Mrs Flanders had slipped out five minutes ago and told her to keep an eye; she leaves the girls a full minute, before calling out for the next batch. It is Fanny who brings over the basket of laundered clothes, an air of mischief about her, as she dumps it on the floor.

'Not a stain on 'em,' she says with a smirk. 'Scrubbed and jiggered so hard I thought my heart would burst, ain't that right, Lizzie?' and Lizzie giggles and calls her a terror, and as Fanny saunters back to the tubs, Ellen wonders if she is the only one to notice her hand lingering upon Lizzie's hip as she reaches across the trough for the dolly. Fanny sees her watching and grins at her without shame, without malice, and there in the fog and the damp and the sweat, something strange happens. Ellen finds herself smiling back.

After a month of good behaviour, she is allowed pen and paper. Ellen settles herself down to compose the letter she has been writing and rewriting in her head ever since she was sentenced, but the starkness of the recipient's name on the page stymies her and the words won't come.

Dear Miss Smart,
I wish to offer my heartfelt thanks and appreciation for your
intervention during my trial.

I was most appreciative of your kind gesture during my . . .

I would like to thank you for . . .

Either too extravagant or too stilted or too aloof – she imagines Harriet opening the letter at breakfast with Blanche Neige on her lap, and reading it with amusement. *She's a rum one, that mistress of yours,* she will murmur, spreading her toast with marmalade. *Never got the measure of her.*

Ellen saves her last leaf of paper for Clem, a sense of hopelessness overcoming her as she writes, for no asylum matron will sanction a letter from a prison inmate to a patient, no matter how careful and coded the note.

Dear Mrs Williams,
Recent events have left me most concerned as to your welfare.
Might you send word if you are able?
Your friend,
Mrs Holywell

She hands it to the postmistress, telling herself that to try is better than doing nothing, and that with any luck Clem's oaf of a husband will have released her from Ticehurst House, and there remains a wisp of possibility that the letter might be forwarded to the Crescent.

And then one day, on visitors' afternoon, as Ellen is scrubbing flannels in the laundry room, a warder tells her that someone has come to see her, and never has Ellen wished more for a puff of powder to take the shine from her face or a mirror to tidy her hair. It is Clem, she is sure of it, and as she follows the warder through the corridors, she is already imagining Clem's greeting from the other side of the bars. Why, Mrs Holywell, she hears her exclaim, and for a moment everything will be right again, and it will be as if it is just the two of them in Clem's sitting room at the Crescent, planning the next edition of the Golden Hour. But when she enters the visitors' room, scouring the sea of distressed, reddened faces as she might search a pebbled beach for the pearly sheen of a shell, someone raises a hand and comes to the bars, and Ellen sees Harriet Smart.

Her first instinct is to go straight back to the laundry. She thinks of the letter that remains unwritten, and that she wishes now she'd been brave enough to send. Miss Smart must think her the rudest, most ungrateful woman in the world.

But the look on Harriet Smart's face as she greets her is warm. 'Miss Harper – Ellen. May I call you Ellen?'

Ellen's words come out in a rush. 'Miss Smart, I . . .'

'Harriet, please.'

'Harriet.' How is it possible that a simple name should make her blush so? Ellen struggles on. 'I don't know how to begin to thank you.'

'For what exactly?'

'For your assistance. At the trial.'

'Much good it did you.' Harriet looks around with a grimace. 'How is it?'

Tolerable, Ellen says, particularly now she is out of confinement. She rubs at a piece of roughened skin on her wrist. 'Do you have any news from Reynold?'

'None, I'm sorry to say.' Harriet looks soberly at Ellen. 'I meant every word I said in court. He should never have left you.'

'He tried to persuade me to go with him.'

'But you were too intent on punishing yourself. Oh, Miss Harper.' Harriet gives her a sad smile. 'There are times you just about break my heart.' Her dark eyes are liquid; they are the truest, simplest thing Ellen has ever seen, and she vows that if she is ever fortunate enough to operate a camera again, she will photograph Miss Smart as she is now, not Harry from the Empire, but Harriet, in her tweed skirt and jacket, with sleek short hair.

'Is there anything you need? Soap? Toothpaste?' Harriet glances at one of the warders. 'I've heard these prison ladies will turn a blind eye for a bag of sugared almonds.'

There is nothing she can think of, Ellen says, wrestling with the untruth, for there is something she needs much more than lavender soap or dentifrice.

'What is it?' Harriet asks. 'Let me help you,' and so taking a breath, Ellen tells her. She is concerned – very concerned, she says, about her former employer—

'Mrs Williams?' Harriet's gaze is steady, and Ellen's voice quivers as she tells Harriet it would bring her much peace of mind to know if Mrs Williams was released yet from the asylum – and if so, that no harm had come to her since.

'Mr Crocker . . .'

'What of him?' Harriet's face darkens, but then a warder starts to ring a handbell and there is no time to explain about Reynold's debts and what the Croc had threatened.

'I'll make some enquiries about your friend.' Harriet reaches through the bars and briefly squeezes Ellen's fingers. '*Bon courage.*'

Ellen watches her leave. Harriet understands, Ellen thinks, she understands her attachment to Clem as keenly as if the experience were her own. She thinks again of the woman at the party in the orange dress. Six months ago, even a month previously, she would have flatly – stupidly – denied that she and Harriet had anything whatsoever in common. As Ellen returns to the laundry, she is thoughtful. It has taken the self-ishness of a love affair and the tragedy of a drowned girl, a trial and a prison sentence for her to understand what Harriet has known all along: that the two of them are the same.

A week before her release, Ellen is called to the governor's office. He tells her that she should consider herself most fortunate: she has received an offer of employment.

'A laundry matron,' he says, glancing at his notes. 'At the Home for Female Penitents.'

When Ellen does not immediately respond, the governor frowns, his pen hovering over his papers. 'Well – are you in agreement? Mrs Flanders, who has been supervising your work in the laundry here, recommended you for the role.' He looks at her with impatience. 'Or am I to assume you have a superior offer of work awaiting you, Harper? It's a live-in position, and an admirable act of charity and forgive-ness, in my opinion.' The man regards her sternly. 'You are aware, I suppose, that the institution is administered by the local branch of the Vigilance Association.'

'I am fully aware, sir,' Ellen murmurs, and he gives her a sharp look.

'I won't ask again, Harper. Will you take it?'

'Yes, sir. Thank you, sir.'

It is always the same with prisoners from the more respectable classes, the governor thinks, as Harper is taken away: they never quite accept their sentence as their due. He signs the paperwork with his habitual scrawl. If you asked him, the vigilants were mad to take her; there was something about Ellen Harper that was distinctly off.

A note comes from Harriet Smart. Ellen will be pleased to know, she writes, that Mrs Williams is no longer at Ticehurst House; however, the house in the Crescent is up for sale and none of the family has been seen in Brighton for several weeks.

> *On another matter, the girl who used to dress me at the Empire has left to marry a chap. Any interest in acting as her replacement? For as long or as short a time as it pleases you, full bed and board. Something to chew over at any rate.*
>   *Best regards*
>   *Harry*

For a moment Ellen considers it. She imagines standing at the ironing board, pressing creases into Harriet's pinstripe trousers, sewing on loose buttons, dusting powder onto her cheeks and forehead with a rabbit's-foot puff, waiting in the quiet of the dressing room until the show is over before returning to the villa in Hove. But here her nerve starts to fail her and the old terror returns. People will talk, there is no doubt of it – the image of Harriet bobbing like a swimmer between the legs of the woman in the orange dress remains vivid. It is out of the question; it cannot be. But as her last days in prison pass, Ellen's decision worries at her, and as she tosses and turns on her bed at night, it doesn't take long to excavate the real reason why she has agreed to work for the vigilants. It is her last chance – albeit a slim one – of seeing Clem again.

Chapter Thirty-Five

She should never have rented a room to a foreigner, Madame le Prevost thinks, even one who spoke French as nicely as the young Englishman with the camera, whom she'd come upon wandering the streets of the 18th arrondissement in the heat of the summer. Once the deposit was paid, it was clear he didn't have two sous to rub together, and he was a peculiar type, always petting the mangy street cats and feeding them scraps. He'd seemed in perfect health when he arrived, which is far from the case now – and she doesn't like the sound of his breathing, which crackles like a fire in the cold attic room. Madame le Prevost sets down her knitting and leans over the bed, pressing her hand against Monsieur Harper's forehead, rolling her eyes as he calls once again for his sister. Clammy with fever and skin as pale as candlewax – the man has no more chance of seeing his relatives again than she has of high-kicking alongside the girls at the Folies: Madame le Prevost smiles at the thought and examines the photograph of his sister on the bedside table. A distinct absence of jewellery, not even a brooch at her collar, and her clothes, while respectable enough, are work-a-day muslin and wool. Nonetheless, one mustn't jump to conclusions, and that smart-looking camera of his must have cost a bit.

The woman sets about going through his things, noting

that her lodger is clearly not a man of sentiment for there are no letters to be found among the pile of photographic journals, no locks of hair or flowers pressed between the pages of the few books he possesses. She finds crumpled receipts, a discarded museum ticket, a name scribbled on the back of a napkin stained with red wine. A foreigner with next to no people, she thinks grimly, and now here she is caring for him as if he is her own son, and next thing you know, she'll be expected to pay for his funeral too. Then just as she is returning a book to the shelf, she notices a photograph that has fallen from its pages. She picks it up and sees a woman dressed as a man, and looking mighty pleased about it, twirling her top hat on a cane. A woman of the stage – by way of the street, more than likely; but that watch chain could be real gold, and the clothes appear good quality. On the back of the print is a name – Harry Smart – and an English address.

Madame le Prevost goes to the window and whistles to one of the children in the street below. Reaching in her pocket, she tosses down a coin, and tells the boy to fetch a doctor. Likely she's wasting her money, she thinks, as she wets the Englishman's purple lips with water – he'll be dead before the ink is dry on the letter she is about to write; and taking a pen, she begins, offering her sincerest condolences to Mademoiselle Smart, while taking great care not to omit a single detail of her own tireless efforts to ensure Mr Harper's utmost comfort during his final days.

'Sign here.' The warder who is discharging Ellen pushes a form across the desk and then disappears into a back room, returning with Ellen's suitcase. She hands it to her with a sniff.

'There's no excuses for the likes of you,' the warder says. 'I've had girls in here who've never been taught to write their name.' She stares at her. 'You're to take the train to Brighton and walk to the reformatory from the station. They're expecting you.'

She calls to one of the guards, who accompanies Ellen across the wide courtyard to the gates. A fizz of excitement to be in her own clothes again, musty as they are, and reunited with the Golden Hour watch. As she'd walked past the cells, several women had called out to her – *Goodbye, Harper, good luck to yer* – and Fanny had whistled and blown her a kiss. It occurs to Ellen now, as the guard unlocks the gate, that she will likely have to wear a uniform at the Penitents' Home – whoever heard of a laundry matron in a blouse and a gold watch?

Ellen looks up at the sky, an expanse of blue against which clouds merge and split at their will above the green hump of the distant hills: she is free, she is free and she could weep with the relief of it. She doesn't know in which direction the station lies, but no matter, she will take pleasure in finding it, and just as she is setting off down the road she sees someone hurrying towards her: it is a woman, it is Harriet Smart. And she feels a spark of pleasure that Harriet should have come to meet her, and she wishes that she didn't have to tell her that she has accepted a job at the Home. She smiles as Harriet approaches – this woman in her tailored jacket and green hat is part of the joy of the day – so why is Harriet looking at her as if Ellen were returning to prison, not coming out of it?

'Oh, Ellen,' she says, and Ellen's heart plummets and she glances at the grey fortress behind her and wishes she were back inside it, for, as sure as anything, Harriet's pain is about to become her own.

'It's Reynold,' Harriet says, so solemn and serious that it

would be hard to believe she had ever joked about anything in her life. 'He's dead.'

Later Ellen won't remember the journey from Lewes prison to Harriet's home in Hove. It is as if she has died herself, and all physical sensation – the screech of the train, the gusty sea-salted air, the softness of the feather bed in the room overlooking the sea – is diminished. It is the letter from France that finally jolts her, and she hears the waves for the first time as she takes it from the stained envelope, smells the tea that someone has poured for her, notices Harriet with her hand to her chin, standing by the tall windows with the same sorrowful expression that she wore outside the prison.

Ellen does not want to believe it, but the roughness of the paper, the misspellings and the smudges, and the grasping tone of its author, this Madame Le Prevost of the 18th arrondissement, transports her to the streets of Paris and makes it true. She knows them, she smells them – the pig fat and the ordure – and she sees her brother in a chilly *chambre de bonne*, slowly dying as his landlady roots through his possessions for evidence of a wealthy relative to extort or, failing that, something to sell to cover the rent he owes. There is no mistake – it is Reynold, Reynold with the weak lungs, who could never run as far or as fast as she could when they were children. Mr Harper had become very ill, the woman writes, with an inflammation of the lungs, and although she had spent much of her own money on doctors' visits and medicine, there was nothing could be done. *Le jeune anglais* had died peacefully nonetheless and Ellen puts the letter down and cannot read on. No one dies peacefully when they drown, and Reynold will have drowned in the rising tide of his lungs, he will have struggled and sweated and called for her to help him. Might we close the window? she asks Harriet, for all she can hear now is the relentless surge of the sea through the pebbles, becoming louder and louder, and with it the room sways and tilts as if it is being tossed from one wave to another.

'Mattie!' Harriet calls out. 'Matilda!' A frenzy of footsteps follows, and the last thing Ellen remembers is the sensation of being caught in the soft strong cradle of someone's arms.

Clem had never imagined that the business of carrying a child would be so undignified. Little wonder that illustrators like to depict the whole sorry business with storks bearing white cloth bundles, if what she is experiencing now is a warning of worse horrors ahead. She is fat and clumsy and uncomfortable – her ankles, usually so finely turned, are swollen as ripe figs, her stomach as taut and tight as the skin of a drum. She can no longer tolerate the smell of coffee nor the taste of red wine, and on occasion, usually after breakfast, she farts like a peasant. The other morning, her sister-in-law had sternly reprimanded her. You forget yourself, Clementine, she had said with a frown, to which Clem could only silently agree. She *was* forgetting herself, a little more each day.

She is permitted only the gentlest of exercise, and then only in the company of either Caroline or Mrs Gately. If it is too cold or wet or windy, they will not allow it and she is confined to the drawing room, where if she is particularly unlucky, one of Caroline's new acquaintances from the League of Friends will pay them an impromptu visit. Her sister-in-law had wasted no time in making her presence known in the small village and had infiltrated both the church committee and the local sewing circle, and recently delivered a lecture to the Temperance Society on 'The Suppression of Vice in Provincial Theatres' of which she was most proud. As they sit, morning after interminable morning in the breakfast room, Clem prays that urgent vigilant business will one day send Caroline on her way, but so far the contents of the committee-meeting minutes that arrive regularly by post have failed to dislodge the sentinel from her watch.

Herbert spends his time on the estate or on horseback – he is rarely at home during the day and retires to his study, a room which is now always locked, directly after dinner. He hasn't come to her bed, not once, since she arrived, and sometimes Clem finds herself wishing he would, just for the novelty of it. She spends long lonely nights thinking of Ellen, imagining her broad smooth hands caressing the parts of her which have not been contorted by the baby. She thinks of the Golden Hour photographs and wonders how many men have looked at her and desired her, remembering how naive she'd been on that day she and Ellen went bathing, when she'd insisted that she didn't care about the consequences, that she wanted a divorce, that she had nothing. Ellen had been right to resist because now she has lost Ellen too – and no one will say what has become of her, because Herbert won't have mention of her name.

One rainy afternoon in the middle of November, Clem finds herself alone and unsupervised. Caroline is at the church bazaar; Mrs Gately is visiting her sister who has shingles; Herbert is out riding. There is always a reason why a room is locked, Clem thinks idly, turning the door handle of her husband's study back and forth, and at the same moment one of the girls who comes in to clean from the village walks past with a basket of cloths and dusters.

'Do you want to go in, madam?' she asks. 'They told me to lock it when I was done,' and she pulls a set of keys from her pocket and slides first one and then another into the lock, and before Clem can reply, the door is opened and the maid has gone on her way.

With quiet triumph, Clem steps into the darkened study. As she looks about her, she smells the secrets of which Herbert is so ashamed, feels Ellen's presence as if she were there with her. He thinks he can just bury what has happened as if it is a dead dog – well, it is time to uncover the truth. Clem starts to sift methodically through the drawers, uncovering bills, receipts and several pleading letters from Ottilie in Lausanne, begging her uncle to let her come home. She should enjoy what little freedom she has while it's available, Clem thinks; the poor girl will be married by the time she turns eighteen, and she'd tell her as much if it weren't for Caroline reading every letter she writes before it's dispatched. She opens the bottom drawer and finds a bundle of her sister-in-law's recent correspondence, all unremarkable, until she comes to a letter from Miss Hinchlin, dated 2nd October, from which Ellen's name leaps from the page.

Upon her release from prison, Miss Hinchlin writes, Miss Harper had not reported for duty at the Home for Penitents. Some enquiries were made and she was found to be living in Hove, having been taken in by Miss Harriet Smart, who is known of course to the association and whom Mrs Yorke-Duffy will doubtless also remember from the woman's futile attempt to convince the jury of Miss Harper's good character. The position of laundry matron, Miss Hinchlin goes on, still remains vacant, which – of course – is most inconvenient.

Clem glares at the painting of a cocker spaniel with a

pheasant in its jaws on the wall opposite, and utters a word that had once had her confined to her room in the asylum for two nights and a day. So this was how Herbert had exacted his revenge; he – and the vigilants – had put Ellen on trial, so that she too could be locked up, before then humiliating her further by offering her work in the reformatory, that Ellen likely had little option but to accept. Yet Miss Smart had stepped in to help her, and Clem feels peculiar at the thought of it. She remembers the night at the theatre – Harriet Smart's song about the 'prudes on the prowl', her teasing looks towards their box. Was the performance prompted by jealousy, had Harriet perceived her as a threat? Clem curses her husband again. It should have been her standing in the witness box defending her friend, not some attention-hungry music-hall artist – it was she who should have been there when Ellen came out of prison. Ellen will think that she has abandoned her, forgotten her completely.

Clem slams the drawer, her breath coming quickly as she thinks. Her beloved husband has hypocrite running through him like 'Brighton' through sugared rock: he must be up to something, locked away in here every night – does he honestly expect her to believe that the Golden Hour photographs were the first of that kind he had seen? Don't let me down, Herb, she mutters, drawn again to the secret compartment where she first found his snuffbox. The drawer releases and the snuffbox, of course, is still there. It makes Clem smile now to see the woman under the lid, to remember herself so shocked little more than a year ago; she takes the key and unlocks the drawer. And there, underneath Barnaby's reports from Eton, wrapped in white tissue like something precious, are the six Golden Hour photographs that Ellen had taken of her. The corners are worn, she notices; they have been thumbed through, pored over, used.

Clem gathers up the photographs. She leaves the drawer half open, the snuffbox on the desk. As she comes out of the study, she sees a maid passing with a tray of dirty plates from lunch – Clem slips one of the prints into the girl's apron pocket.

'Yours,' she says, with a smile. 'To keep.'

Then she goes to the kitchen, where the cook and the kitchen maid are chopping vegetables, and tosses two more on the table like playing cards. 'I think they've come out rather well, don't you?'

She hands one to the boy who is cleaning boots in the passageway, another to the merchant who has just arrived with the coal. 'Someone fetch the master,' she hears the cook say with rising panic, but she turns and says that won't be necessary, for the master has already seen them many times. The servants stare at her in horror – and oh, what fun it is to play the mad woman – and here now is Mrs Gately, shaking out her umbrella, back from seeing her sister, and frowning at the sight of Clem below stairs.

'Are you quite well, Mrs Williams?' she asks, and Clem presents her with the remaining print of herself sipping tea bare-breasted by the mantelpiece and watches the woman's face flush and crumple.

'One of my husband's favourites, Mrs Gately,' she says. 'When my figure was unspoiled. I'll be in my room if Mr Williams needs me.'

And smiling pleasantly at the silent servants, she goes upstairs and waits.

Chapter Thirty-Six

R eynold's remains arrive by boat a week later in a copper urn. They sit above the fireplace in the bedroom which Ellen has barely moved from since she first arrived, and to begin with she hardly notices them because she is certain that she is dying. Her heart scampers, she wheezes and gasps, her skin is either hot with fever or frozen with chills. A doctor comes and diagnoses pneumonia, prescribes absolute rest and plenty of it. Every morning Mattie brings beef tea and buttered toast, and opens the windows wide to let in the 'good air', and every afternoon before she goes to the theatre, Harriet – and Blanche Neige – come to sit with her. Ellen wakes one day to find Harriet practising her steps for that evening's performance in front of the wardrobe mirror, twirling the fire poker as she hums out a tune.

> *I'm in love with the girl from the gallery.*
> *I'm in love with the lady from the box.*

The cat cries for attention and Harriet scoops her up, petting her in exactly the way that Reynold used to, and for the first time since the news of his death, Ellen starts to cry, and it is a long time before she can stop. Harriet sits on the edge of the bed and rubs her hand. She tells her there's nothing she can say that will make it better, and she's sorry, but perhaps when Ellen is back on her feet, she might want to think about giving Reynold a send-off? Harriet nods towards the urn. The tableaux gals have been asking, she says, adding that anyone would think it was their own brother who had died they were that upset, and she wouldn't be surprised if Corry exchanged her body stocking for black crepe! They send their regards to their old Governess, she goes on, and hope she's on the mend soon.

'I always thought they rather despised me,' Ellen says, with a small smile.

'They just like to lark about.' Harriet shrugs. 'You – of all people – know what girls are like,' and then her face loses its humour as Ellen's tears start up again. 'And now I see I've upset you.'

'What that man – Mr Steadman – said at the trial was true.' Ellen wipes her eyes. 'If I hadn't taken Lily's photograph, she would still be alive today. I'm sure of it.' And she tells Harriet about Lily's uncle finding the photograph, and how distressed Lily had been.

Harriet considers this. 'Seems to me it's Uncle Jack who should have been in the dock, not you.'

'You didn't see her – she was distraught. She came to me for help – and I was too . . .' Ellen looks away. 'I was preoccupied with another matter.'

'Forgive me if I speak out of turn.' Harriet gets up and walks to the window. 'But from what I've seen, Mrs Williams takes a rather fine photograph and I doubt very much she's about to throw herself from the pier, any more than Corry or Sal or Jemima ever would.' She looks at Ellen gently. 'I assume that was how you found yourself strung up before the vigilants? Mrs Williams' husband found out about the photographs of his wife, and you were forced somehow to come forward?'

'You knew?' Ellen stares at her. 'About Clem ... Mrs Williams?'

'I was there one afternoon with your brother when the prints were drying,' Harriet says in her nonchalant way. 'Very accomplished, incidentally – strides above what Reynold could do.'

When Ellen next speaks, she cannot meet Harriet's gaze. 'You have heard no further news, I suppose?'

'Of Mrs Williams?' Harriet shakes her head. 'But I'll keep my ear to the ground. Anyway –' she glances at the clock – 'duty calls. Be sure to call Mattie if you need anything.' As she goes to the door, she lays her hand on Ellen's shoulder. 'You let your heart take you to the wrong places, my dear, if you don't mind me saying. I've wanted to tell you for the longest time.'

She is gone before Ellen has a chance to reply. Blanche jumps on the bed and curls up next to her, purring loudly. Absently, Ellen strokes her, and as she stares at the urn, another scattered piece from the past months falls into place and she is back in her cell, looking into the kind concerned face of Mr Limbrick, the lawyer she had sent on his way. She exclaims out loud and the cat yawns, as if to say how tiresome it is to keep company with a person so dull-witted and slow. It was Harriet who had sent Limbrick, Harriet who had offered the lifeline she had so stubbornly refused to take.

When Ellen is well enough, she and Harriet start to take daily walks along the promenade, short distances at first, not even as far as the pier. And Ellen begins to look forward to them, even when the wind howls and the rain falls horizontal, for every time she comes back knowing a little more about Harriet Smart. Afterwards, when Harriet has left for the theatre, Ellen will sit in front of the fire and try to marry what she has just learnt with what she already knows of her host; it is like turning the lens of a kaleidoscope and taking delight in the new pattern in which the coloured particles fall.

Harriet was brought up in an orphanage in Bermondsey, Ellen discovers, a strict, sad type of place, run by nuns, where there was no sight more fearsome than a certain type of nun with the power gone to her head and a birch whistling as it flew through the air towards its victim's trembling upturned palm. They called her Teresa after one of the saints, a name Harriet had to share with five other girls, and the only thing she liked about the place was singing hymns on Sundays and acting out Bible stories for the patrons who came at Christmas and Easter to sip tea and give each other a pat on the back for how charitable they were.

And then, just after her seventh birthday, Theresa's life changed. A few times a year, visitors would come to the orphanage, people who couldn't have children of their own and wanted to fill the emptiness. In warmer weather, they would stand and watch the children playing outside, and if a nun came and took you by the hand, you knew you had to be on your very best behaviour, and say 'ma'am' and 'sir' after everything, and hold out your right hand to be shaken, even if it made the grown-ups laugh. It was usually the girls that got picked – and always the sappy, pretty ones, Harriet said, with the curls and pink cheeks, who looked like they'd stepped out of a picture book. She'd never once been selected and she'd given up hoping for it, and so on this particular Visitors' Day she had snuck off to play marbles in a corner of the yard with a very wicked boy named Albert, whom everyone called Birch because he was on the receiving end of it so often. One of the visitors that day was a large, red-faced man with a booming voice and a shiny yellow waistcoat, and he didn't look at all sad and sorrowful, and there was a woman with him, in a bright blue dress with ribbons in her hair, who made the nuns' faces pinch and purse.

'I wanted more than anything for them to notice me,' Harriet told Ellen, 'and so I started larking about.'

She'd begun singing 'All Things Bright and Beautiful', but the yard was noisy and no one paid much attention, so then she sat on Birch's shoulders and made him stand and there she was, with her skirts and petticoats rucked up, stockinged legs dangling around his neck, belting out the hymn as if she were born to the music hall. She got as far as *Each little flower that opens*, before Sister Carahew bore down upon them, and if it hadn't been Visitors' Day, she would no doubt have birched them or worse on the spot. The nun had just pinched Harriet's ear and called her a little heathen, when the jolly couple in the colourful clothes sauntered over.

'What's your name, Miss Mischief?' The man in the waistcoat bent down and smiled at her.

'Teresa, sir.'

'What a pretty name,' the lady said, and then Harriet, whose ear was still stinging and who knew she would be getting the birch the minute they'd gone, had said she didn't like it, which made the lady turn to the gentleman and laugh. And they didn't ask her if she said her prayers every night and respected her elders, but instead whether she liked to sing, and she told them she did very much, and act out the story of Noah and his animals too, and all the time poor Birch stood there next to her and no one paid him any attention at all.

'How would you like to learn to play the piano, Teresa?' the man asked, and she said she would but more than likely the sisters wouldn't let her, and he said they'd see about that, and before they left the lady patted her cheek and said she was a funny, dear little thing and they would be back to visit her next week, if she'd like it.

'And they became my parents.'

They are in Harriet's study, on a Sunday afternoon, with the weather too foul to walk, looking at the photograph of Harriet and the beaming couple outside the music hall that had roused such envy in Ellen on the night of the Christmas party.

'Ambrose and Eliza Smart,' Harriet goes on. 'Best thing that ever happened to me. He managed a music hall in the East End, and safe to say I never sang 'All Things Bright and Beautiful' again.'

And Ellen remembers the Bible, with the inscription to Teresa Middleton of St Mark's Orphanage; as if following the train of her thoughts, Harriet goes to the bookshelf and passes the Bible to her.

'I keep it to remind myself of my good fortune,' she says. 'Not everyone was as lucky as me.'

Ellen looks at the cheap cloth binding, the starkness of the lettering on the cover, and it brings with it a certain feeling – of fear, uncertainty, a desire to flee. She has seen this same Bible somewhere before, and the feeling becomes stronger, and the picture comes into focus. A fish tank, the jaws of a pewter crocodile, and then Mr Crocker himself, opening up an identical edition and taunting her with the photographs he concealed in its pages.

'What happened to the boy – Birch?' she asks, and Harriet says nothing for a moment, but she doesn't have to for it is all making sense – Mr Crocker in the best box at the Empire, Harriet's photograph on his mantelpiece, Harriet coming out of his house and slipping away into the mist.

'He turned bad, I'm sorry to say.' Harriet returns the Bible to the shelf. 'And now there's no way back.'

'Are you still friends?'

'I wouldn't say we were friends. More like estranged siblings. And as you know, brothers are not always as receptive as they might be . . .'

'To the opinions of their sisters, yes.'

They smile at each other in the flickering firelight, before Harriet looks away, calling Blanche to her lap, and as she sits there, crooning to the cat, she seems a little shy, a little awkward, and it is Ellen who desires to draw her back.

'You warned me about Mr Crocker,' Ellen says. 'And of course, you were right.' She pauses. 'The last time I saw him, he threatened me. Not just me, but other people . . .' She hesitates. She remembers Fanny and Lizzie in the prison laundry; she must stop being ashamed and say what she feels – this is Harriet, and the least she owes her is the truth. 'People he knew I cared for,' she goes on. 'Reynold. Ottilie, my pupil. And Mrs Williams – Clem.'

Harriet gets up and lights a cigarette. She stands by the mantelpiece, shirtsleeves rolled to the elbow of her slim arms, one hand rubbing the nape of her bare neck as she regards Ellen thoughtfully through a haze of smoke.

'And there are still debts that I must settle,' Ellen says, and there Harriet stops her.

'The debt is cleared.'

'But how?'

'Let's just say that there are times when Birch can be made to listen.' Harriet flicks ash into a tray. 'He won't be troubling you again.'

'Did you pay him?'

'I may have given him a small financial incentive. But mostly I convinced him. I know him, you see, as no one else does.' Harriet shoos Blanche from her chair and sits down again. 'But the proof – as they say – is in the pudding. Perhaps you might like some assurance that it's baked?'

'Meaning?'

'Meaning that if you feel well enough, it might be time to pay Mr Crocker a visit.'

Ellen stands with Harriet on the Croc's doorstep, her nerves dissipated somewhat by the defiance of Harriet's cologne and Reynold's voice inside her head. *You see, Ellie,* he is saying warmly, *she* is *our friend!* And it is pleasant indeed to have this brother back, not the one who left her, or who tried to persuade her to marry, but the Reynold whom she grew up with, playing hoop and reading stories and helping with the arithmetic he could never do, the brother whose hand she used to reach for at night after Maman had left. She glances at Harriet. Reynold had recognised what she herself had refused to: Harriet's extraordinary light, her bold appetite for both the pleasure and the pain of life that means she will always choose to sit on a boy's shoulders and sing, even if it means the birch; she will host raucous parties with cancan girls who show their legs, and never mind what the neighbours think; she will find love where it pleases her to find it, and Ellen is somehow glad that the woman from Christmas Eve has not reappeared at the house. And it is as if Harriet can sense her thoughts, for she turns to Ellen just as the door opens and smiles.

'Oh my. What a pair you make.' It is the Croc himself, not the bearded man as usual; he leans against the door jamb and appraises them.

'Where's your gorilla, Albert?' Harriet folds her arms and appraises him back. 'Run off to join the circus?'

'Called away on urgent business.'

'Is that so?' Harriet and Mr Crocker shake hands in a manner that is more wrestle than greeting. 'Are you going to let us in?'

Silently, he stands back, and Ellen follows Harriet downstairs to the basement, where a low fire spits in the grate. Tossing a crumpled copy of *Racing Illustrated* from the couch, Harriet sits down, gesturing to Ellen to do the same.

'You know why we're here, Albert.'

Mr Crocker ignores her, his gaze fixed on Ellen. 'You didn't put up much of a fight in court, Miss Harper – almost like you were asking to be sent down.' He looks from her to Harriet and laughs. 'Harry was wasting her breath. And to think you always looked at me like something that had dropped from a horse's arse.'

'That's enough,' Harriet says sharply, telling him to fetch the paperwork they talked about. Mr Crocker goes to his desk and, with much theatre, takes a document from one of the drawers and signs it.

'Pleasure doing business.' He smiles, dangling the bill of receipt between his fingers, as if it is bait and Ellen the dumb animal to be enticed.

Ellen snatches it from him. The bill states that Reynold's debt is cleared, and as she looks around the sad, squalid room, she reminds herself of what Harriet had told her – that this man who is feared across Brighton, who has created his own mythology, was once a boy abandoned by his parents, and beaten by nuns for wetting the bed. And there is the evidence in the Bible on the shelf behind him, the white threaded veins of the spine.

'Haven't you forgotten something?' she says. 'The photographs. I'd like them back, please.'

'I'm sure you would,' the Croc says. 'But that ain't part of the deal.'

'The "deal",' Harriet says icily, 'was that you behaved yourself – Birch.'

He flinches, a new uncertainty in his eyes, as Harriet strides across the room and pulls the Bible from the shelf. She delves in the pages for the photographs, removing them one by one.

'How would you like Birch to dispose of these, Miss Harper?'

'Don't call me that.' His teeth – misshapen, neglected – are bared, but he cowers a little as if he expects to be hit.

'Burn them,' Ellen says.

'Do as she says.' Harriet glares at him. 'Or I'll tell your men – every last filthy one of them – that their precious Croc is Bedwetter Birch from St Marks who used to soil his sheets every night for a month after Visitors' Day.'

'Pair of bitches,' he mutters and then, seizing the prints from Harriet, he calls them far worse as he throws the photographs one by one onto the flames. The pictures blister and shrivel as the room fills with an acrid, bitter smell.

When the last photograph has been destroyed, Harriet offers him her hand. 'No hard feelings, eh, Albert?'

The string of curses that follows is sign enough that it is time to leave, and as the two of them emerge onto the street, Harriet raises a quizzical eyebrow.

'I'd almost feel sorry for the man,' she says musingly, 'but I could never forgive him for what he did to Flossy.'

And she takes Ellen's arm for the first time, and it feels like the most natural thing in the world to walk that way, with the smell of burning in their hair and clothes, laughing at the ruthless moneylender, who could be reduced so easily to who he was by a childhood nickname.

The day they scatter Reynold's ashes is cold and sharp and bright. He would have appreciated the light, Ellen thinks, the sun slanting low across the shingle, the pebbles glistening with frost, as a small group congregates: Harriet, the three tableaux girls, the Ice King, and the landlord from the Jolly. On the promenade a brass band plays carols, and the smell of roasting chestnuts wafts across the beach. Corazón, in a berry-red cloak, cries when she sees the urn, and says it isn't right that they burnt him, and Jemima and Sal tell her to hush for she'll upset Miss Harper with all her carrying-on, and Ellen feels a fondness towards them. Harriet was right – they mean no harm.

There are to be no prayers, she'd told Harriet, Reynold wouldn't have liked it, and Harriet reminds everyone of this as the urn is passed from one to the other and a murmuration of cinders flies into the silver sea. Tears course down Ellen's face as the waves swell and retreat, and she thinks of Lily again – and she is sorry. This grief, the circling, wheeling nature of it, is as much part of her now as her own blood; it is hers to live with, hers to survive.

Harriet has brought champagne, and the mussel and whelk and cockle sellers watch from their barrows with curious expressions as Ellen raises a toast.

'To Reynold,' she says, 'and to Lily,' and she looks at

Harriet, in the navy peacoat that suits her so very well, the peacock feather in her hat fluttering in the wind, and the hollowness of her loss seesaws briefly with an entirely different emotion – and her heart skitters.

There's champagne on ice at the house, if anyone should want it, Harriet says, and they all agree that they would, and as they walk to the villa, Ellen asks Harriet if she still finds herself in need of a dresser at the theatre.

'Are you sure you feel ready?' Harriet asks, and Ellen nods.

'Then I should like that very much.' Then Harriet takes hold of her hand and presses her thumb into Ellen's palm. This is not a pat on the shoulder, or a linking of arms, it is a caress or it feels like one. But then the moment is over, and they are at the villa and Harriet is ushering everyone inside and asking for oysters to be sent up with the champagne. Mattie glances at Ellen as she takes their coats and hats.

'There's a visitor come for you, Miss Harper. I told her you weren't at home, but she wasn't for leaving and I didn't want to put a lady in her condition out.' She winces apologetically. 'I showed her to the parlour.'

'Who is it, Mattie?' Ellen asks. She fears the answer suddenly – 'a lady in her condition'; what can she mean? – and as she takes off her glove she feels again the pressure of Harriet's thumb, as if it were still nestled there.

Harriet picks up the visiting card from the salver. 'Well,' she says. Her mouth works as if she doesn't quite know what to do with it as she hands the card to Ellen. 'It seems that Mrs Williams has arrived.'

Chapter Thirty-Seven

The longer Clem sits waiting in Miss Smart's parlour, the sharper her feeling of envy. It is not the villa itself, for her former residence in the Crescent was far bigger – and much smarter too; and there is much to criticise here, if one were inclined – such a number of photographs on the wall there is barely any need for wallpaper, and many would say it is the height of vulgarity to put so many pictures of oneself on public display. The baby chooses this moment to deliver a robust kick to her insides, as if to remind her that she is not one to lecture on the subject of vulgarity, and Clem strokes her belly as she continues her appraisal of Miss Smart's living quarters. There is a wine stain on the Turkish couch, a book with a broken spine tossed face down on the easy chair opposite, and the whole room smells faintly of cigarette smoke. No, nothing to envy here at all – and yet . . . The woman's picture is everywhere – surrounded by bouquets of flowers and taking a bow on a stage; triumphant outside a music hall, with her name on the billboard; smoking on a wing-backed chair in a gentleman's suit. There is no husband to commit her to an asylum, or prevent her from speaking in court, a state of felicity – and now Clem tries to cheer herself – that will also soon be her own.

Her mother had not taken the news of Clem's impending divorce well. She had sent an impassioned letter, reminding her of the fate of Mrs Burtenshaw, a divorcee from Long Island, who was snubbed wherever she went, no matter her amiable disposition and gowns from Worth. While conceding that the settlement from Herbert was generous, this of itself made her even more furious with her daughter, for she simply *failed* to understand why such drastic measures were required after barely two years of matrimony. Why, they were only just settling in! she had written. Clem lays a hand on her stomach. Her mama would be even more shocked if she knew what she'd had to bargain with.

Mrs Gately had resigned on the same evening that Clem had distributed her Golden Hour photographs among the staff at Feathers. She had thought she was working for a lady, the woman had told Herbert angrily, and the cook had almost followed suit, before Caroline offered her and all the servants affected two shillings more a week. A long conversation had taken place between her sister-in-law and husband behind the closed door of his study, and when he emerged he had come up to Clem's room, and with more weariness than anger had asked her to tell him what she wanted, so that this hell she was subjecting him to would stop.

'A divorce,' she said, and for the first time he had listened.

Clem hears voices and goes to the window. A small group of people are approaching the villa – a dark-skinned girl in a red cloak, and her two companions; a tall rosy-cheeked gentleman who is quite handsome, Clem notes, and another man who is not; and then at the rear of the party she sees Ellen, deep in conversation with Harriet Smart. Clem is unprepared for the surge of jealousy, like two stinging slaps to the cheek, and then the misery that follows it. I have been replaced, she thinks unhappily as she watches them – Ellen, paler and slighter than she remembers, her black hat and cloak more suited to mourning than the festive period. And then, briefly, Miss Smart takes hold of Ellen's hand, and Clem's slapped cheek stings afresh.

She returns to the couch, as downstairs the hallway fills with voices, before a quietness descends, prompted, she supposes, by the announcement of her arrival. Her heart hammers when she hears Ellen's voice, and she checks her reflection fretfully in the mirror. Even her face is fat, with a chin that is beginning to compete with her sister-in-law's – she will be lucky indeed if Ellen even recognises her.

The door handle turns and Ellen walks in and says her name.

'Oh, Clem.' Ellen doesn't move from the door. She has never seen a woman as close to term as Clem is now, and for a moment Clem's distended belly, the ampleness of her bosom, the incontrovertible truth of her pregnancy, is all she can see. Clem eases herself to her feet and stands there expectantly, looking very much as if she might cry.

'I suppose –' her voice wavers – 'that this is something of a surprise.'

'Yes, somewhat,' Ellen says, before pleasure overcomes shock and she smiles at the earnestness in her own tone, and Clem smiles back and then they are in each other's arms – or as best they can with the baby's bulk between them.

'I'm so relieved you're well.' Ellen takes Clem's hand as they sit down, but Clem looks at her oddly and flushes.

'Well? Ellen, I am far from well.'

'Healthy, then.'

Clem draws her hand away and lets out a small angry laugh. 'Yes,' she says, 'I suppose I am healthy, all said.'

Neither speaks. From the room next door comes the warm hum of conversation, the popping of a cork. Ellen has yearned to see Clem for so long, thought of it constantly when she was in prison, but now that the moment is here the right words desert her, and she is no better than a vigilant at a meeting, making inane remarks about Mrs Williams' health.

She tries again. 'I'm sorry.' She looks towards Clem's stomach. 'I know how much you wanted to avoid . . .'

Clem sighs. 'My body clearly couldn't rest easy until duty was done and I was turned into a pumpkin.' She smiles ruefully and lets Ellen slip an arm around her slim shoulders, sighs again as she leans against her, slipping her fingers under the lace of Ellen's cuff.

'You're not wearing the watch,' she says. 'Do you still have it?' and Ellen tells her that yes, of course, but she must have forgotten to put it on when she was dressing earlier – she has been somewhat preoccupied today, she says, and then Clem sits up a little straighter and touches the black ribbon at the neck of Ellen's blouse.

'What's happened?' she asks, taking in for the first time Ellen's red-rimmed eyes, the faint tracks of tears on her cheeks.

And so Ellen tells her, all about Reynold and Paris and how, upon her release from prison, she had become ill herself and how kind Miss Smart has been, and at the mention of her name, Clem stiffens.

'I'm glad there was someone to take care of you,' she says. 'But I am here now.'

And then there is a knock on the door and Mattie appears with two glasses of champagne, and a steaming cup of Darjeeling 'in case Mrs Williams has no taste for the other'. But Clem does have appetite for the other and she takes the glass and clinks it against Ellen's – and as Ellen takes her first sip, she thinks of Harriet instructing Mattie to take some champagne to the ladies, while she entertains Ellen's guests, at Ellen's brother's wake, and if Reynold were here he would no doubt have some choice remarks to make on the subject. And she looks at Clem, at the flower of her face, still open and unchanged despite everything, the gold sheen of her hair, less fussed over than it used to be, blue eyes made indigo in the darkening room; and she remembers lying under her, over her, beside her – and her body reminds her how long it is since she has been touched.

Ellen takes Clem's wrist and presses her mouth to it. 'I really am very pleased to see you,' she says, and when she looks up Clem's eyes are half closed and her dimples are showing.

'Dear Ellen,' she murmurs, reaching out to touch Ellen's hair. 'I'm so glad we can be together again, as we were.' She gives her a roguish smile. 'You must be sure to pack some woollen underthings, for Manhattan winters can be harsh. I shall buy you a sable muffler and fur-lined boots, like mine, and you'll be warm as toast.'

'Manhattan winters?' Ellen looks at her, puzzled.

Clem clasps her hands, her eyes shining. 'The past few months have been unspeakably awful, but it's all come to good. Herbert's agreed to a divorce. Yes,' she goes on, when Ellen doesn't reply, 'I can hardly believe it, either. But we have agreed upon a settlement – he has not been ungenerous.'

Unease steals through Ellen: what has Clem done? 'He must have conditions?' she says.

'Of course.' Her friend takes another sip of champagne. 'The first that I must leave the country. To save him from further disgrace, he tells me.'

'And the second?'

'That the child stay in England to be brought up by its father.' She laughs drily. '*His* father, rather – Herbert seems convinced I am carrying a boy.'

'But . . .' Ellen stares at her. 'You can't mean this. When the baby comes, you will feel differently.'

'How so?' Clem's gaze hardens.

'It's your child. Your –' what were the words Clem herself had used? – 'your bright-eyed terror, remember, with the sticks and stones in his pockets?'

'The child I didn't ask for or want.'

Ellen looks away. Had her own mother felt this way? Was that why she had left her and Reynold eventually? Would she have done exactly what Clem is about to do now, if she'd had the opportunity?

'Ellen.' Clem seizes her hand. 'I can't do it. I'm a bad, self-ish person, I know, but I can't. If the birth of the child doesn't kill me, a life as Herbert's wife surely will. You know that.' Her breath comes quickly. 'I'd like you to come with me to New York. Will you? Please say you will.'

When Ellen doesn't reply, she withdraws her hand. 'I've blown in here like a whirlwind, interrupted your brother's funeral. I've sprung this upon you. I'm sorry.'

'I'm glad you came,' Ellen says, and she means it, so why this weight pressing down upon her, as if Reynold himself were sitting behind her, his arms looped around her waist and his chin on her shoulder, holding her back. She tries to clear her head. 'I need time to think about it, that's all.'

Clem takes a card from her bag. 'I'm at the Metropole for

348

the next two nights,' she says. 'Will you meet me for lunch tomorrow? We can talk more then.'

Yes, Ellen says, she will, and she leans across to embrace her, a clumsy kiss that she wishes she could wipe out like an equation on a slate, for somehow she kisses the corner of Clem's mouth, not the centre, and when Clem tries to rectify the error, their noses collide, and it becomes little more than a brushing of lips, before Clem winces, asking if she might make use of Miss Smart's bathroom: it is the baby being troublesome, she explains, for it will insist on pressing parts of her that should not be pressed upon.

'Besides, I have intruded upon you long enough,' she says, and helping her to her feet, Ellen calls for the maid.

But it is Harriet who comes, her eyes glittering at Clem in a way that is not altogether friendly as she offers her her arm.

'No need to concern yourself, Mrs Williams,' she says. 'I'll have Mattie accompany you to wherever you're going in the cab,' and with a jovial briskness she escorts Clem and her unborn child from the premises.

Chapter Thirty-Eight

B oiled eggs for two as the morning sky glowers and darkens, and the stiff wind shows its temper and tosses small pebbles from the sea to the road. Outside Harriet Smart's villa, a horse whinnies and rears, almost upturning its carriage, and the ladies inside shriek loudly enough for Harriet and Ellen to set down their spoons and go to the window.

'Good Lord,' Harriet says, as the driver soothes the animal. 'We may have to postpone our morning constitutional.' She returns to her chair and looks at Ellen expectantly. 'Why don't you come to the theatre with me this afternoon? I'll introduce you to Mr Juniper and the other chaps, get you settled in.'

Ellen looks out at the sea. With each pitch and roll of the waves she thinks of Reynold's absence and Clem's presence, and how she must tell Harriet that she cannot come to the Empire later after all.

'Could we rearrange for tomorrow instead?' She tries to keep her voice light. 'I'd planned to have lunch with Mrs Williams.'

'She's still in town?' Harriet takes a mouthful of tea. 'Heavens, if I were the proprietor of the Metropole, I'd be rather fearful for my soft furnishings. Forgive me for being crude, but your friend seemed just about ready to burst.'

Ellen gives Harriet a quick smile. 'She's not here for long.'

'Then you should make the most of it.' Harriet picks up her toast then sets it down again. 'You know, this new song is still worrying at me – can't get the scanning quite right.' She draws back her chair. 'I'll be in the parlour.'

'But you haven't finished breakfast.'

But Harriet's only response is a brusque pat on Ellen's shoulder as she passes, and Ellen is left alone with the moan of the wind and then the sound of Harriet cursing – in a rare moment of ill humour – as she plays the same few bars over and over again on the piano next door.

When Ellen arrives at the Metropole, she finds Clem seated in a far corner of the crowded orangery, her table almost completely obscured by a jungle of palms and ferns.

'I have reached the conclusion,' Clem says, as the waiter leaves, 'that the patrons of this establishment would find it less disconcerting if I were to pass among them naked as Lady Godiva, rather than fully dressed and in my current state.'

She beams at Ellen. She wears a port-coloured dress with ruby earrings that dangle from her earlobes like drops of blood, her hair is curled at the fringe and woven into intricate plaits, set off by a white tulle hat trimmed with gold braid. She is the Clem that Ellen remembers, who accompanied her to Holywell Street and negotiated with such vim with Mr Dawson in the squalor of his back room, the Clem who conceived of the Golden Hour, and drafted the very first 'Dear Sirs' letter in her room one evening, presenting it with such amusement to Ellen the next day. Hard to believe, as she calls for champagne – 'for we're celebrating, aren't we?' – that she has been locked up as Ellen has, and likely treated far worse; and that now days pass at Feathers when not a soul speaks to her, such is her disgrace.

'Even my new maid,' she tells Ellen. 'I catch her looking at me sometimes as if I'm Satan personified. Herbert's furious – we had to pay double to get someone, after Mrs Gately left.'

And Clem goes on to explain exactly why Mrs Gately left and describes with much animation the reactions of the servants as she distributed her Golden Hour photographs among them, and how Mrs Yorke-Duffy had packed and left for Brighton that same evening, her indignation resulting in some most unladylike language.

'It's clear you can't control your wife, Herbert, and I'm damned tired of doing the job for you!'

And the palm fronds quiver as the women laugh, and the waiter serving the entrée thinks it wise that the maître d' had the foresight to allocate the ladies this table – usually reserved for men and their mistresses – for the American lady's condition is one thing, and the fact they are unaccompanied by their menfolk another, not to mention the light work they are making of the champagne.

When the waiter has gone, Ellen lays her hand on Clem's, and Clem smiles when she sees the Golden Hour watch, back on Ellen's wrist 'where it should be', she tells her. They sit that way for some time, the clamour of twittering voices and chinking plates fading, until it is just them, and the first time they met outside the Empire, and the second time, on the King's Road, with Clem holding out the handkerchief with Ellen's initials on it, her face full of curiosity, and all the times after that when what could or might happen did.

'You must tell me,' Ellen says, drawing back as the salmon arrives, 'about New York.'

The picture Clem paints is alive with detail. In summer, they will cycle under the plane trees in Central Park, and have peppermint ice cream at Delmonico's; they will take a box at the opera house and laugh at all the dowagers in their furs and pearls; they will disguise themselves as seamstresses and take the ferry to Coney Island and ride on the Flip-Flap Railroad, eat salt-water taffy and go bathing in the sea. They will find the best photographer in Manhattan and have their portrait taken together, and it will hang in the parlour of their apartment, when she has found one that is suitable. Indeed – Clem lets out a cry of delight – and she can't believe she hasn't thought of this before – they shall purchase a camera and set up a darkroom just for fun!

'And you are not to worry about money, Ellen,' she says. 'Don't frown so – I know how proud you are! You shall be my companion, paid, just as you were at the Crescent.'

'Oh,' Ellen says, with a jolt of surprise that strikes her like pain. And then, because she doesn't know what else to say, 'Thank you.'

It is past four by the time they leave, and teatime has replaced luncheon in the orangery. Ellen offers Clem her arm as support, and slowly they make their way around the tables and potted palms, and hats turn and feathers flutter, and looks are exchanged across watercress sandwiches that somehow make more noise than words themselves.

'As I told you,' Clem murmurs, 'there is only one place suitable for pumpkins like me, and that is to be planted in bedsheets!'

Ellen smiles. And then, a woman walks in, of a similar age to Mrs Yorke-Duffy, with sharp, inquisitive eyes that absorb the cut and quality of Clem's earrings and wedding ring as swiftly as she does her advanced stage of pregnancy. As she passes, the woman directs her attention to Ellen.

'You are sorely remiss in your duties, miss. Your mistress should be at rest in her rooms.' She averts her eyes. 'It's a disgrace.'

'There are doubtless many who share your sentiments, madam,' Clem says with a polite smile. 'However, my companion and I do not.'

And, stifling a laugh, she proceeds into the lobby. 'Isn't it fun,' she says, turning to Ellen, 'to behave as one pleases!'

Ellen does not reply. 'Is that what I will be?' she asks. 'In New York. Your "companion"?'

Clem looks puzzled, then laughs again. 'Oh, Ellen, don't be cross.' She lowers her voice. 'I could hardly tell her what we really are to each other, could I?' She beckons to one of the hotel staff. 'Let's take tea in my rooms, before you leave.'

Ellen looks at her friend. She hasn't asked how I should like to live in New York, not once, she thinks, and as the hotel doors swing open, a gust of cold wind sweeps the lobby and her head clears with it.

'I should go,' she says. 'I'd like to take a walk before dark.'

'In this weather? But you'll come back tomorrow, before I leave?' And the merriment leaches from Clem's eyes and she becomes the woman Ellen found waiting in the parlour at Harriet's, fearful and alone. Clem holds her arm tightly. 'And then as soon as the baby's born, I'll send word and book passage for us both to America.'

Ellen wants to believe her. She wants to believe that life can be conducted like an orchestra, that crescendo will descend into peace, after the cymbal's final shiver. But this is a child. Another person with needs and desires and tiny perfect fingers that will curl into fists and squirm and rage and wail for a loss that it doesn't understand.

'You need to rest,' she says.

They say goodbye, and Ellen steps out into the storm, the

ghost of Clem's fingers still clutching her arm, not wanting to let go.

Ellen returns to the villa. The hours before Harriet is due back from the theatre stretch before her. She wanders through the house as shutters bang and hail pelts against the windows, her restlessness keeping pace with the troubled meandering of her thoughts. Why, she asks herself, does she hesitate so? This is Clem who secured her release from a prison cell, Clem who changed everything when she came to her room that night, touching her and taking pleasure from her, when Ellen had thought that no one ever would. She goes to the parlour, pours herself a brandy, tries to conceive of this life in New York, a laundry room turned to a darkroom, a camera on a tripod in the front parlour, the boxes at the opera house and strolls around the park. And the nights, with the servants returned to their own homes, the two of them in Clem's bed or her own – is happiness really so hard for her to imagine?

Ellen sits at the piano and stares at the photograph of Harriet dressed as a sailor, hands pressed to slim hips. What was it Harriet had said – that she let her heart lead her to the wrong places? Was she right? Was that why she couldn't see herself and Clem in the apartment on the Upper East Side, was that why her imagination refused to accompany her across the Atlantic?

Downstairs, the front door slams. Ellen gets up as she hears Harriet, talking to Mattie. The parlour suddenly feels a little warmer, the wind drops; Blanche rouses herself from her spot by the fire and jumps onto the chair arm, her head turned towards the door.

'Evening, all.' Harriet is still in her stage clothes, face shiny with cold cream, necktie hanging loose, waistcoat half buttoned. She ruffles the cat's neck and flings herself into the easy chair.

'Poor turnout tonight,' she says. 'Damned weather kept everyone at home.'

'Drink?'

'Please.' Harriet gives Ellen a small smile. 'Wasn't sure if you'd be here.'

'Where else would I be?' Ellen pours brandy into a glass.

'I don't know, Blanche.' Harriet chucks the purring cat under the chin. 'Where else might our friend Miss Harper be?'

Ellen is firm with herself. She must tell Harriet now, before she loses her nerve completely, but why is it so difficult, why does she feel like a heckler set on ruining Harriet's performance?

'Mrs Williams is going back to America. After the baby's born.' She pauses. 'And she's asked me to go with her.'

Harriet is silent. She puts down the cat and walks to the window, opens the shutters a crack and peers out into the dark night. 'Of course she has,' she says quietly. 'The question is: will you?'

'I . . . I believe so. I haven't fully decided.'

When Harriet turns from the window, her eyes pool with sadness. 'And what will you do when she's finished playing – when she tires of you? When a man takes her hand at a dance, and makes her laugh like you used to, and then invites her for lunch, then another dance, then a weekend in his house by the lake, or the sea, or the woods? You will have to watch, Ellen, as he woos her and she lets him, you will have to witness every excruciating minute of it, every sigh, every indiscretion, each bill and coo – you'll be little more than her chaperone!' Harriet shakes her head in exasperation. 'She'll be married again within the year. Take it from someone who knows.'

Ellen turns away. 'You're being cruel.'

'I'm being truthful!' Harriet drains her glass and slams it on the tray. 'She's not like us, Ellen. Do you understand?'

Her voice is raised, her tone sharper than Ellen has ever known: she feels both cut by it and strangely alive. Doesn't raw honesty always hurt? Isn't that why this life of peppermint ice cream and larks in the darkroom with Clem is so difficult for her to see or smell or taste? It is a concoction, no more real than the Golden Hour photographs of nymphs and goddesses, of tableaux girls pretending to be housekeepers, of Clem playing at being something she's not. And the truth of who she, herself, is stands before her, reflected back, and as Ellen looks at Harriet, it is clear that she is suffering too.

'You must do as you want.' Harriet avoids Ellen's gaze as she walks to the door. 'At any rate, I've had quite enough of today. Goodnight.'

'Wait!' She can't let her leave, not like this; Ellen is on her feet and across the room before she can think better of it and Harriet turns, her hand on the doorknob.

'What is it?'

'It's you.' There can be no going back now; she has Harriet's hands in her own, seized without permission, and although Harriet is looking at her with wide eyes, she makes no move to reclaim them. 'I want you.'

Ellen's heart pounds, but the fear of Harriet drawing away is overcome by the deeper terror of doing nothing. Ellen reaches her hand to her friend's head and strokes her short, boyish hair, and it feels just as she'd always imagined it would, and she can feel the heat from her scalp, she can smell hair oil and cigarette smoke and the woody cologne she has grown to love. Harriet's eyelids flicker and she lets out a sigh as she leans back against the door, before her arm snakes around Ellen's waist and pulls her close. Then they are kissing, and there is nothing hesitant, nothing polite about it, and it isn't like it was with Clem because Harriet – Ellen realises – isn't playing, and neither is she.

Harriet turns the key in the lock. Still kissing, they perform an ungainly dance towards the couch, and then Harriet is astride her and all Ellen can think of is Harriet's tongue and how much she wants it to touch other parts of her, and she must have moaned or cried out or pulled Harriet even closer, because Harriet smiles and murmurs that while anticipation is all part of the pleasure, haven't the two of them waited long enough? And she stands up and unbuttons her trousers, lets them pool to the floor; she is wearing plain flannel drawers that smell of lye soap and lemons, when Ellen wraps her arms around Harriet's pale thighs and presses her head to them. And Harriet takes her hand and moves Ellen's fingers against her, and it is as if there is a thread connecting them, for the quicker Harriet's breath comes then so too does Ellen's, and she pushes deeper until Harriet pulls away.

'Not yet,' she says, and kneeling next to the couch, she draws Ellen onto the floor so that she is lying beside her, and with an assurance that makes it the most natural activity in the world, lifts Ellen's skirts and petticoats, scoops down her drawers and dips her head between her parted legs. At first, Ellen stiffens at the strangeness of it, but Harriet's breath is warm and teasing; it is as if she is whispering to her, saying it's certainly a peculiar sensation when a person isn't accustomed, but over time she might come to enjoy it, and that time might come sooner than she . . . oh! Ellen cries out. Then a finger slips inside her and then another, and Ellen moves against them, and the wind moans down the chimney, as the pace gathers, as the heel of a hand pushes against her. Harriet is on top of her now, and she feels her dampness rubbing against her bare thigh, her breath in her ear, and fleetingly Ellen wonders how many women Harriet has done this with before, and then tells herself it's of little consequence because it is she who is here now. And in this house there is no one to care when they both cry out for the last time and the sound is swept up the chimney by the wind and tossed into the storm outside.

They lie side by side, fingers touching. Coals glow in the grate; there is a small thud as Blanche jumps from the chair and picks her way over the rug towards them.

'Even the damn cat is purring,' Harriet says, and she calls Blanche to her lap and Ellen smiles and leans against her, and she could stay that way for a very long time, she thinks, with Harriet's arm flung around her and the roar of the sea outside.

'Do you have any notion of how long I've wanted you?' Harriet says, curling a strand of Ellen's hair around her finger.

'I rather thought you tolerated me for Reynold's sake.' She looks sideways at Harriet and nudges her playfully. 'You certainly liked to tease.'

'I'm a rough, unfinished thing. All I'm good for is making people laugh.' Harriet traces a finger along the curve of Ellen's cheek, then presses her lips to the pulse at her neck. 'I was just trying to tease you out.'

And taking Ellen's hand, she suggests they go upstairs to bed.

Chapter Thirty-Nine

Ellen wakes early to the sound of lapping waves and the rise and fall of Harriet's breathing. In repose, bedcovers bunched in her fist and her face flushed with sleep, Ellen glimpses Teresa, the mischievous child from the orphanage. She kisses her creased cheek and Harriet stirs.

'Oh good,' she murmurs, 'you're still here,' before her eyes flicker shut again.

As she gets out of bed, Ellen is aware of two things: that she is wearing a man's nightshirt that Harriet had given her to sleep in after they'd made love a third and final time; and that the wind has stopped. She opens the shutters. The sky is turning from grey to pale lavender, and the sea undulates in soft folds, like a counterpane after a good shake. As she takes in the sunrise, she sees that the beach is strewn with pieces of timber, and as she looks east towards the town, she notices that something is missing. Further along the promenade, past the West Pier, a solitary clump of iron rises from the shingle, amputated from the rest of the Chain Pier which she now sees has disappeared completely.

Ellen splashes her face with water and dresses. Clem's watch, discarded among Harriet's cufflinks, glints a reminder and, frowning, Ellen slips it on her wrist.

Outside, gulls swoop and circle. The weaponry of the storm, pebbles and pieces of iron, cover the promenade, and by the time Ellen reaches what remains of the pier, the level of devastation is apparent. A gang of men passes, carrying armfuls of wooden planks, children forage for nails in the shingle. Fishing boats lie on their sides splintered and broken, a woman whom Ellen recognises as one of the dippers sits on her haunches and weeps next to where the bathing machines were once stationed. A discarded sign catches her eye in the rubble and she picks it up, the sunny optimism of the script pressing hard against her heart.

Walter Clarke, Purveyor of Ices.
6d a piece! All flavours!

She walks up the slipway and along the King's Road, stepping over the broken glass, until she comes to Reynold's old studio. It has been boarded up for some time, but the sign is still there, like an inscription on a tomb – *Mr R. Harper, Photographer.* Ellen remembers Reynold's excitement on that warm September day, his plans for the future, feels his arm through hers. Perhaps if she had swallowed her pride and stayed with him, managing his ambition from the shadows, keeping a closer eye on money coming in and going out, they could have made it a success. She wipes her eyes.

'Miss Harper.'

Ellen looks up into the kind, exhausted face of the Ice King. It would be foolish, he says, to ask her what the matter is; besides if ever there was a day for tears, it is this one and he must confess he feels rather close to it himself.

'I've three kiosks gone,' he tells her. 'And Volk's lost his railway. Whole thing smashed to smithereens.'

They talk awhile about the storm and the pier, and how it's enough to make one want to move to the capital, even with all its filth and smoke. And then Wally shakes her hand and says he has a hundred matters to attend to – but – with a nod towards the sign – once again he is truly sorry for her loss: he misses his wife every day, and it's worse when everything is topsy-turvy and things aren't going as they should.

'But I'll let you into a secret, Miss Harper,' he says. 'I'd have lent you the money in the blink of an eye if it had been your name above that door. But with your poor brother, I just couldn't take the risk.'

And he tips his hat and bids her good day.

Ellen stares after him. A few rays of sun pierce the clouds; two children chase each other down the street, laughing as they pass. And she recalls what Harriet had said last night, just before they went to sleep, when Ellen had held her in her arms and told her she was grateful.

'You don't owe me anything,' Harriet said, and she'd kissed the tip of Ellen's nose as if she were an adorable child. And Ellen had felt both very free and very safe, and then she had thought of Clem, who, despite everything, made her feel neither.

The red brick of the Metropole Hotel looms in the distance, but what she has to tell Clem can wait, and Ellen crosses the road and goes down to the beach. She wanders to the water's edge, lets the waves lap around her boots. Then, she undoes the clasp of her watch and holds it in her palm, looks again at the engraving. It is a totem of a time best forgotten: it would take no more than a second to hurl it like a pebble into the eager sea, where it will be left to rust and confuse the fish.

Your name above the door. Wally Clarke's words return to her and she lowers her arm. She remembers the gasps from the courtroom when Herbert Williams had remarked upon the watch's value. Ellen slips the watch in her cloak pocket, replacing it with a stone which she throws with all her might into the sea. The sound it makes as it hits the surf is strangely satisfying, and she does it again. A woman walks past with her daughter, and the little girl gapes at Ellen, and asks her mother why the funny lady's throwing stones.

Ellen thinks of Harriet. *Because I want to, ducky*, she would reply.

She steps out of the shallows, shakes the water from her skirts. Then picking her way through the wreckage, Ellen walks back towards Hove.

EPILOGUE

Richmond, 1913

England is a peculiar country, Edie Rosso reflects as she alights from the train into a station so sleepy that it seems impossible that a photographer of any merit might operate from the town it serves, and she wonders again why her mother was so set on their coming here, when there are any number of establishments in the city which would have done just as well. But her mother – walking ahead as quickly as her tapered skirt will allow – had been insistent, telling Edie that if she is so set on it – this life in front of the camera – then she will need a decent photograph of herself to send to the New York studios.

'I know just the lady to take it,' she had said, but would not be drawn much further, other than to say that the photographer in question had been her paid companion for a short time, when she was married to Edie's father. Strange to have had a father whom one has never known, but Edie has been Edie Rosso for as long as she can remember, and when she and Mama had visited her father's grave a few days ago in the small muddy village where people gawped and stared at them, all Edie could think was how glad she was not to have grown up there, a sentiment which was compounded when she met her surviving relatives. How Papa – the real one, Alberto Rosso – would have laughed if he'd been there. Her aunt was straight out of a Dickens novel, with a hat as old as

Edie herself, and opinions to match, and as for poor Cousin
Ottilie, she was the living embodiment of an old maid,
although afterwards Mama had told her that Ottilie was
perfectly happy that way. Not everyone wants to get married,
she said, adding that it was lucky for Edie that her father had
seen sense and left it to her mama to raise her in America,
for Edie could be sure that there would have been no audi-
tioning for parts in the pictures if he and Aunt Caroline had
had anything to do with it.

Now she walks with her mother through the quiet streets
towards a grey-green ribbon of river, and then along its
banks until they come to a large white house with a sloping
lawn and a veranda filled with red geraniums. A figure moves
behind the tall windows, and her mother turns and briefly
cups her cheek.

'I'm so proud of you,' she says, and her bluebell eyes, the
exact same colour as Edie's, fill with tears. 'And she will be
too.'

Edie follows her up the path to the front door, where a
discreet copper plaque bears the name *Harper's Photographic
Studio.* As her mother lifts the door knocker, her intake
of breath is audible; she is nervous, Edie realises, looking
at her curiously, for this in itself is an uncommon enough
occurrence.

'Ladies!' A woman dressed in men's trousers and a crisp
white shirt, unbuttoned at the neck, opens the door. She has
daringly short hair, speckled with silver, and an expansive
smile: Edie likes her instantly.

'Miss Smart,' her mother says, with a touch of coolness at
which Miss Smart laughs and holds the door open wide,
saying that the past is another country, as far as she is
concerned, and that she is most glad to see Mrs Rosso and

her daughter, and she knows she won't be the only one. And then they follow Miss Smart into a sunny drawing room, filled with photographs, where a woman with greying hair and a wide handsome face sits at a desk examining a sheet of photographs through an eyepiece. As she looks up, her mother calls out Miss Harper's name, and then the two of them are in each other's arms, and her mother is half crying, half laughing, as the woman whose name is Ellen passes her a handkerchief.

There is something about the way they are holding each other that makes Edie look away, and then Miss Smart, who is watching her watching her mother, takes her arm and says that it is a pleasure to meet a fellow artiste, and that if she were twenty years younger she wouldn't mind having a shot at the pictures herself, although she fears she likes the sound of her own voice too much to have ever been a success. I can't help it, I'm terribly Victorian, she tells Edie with a wink; and when the music hall dies – which it will – I go with it! And she takes Edie on a tour of the photographs lining the wall, where there are several of Miss Smart, both on stage and off, in men's clothes and women's, and one, set in a silver frame, of her and Miss Harper standing with their bicycles by the curlicued railings of a seafront promenade.

Her mother calls her over and Miss Harper shakes Edie's hand, studying her with the same intensity with which she had been appraising the prints when they first arrived.

'She's all you, Clem,' she says – and *thank heavens for it!* her mama responds – and as the two of them chatter on, Edie's attention is drawn to a photograph on top of Miss Harper's desk, showing a young woman in old-fashioned clothes, sitting on a worn armchair, with a cat on her lap.

She asks who it is, but Miss Harper pretends not to hear her and changes the subject.

'Let's start with your pictures, Edie,' she says.

And Edie follows her mother's friend into the studio.

Later, they all have tea outside on the lawn. As the sun begins to dip behind the trees, tea is replaced by champagne, and once the dregs lie warm in their glasses, and they are flushed and dishevelled with sun and chatter and laughter, Clem suggests that Ellen take one last photograph, of her and Edie. And so they all go back into the studio, and Clem and Edie lie each one end of the couch, the soles of their feet touching, red-gold hair falling loose across their shoulders, as Ellen sets up the camera.

I always said you had an eye, Ellie. Reynold is back, he is studying the composition beside her, and it isn't the time to retort that he didn't say it often enough, because seeing Clem again, and the daughter who is so like her, has made Ellen happier than she thought possible and she wants nothing to spoil this day. *Of course,* her brother goes on, *Mrs Williams always was the type to fall on her feet* . . . and then she silences him, for he has no place here, not today.

A breeze stirs the air with the scent of the river and Ellen looks at Harriet who sits, legs outstretched, by the open window, watching her, with nothing more complicated than love in her eyes.

Ellen stands beside the camera. This time she doesn't tell the women to hold still. She presses the shutter and lets in the light.

Author's note

The initial inspiration for this novel came from some early research that led me to Linley Sambourne, an illustrator and cartoonist for *Punch* magazine in the last decades of the Victorian era. Sambourne was also a keen amateur photographer, taking photos of family members often in outlandish poses, which he would then develop in a makeshift darkroom and use as studies for his illustrations. I didn't have to dig very deeply to discover that Sambourne's passion for photography included a proclivity for photographing nudes – an activity which his wife, Marion, was likely aware of but chose to ignore. In excerpts from Sambourne's diaries, the models (always women) are described in pithy, sometimes cruelly objective terms, with those whom Sambourne found less suitable or compliant described as 'bad', 'ugly' or 'stupid'. A throwaway line in a footnote stopped me in my tracks and I became increasingly intrigued by these women. Who were they? Where did they come from and how did they feel about what they were doing? The fictionalised answers to these questions can be found in part in *The Golden Hour*.

The National Vigilance Association, established in 1885, was active in Britain for over sixty years. Founded at a time when prostitution was rife, and protection for vulnerable young girls negligible, the organisation grew swiftly and local branches sprang up around the country. Thanks to the Women's Library at the London School of Economics, I was able to browse committee-meeting minutes which proved a fascinating insight into the social mores of the era. It is clear that the NVA greatly assisted a lot of women who had scant resources of their own, even if on occasion the concern of certain members for the moral well-being of the public was somewhat overzealous . . .

The music hall craze for living statues – or *tableaux vivants* – was at its height in the mid-1890s. Inspiration was drawn from classical statues, such as the *Venus de Milo*, and popular paintings by Royal Academy artists, as well as lesser-known, more provocative works from the likes of European painters Luis Falero and Jean-Leon Gérôme. By means of an innovative stage mechanism, several living statues could be shown consecutively, with performers, usually female, striking poses that emulated the works of art in question. The 'nude' tableaux, in which models wore flesh-coloured body stockings, were highly controversial and anathema to social purity groups such as the National Vigilance Association, who campaigned to remove them from theatres.

The Eton College incident is based on a real-life scandal at an unnamed public school in 1881, recorded by an Inspector Brennan in his memoir, *Stories from Scotland Yard*.

As a final note, all the characters in *The Golden Hour* are the work of my imagination, only as real as readers might believe them to be . . .

Acknowledgements

I would like to thank the following:

My former editor Olivia Barber at Hodder and Stoughton, who worked with me on this manuscript from its inception and whose astute editorial insights and unwavering support have helped shape it into the book it is today. My thanks and gratitude also to the rest of the publishing team at Hodder, particularly Amy Batley for so efficiently taking the reins, Phoebe Morgan, Kimberley Atkins, Charlea Charlton, Becky Glibbery, Natalie Chen, Jenny Platt, Purvi Gadia and Talya Baker.

My agent Broo Doherty of DHH Literary Agency, who breezed into my literary life when I most needed it, bringing warmth, wisdom and expertise – thank you for your belief in me and my writing.

The museums and research libraries that make writing historical fiction a real labour of love, in particular the Hove Museum of Creativity, Brighton Museum and Art Gallery and Digital Image Bank, the Keep archives, the British Library, the Bishopsgate Institute archives, the Museum of the Home, the Victoria and Albert Museum, the Women's Library at the London School of Economics and Sambourne House. Special thanks go to the Jubilee Library in Brighton – for always being there.

The Society of Authors' Foundation grant which bought me some much-needed writing time – I am hugely grateful – thank you.

There are no friends like writer friends and particular thanks go to Frances Merivale, Sara Sarre, Jayne Watson and Pam Jobs, who all read at least one draft of this novel, and in Fran's case, two! Your insights and encouragement have been invaluable – and mean so much to me. Thanks also to Anita Frank for warm and wise advice and support.

Allie Helm for the loan of her Aldeburgh cottage – and Sara for so generously inviting me to join her on several writing retreats there.

Alex James for setting me straight on photographic processes (all errors are, of course, my own!) and David Simkin (www.photohistory-sussex.co.uk) for sharing such a comprehensive reading list.

All the family, friends, fellow authors, colleagues and total strangers, who read, reviewed and recommended my first novel, *The French House*. I hope you enjoy *The Golden Hour* just as much! A special thank you to Joan Udell for so warmly supporting and celebrating my debut's first steps into the big wide world (aka Canada!); and Cathy Hayward and Mariateresa Boffo from the Kemptown Bookshop, Brighton. Also, Denise Tyler, Clare Dyer, Bill Buckley and Josie Lloyd for sharing *The French House* love across Sussex and Berkshire!

The late Wayne Milstead, co-founder of the Circle of Missé writing retreat, who died suddenly and tragically in 2023. I wrote several chunks of *The French House* at Missé, as well as the final chapters of *The Golden Hour* during my last stay there, in the summer of 2022. Every trip to Missé – and conversation with Wayne – was a reminder that the writing itself and the act of creating is what really matters; the rest is just noise. I miss him.

My adopted home of Brighton – for being such a rich source of inspiration.

Jeff for riding the publishing roller-coaster alongside me, for the autumnal plot walk in Stanmer woods and for being quietly proud.

And my parents – for everything.

The following publications have greatly helped with my research for this novel:

The Photographic Studios of Europe, H Baden Pritchard
The Victorian House, Judith Flanders
Walking on Water: The West Pier Story, Fred Gray
Victorian Photographers at Work, John Hannavy
Palaces of Pleasure: How the Victorians Created Mass Entertainment, Lee Jackson
Public Artist, Private Passions: The World of Edward Linley Sambourne, curated by Leighton House Museum
A Victorian Household, Shirley Nicholson
Making a Spectacle of Themselves: Art and Female Agency in 1890s Music Hall, Elena Stevens, University of Southampton
'Victorian Erotic Photographs and the Intimate Public Sphere', *Nineteenth Century Contexts*, Rachel Teukolsky (2020)
The Victorian Underworld, Donald Thomas

Reading Group Questions

1. In the opening of the novel, Brighton is described as a 'shoeless, well-heeled town'. What do you understand this to mean? Why did the author choose to set the story in Brighton, do you think?

2. Early on in the novel, Ellen describes her relationship with her brother, Reynold, as being 'tethered to a person you long to be freed from, yet cannot imagine being without'. How has this dynamic come about? Discuss the relationship between the two siblings.

3. What was your reaction to the character of Ellen? Did your feelings towards her alter as the novel progressed?

4. The friendship between Ellen and Clem is an unusual one. How does the relationship develop and what does it teach them about themselves and each other by the end of the book?

5. Ellen, Clem and Lily are from very different social classes but each finds herself struggling against the constraints of her individual circumstances. What does freedom mean to each of them? Discuss the relationship between class and freedom in the novel.

6. Discuss the relationship between Ellen and Harriet Smart. What does Harriet Smart represent to Ellen and how does this change over the course of the novel?

7. Discuss the character of Mrs Yorke-Duffy: meddling busybody or a woman ahead of her time? Why might educated women like her have been keen to join organisations such as the Vigilance Association?

8. The underground trade in erotic photography plays a central part in the novel. Are there any situations which resonate with modern life today?

9. What did you learn about life in late-Victorian England from this novel? Did anything surprise you?

10. What did you think of the ending? Was it the ending you were expecting?